Rowe is a paranormal star!" ~J.R. Ward

D1225842

one of the best romances I have read. I can't wait till it comes out and I can tell the world about it." ~Sharon Stogner, Love Romance Passion

"*No Knight Needed* is contemporary romance at its best....There was not a moment that I wasn't completely engrossed in the novel, the story, the characters. I very audibly cheered for them and did not shed just one tear, nope, rather bucket fulls. My heart at times broke for them. The narrative and dialogue surrounding these 'tender' moments in particular were so beautifully crafted, poetic even; it was this that had me blubbering. And of course on the flip side of the heart-wrenching events, was the amazing, witty humour....If it's not obvious by now, then just to be clear, I love this book! I would most definitely and happily reread, which is an absolute first for me in this genre." ~Becky Johnson, Bex 'N' Books

"*No Knight Needed* is an amazing story of love and life...I literally laughed out loud, cried and cheered.... *No Knight Needed* is a must read and must re-read." ~Jeanne Stone-Hunter, My Book Addiction Reviews

DARKNESS ARISEN

ISBN-10: 0988656698

ISBN-13: 978-0-9886566-9-7

For further information, please contact Stephanie@ stephanierowe.com

Acknowledgements

Special thanks to my beta readers, who worked incredibly hard to get this book read in time for my tight deadline. Thank you for all your support and hard work! This book is a far better book because of your contributions, suggestions, and support. I love you guys!

There are so many to thank by name, more than I could count, but here are those who I want to called out specially for all they did to help this book come to life: Leslie Barnes, Alencia Bates, Jean Bowden, Shell Bryce, Holly Collins, Ashley Cuesta, Courtny Eskew, Sandi Foss, Valerie Glass, Tamara Hoffa, Heidi Hoffman, Jeanne Hunter, Rebecca Johnson, Dottie Jones, Janet Juengling-Snell, Deb Julienne, Bridget Koan, Felicia Low, Carol Malcom, Phyllis Marshall, D. Alexx Miller, Jodi Moore, Evelyn Newman, Mary Lynn Ostrum, Judi Pflughoeft, Emily Recchia, Kasey Richardson, Karen Roma, Caryn Santee, Dana Simmons, Julie Simpson, Summer Steelman, Sharon Stogner, Amanda Tamayo, Nicole Telhiard, Linda Watson, and Denise Whelan.

And lastly, thank you to Pete Davis at Los Zombios for another fantastic cover, and for all his hard work on the technical side to make this book come to life. Mom, you're the best. I love you. Special thanks also to my amazing, beautiful, special daughter, who I love more than words could ever express. You are my world, sweet girl, in all way

Dedication

For Jan Leyh, a courageous, lovely, amazing woman who makes my life better simply because she is a part of it.

Onward, Jan, to victory! I know you will triumph.

DARKNESS ARISEN

THE ORDER OF THE BLADE

STEPHANIE ROWE

CHAPTER ONE

Naked on a public beach at midnight under an eerily full moon was not where Alice Shaw wanted to be.

At all.

But she knew she had no other choice, not with the way the deep red glow of the night sky was streaking across the still waters of the Oregon coast.

The only sounds were the soft lapping of the ocean on the rocky sand, the distant roar of waves further out to sea… and the thudding of her heart, of course. The air was hot and thick, unusually humid for Oregon, even in the summer. Sweat ran in disordered streaks down her chest…nerves or humidity? She wanted to believe it was the weather. Her gut knew it was fear.

Fisting her hand tightly around the precious item she dared not drop, Alice untied the drawstring of her shorts and let them fall. They hit the sand with a whisper that made her jump, and she quickly scanned the beach again for any sign of humanity, or any other living creature.

She saw nothing. Heard nothing. She appeared to be alone, which she knew could be a lie. But it was the best she could hope for.

Quickly, she turned back to the water that was a glistening red, mixed with the unnatural blue-green of the moon. She swallowed hard, then yanked off her underwear and pulled her tank top over her head. They joined her shorts, flip-flops, and car keys on the sand, a tiny pile that had been her last defense against anything. Now, she had nothing. Nothing but the blood-red natural pearl clenched in her hand, one of three so precious that no creature on earth even knew she had it in her possession. Only her mother had known, because she'd given it to Alice, but her mother was long gone.

The pearl was a secret she had sworn to keep. A secret she was going to betray tonight.

She moved up next to the water, so her toes were right on the edge of where the damp sand met the dry beach, where hard met soft, where cold met hot. The warm breeze seemed to caress her like invisible fingers of sin, and she shivered, wishing for her clothes.

But the Mageaan would never accept her if she brought anything into the ocean with her. All she was allowed to bring was herself. Vulnerable. Defenseless. Pure.

Pure? She laughed softly. Purity was an area where she had failed completely, and if all went as planned, her fall from grace would become even greater.

But for Catherine, she would do it. Once she fulfilled her promise to Catherine, death would no longer be the threat that it currently was.

Alice raised her eyes to the sky, watching, waiting, and searching the vast night. The sky blazed crimson, becoming angrier by the minute, and yet she did not move. A glowing ring of red light drifted near the moon, and she sucked in her breath, her heart racing in anticipation. That was it. The sign that the moment was close. So close.

Her muscles tensed. Her blood rushed with searing heat through her veins as she watched the inexorable approach of the bleeding red cloud as it crept closer and closer to the turquoise moon. She began to count under her breath. Five. Four. Three. Two. One.

The edge of the ring drifted over the rim of the moon, breaking the perimeter. The night flashed with a vicious violet energy as the moon seemed to ignite. A firestorm of luminescence thrust the entire earth and ocean into a bath of thundering violet flames.

Now! Alice leapt forward, launching herself into the air, her arms outstretched to her sides like a sacrificial virgin. She threw her head back, baring her throat, and pointed her toes behind her like a ballet dancer in mid leap, exposing her stomach, a position of ultimate surrender. She closed her eyes, relinquishing all defenses as she let herself fall into the water that was only inches deep.

The cold ocean was shockingly brutal as she hit the surface, but she didn't change her position. She didn't try to protect herself from the impact on the sandy bottom. She simply whispered the words she'd paid so dearly for, "May death become my freedom."

Then she plunged into the water...and didn't hit the bottom. She gasped in shock as she was sucked downward, the violent turbulence of the ocean spinning her away from the surface. Violet light burned through her closed eyelids, and her instincts screamed at her to fight, to swim for the surface. But she didn't move, willing herself to hold the same sacrificial position she'd held upon entry, even as she tumbled in all directions, the disorienting movement stripping her of any sense of which way led to the surface.

She knew it was a test. A test she had to pass. A test of courage. A test of fear. A rite of passage to see how much control she had over terror and her survival instinct. The water grew colder, the undertow more violent. Her lungs began to burn with the need to breathe, and real terror began to build inside her.

What if she were wrong to let herself be sucked down? What if surrendering to the sea was actually the opening that death was waiting for, instead of being the one chance she had?

Panic began to beat at her, and her muscles burned with the need to strike for the surface, to fight to live. *No!* She screamed the orders at herself. *Don't fight!*

She squeezed her eyes shut, willing her body not to resist. But still the fear crept through her, growing in strength as memories surfaced of the last time she'd died. She vividly recalled the pain, the panic, and the terror that she wasn't going to make it back to life. Fear lashed through her, screaming at her to fight to save herself before she died again, for a final time. Her skin burned with the bruises still present from the demons who'd tortured her, damage that should have been healed when she came back to life, damage that showed exactly how close she still was to death, a grim reminder that she might have finally used up her "come-back-to-life" frequent die-er card.

If she died today, it might be the end. Her final death. The destruction of her last chance to save her sister.

Her chest constricted, and her body began to shake as terror plunged through her. *No,* she screamed. *Don't give in!* But even as she shouted the denial, her body tore free of its defenseless pose, thrashing violently toward the surface, fighting desperately for another chance at life, shredding her last chance to save the one person who mattered to her. *Dammit!*

Panic took over, and she succumbed to the terror, swimming frantically toward the luminescent glow of the blue-green moon invading the black ocean. Harder and harder she swam, her lungs screaming with the need to breathe, but she couldn't get any closer. It was too far.

Horrifying realization plunged through her. Dear God, it was true. The rumors were true. Because she'd failed the test, the ocean would kill her. No, not the ocean. She would be murdered by the Mageaan, the magical beings she'd been trying to reach when she'd leapt into the water. Elusive creatures who were her last hope. Bitter, angry beings who welcomed no one into their world, unless they were brave enough not to fight death.

She hadn't passed the test. So now, the sea would obey its mistresses and kill her.

No! She couldn't die. She had to get to Catherine. *Catherine!* Alice stretched her hand toward the moon as her mouth opened, compelled by her lungs to take a breath. Water poured into her mouth and filled her lungs—

Something grabbed her hair and yanked her downward, away from the surface, away from her last chance at life, away from Catherine's final hope for survival.

She knew she was dead.

Dammit. She absolutely did not have time to die again.

Calydon warrior Ian Fitzgerald swore as Alice's hair slipped out of his grasp. Her ponytail tore from his hand as she fought against him, trying to swim deeper into the ocean, as if she had no concept of which way led to the surface. "Alice!"

He lunged for her, diving into the water that should be only inches deep, yet was somehow a bottomless pool of blackness. The green-blue moon cast shadows deep into the water. He almost reached her...his fingers brushed her hair... and then she was swept out of his reach, tossed ruthlessly by the violent water. As she tumbled away from Ian, that all-too-familiar sense of despair and anguish arose within him. That same voice, that fucking voice that had tormented his father and grandfather into lethal hell beat at him, taunting him. *She is lost. You have lost her. Die, soldier. It is the only choice.*

Ian swore as his brands burned in his forearms, his weapons straining to be released so he could plunge them into his chest and carve out his own heart. The despair was agonizing and fierce, an onslaught so sudden and visceral it knifed through him before he had a chance to stop it.

Fuck you, he snarled and spun around, focusing his gaze

on Alice. He felt his soul shatter as the ocean dragged Alice down to its depths, dragging her out of his reach after he'd finally found her again. The curse rose within him, sucking him dangerously down into the pits of despair, but at the same time, Ian focused on the woman: the billowing of her auburn hair in the water, her arms as she fought helplessly, the curve of her spine as she twisted and turned. His woman. *His soul mate was in trouble.*

Six hundred years of instincts as a Calydon warrior roared to life within him. His need, his commandment, his duty to protect his mate broke the grip of the curse, and raw male determination exploded through him. *She cannot die.*

With a roar of outrage, Ian launched into action, keeping his entire focus on the woman tumbling toward her death. He allowed no thought other than that she needed him, that he was her only chance for survival. If he died, so would she. *Fuck dying.* He couldn't die, couldn't kill himself, until his woman was safe.

He slashed his way through the water, moving with a speed that was far beyond human capacity, far beyond what the ocean could stop. He called up six hundred years of training as an Order of the Blade warrior, six centuries of a brutal physical life that had honed his body into a mass of muscle coiled so tightly that it was a weapon unto itself.

He called upon all his preternatural strength and streaked through the water, straight down into the endless depths, focused solely on his woman. He saw her below him, a faint pale outline that wasn't struggling anymore. She was floating helplessly, capitulating to the death hunting her, her body limp except for her left hand, which was clenched in a tight fist, as if she was clutching her greatest treasure just before her final death. Renewed urgency roared through Ian as he swam harder, his body undulating fiercely as he plowed relentlessly toward her. *Alice! Wake up!*

But she didn't respond. She just continued to drift

further away from him. Faster he swam, getting closer and closer... and then he saw a black chasm in the bottom of the ocean, a murky darkness flowing from it.

Jesus. The sight of it was like a jolt to his system. The appearance of the black shadows was exactly what had happened when she'd died before. Demons coming out to steal her soul from her body. "No!" he bellowed. "Back the fuck off!"

He called forth his weapons from the brands on his forearms. With a loud crack and a burst of black light, the steel flanged maces appeared in his hands, their blades glistening even in the deep ocean. He hurled them instantly in a one-two strike that cut through the murky darkness. It parted with a screech of insult, torn apart by the demon magic that empowered Ian's weapons as he called his weapons back to him.

He lunged for Alice, knowing he had only a split second before the deathly essence regrouped and took her. *Alice,* he commanded, thrusting his order into her mind. *Give me your hand. Now.*

Her body jerked suddenly, and her eyes opened. She looked right at him, and her eyes widened in shock. The impact of meeting her gaze reverberated through him, stripping the breath from his lungs. Her eyes were still a radiant green that reached right into his core. She hadn't changed.

He had to save her. There was no other option.

Alice. Now. As he said the words, he thrust all the strength he could into their connection, trying to empower her to fight the current trying to take her, infusing his life force into her depleted body, past her mental shields that had fallen with her being so close to death. *Don't block me, Alice. Not this time.*

Her body jerked, and for a split second, she recoiled from him, fear flashing across her face.

Hellfire, woman! I'm not the one you need to fear. He couldn't keep the snarl out of his voice, the frustration of two months of searching for her, the raw desperation of his need to stop her from dying this time. After having her die in his arms three times, the fourth time was going to be a charm even if he had to be a complete bastard to make it happen. *Give me your fucking hand, now.*

Alice blinked, and then she moved her right hand, her fingers stretching toward his, even as she kept her left hand clenched in a fist.

Triumph rushed through him. *Yes!* He gave a final thrust forward, and their fingers touched. The jolt that leapt through him was instantaneous, just like it had been the last time they'd connected. Victory rushed through him. He'd found her. Son of a bitch. *He'd found her again.* He grabbed her hand, locking his fingers around her wrist as she tightened her grip on him.

Ian? Her voice was tentative and faint. Unsure. Testing his name as if she wasn't sure it was right. As if she weren't certain he was real. But son of a bitch, hearing her voice in his head again was like a choir of angels singing a fucking chorus of hallelujahs.

Yeah, it's me. He shifted his position and began to swim backwards, away from the chasm trying to suck her down. Beneath them, the black shadows swirled restlessly, not pursuing them. Of course they weren't going after her. They only got her if she died, and she wasn't going to die, was she? No chance of that. With her hand locked securely in his, Ian felt the grip of his curse begin to fade, defeated momentarily by the fact his woman was alive and with him. *Did you miss me, sweetheart?*

Miss you? Alice began to kick again, her lithe body moving fiercely against the undertow as she committed to going with him. *I thought you were a dream.*

What? She didn't sound overwhelmed with joy to discover he wasn't a figment of her imagination. What the hell was up with that? *You thought you imagined me?* A dream? He'd made the most incredible love to her and she thought he was only her imagination? *I am definitely insulted that you don't remember me. I gave you some of my best stuff—*

A violent torrent of water rushed over them, thrusting them down toward the chasm. He swore as the force of the current swept them both up, his strength overwhelmed by the sheer fury of the ocean. He thrust more effort into his kicks, but the current still hauled them both down toward the pit.

There was a wail, a high-pitched scream as if the ocean itself was a scorned woman being murdered, and then a burst of cold water wrenched Alice from his grasp, catapulting her ruthlessly toward the chasm.

Anguish ricocheted through him as she slipped out of his reach again, and he saw the dark shadows of demons rise to take her. The curse rose with opportunistic speed, shoving its way through his shields with lethal determination. *She is lost. You have failed. Die with her.*

For a split second, the curse was too powerful, and Ian swore, gripping his head against the onslaught of doom and despair trying to take him, trying to force him to give up, to suck him into such hopelessness that the only option was to surrender to death and kill himself.

For months, he'd fought the despair, keeping his shields up as he'd searched for Alice. But he'd had to open himself completely to connect with her this time, which gave him no defenses against the terror of her death. It was too late to block their connection, and the curse was taking advantage, preying on his need for her. He knew instantly that his only chance was to open his connection with her even further, to plunge into the very thing that made him vulnerable, and to use his need to save her life as a fuel to keep himself alive.

Get out of my head, he ordered the curse, keeping his gaze focused on Alice, opening himself to her, trying to connect with something stronger than the curse that had killed every one of his male ancestors.

Alice needs me, he reminded himself, quickly spinning

words and truths that would empower him against the curse. She would die without him. *She. Will. Die.*

Denial roared through him, as the primal instinct of a Calydon warrior to protect his woman exploded to life. Rage tore him from the grasp of the curse, and he spun toward the chasm, trying to right himself against the raging undertow. He stroked desperately against the water, but he was too far away from her, with nothing to leverage off of to propel himself. All the strength and quickness that made him so deadly on land was useless against the rage of the ocean. It was too late. Those few seconds he'd spent fighting off the curse again had given death the head start it needed. Ian roared with fury as he watched Alice get sucked past the rim of the chasm. *Alice!*

You stupid bastard. The voice of his teammate, Ryland Samuels, cut through the despair trying to consume him. *We don't have time to fish you out of there. Don't you have a fucking angel to save? If you let her die, I will carve you up myself.* There was a loud crack and black light flashed from above the surface, and then Ryland's steel machete was streaking through the water, leaving behind a trail of foamy bubbles. *Catch a ride before my woman dies. I threw the damn thing as hard as I could, but it won't keep up the speed long in the water.*

Your woman? Fuck that. She's mine. Get your own damn woman. Ian lunged for the machete as it passed by him. His fingers closed on the engraved handle, and he grunted as it yanked him forward, nearly ripping his shoulder out of its socket. He ducked his head against the current to cut down on drag, turning just enough to keep Alice in his range of vision as she fell into the crevasse. He was gaining on her. Getting closer. Closing the gap. *Come on!* He reached for her mind, but there was no connection. He couldn't access her again. What the hell? She was his soul mate. Why was she so inaccessible to him?

Closer and closer. Almost there—

He reached the rim of the crevasse. Only yards away—

The machete began to slow down, and Ian let go of it as Alice began to pull away from him again. *No!* He called out his mace and hurled it past her. It slammed into the side of the crevasse just below Alice, its handle sticking out from the wall of the cliff. Alice crashed into it, like a tree branch breaking her fall. She bounced off it, and for a moment, his heart stopped. Then she grabbed it, locking her arms and legs around it, using his mace to resist the pull of the chasm.

Her hair was still streaming toward the bottom of the chasm, and the mace was bending downward, barely able to resist the force that was pulling them. Ian had a second, maybe two, to make it happen. He put on a burst of speed, swimming as hard as he could toward Alice, keeping his gaze fixed on his mace. Calculating how long he had until it was torn out of the wall.

Now! A split second before it ripped out, he threw his second mace. It hit right below Alice, and as the first mace tore away from the wall, she landed on the one he'd just thrown. She clung to it, her entire body wrapped around it as she fought against the sheer strength trying to suck her down. Black clouds swirled around her, demons waiting until she broke, so they could take her soul.

This time she's mine, Ian growled as he called back the mace that was free-falling into the chasm. It slammed into his hand just as he reached Alice. He smashed it into the wall, anchoring himself, then grabbed Alice, wrapping his arm around her waist just as his other mace was torn out from under her. She threw herself around him, her lean limbs wrapping around his neck and waist, her face buried against his chest. Her naked body plastered against him.

Jesus. For a split second, he couldn't move. He was overwhelmed by the shock of feeling her body against his. The heat from her body penetrated his clothes, and her skin was soft and vulnerable beneath his arm. The strength of her hold on him was riveting. It felt so right the way she was holding

19

onto him. This was it. This was what he'd been pursuing for so long. Alice. In his arms—

She slipped slightly in his grasp, the movement jerking him back to the present and the force of the current still pulling on her. Shit. What the hell was wrong with him? He was a warrior, and this was battle, not time for a little nookie.

Ian immediately called back his still-falling mace. He sheathed it into his arm, beneath the brand that matched it. One arm was still locked around Alice, and his other hand was gripping the handle of the mace he'd jammed so deeply into the wall of the cliff, anchoring them against the forces trying to pull Alice downward.

He quickly took stock of his surroundings, assessing his best exit. With one arm wrapped around Alice, he could use only one weapon to get them out. The pull on her was extreme, and he could feel it working on him as well. Above him loomed a hundred-foot cliff that he'd have to climb before he'd reach the top of the chasm, let alone get back to the surface.

Shit. These were not optimal circumstances, even for him.

His Order of the Blade training would demand he choose his own life over hers if the choice had to be made, in order to fulfill his oath to trade the life of an innocent when necessary to save the greater good. The Order deemed all its members as critical for the protection of the greater good, so everything had to be sacrificed to keep the individual Order members alive. He was honor-bound to save himself instead of her, but the male within him disagreed big time. No chance would he let his woman die while he swam for freedom like some pansy-assed wuss who couldn't take care of his mate.

He had to make a move, and fast. His lungs were tight from holding his breath for so long, but he knew he still had time before he needed to surface. But Alice? He suddenly realized he didn't know what kind of powers she had. How bound was she by ordinary human-type limitations? *Alice. Do you need to breathe?*

She didn't lift her head, and he realized she hadn't heard him.

Shit. She'd shut him out. Once they got out of this mess, he was going to have to make it clear that jamming their mental connection was not a good plan when they were fighting for their lives. And how in the hell was his soul mate capable of shutting him out anyway? It shouldn't even be possible, and that realization made a shimmer of foreboding echo through him. What if he couldn't claim her? What if she was within his reach, but never ever his?

The idea made pulses of fear ripple violently, and the curse reverberated through him. Shit. Maybe he would have been better off not finding her...

Too late now.

He had her, and he was keeping her alive. *Alice.* Keeping his grip tight on both her and the mace lodged in the wall, he shrugged his shoulder, trying to communicate with her. At his nudge, she looked up. Her eyes were wide with terror.

He met her gaze, drilling into her mind. *Do you need to breathe?*

Her eyes widened, and he knew she'd heard him in her mind. Satisfaction and relief coursed through him. Yeah, that was the way it was supposed to be.

She nodded desperately.

I can breathe for you. Her gaze went to his mouth, and sudden heat radiated through him as he recalled exactly what her mouth tasted like. The sinful softness of her lips. The passion that simmered inside her, buried so deeply that he knew it wasn't ever supposed to come out...but he'd accessed it anyway.

Raw, intense physical need burned through him, and desire pulsed at him. She swallowed, nervousness flickering across her face, and he laughed softly. *Sweetheart, trust me, I want to ravish you, but first I want to get out of this damn sinkhole. Breathing first. Sex later.* But even as he said it, lust coursed through him, thick and dangerous, and he knew that he was lying. He burned for her so badly he'd take her right then and there if he knew she wouldn't drown in the process.

Alice hesitated, then nodded her assent, her gaze searching his. In those green eyes, he saw fear and more than a hint of desire. But there was something else in there too. A fierce determination to do whatever it took to survive. Her will to survive was stronger than her fear of who he was. Respect flashed through him, a connection, because he called on that same survival instinct every single day to fight off the curse and live another day. Suddenly, offering to help her breathe was no longer simply a chance to ravish those decadent lips of hers.

It became so much more than that.

It became about preserving a spirit that was fighting to live. That was what he was all about. That mission defined the very essence of who he was, and what he'd been doing for six hundred years: protecting others. And now, to protect the woman he was meant to be with? It was what he was born to do. *You will live, Alice.* He tightened his grip on her and lowered his head toward hers. Satisfaction thrummed through him when she raised her face to his, entrusting herself into his protection, exactly how it was supposed to be. *I will keep you safe.*

Then he took her mouth with his, and offered her life.

CHAPTER TWO

Alice was too panicked about drowning to worry about the fact that Ian's lips were about to be on hers. Her head was spinning, and her lungs were burning so badly she could barely think. All she wanted was air. Oxygen. Life. If Ian's kiss meant she had a chance for all that, then she was all on board. It would be a salvation, not a sensual decadence.

Still fisting the pearl of Lycanth in her left hand, she raised her face to his and accepted his offer.

The moment his lips met hers, everything changed. Unbelievable warmth filled her. A burst of air raced through her, inflating her lungs like a gift from the heavens. His kiss was soft and tender, his lips a seductive caress that seemed to strip away all her defenses and catapult her into a place of safety and well-being. Her muscles shuddered with relief, and her heart seemed to expand in her chest. The agony in her lungs dissipated, and the muscles in her chest released their tight hold. The relief of being able to breathe was incredible. A gift. Somehow, he was filling her lungs with oxygen, or at least making them not need oxygen any more. She didn't understand, and a ripple of unease pricked at her. *How are you doing this?*

Don't fight me. Ian's voice was a caress in her mind, nothing like the angry orders he'd barked at her before. *It wastes oxygen if you fight me. You can make this easy, sweetheart.*

Tears filled her eyes at his tenderness, at the gentle coaxing in his voice, at the intoxicating sensation of his kiss. Memories flooded her mind now, images of the time she'd met him before, the last time she'd been with him. She recalled the way he'd kissed her: not a kiss of life-giving tenderness, but a raging possession of heat and lust that had almost torn her apart. How could she have forgotten how he'd stoked all that desire in her, along with all the other emotions she wasn't supposed to be able to have? How he'd made her come alive with a fierce, raging intensity that ripped her from her cocoon of isolation and hurled her ruthlessly into a vortex of passion, fire, and *life*.

She'd forgotten all that. All of it. Until his kiss. Until his whispered caress. Until this moment.

When she'd first seen him coming toward her in the ocean moments ago, all she'd remembered was that he'd been there when she'd died three times. As he'd reached out for her, he'd seemed to be death incarnated, trying to kill her for the final time. For one terrifying moment, she'd been certain, so certain, that he was death finally coming to claim her...until she'd heard his voice in her mind. Until that rough and tender sound had filled her with a yearning so strong that it had obliterated all fear.

Yes, he whispered as he deepened the kiss, as his tongue flicked against hers, igniting a spark of desire that seemed to simmer through her. *Like that. Let me in, Alice.*

His reassuring warmth began to flow through her, a heat that chased away the cold of the ocean, the iciness of fear. She became aware of the strength of his body against hers. The steel core of his torso, the unyielding muscles in his arm where he had her locked down, the raw, untamed masculinity pouring off him. The button on the fly of his jeans was rough against her bare stomach.

His lips were soft and hot against hers, moving in a

tantalizing rhythm that stripped all resistance from her. His tongue a seductive master, coaxing her response in a decadent invasion that made her want more. His kiss was more than a kiss. It was the offering of life, not just in that moment, but so much more. Her liberation? Her hope? Her future? Or...was he merely the *illusion* of safety, obscuring a threat that would result in her death for a fourth and final time?

Sudden fear congealed in her belly. Any man who could invoke such a response with his kisses was dangerous to her. And he'd been present every time she'd died. What was he really? Her salvation, her doom, or something else? What was she doing kissing him and entrusting herself to him? This was risky on so many levels—

Hey, hey, hey, he said softly, his arm tightening around her back, crushing her breasts against his chest, making her nipples ache with need. *Don't pull back. Think good thoughts. Like how my mouth-to-mouth is better than any other guy's kiss... no, fuck that. Don't think of anyone else's kiss. That's a crappy idea.*

She almost burst out laughing at his disgruntled tone, her laughter chasing away the fear that had been building in her. She realized she was in no position to be saying no to this man, not right now. Ian was saving her life, and heaven knew she pretty much sucked at saving herself. The larger threat he represented would just have to be dealt with later, when there was enough air around for her to breathe on her own. *You're jealous of another man kissing me?*

Shit, yeah. You might not remember what happened between us, but sex of that magnitude has an impact on a man. His mouth tightened on hers, and suddenly, it became more than an offering of air. It became the kiss of a man who wanted to possess, seduce, and devour the woman who was naked in his arms.

Oh... This was good. Really good. Terrifying...but it was also delicious and incredible to be the recipient of a kiss so full of lust that it couldn't be contained.

Heat and desire burst through her, coiling through her body like a hot wind on a summer night. Desperate need raced along her spine, and her resistance to him crumpled under his onslaught. He growled and amped up the intensity of the kiss, his mouth demanding and hot, his tongue no longer a tease, but an aggressive, dominating force that thrust past her defenses, igniting a fire that seemed to burn through her skin. The kiss became about heat and desire and passion. And need. Dear God, she craved him so deeply she wanted to tear off her skin and plunge inside him until there was nothing separating them, until they were one.

She wrapped her arms more tightly around his neck, pressing her body against his, meeting his kisses with a carnal desire of her own. Her tongue met his in a sinful dance of promise and temptation—

Jesus, Alice. Ian broke the kiss suddenly, stripping her of the heat he'd been generating.

She gasped in protest, barely remembering to close her mouth before the saltwater poured down her throat. She wanted to yank him down toward her and make him kiss her again and again. Down her neck, over her collarbone, and across the swell of her breasts. Then he would take her nipple in his mouth and—

Don't finish that thought, he interrupted, jerking her out of her fantasy, making her realize exactly how much she'd fallen under his spell with her erotic fantasies.

Oh, God. He was so much more dangerous than she'd even realized.

Ian was staring at her intently, his brown eyes stormy with dark clouds of desire, and her body throbbed in response. Ian growled, his jaw tight. *We are so going to finish that when we get out of here.*

Out of here? she echoed blankly, trying to gather her thoughts when all she could think about was his mouth trailing over her skin, his hands moving lower and—

Yes, here. He grinned, a cocky grin, as if she'd just dubbed him king of the world because his kiss had made her forget everything else. *At the bottom of the ocean, dangling precariously over a chasm that's haunted by demon spirits who are trying to claim your soul. That's the here I'm talking about.*

Oh... His words wrenched her back to the present, to the fact they were hanging on the side of a cliff, protected from death only by his mace jammed into the rock. Oh, yeah, *that* here. Fear bubbled back up to the surface, and she glanced down. Only a few yards below them was the thick, shadowy mist from the demon world, waiting to take her soul. Ian was the only thing keeping her out of their reach.

She quickly jerked her attention back to her savior, to the bulging muscles in his arm as he held them in place with his mace. He was clearly straining now, calling upon his reserves to resist the vacuum trying to suck her down. How long could he fight it off? And how long would the Mageaan allow her to live and evade their trap? If they realized she had survived the assassination, they would soon be back to finish what the ocean and the demons hadn't been able to complete. Either way, she would die—

No. Ian's eyes flashed with outrage, as if he'd read her mind. Had he? Oh, man, that wouldn't be good! *Today is not your day to die, Alice. For once I'm going to get it right and save your cute little ass.*

She blinked, his reference to her rear end making her realize he'd been having a clear view of her "cute little ass" and all her other body parts from the first moment she'd encountered him, since she was stark naked. After a flash of embarrassment, she quickly decided that nakedness was not her biggest concern right now. Nothing like death, being hunted by demons, and being swept away by dangerous kisses to make a girl put nakedness further down on the "things to worry about" scale. Right now, it was about living.

Hey. Ian interrupted her thoughts. *Did you hear me? I'm not going to let you die this time. I'm stubborn like that, and I never allow a woman to die four times on my watch. Three, yeah, sure, no big deal, but never four.*

Well, I'm glad to know that four is your limit, you know, given the situation and all. But how could he promise that? She wanted to believe him. She wanted to have another chance to save Catherine and to live, but she wasn't blind to their situation. He was using his mace as an anchor because he couldn't fight the force of the pull by himself. The surface of the ocean was still so far away. And the truth was, she really wasn't predisposed to defeat death these days. It was pretty damn determined. *How? There's no way to swim against this current.*

Have faith, sweetheart. I didn't come alone. Then she felt him turn his focus outward as he reached out with his mind in a different direction. She felt the moment he connected with another male. This male's energy was dark and turbulent, almost violent, with flashes of evil so intense that she recoiled.

But Ian didn't pull back. *Ry. How about another ride? I got the girl.*

About damned time, Ry said. *Is she okay?*

Ian looked at her and raised his brows, telling her to answer the stranger. What was going on? She wasn't telepathic. How was she connecting with both of them? Suspicion rolled through her, a grim realization that she knew very little about Ian, other than the fact that he'd been present all three times she'd died, and that he evoked emotions and desires in her that she wasn't allowed to have, emotions that she'd felt only once before. That other time, the payment had been brutal, too brutal, and too horrific to endure again. And now Ian was dragging her right back to that place.

Ian. Ry's voice grew darker, almost angry, churning with emotions so intense she knew instantly that this man Ry was close to the edge of demon, creatures she was all too familiar with.

Tell me the angel is okay, he commanded. *Now.*

Alice went cold. They knew she was an angel? That was impossible. And so very dangerous. Frantically, she shook her head. *I'm not an angel.*

Ry's relief flooded her once she spoke, as if all he'd focused on was the fact she'd spoken, not her words. She felt him touch her mind, as if searching for reassurance that she was truly all right.

Unease rippled through her at his contact, and she pulled back from his mind as he spoke to Ian. *Way to go, Fitz. I'll let you live today.* Then a flash of black light flooded the water, and a loud crack echoed violently through the depths.

The effects of Ian's life-infusing kiss fading, Alice's lungs began to burn again as a machete streaked through the water directly toward them. She instinctively tried to duck out of the way, but Ian held her tight. The machete sailed past them down into the chasm, then suddenly screeched to a stop. It reversed direction and started to speed back up to the surface, as if Ry had thrown it and called it back to him, just as she'd seen Ian do with his maces.

That's our taxi, sweetheart. Ian adjusted his grip to anchor her more securely against him, and then as the machete raced by, he released his grip on his own weapon and reached his free hand toward the handle of the machete. For a moment, they were suspended in the water, and she felt the force of the current as it tugged them down.

Then Ian grabbed the steel weapon. Their descent stopped with a violent jerk, and then the machete began to tow them effortlessly through the water as it tore back toward the surface.

Relief flashed through her as they sped to the top, but almost immediately, her body began to hurt, she became dizzy, and black spots began to dance across her vision. *Ian! Something's wrong.*

His mind brushed hers briefly as if to scan her body, then Ian's voice shouted in her mind. *Too fast, Ry! She can't ascend that quickly! Stop it!*

You know the damn thing doesn't have speeds, Ry said. *Protect her yourself!*

Ian didn't hesitate. He yanked her tighter against him and slammed his mouth down over hers. This time, the kiss wasn't a breath of fresh air or careful desire. It was raw, sheer passion, an invasion into her soul that shredded her defenses and thrust her under his spell.

Stop! Frantically, she shoved against him, terrified of how he was attempting to possess her. *Don't—*

But then he deepened the kiss, and he thrust the fierceness of his lust right into her body. It ripped a gasp from her, and fire seemed to explode through her veins, tearing her from her own mind and yanking her into a raging cauldron of want and desire. There was no chance to resist, no hope of escaping, no possibility of stopping him.

He simply consumed her.

† † †

Ian didn't care what Alice wanted.

He didn't give a shit if she wanted to distance herself from him. It didn't matter if she wanted to block him and keep him out of her mind. Not if it meant letting her die, which is what was going to happen if he didn't protect her from their rapid ascent to the surface.

The only way to do that was to give her access to his immortality, to his legendary strength as a Calydon. It was pretty damned clear that she would not survive the fast pressure changes if she weren't shielded by his power. That kind of sharing was impossible except between Calydons, or between a male and his *sheva*, his soul mate. Since he was still certain that Alice was his soul mate, wrapping her up in his metaphysical protection should be easy.

But nothing about their connection was how it should have been. His brand hadn't begun to form on her arm after they'd made love, which was one of the five bonding stages. She shouldn't have been able to block him from connecting telepathically, especially not when they were so close to each other physically. Yet, it had happened. Somehow, she was resistant to their bond, and it worried the hell out of him.

Not that he was going to let that stop him from saving her life. He knew the curse would flare up if he tried to connect with her, only to have her reject him, so he mentally prepared himself for a whopping failure as he used the intensity of their kisses to try to breach the walls between their beings. He reached for her, he opened his mind to her, he fought to connect with her, but sure enough, as he tried to merge, he ran into the same walls he'd encountered before when they'd made love and he'd tried to draw her to him.

He could feel some of her emotions, her desire, her fear, but there was a part of her, a deep part of her, that he simply couldn't access. There was no way there should be that kind of block between the two of them. Fuck! He fought harder, racing against time as her body bowed in agony. With the ocean trying to kill her, he couldn't afford to let go of Ryland's machete and stop their ascent. They had to get out, which meant that he needed to help her survive.

Let me in, Alice. I can save you. He hauled her tighter against him and kissed her even more fiercely, opening himself fully to the desire and passion that had been building inside him since the last time they'd met. He unleashed his need into her, filling her with the intensity of his emotions. With grim determination and full realization of the risk he was taking, he dropped every last shred of the emotional shields he'd erected within himself to defend against the curse. He exposed himself to her completely, allowing her into the very depths of his soul.

Emotions crushed him, spewing through him with violent intensity. They screamed through his mind, like black wraiths streaking through him. The agony of desperate need. The crushing force of the ultimate despair of being unable to connect with her or save her. The stench of torment and failure. The blood-red streaks of the terror of losing her. He swore, fighting to hold onto sanity as the emotions flooded him, as the curse screamed its laughter at how defenseless he had just made himself. The despair thickened, tearing apart his sanity, sucking him into the miasma of doom—

Fuck that. He wasn't going down like that. Not now. Not when Alice was counting on him.

Ian focused on the feel of her body against his. On the shivering of her flesh. On the deadly tautness of her muscles. On the waves of pain cascading off her. On the feel of her mouth beneath his. The taste of her lips. The softness of her skin beneath his hands. His need for her. His desire. The raw and burning thirst to consume her on every level of her being. He opened himself to every emotion threatening to overtake him, using the kiss as a conduit to infuse her with his spirit, using the bare and ragged depths of his soul to hammer away at the walls wrapped around her soul that kept her from him. *I burn for you, Alice,* he whispered. *Can you feel that?*

Yes. Her voice whispered through his mind, and he felt her barriers tremble. He kissed her mercilessly, demanding her response, allowing her no respite from the sensual assault, from the intensity of all that he was.

And then she was kissing him back, a kiss so fierce that it skyrocketed the passion between them. Barriers fell, and an inferno ignited. He injected his energy into that fissure, imbuing her with the legendary healing capacity of a Calydon. It flooded her, wiping out the damaging effects of the rapid ascent, empowering her to withstand it. He felt her jerk in response, and then her pain vanished. She relaxed in his arms, her body no longer fighting the poison that had built up in her system as she allowed him to heal her.

Victory exploded through him. He'd saved her in a way

that could work only between a Calydon and his soul mate. Maybe she didn't carry his brand, but he'd just claimed her. *You're mine, Alice. Forever.*

She broke the kiss and stared at him as the water rushed past. *No, Ian. You're wrong. I'm not yours. I'll never be yours.*

The conviction in her eyes was like a knife jabbing through him. His *sheva* should never be able to deny their connection like that. It was impossible. A violation of what defined him as a Calydon male and Alice as his soul mate. But he saw it in her eyes, her conviction, her certainty, and he felt his heart stutter. Holy fuck. What was he getting into?

Then they burst out of the water into the air, the hot, humid atmosphere like a heavy blanket on their skin. Ian released the machete as their arc crested, then looked down to see that the water had become shallow again, only inches deep as they plummeted back down toward the earth.

So, yeah, victory that the bottomless chasm was gone, but also...shit. There was no water to cushion their landing, and they were a good thirty feet in the air and moving fast. Because they hadn't had enough drama already, right? He cradled Alice against him, his only focus to ensure she survived the landing.

Then, he would deal with what had just happened between them.

Then, he would find a way to truly claim the woman he was destined to be with...the woman who was his only chance to resist the curse... and the thing most likely to push him over that very edge.

Chapter Three

Even cradled in Ian's arms, the thud of hitting the sand was jarring. But worse for Alice was the realization that the landing had been hard because the water was shallow. The ocean had closed to her again. All that was beneath her was sand. Ordinary, shallow water. Broken shell fragments. Pebbles. Seaweed.

Dismay tore through Alice as she wrenched herself free from Ian. The pearl clenched in her hand, she scrambled to her feet and checked the sky. It was still blood red, and the turquoise moon was still full, but there were no more clouds. It was a crystal clear night with millions of stars, and no way to access the Mageaan.

"No, no, no," she whispered, frantically searching the sky. "It can't be over. It can't be." This night, the opportunity to enter the Mageaan kingdom by an outsider was a rare occurrence, one that came with little warning under the blood red sky.

"The woman was naked in your arms, and yet she's more interested in shooting stars than you," a deep male voice said, jerking her attention back to the present. "There's no way you can claim she's yours, Fitz."

Alice jerked her gaze off the night sky and looked around. Aside from Ian, who was still in the water behind her, two other warriors were standing on the edge of the beach, watching her intently. Both of them were tall and heavily muscled, but the one on the right looked like death himself. His eyes were a turbulent black, his face angular and furious, his fists clenched as if it was all he could do not to erupt into a murderous rage. Thick black brands slashed across his forearms in the shape of a machete, and she knew he was the one who'd helped them. He was also the one that she'd sensed so much evil in, the man Ian had called Ry.

The other one was less readable. His light brown hair was tousled, and his jaw was chiseled. He was almost as large as Ry, but there was a litheness in his stance that made her half-expect to see him turn into a wild cat and leap a hundred feet onto one of the massive black rocks rising out of the coastal waters. His eyes were dark, but there was a faint green tint around his pupils. A green tint that reminded her of Flynn Shapiro, her best friend and the last person to kill her.

"Alice," Ian rasped out, his voice raw with agony.

She turned quickly to see him on his hands and knees in the water. His head was bent, hanging toward the ground, and his muscles were flexed, as if he were in great pain. His hair was drenched flat against his head, showcasing the angular lines of his skull.

Her heart tightened, and she had to force herself not to run to him. "Are you okay?"

"Yeah. Of course." He suddenly lurched to his feet, staggering as if it had taken supreme effort to pull himself upright. He faced her and stripped off his tee shirt, still swaying as he fought a battle she couldn't see. With a muttered curse, he thrust the shirt toward her. "Put this on," he ordered her. "Now."

For a split second, she was too shocked by the sight of him to respond. In the water, she'd been fighting for her life, almost dead, desperate to breathe. She hadn't had time to notice him, to really see him, but now... Dear God...to call him a specimen wouldn't even begin to do him justice.

Stripped bare to the waist, the strength of his frame was undeniable. He was so chiseled it was as if a sculptor had carved every muscle in great detail. Unlike Ry and the other male, Ian wasn't a bulky mass of muscle. He was wiry and cut, making every curve of each muscle strain against his skin. His shoulders were broad, but he was so fit he seemed to be only bone and steel cords of muscle. A smattering of hair across his chest, and an eight-pack of abs across his stomach were untamed male perfection. Desire leapt through her, hot, throbbing need for the man walking toward her. She swallowed, her pulse pounding in her throat as she watched him approach, each step he took making her body clench in anticipation.

He reached her, and for a long moment, neither of them moved. All she could do was stare into the brown eyes that had haunted her all those days she'd been in demon hands. She'd been so confused, in so much pain, that her mind had barely been able to process what was going on. All she knew was that those intense eyes had provided comfort and strength, that they made her feel like she had hope. How often had she clung to that image in her mind, summoning it to survive one more day? She hadn't seen his face or heard his voice. She'd just seen his eyes.

She'd thought she'd imagined him. She'd thought he was a figment of her imagination, created as a self-preservation tool to survive. But here he stood before her, a thousand times more powerful than he'd been in her mind. "You're real." She couldn't keep the awe out of her voice, and she couldn't stop herself from brushing her finger over his jaw. His skin was rough from the whiskers, but it was the warm, living flesh of a real man standing before her.

"Yeah." He didn't flinch, a statue allowing her to touch him however she wanted. But raw emotion pulsed in his eyes. Desire. Lust. And a male possessiveness so unyielding that her belly clenched in response. "You really don't remember me?"

She laid her palm on his chest, and he sucked in his breath. He slammed his hand over hers, pinning it against him.

"Bits and pieces are coming back," she admitted, her heart starting to race at the way he was invading her space. Heat flamed on her cheeks as a memory of him pinning her up against a wall flashed in her mind. The coldness of the plaster wall against her shoulders and back, the dark lighting of the rear hall of Deliverance, the bar she used to work at, the pulsing heat of his lean hips between her bare thighs...

Sudden heat pulsed through her belly, and she swallowed, embarrassed by the images flashing through her mind. The hot dampness of his mouth on her breasts. The raw strength of his body as he'd driven into her again, and again. The ache in her soul as he'd stripped aside her defenses...

Oh...wow...she hoped that hadn't really happened. For so many reasons. On so many levels. She was always half-insane when she came back to life, and it was always hard to figure out what she'd imagined and what was real. The images of the passionate love-fest between her and Ian had to be her imagination. It *had* to be...but as she felt the thud of his heart beneath her palm, all she could think of was that she also wanted it to have been real. Crap! This was not good. Quickly, she cleared her throat and tried to pull her hand away.

He didn't let her. Instead, his fingers curled around hers, gripping her more tightly, making her pulse jump. "No," he said, his voice raw. "Don't withdraw. Not yet." A sudden chill rippled through Alice as droplets of water beaded down his temples. His pupils were dilated, and his skin was deadly cold. "Tell me you remember me," he whispered urgently. "Even if it's a lie."

Alice swallowed, her heart beginning to pound. Something was wrong with him. So terribly wrong. His skin was too cold. His eyes too tormented. What was wrong? She wanted to help him, even though she didn't understand why.

But she couldn't lie to him. She wasn't capable of it. Not even to help the man who had just saved her life. Not even if he was dying right in front of her. *Oh, no.* What if he was dying? Sudden terror coursed through her and she yanked her hand back, stumbling away from him. "Are you dying? Please, don't tell me you're dying." She couldn't go through that again. Not again. Not with someone who had just saved her life.

Ian fisted his hands and stared at her. His eyes were hooded with agony. "I'm not going to die," he said roughly, "but it would be incredibly helpful of you to at least pretend that my lovemaking was so earth-shattering that you haven't been able to think of anything else since."

"I have moments where I have flashes of it," she admitted, still backing away from him, needing to put distance between them. "But I'm not sure what really happened and what didn't."

"Moments? Flashes?" He closed his eyes and took a deep breath, as if he were summoning intense inner strength to fight off a demon she couldn't see. "That's it? That's all you've got?"

His words were light, a quip, but Alice felt the depth of torment beneath the surface. Something was terribly wrong. Why did he need her to remember? Quickly, she tried to explain. "When I die, I lose many of my short-term memories, or they come back only as fragments. The fact I remembered you at all is something that shouldn't have happened—" She realized suddenly that she'd just revealed too much about herself. Oh, God. What was he doing to her? Making her break rules left and right? Suddenly scared of how dangerous he was to her, she tightened her grip on the pearl, comforted by the fact she still had it as her protection. "I mean—"

"I know you die and come back," Ian interrupted. "You don't need to hide it." He held his shirt toward her again and this time there was no mistaking the blazing heat in his eyes. "But I'm glad to know that our lovemaking was so significant that you recall it at least on some level, even though you shouldn't have been able to. Clearly, I really did blow your mind." And just like that, his torment seemed to disappear, swallowed up by the sheer force of his will, shoved back into whatever dungeon he kept it in, as if the mere acknowledgment that he had affected her had given him some sense of peace. "Put this on, Alice."

She stared at his tee shirt, still dripping with ocean water. "What? Why?" She didn't understand this man. Not her response to him, not his response to her, and now? His shirt? "Are you trying to claim me like some teenage couple? Wear my letter jacket and we'll be going steady?"

He cocked his eyebrow. "No, but if that would work, I'd go back to high school and join the football team. It'd be easier than dealing with you cutting me off all the time."

She blinked at his haunted tone. Was he really affected by her trying to put space between them? "Then why do you want me to wear your shirt?"

"Because," he said, his voice low with desire so intense that it vibrated through her, "as absolutely breathtaking as your naked body is, and as much as I want to haul you into my arms and run my hands over every inch of it, the fact that there are two other men watching you is not something that I'm going to handle well in about thirty seconds."

Alice's stomach dropped at his possessiveness, and fear pulsed more strongly through her. Fear not just of the way he was behaving, but also of the fact that a part of her seemed to preen and bask at his claim on her. Using any excuse to break from his stare, she glanced over his shoulder at the other men, the ones she'd forgotten about completely the moment she'd seen Ian rise out of the water like the god of the sea himself.

Both Ry and the other man were still watching her. They didn't seem to be checking out her body. They were watching her face, and their feet were braced in a battle stance. Warriors who were waiting for something to happen, who were primed to leap into action. What were they expecting? What did they all know that she didn't?

Ry nodded once, his eyes turbulent with evil and darkness. "He's right, my lady," he said, his voice far more deferential than she would ever have expected from a man who carried such a dark presence. "You being naked is going to be a major problem very quickly. Ian's a little unstable these days, I'm no ball of sunshine, and we don't have time to get in a brawl."

She glanced back at Ian, and was startled to see that he wasn't denying Ry's comment. "He's right, Alice. I'm a fucking mess these days. Humor me." Violence began to swirl around her, and it was coming right from Ian. "Now, Alice," he said. "Just do it."

His eyes had darkened to a possessive dark brown that made chills run down her spine. She couldn't belong to him. That would destroy everything. "No," she protested, taking another step back, trying desperately to take back her space. "I have my own clothes. I'll put those on." She turned to head toward the beach, but Ian caught her arm, stepping in front of her so he blocked both her own path and the view of the other men.

"I know where your clothes are," he said, his voice low and rough, as if he were fighting to contain himself. "I saw them when I got here. If you go get them, you will be walking right toward Ry and Vaughn with every inch of your unbelievable body exposed." His grip tightened on her arm and he bent his head so his breath was warm against the side of her neck, sending shivers shooting down her spine. "Don't do that," he whispered. "It's not a good idea. I won't respond well to that trigger. I'm not having the best day, and I need a little bit of help on this one, sweetheart."

She stared at him, her instincts screaming at her to pull away, to declare her independence, to make sure the world understood she didn't belong to him. But when she looked into his eyes and saw the depth of pain in his expression, her protest died in her throat. She'd heard enough about the intensity of Calydon males, and the Order of the Blade warriors were more intense than others. She had no idea why she was apparently a catalyst for Ian, but she didn't have time to deal with the repercussions. She had one mission, and it wasn't to break up a fight among men, or to be naked in front of Ian Fitzgerald any longer. "I'm not your woman," she said, as softly as he had, words just for him. "But I don't have time for some territorial battle between oversexed males. Hand me the damned shirt."

A slow grin spread across his features as he realized she wasn't going to resist any longer. "Female nudity has that effect on me. I appreciate the accommodation."

In a teasing manner completely uncharacteristic of her, Alice raised her brows as she took the wet shirt from him. "All naked women?"

His face darkened and he moved closer, until his bare chest was less than a breath from her breasts, forcing her to crane her neck to see his face. "No, Alice," he said. "Just you."

"Oh." The word came out in a breathless whisper, and she felt a disconcerting sense of satisfaction pulse through her. Why did she care whether Ian noticed other naked women? She didn't even know the man. And the lovemaking incident that was floating in her mind, in and out of focus? It had to be a fantasy created because he was so hot. Seriously. She couldn't *really* have done that, right? Wanton sex with a stranger in a back hall at a bar was so not her style. Ever. "Get away from me." Careful not to drop the pearl, she yanked the sodden fabric out of his hand and jerked it over her head, not as an accommodation to him, but because she knew all too well the damage that these males could cause. If someone died because of her today, she would be helpless to save them, and that was not a memory she wanted to dredge up from her past.

The wet cotton was heavy against her skin, and the shirt came all the way to her mid-thigh. Ian nodded with evident satisfaction. "My shirt belongs on you."

"No, it doesn't." She set her fists on her hips, trying not to notice the scent of cinnamon and male emanating from the shirt that was clinging to her body. "It's a covering, Ian. Nothing else."

He moved quickly then, so quickly that she jumped in nervousness. He grabbed her wrist and flipped her arm over so her forearm was exposed. "Son of a bitch," he muttered. "How is it possible there's nothing there? How are you able to resist me?"

Alice pulled her arm away, needing her space. "What are you talking about?" Something nagged at the back of her mind, as if she knew what he meant, but couldn't quite remember.

"You're my *sheva*."

She frowned at him. "*Sheva*? What's that?"

"It means soul mate."

She blinked, and then shook her head frantically. "Oh, no, no, no. I'm not your soul mate—"

"Stop arguing with me for one damn minute." Ian scowled and took a deep breath, as if he were trying to summon intense inner control. "Since you're my soul mate, as we complete the stages of the *sheva* bond, my brand will begin to appear on your arm. There are five stages, and each one makes the brand more complete. The stages are sex, which we did."

She cleared her throat. "Well, I don't know about that—"

"And trust, where each of us trusts the other with our darkest secret or give the other the power to kill us. There's also death, where we risk our lives to save the other. Transference occurs when you develop the ability to call my weapon. Blood-bonding is another stage which brings us together. They can be done in any order, but with the completion of final stage, our bond and our fates are sealed."

She blinked. "Our bond and our fates are sealed? What does that mean?" Even as she asked it, chills ran down her spine. It sounded too ominous and relentless, things that weren't her cup of tea even on a good day.

"The Calydon destiny is to bond with his mate," Ian explained, tracing the shape of his brand on her arm with his fingers, as if he could manifest it by sheer will. She started to pull away, and then stopped at the flash of tension on his face. "The moment the Calydon completes the bond, he will become so consumed by his woman that her breath becomes the only thing that fills his soul. He's then destined to lose her, and the moment he does, he will snap and go rogue."

Alice instinctively looked over at Ry, who was treading close to rogue already. She'd heard about rogue Calydons, and the swath of destruction they always left behind. "Ian, I don't believe—"

He caught her arm, his eyes blazing with intensity "He will destroy everyone and everything that matters to them. They will both lose that which they hold most dear. The only one who will be able to stop him is his soul mate, who will kill him. Once he dies, she will be so devastated by the loss, that she will kill herself. Everyone dies. No one wins."

Alice stared at him, at the absolute conviction in his face. "That can't be true—"

"It is. Lucky you. Lucky me. Love kills and all that fun jazz. I'm not one of the stable few who will be able to will himself to victory and stave off destiny, so I'll be going down for sure." His voice softened, and his grip on her arm softened to a caress as he rubbed his thumb over the inside of her wrist. "But the ride...the ride is incredible. Love. Passion. The knowledge that you have a partner who will defend you to the death, at all costs, no matter what. It's addicting. Intoxicating. Irresistible." He leaned forward, his mouth a mere breath from hers, tempting her like the devil himself. "Worth every minute, from what I hear."

Her heart began to pound, and it felt like heat was rising from her skin. "Like how you make me feel when you kiss me?"

He grinned at her admission that she was affected by his kisses. "Yeah, exactly like that, only a thousand times more."

"More?" she echoed faintly. She wasn't sure she'd survive more.

"Hell, yeah." His jaw hardened as he resumed tracing the shape of his mace over her forearm. "You don't carry my brand." He tapped her arm. "There's nothing there, Alice. Not a damn thing."

"Of course there isn't," she said, her voice more throaty than she liked. She knew she should be terrified of his little story, but there was something about the way he'd spoken about the soul mates that called to her. The intimacy. The connection. The knowledge that there was someone there for her, always, no matter what. "I'm not your soul mate." She managed a weak laugh. "My soul is already busy with other stuff, you know? No split loyalties. It's against the rules. I'm like a nun."

He snorted. "No nun makes love like you do." He met her gaze. "You are my *sheva*. We satisfied one of the bonding stages when we made love, so you should be marked."

Alice swallowed, her skin suddenly hot. She wasn't sure which to respond to first, his statement that they really had made love, or his continued claim that she was his mate. He'd already ignored her repeated assertion that she wasn't his, and as for the making love…she really didn't want to get into that debate. Instead, she simply raised her arm, showing him the unmarked skin. "No brand. Not yours." End of story. Please? Yeah, the whole intimacy of the bond was appealing, but the doomed fate? Not so much. She had enough on her plate, thanks so much.

"You *are* mine—"

"You still haven't marked her." Ry strode toward them, his eyes as turbulent as they'd been before. Alice instinctively stepped behind Ian, using him as a buffer to protect her from Ry. The warrior's eyes flashed with darkness as he recognized her retreat. "Trust me, Alice, if you are what I think you are, I'm the one you can count on, not the one who will kill you."

She stiffened. "What do you think I am?" She really hoped it wasn't the angel thing again.

"An angel," Ian was the one who answered. "Ry thinks you're an angel. That's why he's here. Are you?"

Ohhh…this wasn't good. It hadn't been a coincidental term of endearment when he'd called her an angel before. They actually meant it.

Alice looked back and forth between the two men, her heart starting to pound. The cost of exposing her identity was so great. Angels of life weren't allowed to connect with anyone. One job. One loyalty. That was it. She couldn't risk revealing angel secrets to them, but the idea that they already knew made her worried. How did they know? As much as she wanted to find out who they were, why they'd come after her, and why Ian had appeared right at the moment when she'd almost died, she couldn't afford to have them around. She needed to get rid of them, and fast. "I need to go—"

"What? You're not walking out on me." Ian clasped her arm. "I've been searching for you for two months."

Another chill rippled over her. Why had he been searching for her? That couldn't be good. But she didn't have time to engage. Not now. Who knew how long she had until death succeeded in claiming her? Minutes? Hours? Days? She couldn't afford to take the time to interrogate the warriors. "I have to get dressed." She glanced up again at the sky. Still a dark red sky and a turquoise moon, but a clear sky. Desolation flooded her. What would she do if she couldn't get the help of the Mageaan? Seeking their help had been a risky choice, for sure, but without their assistance…how would she find Catherine?

She pulled out of Ian's grasp and hurried toward her stash of clothes on the beach. The third warrior hadn't moved. He was still standing there silently, watching her, and she noticed that he didn't have brands on his forearms. So, not a Calydon. Then what was he? What kind of male would the elite Order of the Blade allow on a mission with them? Her skin prickled as she bent to pick up her clothes, then she froze when he crouched beside her, his shoulder against hers.

"Where is Flynn?" he asked without preamble.

She stared at him, her heart starting to pound at the mention of the man who had betrayed her. The man who had once been her best friend, her only friend, who had killed her two months ago. "I don't know." She looked quickly down the beach, suddenly nervous that Flynn had found her again, but she saw only empty sand.

"I tracked him here." The man leaned closer toward her, his gaze intense. The green glow in his eyes was getting stronger, and she felt the air temperature begin to rise. Was he making it change? What was he? "You have Flynn's blood in your system," he said. "You and he are connected. So, where is he?"

"His blood is in my body?" Fear congealed in her belly. "What are you talking about?"

"Vaughn." Ian's mace was suddenly at the man's throat. "You need to back off. You're giving off a bad vibe right now."

For the second time in five minutes, Alice felt relief as Ian stepped between her and another man. Why was she feeling so many threats right now, and how come Ian seemed to be able to give her peace? It didn't make sense. It shouldn't be able to happen. She shouldn't be able to get peace from anyone. It was forbidden and impossible, at least for her. She was a special angel. For her, there were more rules, more limitations, and so much further to fall.

But there was no mistaking that she felt safer with Ian between her and the other men. Dammit. She had no idea what was going on, and she hated feeling out of control.

Vaughn didn't move away. If anything, he leaned closer to her, ignoring the trickle of blood running down his neck from Ian's mace. "Where is Flynn?" he asked again.

"I don't know," she shot back. "Why would I know?"

"Because he claimed you."

Ian growled, and nausea churned through Alice. "Another man claimed me?" The pressure was mounting from all sides, from all these men, Alice grabbed her underwear and yanked them on, keeping her body hidden beneath the long shirt as she did so. "Flynn hasn't claimed me. He was my best friend until he killed me. I hope to God he doesn't find me again—"

"He will." Vaughn stood up, giving her space as he surveyed their surroundings. "He'll always be able to find you since you carry his blood, just like I tracked you here, thinking it was him." His gaze fixated on the horizon. "He'll be back for you, and I'll be waiting."

Alice stared after him as he walked away, striding slowly across the beach as he scanned the area. Chills ran down her spine, and she swallowed. "That's how you found me?" She looked up at Ian, who had sheathed his mace back into the brand on his arm once Vaughn had left. "He tracked me?"

"Yeah." Ian picked up her shirt from the sand and shook it off. "I owe him. I wasn't getting anywhere on my own, but I gotta say, it makes me a little cranky to think of another man's blood in your system. I'm not good with shit like that."

"I've noticed." Alice grabbed her tank top, flinching when her fingers brushed against Ian's, shocking her. "Why are you hunting me?" She checked the sky again, but no clouds.

"Hunting you?" He narrowed his eyes. "Is that what it feels like to you? You think I'm a *threat*?"

"Yes. No. I don't know." Flustered by his intensity and her response to it, Alice turned away and tugged his shirt over her head. She tossed it over her shoulder at him without turning around, then pulled her tank top on. The navy blue material was soft and dry against her, and the built-in bra made her feel safer and more protected. She quickly donned her shorts, then carefully zipped the pearl into the front pocket, making sure it was secure. Then she shoved her feet into the flip flops. She grabbed her car keys, clenching them in her fist as she turned back to him. "Listen, Ian, I don't know you at all and—"

"Stop it!" Ian grabbed her upper arms, yanking her against him so her breasts were against his chest. "You're killing me, Alice. I need you to remember me. *I need it.*"

The instant her nipples brushed against him, hot desire flooded her. Not just desire. Need. Yearning. A sensual lust that crawled like hot lava over her skin. It shouldn't be happening. No man could break through her singular connection to the angelic realm and make her respond to him...and yet there was no way to deny her response. Real fear rippled through her at the realization of how easily this man could destroy everything that mattered to her, including the life of the only person on this earth that she loved.

"Alice. Stop resisting me. It won't work. There's no out."

She stared at him, seeing his commitment to claiming her. He would never let her go, not until he'd destroyed everything. No way. No chance. It didn't matter how fantastic it felt to be kissed by him, to feel responses so human and amazing. It wasn't worth it. She couldn't risk it.

Ian's eyes narrowed in warning, as if he sensed she was about to make a break for it. "Alice—"

"Leave me alone!" She tore herself out of Ian's grasp and sprinted for the ocean, for the water that was her only chance to find Catherine, away from the man who could destroy everything that mattered to her.

Everything.

CHAPTER FOUR

And here we go again...

The moment Alice cut Ian off, the damned curse came roaring back, ready to party. Champagne and streamers flew as the "get Ian to kill himself" celebration launched into full gear, a twelve-piece band breaking into a blistering rendition of the "stab yourself in the heart" polka.

Because she hadn't just walked away. Nope, she'd severed their emotional and mental connections as well, leaving him stranded worse than a gnat in the middle of a raging forest fire.

Since Ian had softened his shields so he could connect enough with her to save her life, he now had no safeguards to prop him up when she cut him off. Like a pathetic wuss, he had no answer for the emptiness that assaulted him. Virulent and poisonous, it was as if someone had jammed Ry's machete into his gut and was twisting it around just for shits and giggles.

He did not have time for this crap. Really. He didn't. Ian fisted his hands as he tried to summon the internal walls that would protect him from the destructive emotions that were toasting his anticipated demise. Even though he rebelled against the despair pouring through him, it came anyway, tearing apart his carefully erected protections with the force of a tsunami shredding a defenseless beach. "Alice!" Her name tore from him, ripping the last shreds of his control and thrusting him ruthlessly into the emotional torment of love wrested from the deepest of souls.

Ian lunged forward, trying to catch her as she raced down the beach, but the curse slammed into him, throwing him to his knees, like he was some minion genuflecting to the power of death. Jesus, he was getting tired of this. The curse hadn't gotten to him this badly in months, and yet it had brought him down three times in twenty minutes now that he was near Alice?

Things were definitely not heading in the right direction.

The voice that had killed his ancestors began to swirl though his mind with its annoyingly familiar refrain. *You can't survive without her. It's too much. Too lonely. You must die.*

The image of the graveyard that housed all his male ancestors flashed through Ian's mind and he swore. Shit. He was not in the mood to be buried right now. Seriously. "I appreciate the offer, but it doesn't fit in with my plans," he gritted out, fighting to keep a sense of humor, a sense of perspective, a sense of humanity in the face of such debilitating loss.

She's gone, the voice taunted. *She's dead. You lost her. Alice is gone.*

"She's not gone! She's in the ocean twenty yards away, for God's sake. I know it. You know it. So leave me the hell alone." But despite his words, agonizing loneliness filled Ian like he was some sorry-assed, love-struck sap. All he could think about was Alice's green eyes, the depth of pain and fear in her expression when he'd held her as she'd died. Three times she'd died in his arms, taken despite the fact that her own protector had been standing over her. And now she was heading off on her own again, no doubt to another death, because that seemed to be how the woman liked to fill her days. How many times was she going to die?

You failed to keep her safe. You suck.

Suck? He sucked? What the hell was that? But he knew it was true. He'd failed to keep her safe. *Failed*. It was his fault she'd died. It was his fault she'd suffered. It was his failure to fulfill his duty. What kind of a man was he, if he couldn't keep his own soul mate alive? The familiar emotions of shame and despair spread through him, like a powerful poison eating away at him, and he swore, steeling himself against the onslaught he knew was coming.

He had to be stronger than the curse. It was getting old, so fucking old, and he was getting tired of being brought down by it. Ian fought to regain control of his emotions. If he died, if he killed himself, he would leave Alice unprotected. *Alice needed him.* Without him, Alice would not come back from the dead this time. He repeated the same litany of reasons why he needed to stay alive, how it was his duty, how his reason for being was to keep her safe, but this time, it wasn't working. The despair was getting stronger instead of weaker.

He was too vulnerable to her. He'd dropped too many damn shields, and he was treading in that dangerous position his father had been in before he'd killed himself—

"Pull your shit together, Fitzgerald!" Ryland swung a piece of driftwood the size of a telephone pole at Ian's head.

"Shit!" Ian raised his arm to block it, and the log slammed into his forearm with enough force to shatter every bone, if he were human. Conveniently, he wasn't. As his arm made contact with the wood, a loud crack split the night, and the log snapped in half, breaking harmlessly around Ian instead of crushing his skull. His arm throbbing and his fingers bordering on numb, Ian scowled at his partner. "Son of a bitch, Ryland. What the hell was that?"

Ryland shrugged, his eyes a bottomless pit of anger and violence. "We don't have time for you to lose your shit over a woman. I figured that saving your own life would get your priorities back in line." He cocked an eyebrow. "You feeling better now? You look better. Not so sweaty and weepy."

"I'm not weepy." Adrenaline racing through him, Ian leapt to his feet and slammed his fist on Ry's shoulder. "Thanks, man."

"My pleasure. Always happy to help. Kinda enjoyed trying to kill you, to be honest."

Ian eyed his teammate. "Dude, you're so fucked."

"Tell me something I don't know." Ry raised his brows. "You gotta ditch that curse, though, Fitz. You won't always have me around to try to take you out and trigger those self-preservation instincts."

"The curse can go to hell." But Ian knew it wouldn't. The curse was an unstoppable, persistent little bugger. It was irreversible, except by Warwick Cardiff, the black magic wizard who'd tossed the curse at his family in the first place. The spell had dragged every one of his ancestors into the grave, their will to live destroyed by the loss of the women they loved.

For six hundred years, Ian had fended off the need to slit his own throat, and he wasn't going to start sticking his fingers in electric sockets just because he'd finally found the woman his soul was meant to connect with. Yeah, he wanted her. Yeah, he needed her. Yeah, he was completely at her mercy every time she turned those green eyes in his direction. So what?

It was time to man-up and be the emotional island he was meant to be. Ian fought down his need for her and his connection to her. He called upon the survival tools that his father had taught him to keep from becoming too emotionally connected with any woman.

Regret and loss filling him even as he did it, Ian blocked from his mind the desperate need in Alice's green eyes, the softness of her skin beneath his palms, the beauty of her kisses that had awakened in him something that he hadn't dared access his whole life. Resistance surged through him as he tried to separate himself from her, a desperate need to keep the connection with her open, to carve every memory of her onto his soul forever.

Shit! It wasn't working. Why in the hell did she have to be so damned addictive?

He had to be like his father, before he'd finally succumbed. He had to shut her out. Ian looked down at the ring on his left index finger. He was wearing his father's signet ring, which was decorated with the Fitzgerald family crest and emblazoned with the symbol of the Order of the Blade. Their mission was to save the world from rogue Calydons, warriors who had turned their immense power against innocents. No one else would ever fall victim to the Order, no one but rogue warriors, but against them, the Order was ruthless. They had to be. The lives of many depended on the Order's ability and willingness to sacrifice a single life.

Ian took a deep breath, drawing his shoulders back as he allowed the significance of the black onyx ring to settle over him. After six hundred years of keeping it locked away because he hadn't earned the right to wear it, Ian had finally put it on a month ago. Remembering his debt of honor had been the only thing that had enabled him to survive Alice's death the last time.

And now, he needed it to survive her being alive, because it was a hell of a lot harder to keep himself distant from her when he could feel her very soul with every breath he took. Shit.

He'd thought finding her would be his key to staying alive. He'd figured that his instinct to protect her would give him enough incentive to fight off the curse because he couldn't wave his manly weapons and beat down her assailants if he were lying belly up in a graveyard.

Yeah, well, that plan had worked out great. He'd managed to find her, but as it turned out, her impact on him was too strong. He understood now why his ancestors had all died from the curse. They'd been brave, powerful leaders who had crumbled. The truth was, the power of a woman over a Fitzgerald male was just too damned much. He sighed and ran his hand through his hair, still damp from his dive in the ocean. "I can take down entire armies of rogue Calydons, but

I'm no match for a green-eyed siren who weighs a buck twenty and kisses like the devil."

Ryland grinned. "She's one hell of a woman. All angels are. They're more than we are, that's for sure."

"Yeah, I'm getting that now." Ian realized now that it had been a mistake to find her. A huge mistake. He'd been better off when she'd been invisible to him. Now? It gave the curse too much ammunition.

Ryland raised his brows. "You okay?"

"Yeah, sure." He shook out his arms, refusing to turn toward the water to see what she was doing. "I'm good."

The most deadly and almost-rogue member of the Order of the Blade shot him a skeptical look as he folded his arms over his chest. "Are you? Because you still look like shit."

"Thanks. You do, too."

A brief grin flashed over Ryland's face. "That's because I'm a totally fucked-up bastard. I'm okay with it. I got no girl to impress." He jerked his chin toward the ocean. "She's getting away, in case you hadn't noticed."

Against his instincts, Ian glanced toward the water. Alice was swimming hard out into the open ocean. The waves were rough, whitecaps rising high out of the water. Further away from her, the water was quiet, but all around her, it was rough, as if the ocean had decided to make her way a little more difficult.

Damn. What was it with this woman and the ocean?

Not that he could let it matter to him. His only chance was to figure out how to stop worrying about her, and divest himself of the need to take responsibility for her. Or to imagine her naked. Or to think of kissing her. Or to recall what it felt like to make love to her.

Shit. He was really not doing a good job at forgetting the girl, was he? Ian let out his breath, steeling himself against the sight of her putting herself in danger. His happy place was a lot harder to find now that Alice had gotten to him. "Figures I had to get paired with a woman who won't bond with me *and* who keeps trying to get herself killed." If she'd been uncomplicated and simply fallen into his arms and let him keep her safe, his plan would have worked. Finding her would have helped him.

But she was not the woman he needed, and it was a mistake to hook up with her.

"She's not trying to get herself killed," Ry replied. "She's on a mission. I admire that. And the fact she thinks you're a pain in the ass she doesn't want around? She's a smart woman, seems to me."

"You're the pain in the ass." Ian narrowed his eyes as he watched her lithe body stroking through the water. There was a focused determination in her movements, and her gaze was fixed on one of the huge black rocks jutting out of the water a few hundred yards from the beach. He shifted restlessly as she neared it, willing her to make it safely to the rock, willing himself not to dive into the water and chase after her again.

He had to let her go.

Ryland was on alert beside him, and Ian knew his teammate was equally primed to go after her if she needed help. "She's sure a firestorm," Ry said. "I'm digging on her."

"Shut up." Because getting jealous would really help his mental state.

Ian ground his jaw as Alice reached the base of the rock. She dug her fingers into the porous volcanic rock and hauled herself out of the water. The muscles in her delicate arms flexed as she crawled up the steep incline, her hair streaming behind her. "I buried her three times. I watched the demons take her soul. It's not easy to forget that."

"I know." Ry's voice was soft. "Trust me, I know."

Ian glanced at Ryland in surprise, wondering who had died in the warrior's life. But before he could question him, the images of Alice's deaths flashed through his mind. Too real. Too visceral. Too debilitating. Those thoughts were really not helping his cause.

Ian ground his jaw, fighting to distance himself from the agony of losing her. He focused on her as she crested the rock, drinking in the glint of the turquoise moonlight on her wet hair. He breathed deeply, inhaling her scent even from a distance. She was alive. In front of him. Not dead. Not right now. See? It was a rosy day on the beach, right? All good.

As he watched her, he felt himself beginning to separate from her as he rebuilt the walls that had protected him from the curse. The emotional shields that had kept him from noticing any female, let alone bonding with one.

"Hey." Ryland glanced sharply at him. "You going to go get her or what?"

"Nope." Ian knew he had no choice. "She's alive. I saved her. My job's done."

Ryland's eyes narrowed. "What the hell are you doing?"

"Paying my debt to my father." Ian felt the familiar lack of emotion settle over him, wiping away the flash of regret that he was isolating himself from her. He'd had to rebuild himself after Alice had died in his arms the first time, and he was better at it now. No more spending months in chains just to stay alive. He was a veritable rock. Go, him.

Now that he knew she was safe, he had to let her go. He had a promise to keep, a debt owed, family honor to restore. He had to find a way to release the souls of his seven dishonored ancestors from their ignominious hell reserved for Order of the Blade members who died ignobly...by their own hand.

Until Ian broke the curse and freed the souls of his father and grandfather, they would suffer in eternity. And if he died before he broke the curse? Eternal hell for all. He was the last Fitzgerald. There would be no one left to save them. There was no way he was going to risk that just because he had the hots for a certain angel.

He'd spent too long chasing her down. It was time to move on. Refusing to acknowledge the regret, he forced himself to turn away. He grabbed his shirt off the beach, the one she'd rejected. He yanked it over his head and began to stride back toward the road, toward the SUV that had brought the three men there.

"Hey!" Ryland jumped in front of him and shoved at his chest. "What the fuck are you doing?"

"Leaving." Ian sidestepped him and kept walking, keeping his back toward the water and the woman who could so easily reach into his soul and crush it. Because who had time to have their soul crushed? No one he knew.

"The hell you are." Ryland grabbed his arm and spun him back. "Some bastard we don't know is trying to destroy the Order, and he's trying to wipe out our trio of guardian angels. We've found Sarah, but there are still two more, one of which we're pretty damn sure is the woman who's got you all twisted up."

"What are you talking about?" That was the first Ian had heard about someone trying to destroy the Order. He knew they'd had some close calls recently when one of their teammates, Kane Santiago, had tracked his *sheva* into a hell storm, but Ian had been hunting for Alice at the time, and he'd missed out on it. "Who's trying to take down the Order?" Battles were one thing, nothing more than a typical day, but someone targeting the Order specifically was a different matter. No one dared take them on.

Frustration flashed across Ryland's face. "We don't know. Kane saw him, but he was insane at the time, so he doesn't remember much. Gideon and Quinn are trying to track the guy. You and I have been assigned to find Alice and determine whether she is one of the Order's guardian angels."

"*Him*? What do you know about him?" A dark foreboding began to seethe inside him, an ominous sense of something seriously wrong. "What did I miss?"

"What did you miss?" Ryland spat at him in disgust. "You missed a hell of a lot over the last year while you were pining over the death of your *sheva* instead of being where you needed to be."

Ian was not interested in revisiting the months he'd spent chained up because he'd been too pathetic to keep himself alive after Elijah had done his Order duty of protecting his teammate by murdering Ian's *sheva* before she could turn him insane. Ian was aware that he'd failed to deliver as an Order member, and it was a bitter taste in his mouth. "I'm not talking about what happened back then. I'm talking about what's going on now." The past was a done deal, but if there were problems now, he wanted to be a part of the team that would handle it.

Ryland shook his head, and Ian didn't miss the unflinching evasiveness in Ryland's gaze. "You and me pulled angel duty. That's all that matters. If Alice is part of the trio that protects us, then we bring her back to Dante's mansion where we can keep her safe. That's why we're here."

Dante Sinclair, their former leader, had been murdered several months ago. He was a legend, a man of such intense power that he'd been able to lead a team of ruffians. Since his death, the Order had been vulnerable and fragmenting, as no one had ascended into the role of leader. According to Calydon lore, a leader would naturally emerge when the time was right, but no one had landed in the middle of the ballroom with a nametag declaring him as the next Order leader, so they were still flying solo and it wasn't going well. They were running missions out of Dante's mansion, which now served as their headquarters.

Why would they want to take Alice back to Dante's place? "I came after Alice because I thought she would help me fight off the curse. That's why *I'm* here. What the hell else is going on?" He hadn't been in close contact with the rest of the Order in almost two months. He and Vaughn had been searching relentlessly for Alice and the man who had murdered her, a man named Flynn Shapiro who appeared to be the same race of beings as Vaughn, whatever that was.

Ry shook his head once. Sharply. "You've been cut out of

the loop. You're in no shape to handle the truth, Fitz."

Ian stiffened. "What does that mean?"

"No more fighting for you, Fitz. Not right now. Your job is to get the girl and bring her home."

Ian saw the unyielding set to Ryland's jaw and realized he spoke the truth. He'd been banned from the front lines, and cut from the inner circle. Son of a bitch. "I can't be benched. The Order is what I live for—"

"Right now, you're a vacuum for despair and hell, and you can't see past your own issues. We needed you in the woods with Kane, and you weren't there. The team made a decision. Until you pull your shit together, you're out of combat and out of the information loop." Ry's eyes flashed. "Be a fucking man, Ian. Do your job. There aren't enough of us to save this ship without you. We need you." Then he turned on his heel and strode back toward the water, toward Alice.

Ian ran his hand through his hair as he watched Ryland stride toward the water to pursue Alice, the woman who had destroyed everything for him. Before he'd met her, he'd been in control of the curse. He'd also been tracking well toward finding the bastard who'd issued it, and he'd been honoring the legacy of his father and grandfather by becoming one of the most deadly members of the Order of the Blade. He'd been surviving, shoving forward to discharge his oath, until he'd met her a year ago. All had been good until Alice had landed in his arms and his teammate had killed her in the name of the greater good, sending him into a year of hell.

She was his Achilles heel, his vulnerability. She was the reason he'd been derelict in his duties lately. Escorting her back to the Order? Exposing himself to her again? He knew now it wasn't worth the risk of jeopardizing everything that mattered to him: the Order, his oath, restoring his family honor.

It was time to go. Ryland had it under control.

But as Ian turned away, his instincts roared at him not to leave Alice. He clenched his fists and kept walking, knowing his only chance to stay alive was to get away from her influence. He would be doing no one any favors if he died, and now that Ryland was convinced she was one of the Order's three guardian angels, she would be well-protected.

So she was safe. It wasn't his job to protect her anymore.

But as he got further away from her, a sheen of sweat broke out over his skin, and his head began to pound. His muscles were so taut that they pulsed with pain, like an invisible cord was binding him to Alice, and it was stretching to the breaking point.

Ian fisted his hands and lowered his head, as though he were fighting a hurricane force wind trying to stop him from leaving. He focused on things that mattered: the cold metal of his father's ring, his connection to a family that was long dead, a father who had died because of what he'd done, and what he had to fix.

There was a loud splash that made Ian jump, and instinctively, he spun around, searching the water for Alice. She wasn't at the rock where he'd last seen her. Panic hit him before he found her at the base of one of the massive black rocks further out to sea, stretching at least a hundred feet out of the water. She'd clearly decided the first one hadn't been far enough offshore, and had struck out for one further away.

The splash had been Ryland hitting the water, and his hard body was striking fast against the waves as he swam after her.

Alice glanced over her shoulder at Ryland, and Ian saw her stiffen when she realized she was being pursued. She tore her gaze off Ry and looked up, searching the shore. She saw Ian, and for a split second, his heart stopped beating, sucked into the depths of her being. The air seemed to go utterly still, and the sound of the crashing waves went silent, until all that remained was Alice. She froze, her fingers digging into the black rock, her body undulating softly as the waves pushed her around. Her blue tank top was plastered to her skin, and her long hair was cascading down her back. She looked small and vulnerable out there, a tiny thing in a massive ocean, clinging to the base of a black rock that loomed so high and threatening.

She was a woman with a death sentence on her head... just like him. Destined to die.

Shit. They were the same. At least in that way. Involuntarily, Ian took a step toward her, then stopped. Jesus. What was he doing? She was too dangerous to him.

Alice shivered and then tore her gaze from his. She turned her back on him, and started to climb the rock. She was struggling to ascend, and for a split second, she wavered, and he thought she was going to fall—

His mind suddenly flashed back to the first time he'd seen her. It had been when he and his teammate Elijah had been closing in on the trail of the warrior who had cursed his great grandfather. After hunting him for so long, Ian had scented victory and been so close to his prey...until Alice had come tumbling down the side of a massive cliff that was too damned reminiscent of the rock she was currently trying to climb. She'd jerked him instantly and completely from his single-minded focus on the wizard. He'd had no time to react or think. He'd simply leapt beneath her and caught her, breaking her fall before she crushed herself on the rocks...

Holy shit. His adrenaline kicked on as he finally connected the facts...realizations that had eluded him because he'd been so busy trying to stay alive. "Son of a bitch," he muttered. "She was there." Alice had been there, in that abandoned, stark section of high desert, when he'd almost nailed Warwick Cardiff, the black magic wizard who had cursed his family. Did she know him? Could she find the wizard for him? What was her connection to the wizard? Or had it been a fluke?

Fragments of information began to circle in his mind, pieces that didn't quite fit. Suddenly, Ry's evasiveness made sense. "Hey!" He broke into a run, sprinting after his teammate. "Ryland!"

The Order of the Blade member didn't even look back.

"Ry!" Ian called out his mace with a loud crack and a flash of black light. "Hey!" He hurled his mace, and it crashed into the water a fraction of an inch from Ryland's face.

Ry immediately stopped swimming and spun around. "What the hell was that?"

Ian charged through the water, the foamy white spray lashing out into the air as his boots broke the surface. "Who's trying to kill the angels? Who's after the Order?" It couldn't be who he thought it was. A coincidence... it *couldn't be.* But it made sense. It explained why the Order thought cutting him out was a good idea. "Who is it?"

Ry stood up in the deep water, the streams of water glittering on his shoulders in the darkness. "You're out of the loop—"

"It's Warwick, isn't it? Warwick Cardiff? That's who it is?"

Ry frowned. "Who is Warwick Cardiff?"

Ian swore, realizing that Ryland really didn't know. But Gideon and Kane and a few of the others knew the name. Ry was too obsessed with his own hell to bother with anyone else's problems. They might have realized the connection, but not told Ryland the details. Ian decided to fill him in, not caring why the others might have wanted Ry in the dark. "He's the wizard who cursed my family—"

Ryland snorted in disgust. "Shit, Ian. Let it go. We don't have time for that—"

"We might." Ian looked past Ryland to where Alice was almost to the top of the rock. "When Elijah and I were tracking Cardiff, Alice was there. We were in the middle of the high desert," he said. "No one was around for a hundred miles...except Alice. The only footprints we saw there were the hoofprints of Cardiff's horse. Why else would she be there?"

If Alice could help him find Warwick, there was no way he was letting her go, no matter how dangerous she was.

Ry stared at him. "Hoofprints," he echoed. "Your wizard rides a horse?"

"Yeah, a black stallion that can fly. Deathbringer." Ian's adrenaline suddenly went on alert at Ry's stunned expression. "What is it?"

"Nothing." Ryland turned quickly away, but not before Ian saw the evasive flick of his eyes.

Ian knew then. Without Ryland even saying a word, he knew. The man trying to destroy the Order had been riding a black horse. Warwick? The bastard wasn't satisfied with taking out the Fitzgerald clan? "You need me," Ian said softly as he looked toward the rock. "If it's Warwick, you can't do it without me." Ian had spent thousands of hours researching demon magic to try to find a way to break the curse. He hadn't succeeded, but he understood a lot more about magic than the rest of the team did.

"Alice is the one we need," Ryland said, quickly, softly, but there was no mistaking the determination in his tone. Alice was not getting away from the Order. Not today. "She's one of our angels. Without her, we are nothing."

Ian looked toward the rock, and anticipation pulsed through him as he watched her pull herself up onto the top. Her body was lithe and strong, her hips curved and appealing. The turquoise moon cast a vibrant tint across her skin, making hot desire surge far too powerfully.

Dangerous didn't even begin to describe her, but at the same time...was she his chance? The opening he'd been searching for?

She looked back over her shoulder at him, as if she'd felt his stare. She tensed when she saw he was closer to her now. This time, there wasn't heat emanating from her gaze. Her eyes narrowed, her muscles tightened, and she shook her head once. Rejecting him without caring what he wanted. Telling him to back off.

If she could lead him to Warwick, there was no chance of that happening. No matter how badly they both wanted to go their separate ways.

"Stay here," he ordered Ryland, without taking his gaze off Alice. "I'll handle this."

Without waiting for an answer, Ian shoved past him, but Ryland grabbed his arm. "Fitz."

Ian looked at him. "What?"

"The future of the Order is at stake. If Alice is involved, if your wizard is involved, you need to step aside. You aren't capable of handling either of them."

Ian's eyes blazed at the insult. "You've fought beside me for six hundred years. You're questioning my ability to be a warrior?"

Ryland didn't look away. "Yeah, I am. Now that Dante is dead, we still have no one who has stepped into the role of our leader. I will not let the Order die. It's more important to me than your ego." Fury began to simmer through him. "I am descended from—"

"A line of males too weak to keep themselves alive," Ryland said.

Ian stiffened. "That's all you see when you look at the legendary men who were the best Order of the Blade members ever to exist? That's all you fucking see?"

Something flickered in Ry's eyes. "No, it's not all I see," he admitted. He met Ian's gaze and gave a slight nod. "Okay, Fitz, you have one chance. Get the girl, bring her back here, and we'll return to the mansion. If you snap, if you fail, you're done, and I will lead the team sent to strip you of your title. Got it?"

Ian's lip curled in disgust, but he said nothing. He was worthy of being in the Order. It was all he lived for. He would not let them cut him out. If Warwick Cardiff was indeed the one trying to take down the Order, they needed him...and they might need Alice, depending on what her true story was.

He gave no response to Ryland. He simply pushed past him, heading right toward the woman who was more than he could handle, toward the woman who could die any second, toward the woman who was supposed to be his *sheva*, and yet inexplicably didn't want a damn thing to do with him.

Too bad for her.

They were about to get involved, whether she wanted to or not.

Risky as it was, he couldn't help but feel damned pleased at the idea of making things happen with the angel who could bring him to his knees with a single kiss.

Self-preservation? Fuck it. He was going in, and he did nothing halfway.

CHAPTER FIVE

Alice's heart began to race as she saw Ian dive through the waves in pursuit of her, his powerful body breaking through the whitecaps with minimal effort. Just like before, the mere anticipation of his nearness sent waves of awareness and desire rushing through her...along with a sense of danger.

He was too determined, and the look on Ry's face was too arrogant as he followed Ian through the waves. She didn't know what they wanted from her, but she knew she couldn't afford it.

She quickly turned her back on them and moved to the edge of the rock, scanning the surface of the ocean for the bumps that were too sleek and too misty to be natural. The pearl was secure in her pocket, still hidden there despite all that had happened since she'd thrown herself into the water.

The Mageaan had known she was in the ocean. They'd tried to kill her, which meant they were nearby, or they had been at least. Were they still around? Trying to ignore the sound of Ian getting closer to her, Alice inched toward the edge of the rock.

She quickly unzipped her pocket and removed the pearl. Glittering streaks of red, orange, crimson, and silver sliced across its surface, like the clouds at sunset on the eve of a hurricane. "Please let this work," she whispered. It was such a risk to reveal that she had the pearl. To give it away was to surrender the one safeguard she had against an eternity of hell, against the future that Ian seemed to be pushing her towards.

But without the help of the creatures in the water below, she had no chance to find Catherine. The Mageaan owned the oceans. They knew everything and everyone that passed through their waters. They would know where Catherine was, but they would never reveal it to an outsider. Not to someone who represented all they had lost…unless she had something to offer them that was more than they could resist.

The pearl was that item. She might be able to convince the Mageaan to trade information for the jewel. Of course, once she reached Catherine… A cold chill rippled through her. How would she accomplish that without Flynn? She couldn't manage by herself what needed to be done.

No. She couldn't worry about that now. None of it mattered if she couldn't find Catherine in the first place, and the Mageaan were the only ones who would know how to find the hidden lair that was obscured by magic and spells, so that no one could find it. No one knew where it was except the man who had created it, and those who haunted the ocean.

She carefully held the pearl up between her thumb and index finger so that the moon's blue-green rays seemed to refract through it, bringing it to life. She glanced over her shoulder and saw Ian was almost to the rock, his muscled shoulders churning powerfully through the whitecaps as he neared.

Alice quickly extended her hand out over the ocean. It was risky, exposing it like that, but she was over a hundred feet above the water. The Mageaan were ocean-bound, and they would not be able to steal it from her up here. "I have one of the Pearls of Lycanth," she shouted. "I will trade it for your help!" The wind seemed to strip the words from her mouth and thrust them out across the water, reverberating again and again. "You can have it," she yelled, even as fear rippled through her at the idea of giving it up. "I will offer it freely!"

A haunted call sounded across the ocean, making the hairs on her arms stand up. Faint drifts of mist formed on the horizon. Excitement shot through her. Was that the Mageaan? "I have the pearl," she yelled again, holding it out for them to see. "It's genuine. I'll trade it for your help!"

The mist swirled closer and thicker, the water churned more violently, and the wind began to howl. Her hair slashed her cheeks, her clothes snapped in the gusts. On the edges of the wind, Alice thought she heard the sound of a woman screaming. Dozens of women wailing, the kind of shrieks that heralded the coming of a brutal death. Their torment was horrific, the pain of souls being ripped apart for an eternity of suffering.

She froze, horrified by the sound. What was that? Was that the Mageaan? If it was, it was so much worse than she'd expected. She'd heard the stories. She'd been warned a thousand times. But there had been no way to comprehend the depths of such suffering. The edge to their screams was like a blade shredding the night. Was that her future? Was that what she would become without the pearl to protect her?

Real terror rippled through her. *I can't do this.* Her hand faltered, and she started to lower it—

A violent gust of wind slammed into her shoulders from behind, thrusting her forward off the edge of the rock. She screamed as she was thrust into the air, and then the wind tore the pearl from her grasp. "No!"

Anguish tore through her as she lunged for it, but her hand closed on empty air as the pearl plummeted down toward the water, the wind howling in triumph, as if the Mageaan themselves had compelled it to help them. Beneath her swelled the mist, but it was no longer white. It was a seething, frothing purple and black pool of poison—

"Hey!" A hand clamped around her wrist, jerking her backwards.

Alice gasped as she ricocheted back against the side of the rock, her body slamming into hard granite, suspended above the tumultuous ocean by one arm. She looked up, and her heart stuttered when she saw Ian down on one knee on the top of the rock, his fingers locked around her wrist. "No, no!" She tugged at her arm. "Let me go! I have to get the pearl! I dropped it in the water!" Frantic, she kicked at the rock, trying to tear herself out of his grasp.

"Hey!" He tightened his grip, ocean water streaming down his arm over his hand. "A pearl? You're serious? You'll never find a pearl down there. That ocean is trying to kill you."

"I don't care! Let me go!" Without the pearl, she had nothing: no future for herself *and* no way to find Catherine. "I have to get it!" Frantic, she twisted around to search the frothing depths, but her heart sank when she saw the ocean churning beneath her. Hate-filled green and purple swells were fighting to get to her, to reclaim the victim they'd lost once. Deadly mist swirled over the surface of the water.

She couldn't survive that. There was no way she could reclaim her pearl from that. Despair coursed through her, utter despair. It was gone. Without it, Catherine was lost to her. One moment of fear and hesitation for her own stupid life, and she'd lost her chance. Frustration and guilt burned through Alice, and all the fight drained from her body. She hung limply from Ian's grasp, the cold wet rock pressing against her as she dangled over her death. This couldn't happen again. She couldn't fail again.

"Alice." Ian's voice was low. Impatient. "Look at me."

She pulled her gaze from the ocean and looked up, compelled by the urgency in his voice. The moment she met his intense gaze, awareness coursed through her. Awareness of the man, of herself, of something more personal than it should have been. Fear rippled through her, fear of the warrior who held her wrist.

"I've never met someone more likely to die than I am," he

said conversationally, as if he weren't the only thing standing between her and a nightmare. "It's damned inconvenient."

She met his gaze, her jaw jutting out. "I'm not afraid of death."

"No, I can see that." One eyebrow was raised, but his eyes were cool and calculating. Water was streaming down his arm over hers, but his grip was tight and secure. "What is it that you *are* afraid of, Alice?"

What was she afraid of? Unbidden, the memory flashed into her mind. Her mother, blood pouring from a wound in her chest, laboring to breathe. Her mother's blond hair matted with blood and dirt, her bright blue eyes glazed over with the onset of death, her lips parted as she fought to share those last words while Alice sat there, inches away, unable to do the one simple thing that would have saved her life—

Ian's gaze sharpened. *Who is that in your mind,* sheva? *Who died like that?* His voice was soft and gentle, reaching deep into her soul, tearing away at the protective shields that enabled her to get through her life every day.

She quickly stiffened, and shook her head. "Leave me alone."

Ian's eyes narrowed. "Maybe you should save that request for after I pull you back up."

Alice grimaced, and glanced down, the sea was still churning beneath her. Waves splashed up, reaching for her ankles. Instinctively, she pulled her feet up, bracing them against the rock. "You have a point."

"As I thought." Ian grinned and braced himself on the rock. "Ready?"

She met his gaze, fighting not to be swallowed up by his piercing stare. "Ready." She dug her toes into the rock.

"On three." He cocked an eyebrow. "One." He held his other hand out to her.

After a split second of hesitation, she reached up and took his hand. His grip was strong around her wrists. Damn, the man was powerful. How was that fair? He could probably take down the world, and she, an angel of life, couldn't save even a single person, no matter how simple a task it would be to help them.

He braced himself. "Two."

She wrapped her fingers around his wrist, and electricity jumped between them. Dammit. Why hadn't things lessened between them? Why was he still affecting her like this?

"Three." He gave a curt nod and pulled.

She pushed off the rock as he shifted his body, easily swinging her to the top. Her bare feet landed silently on the gritty surface, her toes tiny and pale next to the heavy boots he was still wearing. "Swimming's easier without boots," she said, trying to put distance between them.

He shrugged. "I was in a rush. You were getting away."

There was that sense of being hunted by him again. Alice instinctively pulled out of his grasp. "What do you want from me?"

Ian went still for a moment, and his gaze bore down on her. She felt pressure in her mind as he tried to break past her barriers, connecting with her too intimately. She stiffened immediately and folded her arms over her chest, raising her chin as she faced him, fighting against the swirl of emotion he aroused in her. "You're not stalking me because of the soul mate thing, are you? Because I'm not yours—"

"Yes, you are." His response was instant and unyielding, and she felt her pulse quicken in response.

She couldn't afford to belong to him. She didn't want to crave him so badly that she felt like her own soul would burst into violent flames if he walked away from her…but she did. It was like he'd ignited a raging fire within her, one that he stoked ever higher with each touch, with each word, with each kiss.

And as a smug grin spread over his face, she knew that he was well aware of exactly how he affected her.

"Damn you, Ian," she snapped.

He grinned more broadly, and she suddenly realized that she'd just laid down a challenge that he was delighted to accept. And even scarier was the realization that she didn't want him to be dissuaded from pursuing her.

Oh, God. What was she getting into? "Who are you, Ian? Why are you after me?"

He held up his index finger to silence her questions. "Warwick Cardiff."

Alice froze at the name, and her skin turned to ice. She took a step backwards, frantically looking around her for some sort of defense. There was nothing. She had nothing. She—

"Hey." He caught her arm, and she yelped, jumping out of his grasp. He instantly held out his hands in a show of peace, but at the same time, she felt the intensity of his readiness to grab her if she got out of range. "It's okay. I save you, remember? I don't hurt you."

"Not yet." She eased around the top of the rock, keeping to the edge. "Are you with Warwick? Do you work for him?"

"No." His voice was hard. Triumphant. As if her reaction to that name had confirmed his suspicions. "Do you?"

"Me?" She almost laughed at the absurdity of it. "He's a ruthless bastard who has my sister—" She immediately cut herself off. She couldn't afford to reveal anything that could get them in trouble. As an angel, she was allowed to have no loyalties, and she had to protect all secrets about angels. And yet, she kept spilling those tidbits to him? Why? She didn't understand, but it wasn't good.

His eyes narrowed. "Catherine? Catherine Taylor?"

She stared at him, fear ripping through her. "How do you know her name?"

He gave a sigh of impatience. "Don't you remember anything you told me before you died? I thought that your name was Catherine because when you died the first time, you had Catherine's ID in your wallet. Last time we met, you told me that Catherine was your sister, and your name was Alice

Shaw. You were the one who died the first time, not Catherine, even though you had her ID. You don't remember all that?"

Alice grimaced. "No." When had she told him Catherine was her sister? Why? She reserved that lie for people who were too close to the truth, and for her own private moments of fantasy. What did he know? Frustrated, she shoved her wet hair out of her face. Why couldn't she remember? How much time had she spent with this man? All she recalled were the flashes of passion, of intense desire, of a connection so strong that it terrified her.

"What do you know about him?" Ian didn't move, but he was watching her with raw intensity.

Alice squeezed the water out of the ends of her hair, the strong wind chilly. "Why? Why do you care about him?" Anything having to do with Warwick was dangerous. Was the wizard why Ian had been hunting her? She felt like her world was spiraling out of control, and she was fighting desperately for balance. And the pearl, God, the pearl. Did the Mageaan have it?

"Because he cursed my family," Ian said. "It's time for the curse to end. I need to find him to make it happen."

Alice sensed the urgency in his voice, the desperation in his eyes. For a split second, her shields fell, and his emotions came tumbling over her. Grief, despair, guilt, and intense determination. Recognition pulsed through her, and she touched his arm briefly. It was exactly how she felt, every minute of every day. "I need to find him to save my sister." Again the lie about Catherine's true identity. If she'd chosen to lie to him the first time, she must have had a reason. "Cardiff has her."

Anticipation gleamed in his eyes. "Any leads?"

"Some." Alice instinctively glanced over her shoulder where her pearl had disappeared. "Warwick's lands are on an island in the ocean. It's protected by magic, and it's impossible to find, unless you know where it is."

Ian's eyes narrowed as he looked out across the waters. "A hidden island," he murmured thoughtfully. "That explains why I was never able to find it." He glanced at her, his gaze so sharp she could almost see the wheels turning in his mind. "You've found it?"

She shook her head. "No, not quite. Have you heard of the Mageaan?"

Ian shook his head. "No. Who are they?"

"Fallen angels sentenced to an eternity of suffering in the oceans. Over time, they lose their humanity, both their souls and their physical bodies, until they are mere ghosts, bound to the ocean."

He raised his brows. "Weird that I've never heard of them."

"Angels like to keep secrets," she said. "The Mageaan own the oceans, and they know everything that goes on. But they are vile and hateful and will help no one unless it's to their benefit." She hesitated, and then decided not to tell him about the pearl. No one could know about it. "I had something they might be willing to trade for, but I lost it."

"The pearl."

She felt the blood drain from her face. "What pearl?" she hedged.

Ian laughed softly. "Sweetheart, you have to start keeping track of what you tell me during moments of stress. You were shouting about it when I kept you from plummeting to your death about two minutes ago." He raised his brows. "I'm one of those guys who actually listens when his woman talks. I'm a rare breed. Dangerous, apparently, since you aren't expecting me to hear you."

She would have laughed at his humor, which she had to admit was sort of appealing, except she was entirely too strung-out to find amusement in the situation. He might know she'd lost a pearl, but he had no way of knowing it was the pearl of Lycanth. "Okay, yes, it's a pearl. An old one that was reportedly stolen from their treasures a thousand years ago. It has no value, except to them." A partial truth, enough to be able to look him in the eye while saying it, but obscure enough to hide the secrets he couldn't know. "But I dropped it in the water. That was my last chance."

Ian cupped her face, his fingers tantalizingly soft against her damp skin. "Alice, there's always another chance."

She met his gaze then, his intense, powerful gaze, and she realized what he was saying. "You? You'll help me?"

"We'll help each other." He edged forward, crowding her space, and he didn't stop until his chest was almost against hers, forcing her to crane her neck to look at him, or else step back. "We both want to find him. I can help you. You help me. The slippery bastard's days of hiding are over."

"I have to find him." It was difficult to breathe with Ian so close. She didn't step back, but her heart started to race. There was no mistaking Ian's intense strength and determination. He was even more powerful than Flynn, who was the backup she'd been counting on when they finally found Warwick's lands. But... "You're dangerous to me," she whispered.

"Am I?" A grim smile flitted across Ian's hard features. "And you're my doom, in too many ways. But I'm willing to take the risk. Are you?"

She stood taller at the challenge in his voice and lifted her chin. Fear burned through her, but deeper still was her need to help Catherine. To end the nightmares that had been haunting her for years. If he could do that... "When we find him, will you help me...save...Catherine?" 'Save' was a close enough word to what she needed to do when she found Catherine, and it would appeal to his Order of the Blade oath to protect.

Because it wasn't enough to simply find Warwick's island. She needed Ian for that final step, the one she couldn't do by herself, no matter how badly she wanted to.

Ian narrowed his eyes for a split second. "I swore an oath

to the Order to put its mission first over all others, no matter what the cost," he said. "I will help your sister if I can, but not if it conflicts with what I'm sworn to protect."

"What?" She stared at him. Hello? Hadn't she just offered him something to protect? "What kind of answer is that?"

"The Order of the Blade is an elite team created two thousand years ago to protect innocents from rogue Calydons. We are not allowed to sacrifice ourselves to protect others, because without us, there is no way to stop them. The greater good triumphs."

She gazed at him in dismay. "You would let an innocent die to save yourself?"

"I would let an innocent die if it was the only way to save a thousand others." Flint glittered in his eyes. "It's what I have to do, Alice." He raised his brows. "If you're an angel, you, of anyone, should understand about the greater good. Isn't that what angels are all about?"

She swallowed and looked away for a split second. "Yeah, sure, the greater good," she agreed. "That's what I do every day. Save the world." She couldn't quite keep the bitterness out of her voice, and she grimaced when she saw the flicker of interest on Ian's face. She immediately faced him again and raised her chin. "Promise me you will help me with Catherine," she said.

"I don't make promises unless I know I can keep them," he said. "I don't know what I'll find at his place, but if there's any way at all that I can save her, I will." He met her gaze. "My promise is that I will do my absolute best to save your sister. If there is a way to do it without violating my oath, I will find it and do it. I promise you my best, and trust me, that's a damn good offer. Deal?"

Alice grimaced, shifting under his stare. Did she really dare align herself with a man who was too smart to trap himself with a simple promise? A man who unsettled her far too deeply? A man she couldn't get out of her mind? A man who had saved her life twice in the last ten minutes? A man who claimed her for his own, threatening to strip her of everything she was?

She thought of her mother dying in her arms, and she knew the answer was yes. Absolutely, unequivocally, without a doubt, yes. Anything to keep the past from happening again. She met his gaze. "It's a deal."

† † †

Relief poured through Ian at Alice's acquiescence. She was on his team. *Hot damn.* She was the first person he'd come across in years who had helpful information about the elusive wizard who had cursed his family. She was the break he needed.

But at the same time, dark foreboding settled around him. A Calydon's *sheva* spelled doom for both parties even under the best of circumstances, and for Ian, his soul mate was the key to an even darker fate.

Every withdrawal by Alice, every time death tried to take her again, every moment that his mark failed to appear on her arm...it was a constant, inexorable slide from sanity to suicidal madness.

It couldn't stay like this.

Alice's expression grew wary. "What is it?" She glanced over her shoulder, as if looking for something to defend herself against him.

"No. Don't retreat." He closed the distance between them in two steps, forcing himself to stop when she leaped back. Anguish tore through him as his *sheva* distanced herself from him again. Son of a bitch. How had he managed to get the one *sheva* in history that was so damn resistant to her mate? It shouldn't be possible, but it was.

Damn that curse. It knew what it was doing by selecting Alice for him.

Alice pulled back, inching so close to the edge of the rock, Ian knew she was considering jumping.

"Stop." Forcing himself to hold back, he raised his palms in a gesture of peace. "Don't retreat. Stay where you are."

She stopped, and then frowned at him. "Are you in pain?"

"I'm fine." He took a deep breath, fighting not to scare her into bolting. As a Calydon, it was etched in the very marrow of his being to claim his woman, not to stand back and give her space. What he was trying to do now was against his nature on so many levels, and with the addition of the curse, it was hell. The need to lock her down was fierce. If he could just get his brand on her arm, it would help. But without it, she was still an elusive enigma, able to flutter out of his life without a moment of hesitation. "If we are going to work together," he said, keeping his voice contained, "there's one thing that is going to have to change."

She stiffened. "What's that?"

"Your response to me." There was no point in hiding it. It was what it was, and he was too seasoned of a warrior not to know when a threat could not be ignored.

Her mouth tightened, but a faint flush rose on her cheeks, sending heat spiraling through his body. "What do you mean?"

"My destiny," he said quietly, "is to find the woman who touches my soul, and then I have to lose her."

"Yes, you told me." She swallowed, but he saw empathy flash in her eyes. "I know what that's like, to lose someone," she said, her voice softening. "That's awful."

He nodded and inched closer, his entire soul screaming to connect with her. "The curse makes the loss so powerful that it's impossible to withstand. Suicide is the only way out."

Alice stared at him. "Suicide?" She glanced at the brand on his forearm and then back at his face. "But you're an immortal warrior. I don't understand. How could anything affect you that strongly?"

"Apparently, I'm a sensitive guy. You didn't notice that

about me right away?" He moved closer, carefully, slowly encroaching on her space. "I cry at chick flicks and weddings."

The smallest hint of a smile pulled at the corner of her mouth. "Do you now? Why do I find that hard to believe?"

"Just because I'm a badass warrior who is a critical part of the Order of the Blade team, and I spend my days saving the world and killing rogue Calydons, you think I don't have a sensitive side?" Another step, and he was close enough to catch her scent, even though the wind was blowing it in the other direction. She smelled like salt and brine from the ocean, but beneath that was the hint of something fresh and exotic, something pure, like a lily on a spring breeze.

She cocked her head, and he was pleased to see a thoughtful expression on her face. No longer fear or distrust. No longer trying to shut him out. She was analyzing him now, and that was a hell of a lot better than fearing him. "Do you really?" she asked, as if she wasn't quite sure what to believe. "I mean, do you really have a sensitive side? I believe you about the killing bad guys." She met his gaze. "That's why I agreed to team up with you."

He didn't have to feign the look of agony. "That's the reason? It had nothing at all to do with the scorching flames searing the air every time we get close to each other? It wasn't because your soul burns for me and you can't take one more minute without my lips against yours, and my soul entwined with yours?"

Her eyes widened. "No, definitely not that."

"Shit. I don't get how you're so immune to my charms. I'm generally considered a ladies' man, you know." He reached out ever so gently and encircled her wrists lightly with his fingers. She stiffened, but when he didn't tighten his grip, she didn't pull away. "The first time I met you, I was with my teammate, Elijah," he said. "Do you remember?"

"No…" She let the word trail off, as if she wasn't sure what she knew and what she didn't. She cocked her head, and he saw curiosity flare in her eyes, making him realize that she truly did not recognize him or remember what had happened.

Urgency coursed through him. He needed her to remember. The fact he wasn't imprinted in her mind or her soul was brutal, against the laws of what bound them. "We were tracking Cardiff," he said.

Her eyes widened. "You found him?"

He shook his head. "I was following a lead. We were in the mountains of southeast Washington, closing hard when I heard a scream from the heavens."

"The heavens?" She rolled her eyes, in a decidedly human reaction that was pretty damn cute. "Isn't that a little dramatic?"

He raised his brows. "So, now you're calling me a drama queen?"

She burst out laughing. "It hadn't occurred to me, but hey, if that's your claim to fame, it's all yours."

He grinned, loving the sound of her laughter. "I looked up to the heavens, as I said. Know what I saw?"

"Butterflies?   Clouds   shaped   like   hearts?"
"Almost." He tightened his grip on her wrist. "A woman had just tumbled off the edge of a cliff at least two hundred feet above my head, and she was plummeting straight down to certain death on the rocks below." He swore, remembering his shock at seeing a woman catapulting through the air in such a barren place. He could still vividly recall that moment when he saw her: auburn hair streaming out behind her, hands hopelessly outstretched, as if she were reaching for some salvation he couldn't see, the look of shock on her face as she tumbled down toward him. The moment when his world became only about her. "You were wearing blue jeans, a red tee shirt with a sparkly heart on it, and sneakers. Your outfit was so normal and unpretentious, and not at all fitting in with a woman who would be free-climbing those ledges."

She stared at him. "That's my favorite shirt."

He grinned at the stark surprise on her face, as if until now, she hadn't completely believed in their past. "The world stopped when I saw you," he said. "My entire focus immediately switched off Cardiff to saving you." Never in his life had anything taken his mind off Cardiff, not until he'd seen Alice in her swan dive. "I sprinted over there—"

She held up her hand. "I remember now," she said slowly, as if the memories were still coming. "You leapt up to snatch me out of midair. I must have been fifty feet up when you grabbed me."

Ian grinned. "Couldn't let you hit the ground unattended. It wouldn't be chivalrous." Then his amusement faded as he recalled the rest of it. "We landed," he said softly, searching her face for some flash of recognition. "I stood there with you in my arms in the middle of that mountain range and my entire world shifted. For the first time in my life, I felt the power of the curse. I knew you were my downfall—"

"Whoa." She jerked her hand free. "I remember now. You made some announcement about how I was your *sheva* and then your friend killed me."

"No!" He grabbed her shoulders before she could pull away. "Listen to me, Alice. Elijah made that move when the Order was run differently, when it was our duty to kill Order *shevas* before they could kill us—"

"What?" She gaped at him, and it definitely wasn't with love and adoration. "You guys kill your soul mates as a regular thing?"

"We used to. Not so much anymore." At her disbelieving stare, he realized he really wasn't playing the smooth Casanova role well. Shit. "Try this." He grabbed her hand and pressed it against his chest. "Close your eyes, Alice. Feel what I felt that day when you died in my arms."

"I don't want—"

He narrowed his eyes. "If you want to save your sister, then you need to do it."

Alice bit her lip, but she finally stopped fighting. Her fingers were petite and too fragile against his chest. An overwhelming sense of protectiveness swelled inside him, and he pinned her hand beneath his. "Stop fighting me," he said, opening himself to that moment when Elijah had cut her down.

The despair rolled over him like a thick cloud, the agonizing sense of loss that seemed to strip everything else from his mind. He remembered her gasp of shock, and the way she'd reached for him as life had bled from her body. The agony of losing this woman he didn't know. The guilt and shame of being unable to protect her.

Alice sucked in her breath, and her fingers dug into his chest. He realized immediately that she was experiencing his loss, understanding the truth of the words he was speaking.

"Elijah should never have been able to strike before I realized he was coming," he told her. "But I was so consumed by you, and the curse was already working. Every instinct I've honed for the last six hundred years vanished. You were all I saw, until it was too late."

She pulled her hand away, and folded her arms across her chest, hunching her shoulders, as if trying to ward off the taint of his emotions. The intimacy had made her uncomfortable, he could see that, and tension hummed through him. He needed to bond with her, and yet all she did was create distance.

"Every time you die, the curse comes back," he said. "Every time you shut me out, the curse gains strength. You can't do that to me if we have any chance of making it out of this thing alive."

"Shut you out? What does that mean?"

"It means exactly what you think it means." He moved closer, taking her wrist again. "I can deal with only so much loss when it comes to you," he said softly.

"Me? But I'm—"

"You're my soul mate, and the fact you don't carry my

marks doesn't change that. From now on, you don't get to die."

She shook her head. "There's no way to stop it," she said. "Cardiff killed me with a black magic spell. I'm almost impossible to kill, so I keep coming back to life, but each time it gets harder. It's just a matter of time until death finally keeps me and I can't revive. I'm going to keep dying until I finally stay dead—"

"No!" He yanked her against him, and she tumbled into his chest, slamming against his hard body. "You can't die again," he said. "You won't have to come back from death again, because I won't let you die."

Hope flashed across her face for a split second, but was immediately shoved aside by grim reality. "There's nothing you can do, Ian. I'm already dead—"

"Hell, Alice," he interrupted, cutting her off. "All you have to do is talk like that, and it nearly does me in. You make me tread so fucking close to the edge." He lowered his voice, his words like daggers through her chest while his hand locked around her hips. "You scare the living hell out of me, Alice, and I can't let you destroy me."

She braced her hands against his chest, pushing against him, trying to put space between them, but he didn't give her even an inch. "I wouldn't destroy you."

"You would, and you will." He bent his head, until his mouth was only a breath from hers. "No more walls between us, Alice. I can't take it."

He felt her sudden understanding of what he wanted, and the cold chill of raw fear. "You want sex? Emotions? All that?" At his nod, she shook her head violently. "Dear God," she whispered. "Not that. I can't—"

"You can." And then, before she could stop him, before she could twist away from him, before she could fight her own desires, he claimed her with a kiss meant to sear her very soul.

CHAPTER SIX

Alice didn't want to kiss Ian.

She didn't want to feel his emotions.

And most of all, she didn't want to feel her response to him.

But as Ian's mouth captured hers, all of Alice's resistance vanished, just like before. It wasn't simply the kiss. It wasn't simply the raw strength of his body against hers. It wasn't just the fact that he had pledged to keep her alive. It was the sheer force of his being as it filled her through his kisses, his touch, and his very breath.

His hands were firm and unyielding on her hips, pulling her against him. She loved the sensation of being trapped in his arms, as if his great strength could keep all the darkness at bay. The breadth of his shoulders made her feel tiny, as if it was no longer her job to make everything right, to be an independent entity who was incapable of connecting emotionally with anyone.

It was intoxicating the way his lips were soft and yet demanding at the same time, the shocking sensation of his tongue sliding against hers. Her breasts were crushed against his chest, making her nipples tingle with a desire that seemed to vibrate right through her to every level of her being. She'd been kissed before, but never had it been like this. Never had it reached inside her very soul and infused her with life.

She knew it was forbidden. An angel of life was not allowed to connect with anyone, or to develop loyalties to anything but her job. Even her friendship with Flynn had been superficial on some levels. But right now, with Ian kissing her, she didn't care. Though she knew he must be the catalyst sent to be her downfall, she couldn't resist him. It was just too much, this gift, this moment of feeling alive and human. This moment of feeling like there was another being on this planet who was a part of her.

Ian deepened the kiss, asking for more as his hands palmed her lower back, pressing her more tightly against him. Suddenly, and unexpectedly, her resistance shattered. She locked her hands behind his neck and kissed him back.

Yes, Alice. Just like this. His guttural groan of capitulation filled her mind, and she felt his rising ardor, his need for her.

Excitement tore through her, a heady feeling of power that she could have that kind of effect on him. It was intoxicating, empowering. His emotions were stark and raw, exposed to her, filling her with feelings so intense she barely understood them. It was a gift, this moment, this feeling of being alive. She wanted more. So much more.

His hands slipped beneath her shirt, and she gasped at the feel of his palms against her bare skin. Electricity seemed to leap between them, searing her skin, plummeting through her. She felt like she was on fire, burning for this man who carried so much torment that even she could feel it. *Ian—*

Alice. I can't tell you how amazing it feels to hear your voice in my mind. You belong there. Doesn't it feel right? His hands slid over the curve of her bottom, cupping her, lifting her against him.

The hard length of him pressed into her belly, sending desire shooting through her. And now she remembered. She recalled every detail of when they'd made love before. How she'd given herself over to him on purpose, how they'd tried to use their kisses and physical connection to break the barriers between them so he could learn the secrets she wasn't allowed to share. She remembered the intoxicating sensation of the hard wall against her back, the warm heat of his skin on the inside of her thighs, the feel of him sliding into her—

"Hells fire, Ian. That woman deserves more than a tumble on a fucking rock in the middle of the ocean with an audience. She's an angel, for hell's sake." Ry's voice broke through the sensual haze consuming them, and Alice pulled back, horrified by what she'd done.

But Ian didn't release her or even give the slightest acknowledgement of Ry. He kept his hands locked around her waist, his dark eyes seeming to swallow her up.

Her heart began to race, and suddenly she seemed to have trouble breathing. "I can't do that again," she whispered.

"I need it," he answered. "I need you, or I will die."

A sudden chill broke through her, a sudden panic. "I can't keep people alive," she blurted out. "Please don't count on me for that. I can't—"

"Hey." His voice softened, and he touched his finger to her lips. "It's okay," he said softly, his voice low as if it was just for her. "I didn't mean it that way. I'll keep myself alive." He trailed his fingers through her hair, a gesture so tender that her throat tightened. "I just meant that I need a little loving from you." He flashed her a cocky grin that belied all the strain he'd been fighting so hard before. "Just welcome my kisses like that, and we'll be on the right path."

"I can't—"

"You can." He kissed her forehead once, an endearing tenderness that made her want to cry for what she'd never had.

Ry made a grunt of impatience, and Alice finally looked over at him. The warrior was standing on the edge of the rock, water streaming from his body. He flashed her a hooded smile that seemed like an unbalanced compromise between lethal violence, dark anger, and deferential respect.

Once he had her attention, Ry went down on one knee and bowed his head. "My name is Ryland Samuels," he said. "I'm here to serve you, my lady. Accept my protection, I beseech you."

"You're beseeching her? What happened to 'kill first and regret never?'" Ian dropped his arm around her shoulders, a proprietary gesture that felt both good and threatening. "Hell," he said. "You okay, man? I've never seen you like this."

Ryland slowly raised his head, but his eyes were on Alice alone. The black depths were glittering with something so dark and so evil that it made her skin crawl. "What are you?" she asked.

"Order of the Blade," Ryland said. "One of the elite Calydon warriors sworn to protect the innocents of the world from rogue Calydons."

"No." Memories fluttered in the back of her mind. There was something familiar about his eyes, about the shadows moving in them. "You're not. What are you?"

He met her gaze, and this time there was no mistaking the flint in them. "Order of the Blade," he repeated firmly. "And my mission is to take you back to our leader's mansion where we can keep you safe."

She glanced at Ian, who was still relaxed beside her. He had the aura of a man who'd just been well sated from a three day lovemaking marathon, a man who was king of his world and would not be dethroned. Had her kiss done that to him?

Wow. She must be pretty good.

"She's not going anywhere with you," Ian said. "We're going to find Warwick."

"No." Ryland rose to his feet. "If she's who we think she is, the entire future of the Order depends on her safety."

"She's not—"

Alice held up her hand to silence Ian, curious as to what Ryland knew about her. "Who do you think I am?"

Ry met her gaze. "The Order of the Blade has a trinity of

guardian angels. Someone was trying to murder one of them, Sarah Burns, the angel of hope. According to legend, there are two others. If they get killed, the Order is no longer protected. A race is on to find them before the man trying to destroy us brings them down." He gave her an appraising look. "I think you're one of them."

"A guardian angel for the Order?" She laughed softly. "It would be a sorry day for you all if I was. I'm one of those angels who can't quite get it right."

Ian raised his brows. "So you really are an angel?"

"Yes—" She stopped, startled that she'd been able to tell him that she was. The limits that bound her had been inflexible her whole life. No secrets could be shared. No revelations. Just isolation, and, for her, failure. But the rules seemed to be changing now. What was he doing to her? And what ramifications would it have? Sudden excitement rippled through her. Would Ian give her the chance to break free of her angel shackles? Or would he doom her forever?

Probably doom, he said. *It's a* sheva *thing.*

She looked at him. "Please get out of my head."

No.

She narrowed her eyes at him. "You're going to be a pain in the butt, aren't you?"

Ian grinned. *Yeah, probably. Is that so bad?*

"Yes."

"Hey." Ryland rose to his feet. "I'll call Kane to come here and teleport us. We'll head back to the mansion—"

"No." Alice glanced over at the ocean. "I have to find my...sister." The lie she'd uttered so easily both to Ian and to herself for so long suddenly felt awkward. If her connection with Ian was such that he could enable her to break through her restraints... suddenly, lying to him felt wrong.

"Is she an angel, too?" Ryland asked, sudden fire gleaming in his eyes. "Your sister?"

Alice hesitated. How much revelation would save her

and Catherine, and how much would endanger them? Every reveal of angel secrets to outsiders would thicken the taint on her soul.

Ryland swore, taking her silence as confirmation. "I knew it. She is, isn't she?" He slammed his fist into his palm. "She's the third part of the trinity, isn't she? That's it. She's the other one we need to find." He strode to the edge of the rock and surveyed the horizon, as if he could make her appear by sheer force of will. "What's her name?"

She glanced at Ian, uncertain how much to reveal to these warriors. Ian's jaw was strong and powerful, and there was a determined set to his shoulders. In the moonlight, his stance was unyielding, and he was watching her intently. He was so dangerous to her, but at the same time, there was no denying that there was a connection between them, which was more than she'd had with anyone else in so long. She'd felt his agony when she'd died, and she knew his response to her was genuine. Could she trust him?

Warwick killed my father, Ian said. *I will not rest until the wrong is righted. You know that.* He let her feel the raw determination of his words, his commitment to his cause.

It felt exactly the same as her own need to track down Catherine, her own need to find the wizard. A commitment that would not die for either of them until it was over, no matter what else happened between them.

She could trust him, with that at least. *Can I trust your team?*

Warwick might be the one targeting the Order. If it's him, they'll help. Ian glanced over at Ryland. *We'll need their assistance against him.*

Alice took a deep breath, fear warring with the need for help. Alone, she had no chance. With the Order of the Blade at her back? Maybe the nightmare could finally end. She took a deep breath and made her decision. Anything was worth the risk to help Catherine. *Okay.* She turned to Ryland as

Ian locked her more securely beneath his arm. "My sister is Catherine Taylor," she said. "And yes, she's an angel."

Ryland spun around to face her, intensity burning in his eyes. "Is she part of the trinity? Are you?"

She hesitated, and then gave the only answer she could. "I don't know."

† † †

Ian studied Ryland's tense body language, and a rising sense of frustration filled him. What the hell did Ryland know? More than he'd been sharing. "Ry. You need to fill me in on this shit. I need the details."

His teammate ignored him, still focusing on Alice. "What kind of angel are you? What kind is Catherine?"

"Hey." Ian strode across the rock, stepping in front of Ryland and blocking his view of Alice. "What the hell is your problem? It's Cardiff who is after the Order, isn't it? You saw his horse, didn't you? That's why you're cutting me out, because you think I can't handle it."

Ry gave him a cursory glance, revealing nothing. "Fitz, you're a non-entity right now for the Order. You're a liability. At any moment, you could kill yourself, and you see nothing but your own goals. We can't afford that right now. When I said you're out of the loop, I didn't just mean that you're off the front lines. The team took a vote. You are no longer an active member of the Order of the Blade." His eyes glittered. "I gave you a chance when I let you go after Alice just now, and you took that to align with her on your own mission, not the Order's. Trust is over. I'm calling it in." There was no regret in Ryland's eyes. Just the hard commitment built on a life of anger and torment that had consumed him for so long.

"Hell, man. I've been tracking Cardiff for six hundred years. If he's involved, you *need* me." Fury built inside Ian, disbelief that the Order was cutting him out. "I'm one of the best fighters the team has ever had."

"You *were,* before you fell victim to the curse. I know you're good. We all know you're good. But right now, you're not mentally fit. You're a danger to us all, because we can't afford to count on you."

Ian stared at him. "Of course you can count on me—"

"Can we? You think?" Ryland met his gaze. "You still want to know what you missed?" He gave Ian his full attention, his eyes blazing. "We went out in those woods with Kane and Sarah. There was a madman in there, and he took Thano. Fucking took him!"

"What?" Ian was shocked by Ry's revelation about their youngest Order of the Blade member. Thano was only thirty-five years old, but the cocky kid was one of the best warriors he'd ever met, and he always kept a sense of humor the rest of them seemed to have lost. "Took him? What does that mean?"

"It means, you selfish bastard, that this giant pit of hell appeared out of nowhere and sucked Thano into it. I got a good look down its throat, and there was nothing but living hell down there. Everyone else thinks he's probably dead." Bitterness flashed in Ryland's eyes. "I won't believe it until I get proof. Thano's too irreverent to die easily."

Ian swore, running his hand through his hair. He couldn't believe no one had told him that Thano had been kidnapped. Then again, Ryland was the only one he'd seen recently, and Ry had clearly decided to keep him out of the loop. "Where is he? What was the hole? Who has him?"

Ryland shrugged. "The demon who was trying to kill Kane is gone, but there was another male there at the end. Kane saw him, and he was the one leading the show. Once I get the angels secured, I'm going to find that bastard and get Thano back." Bitterness blazed in Ry's eyes. "If you'd been there, we could have saved him. We didn't have enough firepower. You're out, man. You're fucking out."

Son of a bitch. Ryland meant it. And Ian didn't blame them. Not entirely. By not being there, he'd weakened the team and exposed Thano. Bitterness coursed through him, bitterness for the curse that had taken so much from him and his ancestors already. "The team voted? Or is this one of your unilateral decisions?"

"The team. It was my unilateral decision to give you one more chance, and you blew it." Ryland turned away and faced Alice, who had been watching them intently, listening to the conversation. "You're coming back with me," he said. "You need to be protected."

Alice stiffened. "I'm not going back with you. I need to find my sister—"

"I'll find her," Ryland said. "I'll track her down—"

"She'll kill you," Alice interrupted. "You won't be able to get near her—"

Ian raised his brows at her claim. "Kill him? What kind of angel is she?"

Alice glanced at him, and said nothing, making Ian even more curious.

"No one can kill me," Ry said. "Not unless I choose to die. I don't have time to deal with Ian's shit or your loyalty." He held out his hand. "Come with me, Alice. I swear on my mother's soul that I will ensure your safety in a way that Ian never can." He glanced over at Ian, and pity flickered briefly in his eyes. "Sorry, man. But the Order trumps. Gideon and Quinn will decide if you're fit to be reinstated, but I wouldn't lay any bets in your favor right now."

Ian felt a ripple of energy in his mind, and he realized that Ryland had reached out mentally to their team. Had he called Kane? Kane Santiago was the only one of their team with the ability to teleport. He could be there in a split second, and he would be able to take Alice and Ian with him.

The last time the Order had deemed Ian unfit, they'd locked him in a dungeon for three months to keep him alive. This time, they hadn't simply deemed him unfit; they'd actually stripped him of his membership on the team. What would that translate to? Tearing his weapons out of his arms? Chaining him up again? Jesus, the Order was falling apart now that Dante wasn't around to hold them together. You didn't do that shit to teammates. You just didn't. You had to have faith in them.

He needed to be out here, on the front lines, with Alice, finishing this off. He'd been a part of this team for six hundred years, and his ancestors had all been premiere Order members. The Order was his future and his fate. It was the honor of his family. He couldn't be cast out. Dealing with the curse supported the Order's cause because it was to protect one of their best team members. Didn't they get that?

But as he looked at Ryland's stoic face, he realized the answer was no. The Order couldn't see past the failure in the woods, the loss of Thano. Son of a bitch. The curse was doing worse than killing his male lineage. It was stripping them of the very last bit of honor that they'd clung to: membership in the elite Order of the Blade. "Is the decision made?" He'd heard rumors of people being stripped of their Order status for good, but he'd never seen it happen, never heard any actual evidence of it really occurring. What the hell was going on?

Ry met his gaze for a long moment, and regret flickered on his face. "Fitz, you're putting personal agenda over the greater good. It's been too many times, and at too great a cost. They can't afford to count on you anymore. You'd do the same in their position. You know you would."

Jesus Christ. He'd failed the Order? Ian closed his eyes, stunned by the revelation. Shocked by how far things had fallen. If he went back there and they separated him from Alice...nothing would be fixed. He'd still be chased by the curse, fighting a losing battle to stay sane, and unable to focus on the one thing that mattered to him: the Order.

Fuck. There was only one option. To not go home until he'd proven himself the warrior he was. Until he'd broken the curse, freeing him to focus on the Order.

He had to disobey a direct order. There was no other option. *Alice?*

She jerked her gaze to him, but as usual, didn't answer telepathically.

They'll stop us from going after Cardiff.

She looked sharply at Ryland, who was inching toward her, still jawing on about how he would serve her and protect her.

Kane Santiago will be here momentarily to teleport us. There is no way to stop him once he touches us. Our only out is to not be here when he arrives.

She met his gaze, and grim determination darkened her expression. She gave a slight nod.

Satisfaction thrummed through Ian at Alice's agreement, at her unwillingness to yield to the Order's demands. It took courage to go against the Order of the Blade. *You're my kind of woman, Alice.*

She wrinkled her nose at him, but a small smile curved at the corners of her mouth.

Ian did a quick inventory of their options. There really weren't many. *Jump off the rock. The ocean will swallow us up. No scent. No sight. They won't be able to find us.*

For a moment, she hesitated, and he knew she was remembering how violent the ocean had been. How it had been trying to kill her.

I don't have time to die either, he said softly. *I'll keep us alive. I can do it.*

She looked at him, and he saw the emotions warring inside her. Should she trust him alone, or put her faith in Ryland and the rest of the Order? Was aligning herself with the entire team a better choice for finding her sister? She wouldn't do that...but when she looked at Ryland again, Ian stiffened. Would she really choose to leave him? She would. He knew she would. His own *sheva* would walk out on him if she felt it furthered her goals. It was impossible that she could have that ability, but somehow, she did. His *sheva* was not bound to him the way she should have been—

Ian felt a faint disturbance in the atmosphere just behind him. Kane was coming! Time was up. *Now!* He leapt across the rock toward her, urgency making him move faster than Ryland had time to react to. He held out his hand to Alice as he sprinted toward the edge of the rock.

He wasn't going to stop. He wasn't going back to the Order. *Alice.* He thrust all his urgency into his voice. *Come with me.*

"Hey!" Ryland's outraged shout echoed through the night. "Don't pull this shit, Fitz!" Ryland lunged for Alice, two men reaching for her, trying to claim her.

For an agonizingly long moment, she didn't move, her gaze going frantically back and forth between them. Ian didn't hold back. He just ran for her, his hand outstretched, willing her to reach out. *Come on, Alice. You trusted me enough to make love. You asked me to find you when you died. I did.*

Her gaze locked on his. *I asked you to find me? Yes.* He was almost to her now, only a fraction of an inch ahead of Ryland. He couldn't slow down or he'd be caught. It was now, or never. *Alice!*

He raced past her, his hand still outstretched toward her, and she didn't move. She didn't take his hand. Shit—

Ian! She lunged for him, and he reached back, his hand clamping around hers just as Ryland reached for her. Ian yanked her forward, and Ryland's hand brushed down her back, his fingers grasping only air.

Ian had no time to prepare her as they careened off the edge of the rock, free-falling a hundred feet into the still-churning ocean. It howled with fury, reaching up for them as they fell. He hauled her toward him, fighting to control their fall as they plummeted down.

Make yourself like an arrow, he instructed. *We want to go as deep as possible or else Kane will be able to track us.*

Deep? In that? But even as she questioned him, she quickly straightened her body, her hands by her sides, her toes pointed. Ian wrapped his arms around her. He anchored her against his chest, mimicking her pose so that their bodies were pressed together into a single torpedo ready to plunge into the ocean.

The ocean will hide us. It's our only chance. Even as he said the words, he heard Kane's shout from the rock above, and he knew that Kane would teleport into the water and try to snatch them out of it. Unless he couldn't find them. *Now!*

Their feet hit the water, he sucked in his breath, and then violent purple waves consumed them. As they were yanked beneath the surface, Ian was shocked to see dozens of pale white faces appearing around them, like mist in the depths of the ocean. A silent screaming filled his mind, so shrill that Alice hunched over, covering her ears to fight off the pain. The faces swirled in and out, misty arms striking at them, drawing blood with each swipe.

The brands on Ian's arms burned as his weapons strained to be released so he could fight back, but he and Alice were moving too fast through the water. If he loosened his grip on her at all to free his hand for fighting, she would be torn out of his grasp.

So, he simply locked his legs and arms more tightly around her, using his body to shield her from their attackers. As their blades dug into his back, as their screams battered his sanity, as he and Alice plunged further and further into the depths, Ian eschewed six hundred years of training as a warrior and didn't fight back. He didn't defend.

He simply protected the woman in his arms.

† † †

Alice burrowed deeper against Ian, her body bowing under the agony of the piercing screams. Pressure built in her ears, until it felt like they were going to burst. The pain was beyond what she could survive, more than what she'd ever endured from the demons. The water streamed past, feeling like a thousand daggers slicing through her skin. *Ian!*

Ian tightened his arms around her, his legs trapping her and drawing her into his body. *I've got you.*

She felt his warm strength reaching out to her mind, and she quickly dropped her mental shields, knowing instinctively that she needed his help. His power flooded her mind, coating it with a protective shield. The pain from the screams lessened ever so slightly, blocked by whatever he was doing. Gratefully, she clung to him, to the respite he was offering, accepting the window he'd created to allow her to think, to react, to process.

Still holding tightly to him, Alice lifted her head, then went still with shock when she saw the faces of the Mageaan surrounding them. *Oh my God, Ian. They never show themselves.* Their mouths were open in gaping screams, their lips no more than white mist slashing through the water. Their eyes were bottomless pits of torment. Their souls broken and empty. Their faces contorted in fury and hate and the promise of death.

There were so many of them. Hundreds of them, as far as she could see, filling the ocean with an endless swarm of apparitions. The ones nearby moved closer, slashing at them with short daggers made from what looked like oyster shells. She realized that the stabs of pain on her back weren't from the ocean. It was the Mageaan, trying to kill them.

What are they? Ian adjusted his grip on her, keeping her tight as they plummeted downward, still moving at a rapid pace.

These are the Mageaan. Welcome to your first sighting of fallen angels, sentenced to eternity beneath the sea.

Damn. I thought angels were the good guys.

Alice thought of Catherine, and she knew that was so far from the truth. *Not so much—* A massive Mageaan, twice the size of the others suddenly streaked across the ocean toward them, a glittery blood-red blade in her hand. *Um, Ian—*

I'm on it. You need to hold onto me.

Alice quickly wrapped her legs around his waist and tightened her arms around his neck. Ian locked his left arm around her waist, and then let go with his right. There was a crack and a flash of black light, and then Ian's mace appeared in his hand.

He swung just as the apparition struck out, knocking the dagger out of her hand. She screamed and spun toward them, her mouth expanding in a macabre scream of rage. She lunged for them, and Ian reared back to plunge the mace down her throat. But just as he was about to make contact, Alice saw a flash of light blue in the Mageaan's eyes, a glimpse of the angel that this creature had once been. Recognition surged through her for this apparition who had once been a woman. This wraith had once been like her. And now, were it not for the pearl of Lycanth, this could be Alice in a week, a day, or even an hour. How could she cause it more pain? "No!" She grabbed Ian's wrist. "Don't hurt her!"

"What?" He looked at her like she had just lost her mind.

"Don't!" She stayed his arm, and for a split second, she thought he would strike. Then he let his arm fall, lowering the mace just as the Mageaan's mouth consumed them both.

CHAPTER SEVEN

Ian swore as the Mageaan sucked them into her gaping mouth. What the hell was he doing, letting them be taken? But even as he questioned it, he didn't strike. There had been an urgency in Alice's voice that had touched him, and he'd instantly backed off, her will somehow able to affect his own.

But as he watched the teeth coming down toward their heads, he had a bad feeling about it. *This feels like one of those rash decisions I'm going to regret later,* he muttered as the darkness closed down around them. Well, darkness except for the few thousand glittering fangs that lined the mouth of the creature.

She's an angel, Alice said.

Yeah, I got that. So? Does that mean she's not a meat eater? 'Cause I'm feeling like she is.

It means we have to believe in her. In them. No one ever believes in them anymore.

Well, I can see why. Adrenaline burned through him as the Mageaan's mouth continued to close. He tightened his grip on his mace as he rapidly calculated the seconds until the poisonous fangs made contact. He might give Alice the leeway of trusting the Mageaan, somewhat, but he wasn't going to let it get to the point of risking actual death. Those fangs weren't going to get to the point of no return, end of story.

Closer and closer they came. Alice was staring at them, her chin lifted and her throat exposed, as if she were trying to communicate her complete willingness to surrender to their mercy. But the secure hold she had on his neck told him she wasn't quite as convinced as she wanted to pretend.

Ian raised his mace as the teeth descended. "Don't do it," he warned it, his voice carrying through the water. "Just don't do it."

Alice gripped his arm. *Ian. Have faith.*

I have no faith, sweetheart. I'm fresh out. But he didn't strike. He still had time. He could take it down with one blow. Something about Alice's unwavering faith made him want to believe. She made him want to see that there was some good in this hellish existence and crazy world.

"You stole the pearl," Alice shouted into the water, the ocean swallowing up her voice. "It won't work for you. It has to be freely given by one angel to another. What do you really want? Are you really a monster, or do you want more?"

The teeth stopped descending. Two fangs pressed against the side of Ian's temple, and hundreds more were suspended a fraction of an inch from Alice's exposed throat.

Ian raised his mace, muscles straining with readiness for a sudden attack. One breath. One ripple from the ocean. One millimeter further with the fangs, and he would strike it down. "Give the girl a chance to be right," he said. "Make a good choice, or death will be your next date."

Ian. Be nice. Alice was still in his arms, but her fingers were digging into his neck, and he could feel her heart racing against his chest.

You want me to be nice? I have a fang in need of some serious fluoride and breath mints digging into my temple. I think I'm being incredibly tolerant and charming given the situation. "Back the fuck off," he warned again. "Despite my boyish good looks, I'm really not that nice of a guy." The creature didn't back off, but it didn't go for the jugular either. It was poised and waiting, as if trying to decide whether this snack would go right to the hips or whether it would be worth it for the pure enjoyment of crushing some skulls.

"Time is almost up," Ian gritted out, readiness humming through every cell of his being. "Leave the party, or we're going to do some serious dancing with you."

For another long second, there was no response, and then suddenly, the thing simply dissolved into white mist.

The sudden influx of vapor obscured Ian's vision completely within milliseconds, cutting him off from being able to see or defend. Shit! He opened his preternatural senses, sending energy waves into the white foam, immediately locating every creature that was around them. He knew precisely where each one was. He could hear the beating of their hearts. He could feel the darkness of their energy swirling around them.

And he could tell that not one of them was moving into an attack position, despite the fact that he'd just been momentarily blinded. They were close, too close for any kind of comfort, but they weren't lining up for the final attack. Was Alice right? Was it over?

Then the mist dissolved, giving him a full view of what lay before them, and he knew that it had all just begun.

† † †

The sight that greeted Alice when the mist dissolved was not in the top ten of "things she wanted to see before she died."

Apparently, the news of their arrival had gone out, and then some. The welcoming party had just gone from dangerously intimate to a public free-for-all with the potential for really bad fallout. There were dozens of Mageaan encircling them, women who seemed to be mere ghosts, slivers of white mist floating in the ocean.

Alice and Ian had stopped their downward descent. They were now standing on the edge of a vibrant pink and turquoise coral reef that seemed to glow from within, casting light out into the dark water. Alice instinctively sucked in her breath, then stopped in shock when she felt the ocean water slide harmlessly through her lungs. *I'm breathing under water.*

Me too. I'd comment that it's a pretty handy development for us, but given our situation, I'm thinking maybe we shouldn't be so quick to rejoice. Gifts come with a price. Keeping Alice locked against him, he spun them slowly in a circle, his mace still out as he surveyed their situation.

There were Mageaan on all sides of them, including above and below. There wasn't even a small patch of green ocean. Just white, misty figures encircling them. They weren't armed, but she and Ian had already experienced how quickly that could change.

She gripped Ian, not daring to let him go, knowing she had no tools to protect herself against them. *Could you stop all of them?*

Yeah, no problem. A hundred to one odds are totally in my favor. He raised his mace. *But I might need both my hands this time. If I need to go to battle, find a place to hide in the coral 'til I'm done.*

She wanted to look at him to see if he was serious, but before she could turn her head, the Mageaan directly in front of them parted. Their ethereal bodies eased to the sides, opening a pathway between them.

Gliding down the channel were two Mageaan. They were identical, both of them tall and lean. Their aqua-colored hair was streaming out behind them. They were not the pure white mist of the others. Instead, their bodies had a faint blue tint, as if they were glowing. Their breasts were covered by what looked like a crisscross harness of seaweed that matched the elbow-length dark gloves that were their only clothes. Their lower bodies seamlessly transitioned into a scaled tail that glittered even deep under water. They were so lean and fleshless, so devoid of shapely curves, it was as if their very essences as women were slowly dying.

As they passed by the legions of white misty women, the other Mageaan bowed low, prostrating themselves to those who were clearly their leaders.

Alice stood taller as they neared, and Ian moved slightly in front of her, keeping his shoulder between her and the approaching women.

The women floated to a stop just above them, looking down at Ian and Alice in a clear statement of who was in charge: the ocean dwellers, not those from the land above. Their faces were angular and defined, giving them a look of ancient royalty, haughty and brutal. "Who are you?" They asked the question in unison, two voices mingling in the water.

Ian answered for them. "My name is Ian Fitzgerald, Order of the Blade," claiming allegiance to the organization that Alice knew had cut him out. Habit? Or did he not consider himself divested of his role? "Who are you?" he asked sharply. He made it clear he wasn't deferring to them, his voice demanding their response.

Now that the leaders were closer, Alice could see slight differences between them. One of them had delicate red streaks in her hair, and her eyes were a brilliant blue. The other's hair was simply turquoise and green, and her eyes were a bottomless gold that seemed to glitter from within.

The one with the red streaks raised her eyebrows, giving an almost flirtatious look at Ian that made Alice want to be the one to claim him. "We are the Empresses of the Underworld," she said haughtily, her tone making it clear she was answering his question only because it suited her. "To you, we are simply Your Majesties. You have not earned our names."

Ian didn't back down. "The tattoo across your throat says Jada, and hers says Esmeralda. I assume those are your names?"

Jada hissed and bared her fingers, as if claws were about to burst free.

Alice took a step back. *Don't make them mad,* she advised Ian. *We need their help. Their names are tattooed on them so they don't forget who they are. They lose their humanity with each passing day in exile. No one is allowed to say their names anymore. They are no longer individuals.*

"I have not heard my name in too long," Esmeralda said, her voice soft with awe. She was not the one who had first spoken. "Say it again. I want to hear it."

Ian met her gaze. "Your Majesty, Esmeralda is the name of royalty. It befits you."

She preened under his attention, and Alice stiffened. It couldn't be a good thing to have the leaders of the Mageaan looking at Ian as if he were dessert, because they could turn him into that with a snap of their tainted fingers. They might be fallen angels, but their powers were considerable, only they were now twisted and deadly, morphed into hate and pain.

The leaders circled closer, their hair wafting around their heads like the halos they no longer deserved to wear. "You are a strong warrior, are you not?" Again, they spoke together, two voices as one, though it was clear that Jada was the one whose thoughts they were voicing, because only her mouth was moving.

Ian didn't hesitate. "I am."

Alice almost laughed at his arrogance, but at the same time, she was a little jealous. *Do you sell that self-confidence by the case?*

He glanced at her, and she felt his surprise. *You're willing to dive off a rock into murderous ocean after a pearl, with no way to protect yourself, and you think I'm the one with self-confidence? Sweetheart, you're a hell of a warrior.*

She was startled by his assessment, but at the same time, it felt good. Really good. Even if he was wrong, it still was amazing to have someone look at her like she was worth something.

He narrowed his eyes. *You don't think you're worth*

anything? You're an angel, Alice. How is that not worthy?

I'm a really bad one, she admitted.

Ian raised his brows. *A bad angel? Sweetheart, men dream of having one night with a bad angel.*

Heat flushed her cheeks, and she glared at him. *Sex? You're turning this into a sexual tease? I was serious.*

I know. That was my awkward guy-attempt to table the conversation until I could give it the attention it deserved. I'm pretty focused right now on the fact that these two slightly bitter ex-angels are getting closer to us than I want them to. He shrugged apologetically. *Just so you know, I'm warning you now that I'm probably going to suck at the male-female relationship thing.*

She almost laughed at his comment, so self-deprecating coming from a deadly warrior, but there was a sudden surge in the current that pulled her attention back to their surroundings.

Esmeralda was swimming down toward them, making a slow circle around them. Ian turned with her, his mace still ready. He kept Alice behind him the whole time, making it clear that he was ready to defend her, and that he was not at their mercy.

The Mageaan clucked her teeth, her golden eyes bright with interest. Her eyes and hair were the only strong color she carried, as if they were the last things that were going to fade into oblivion. The legions of women surrounding them had pale blue eyes and white hair, and their names had faded into dark, illegible scrawls across their chests. Were Esmeralda and Jada more powerful, or were they simply newer and therefore still able to retain some connection to their humanity?

"You will suffice, warrior." Again, with the two voices, even though it was clear that it was Esmeralda's sentiment that was being voiced. She looked at Alice. "We accept him as your sacrifice. You may live."

"Sacrifice?" Alice immediately moved in front of him.

"I'm not offering him—"

"No." Ian's voice was hard and instant, yanking Alice back behind him so he could block her with his body, even though he was the one they wanted to hurt. Hello? Didn't he realize that they'd just said they wouldn't hurt her? "I belong to her, and no one else. I do not leave her side. *Ever.*"

Oh... how sweet was that? Excitement trilled through Alice at his words, and she had a crazy urge to smile. Yes, her response was slightly insane given their current situation, but it wasn't every day that a man who other women envied publicly aligned himself with her. Or even a man that other women didn't envy. Or, quite frankly, even a mold infested mushroom. The list of people who had hoisted pompoms on her behalf was depressingly short, especially given that her angel status should normally come with some amount of built-in popularity.

Anger flashed in Esmeralda's golden eyes. "You are not in control down here, warrior. This is not your world."

"Everywhere I am is my world," he snapped back.

Damn, Alice wanted to live life that confidently. It must be so cool! Not that it would be helpful if he catapulted them into a war with the Mageaan, of course. Admirable, but not helpful. He was a man in a woman's world right now, and he wasn't adjusting well.

Alice put her hand on his arm, trying to defuse the growing tension. *Ian. We need their help. They're the ones who could take us to Warwick, if they choose. Remember? Let me deal with them. They were once angels, which means I have a connection to them.* They were actually so much more similar to her than anyone knew. Anyone but Catherine.

Her heart tightened at the thought of the woman who meant so much to her. She had to find a way out of this situation. Catherine was counting on her. *Let me handle this, Ian.* She couldn't keep the urgency out of her voice. *Please.*

Ian looked at her sharply, and she saw his mind rapidly

assessing the situation. He didn't lower his weapon, but he gave her a slight nod, turning the negotiation over to her. *I'll cover you. Go.*

Alice immediately moved up beside Ian, relieved when he didn't try to shove his manly shoulder in front of her again. Not that she didn't appreciate his shoulder, but this was a time for estrogen not testosterone. "My name is Alice Shaw. I brought you a pearl of Lycanth to exchange for your help. That is my offer. Not the warrior."

Jada swam down toward her and held out her hand, the red sections in her hair looking like streaks of fresh blood. And maybe it was. Who knew where the leaders had been before showing up for the apparent town meeting? "Let me see the pearl."

Alice grimaced. "I lost—"

Triumph flashed in the Mageaan's eyes, and Ian's voice breathed through her mind. *They have it. I can feel their deception.*

Alice narrowed her eyes at Ian's revelation. Seriously? They'd had it the whole time? Of course they had. They owned the ocean, didn't they? "You already have it," she snapped. "You stole it from me with the wind, but you can do nothing with it unless I offer it to you." She held out her hand. "Give it back to me. Now."

For a long moment, neither of the women moved, then finally, Jada swam closer. She laughed softly, her voice a melodic beauty in the dark water. "Of course we have it. You foolishly lost it. Speak the words to offer it to us willingly, and we may allow you and the warrior to exit alive."

Ian touched Alice's hand. *I can get us out alive. We don't have to bargain for our safety. Negotiate for their help to find Warwick.*

Alice glanced at him. *There are hundreds of them now, and they're really not that nice when they decide to murder you.*

He raised his brows. *I'm not that nice when someone tries*

to kill me, so it'll be a fair fight.

Alice tried again, wanting him to understand the nature of the enemy. *You've heard to beware of scorned women? Well, these women have been scorned, stripped of their identity and their femininity, and left to rot away beneath the sea. Trust me when I say that you've never run into the likes of them.*

They've never run into the likes of me. Ian shrugged. *I'm good.*

His confidence was so evident that Alice almost believed him. He had, after all, fought for the Order for hundreds of years. A man didn't survive that by luck. *You're sure?*

His intense conviction rolled through her. *If I die, I fail my family's honor and leave you unprotected. Seeing as how I won't allow that to happen under any circumstances, the answer is yeah, I'm sure. Get it done, and I'll back you up.*

She grinned, a foreign sensation of freedom filling her. She'd spent her life on the run, hiding from herself, avoiding any kind of conflict that would draw her into actions meant to destroy her. She'd always felt powerless...until now. Until this deadly warrior's offer had given her the freedom to finally stand up for what she wanted.

She'd never had an ally before, but it certainly made things easier. She might be an all-powerful (hah!) angel, but that meant she had no offensive skills. Apparently, an angel wasn't supposed to be murdered by an evil wizard and then chased by death until she ran out of lives. Angels weren't supposed to need to defend themselves, and even if they did, they weren't supposed to inflict harm. Taking one for the team wasn't so appealing when you were actually facing death.

But now? Different rules. She had a warrior at her back, and she was going to take advantage. Rolling in a sense of confidence she'd never had the luxury of enjoying, Alice set her hands on her hips and eyed the Mageaan. "Thanks, but we're going to leave alive anyway. The question is whether you get the pearl or not—"

Ian swore suddenly and whirled around, his mace slicing through the air. There was a furious hiss, like steam had been released from the bowels of the earth. Alice turned just as his mace made contact with a Mageaan who had snuck up behind them. His assailant screamed as his weapon cracked into her chest, and she went tumbling down into the ocean depths, her arms held out beseechingly as she fell. Deep purple blood poured from a wound in her chest as her head fell back in the agony of death.

"No!" Alice covered her mouth in horror as the woman's tail faded to a deadly gray and then split, turning into deformed legs too human to ignore as she reverted back into the decayed human form that remained of who she'd once been. "You killed her!" Alice gaped in horror at Ian, the angel's death feeling like a knife in her own heart. "You killed an angel?"

He stared at her, his brow furrowed in confusion even as he reached behind him, feeling his lower back. "Well, yeah, of course I did. She was trying to kill you. Wasn't that what our entire conversation was about when you asked me if I could take them all on?"

God, yes, she knew it was, but it was different to see an angel die. It was too personal, too real, too close to home. "Yes, but—"

The dying Mageaan screamed, her ashen fingers stretching toward Alice. "Save me—"

"I can't!" Tears filled Alice's eyes, her entire soul burning with the need to save the woman. She felt her death in every fiber of her being, and it tore at her very soul.

Beside her, Ian suddenly went down to his knees, swearing violently. In the middle of his lower back, right where his kidney would be, the handle of a massive dagger was sticking out of his flesh. His fingers were splayed around it, as if he'd tried to pull it out and caused more damage instead.

"Ian!" Alice stared in horror as dark red blood flowed from his wound, mixing with the water around them.

Suddenly, reality came crashing down around her. His fatal strike didn't make him a monster. It had been self-defense against a creature who was so far from humanity that there could be no mercy. Not anymore. No matter what she'd been before.

"I'm fine. My fault for not assuming they'd strike before the negotiations were over." He swore and jerked the blade out of his back in one swift move, swearing as the twelve-inch serrated blade slid out of his body, ripping organs and flesh as he removed it.

Alice's stomach turned as she stared at it, horrified by what had happened to him. How could someone who had once been an angel do that to another living creature? Striking to kill in cold blood, against a man who had made no offensive move or threat? Was that her future? Was that what she would become?

He lunged to his feet, a mace clenched in each hand. "You just broke the rules of engagement," he said with a snarl.

Esmeralda hissed, her golden eyes glowing. "You killed one of us!" she shrieked in outrage. With a swift movement, she slashed her hand through the sea, drawing a symbol in the water.

"No!" Jada shouted, lunging for Esmeralda, but before she could reach her, the ocean erupted as the Mageaan attacked, swarming in from all sides, claws bared, their faces contorted like they had become the very demons they once protected against.

Ian swore and shoved Alice into a crack in the coral reef, and then he launched into a full-scale assault. For a moment, she was mesmerized as he fought, stunned by his sheer raw strength, by the way his body coiled and then released with lightning-fast speed. Even in the water, he was incredibly agile, thousands of times faster than the Mageaan.

And then the sea creatures changed.

There was a low rumble, like the ocean floor was rolling

over in its sleep, and suddenly the Mageaan shifted from white to black and purple. They shrieked with murderous intent, darting in and out like assault weapons, attacking and retreating before Ian could strike them. Poison leaked from their bodies, staining the water like giant squid on a mission to kill.

Aghast at the carnage and the brutality of the sea creatures, Alice watched them fall to Ian's mace, one by one, screaming as they returned to their human bodies at the moment of death. Only then, did they seem to regain their souls, reaching for Alice, begging her for help as they tumbled into the ocean's depths.

Guilt and horror filled Alice as she stood there, doing nothing to save them, like some cruel, heartless bitch. Unable to save them. Unable to do a single thing to save these women who had once been angels.

More and more cuts appeared on Ian's flesh, and as many Mageaan as he took out, more seemed to come. Hundreds? Thousands? The attack was so violent the water began to foam, filled with purple and red bubbles tainted by the blood of all those who were fighting, until Alice couldn't even see Ian anymore. *Ian!*

Stay where you are, sweetheart. I got this covered— A grunt of pain from him interrupted his response, and she felt searing pain erupt from him before he blocked their connection.

Frantic, she looked around for something, anything to help him.

"How long do you really think he can last?"

Alice looked up to see the two leaders peering down at her, hovering just outside the entrance to her hiding place. "As long as he needs to," she retorted, praying she was right.

"Will he?" They moved closer. "And what do you think will happen to him if *you* start getting attacked? How can he save you and himself? Not so easy."

Alice frantically looked past them, but she couldn't see anything except the bubbly foam.

"Offer us the pearl," Jada spoke, but once again, both of their voices were in the air. "Then you may live—"

A loud scream rent the ocean, and both leaders spun around, shrieking simultaneously as another wraith fell to Ian's blade, a clamshell dagger still clenched in her hand. "No!" The leaders rushed toward her, sweeping her up in their arms as the black specter began to transition back into a person.

It was a woman. A young woman. Maybe twenty, at best. Her body was flesh-colored, her curves real and womanly, indicating that she was a new arrival. Hours? Days? Not much longer than that. Not someone who should be in a battle. Not someone who should be condemned to a life of exile and disintegration. She was a girl who should have been dancing on the earth with flowers in her hair.

"Oh, no." Alice held her hand to her mouth as the leaders scooped the woman up, cradling her against their chests as they rushed back toward Alice.

"Save her," they screamed as they laid her at Alice's feet. "Save her now!"

The young woman looked up at Alice, her magenta eyes glazed with pain. There was so much pain in her face, and so much anguish. "I didn't want to fight him," she gasped. "I'm sorry."

"You were forced to fight him?" When the woman nodded, Alice realized that the young woman had somehow retained her humanity when she'd become a Mageaan. She had a living, breathing soul. She had empathy. She had emotions. She had the ability to think for herself.

Alice turned to the leaders, disgusted by what they'd done to the girl. "How could you send her into battle? How could you force her to try to kill another living creature?"

"Save her," Esmeralda shouted. She grabbed Alice by the hair, yanked her out of the crevice, and threw her to the ground. "Save her now!"

Alice fell to her knees besides the young woman, horrified by the spreading stain across her chest. "I'm so sorry—"

The injured Mageaan took her hand, her fingers cold as they began to turn gray. It wasn't the decayed gray of a soul long dead. It was the onset of death, true death. "Save me," she whispered. "I'm not ready to die."

Guilt burned through Alice. "I can't help you—"

Esmeralda grabbed Alice's hair, twisting violently. "You're an angel of life! You can save anyone! Save her!"

"I can't!" Alice lunged to her feet, shoving the golden-eyed woman back. "I can't save anyone!"

"You lie! You're all the same! You can save her if you want to, you just won't!"

"That's not true—" Alice stopped when the young woman's hand closed around her ankle in a silent plea. Alice immediately dropped to her knees. "What's your name?" she asked gently, wishing there was some way to give her comfort.

"My name is Chloe," the young woman whispered, her voice growing fainter. "I'm not supposed to be here. This isn't my fate. Don't let me die here." She reached out, brushing her fingers over Alice's cheek. "Angel of life, grant me this wish to live another day."

Alice bit her lip, fighting the swell of despair and guilt. The memory of a moment too much like this one. "I'm so sorry, Chloe. I wish I could—"

"Try. Please try," Chloe begged. "An angel's kiss is all I need."

Alice stared at her in disbelief as the woman's words registered. "An angel's kiss will save your life? So you're a—"

"Yes," Chloe said, cutting her off before she could say it aloud. "Please."

Alice closed her eyes, agony welling through her. It was just like before, just like when her mother had died: a soul so precious, and yet Alice still couldn't save her. Chloe was so rare, a gift to the very earth. How had she ended up here? How had she found herself at the end of Ian's mace?

"Please," whispered Chloe, her voice growing fainter.

Dammit. She couldn't let Chloe die. Her death would reverberate across the earth. She had to live. This time, please, this time, it had to be different. *Please let me save her.* Fear beating at her, she grabbed the girl's wrist and lifted her hand so her palm was facing up. Alice bent her head, and she felt Chloe suck in her breath in anticipation. One kiss. That was all she needed to do. One kiss.

When her lips were an inch from Chloe's hand, Alice's body froze. Her muscles locked up, completely immobilizing her. She couldn't move. She screamed inside, willing her body to close that last inch so she could press her lips to Chloe's palm, but her muscles were rigid, her body beyond her command. Pain screamed through her cells, and still she fought it, struggling to move that extra inch.

"Oh, come on!" Esmeralda grabbed Chloe's wrist and lifted her hand to Alice's face. A split second before it made contact with Alice's lips, a violent invisible force repelled Alice backward, slamming her against the coral reef. Pain shot through her head, and she knew she'd cut it open.

The leaders refused to give up, hoisting Chloe in their arms and dragging her toward Alice. As they neared, more pain seared through Alice's body, and she screamed in agony. But she couldn't move. She could do nothing but wait as they approached. A third attempt to save Chloe's life would have severe repercussions for Alice. It would be enough to kill her again.

She begged them to stop, even as Chloe looked at her beseechingly. "Why won't you help me?" she asked. "Why?"

"I can't," Alice said. "I can't save any life. Not anyone's."

"You're an angel of life!"

"I know that!" Alice braced herself as the empresses

thrust Chloe at her. She tried to grab her, but her arms were locked down, her muscles rigid. A split second before Chloe reached Alice, a rush of water threw the injured Mageaan aside and slammed her into the coral. The young woman bounced off it and landed on the coral shelf. Immobile. Inches from death.

"You bitch!" Esmeralda lunged at Alice, her eyes blazing with loathing and hate so vile that Alice knew death was her only goal.

Alice struggled to get off the coral, but she was still immobilized, locked down until Chloe was dead, banned from trying to save her again. "I have the pearl!" Alice shouted in a last attempt to draw her attention, but Esmeralda didn't even slow. She simply tore a piece of coral off the reef and sliced it at Alice—

There was a loud crack and Ian's mace appeared in Alice's hand, the cold steel fitting her palm as if it had been made for her. Her hand moving as if it had a will of its own, Alice thrust the mace into Esmeralda's chest just as the Mageaan swung the sharp edge of the coral at Alice's head. Esmeralda screamed, lost her balance, and her piece of coral thudded harmlessly against the coral beside Alice's head.

Horrified, Alice stared in shock as the woman fell, her face contorted in the depths of agony as death took her, the mace in her heart an instant death blow.

Dear God, she'd killed her. How was that possible? What had happened? Shock taking over, Alice looked up and saw the battle had stopped.

The Mageaan were gaping at their fallen leader, their bodies morphing back into white mist one by one. In the midst of them stood Ian. His body was covered in wounds, his chest was heaving, and he was holding a mace in one hand.

His other hand was empty...because she had his second weapon.

Stunned, Alice held up the mace. "How?" she asked, her voice shaking.

119

"She was going to kill you." His voice was soft, and yet ruthlessly triumphant as he strode across the coral shelf toward her. "You called my weapon. Only a *sheva* can do that. It's one of the stages of the bond."

"I killed her. I killed a living creature." Alice's legs began to give away, and she slithered to her knees just as Ian caught her.

He grabbed her around the waist, holding her up as he gently took the mace from her hand. "It was self-defense," he said. "It's okay."

"No, no, it's not." Stunned, Alice looked across the coral to where Jada was sitting on the ground, holding Chloe in her arms, rocking her gently. "Esmeralda is dead, isn't she? And Chloe?" Two women dead because of her. Dead. Just like before.

"Chloe isn't dead yet." Jada's eyes were haunted. "But soon. Esmeralda is gone."

"Oh, God." Alice's whole body began to shake, and her skin felt hot and clammy, despite the cold ocean. "I can't do this." She stumbled away from Ian, fighting against the assault of memories.

Hey. Ian moved up beside her, setting his hand on her shoulder. She closed her eyes as electricity jumped between them at the contact. *It's okay, Alice. Even angels have a right to save their own lives.*

His voice was certain and non-judgmental, and Alice fought to hold onto his strength as she struggled to regroup. She had to be strong right now. They were still in a dangerous situation, and she couldn't fall apart. *You mean that? Because even if you don't, tell me you do.*

Ian brushed his lips over her forehead, an intimate gesture so tender that it said more than words would ever have communicated. He truly believed in the beauty of her soul, despite what she had just done. She closed her eyes and leaned her forehead against his, a perfect unspoken moment of connection. *Thank you,* she whispered.

I mean it, and I'm not just saying that. He turned his head enough to brush a light kiss over her cheekbone, another kiss of tenderness, but this time, with the slightest hint of possessiveness that made awareness simmer inside her. Ian said nothing as he ran his fingers down her forearm, his touch probing lightly where his brand was supposed to appear.

Quickly, she opened her eyes and looked at her arm.

There were still no marks there. Nothing to connect them despite the fact that she'd just called his weapon. Ian swore softly and laid his palm over her arm, covering the expanse of skin. *You calling my weapon is one of the bonding stages,* he said. *Only a* sheva *can do it. That's the second stage that we've completed. There's no way my brand shouldn't be starting to form on your arm. It's impossible.*

And yet, it was what had happened.

An aching sense of loneliness filled Alice, and she was hit with a sudden, burning desire to have his brand on her. To belong somewhere. To be connected with a living being the way she seemed to be able to connect with him. The absence of his mark was a brutal stab of isolation and loss, a taunting denial of all she wanted to be.

She had nothing. She was nothing. She was an angel of life who could not save any living creature, even her own mother. Even Chloe.

Ian ran his hand up her arm, encircling the back of her neck. His eyes were glittering with something dangerous and possessive. *I need to mark you. I don't handle it well when my mark doesn't show up on you when it should. That's twice now. And still you resist me.* His voice was tense, and she felt the supreme effort he was exercising to battle the effects of the curse. His fingers were digging into her neck, drawing her closer.

Excitement leapt through her, a desperate need to cleanse herself of who she was. She wanted to hide from her life, and lose herself in what he awakened within her. To feel Ian's desire for her and pretend that it made sense, pretend she deserved it.

His fingers dug into her hair, and his mouth hovered inches from hers. His body was shaking with the effort of controlling himself, and she felt the waves of despair rolling through him as a result of the fact his brand still hadn't appeared on her arm. The curse was strong and gaining strength. He swore under his breath, squeezing her neck even harder, promising so much unrestrained passion. *Not here. Not now. But it has to be soon.*

Not now? Why not now? She wanted to protest, to shout at him not to withhold the gift he offered, and then she suddenly remembered where they were: on a coral reef in the depths of the ocean surrounded by dead bodies and murderous Mageaan. Not the kind of thing a girl was supposed to forget. *What are you doing to me?* Horrified by the fact she'd been so consumed by her emotions and lust that she'd forgotten where she was, she jerked out of his grasp and spun around.

To her shock, every Mageaan within sight was bent low, their heads bowed toward her. She stiffened, dark foreboding settling deep inside her. "This isn't good."

Ian studied the genuflecting masses. *They're saluting you as their new leader. You killed their current one.*

A ripple of unease went through her. Only fallen angels could be Mageaan. Had she crossed that line when she murdered? She quickly looked at her palms. In the center of one hand was a small, gray dot. The first step. The precursor to losing all that she was. Horrified, she closed her palm, jerking her chin up as she looked toward Jada. "I'm not their leader," she said sharply.

Jada was still sitting down with Chloe in her lap. She looked weary and exhausted. "You are bound to us now. You cannot leave the water. Ever."

Alice shook her head. "Oh, no, no. That's not possible. I

have to leave. I have to find my sister. I won't stay—"

"You don't have a choice. You can't leave. It's impossible." Jada looked at Ian. Gone was the hostility from before, replaced by resigned understanding and bitter camaraderie. "And you, as her mate, are equally condemned. Both of your futures are dead now." She rose to her feet, still cradling the unconscious Chloe. "Welcome to hell."

CHAPTER EIGHT

Ian didn't trust the beauty of the palace they'd entered. Not for a minute.

He strode restlessly behind Alice as they followed the leader of the Mageaan down a long corridor beneath the coral. The entrance had been deep beneath the vibrant reef, and the moment they'd stepped past the threshold into the undersea palace, they'd walked into fresh air. The ocean seemed to be held at the entrance by an invisible shield easily passable with one simple step. The moment they'd crossed into air, Jada's tail had disappeared. In its place were two very human legs, long, elegant, and lean, a reminder of what she had been before being cast aside in the sea.

Along the walls were troughs of salt water, housing assorted bioluminescent fish that were casting a purple and green glow into the tunnel. Was that their only source of light, down here so deep beneath the surface of the ocean? It was ingenious, actually, given that it wasn't as if there could be electricity or solar power illuminating the coral reef castle.

The walls were coated with vibrant plants of the most magnificent colors, and the floors were polished stone. Marble? Coral? Oyster shell? It was beautiful and magical, and he didn't trust it for a moment.

He'd seen ethereal mist turn into women and then

demon specters. He could taste the haunting poison in the air. He'd been stabbed in the kidney by a fallen angel. And he'd watched his brand fail to appear on his *sheva* after two bonding stages.

Yeah, he wasn't trusting that anything was actually how it appeared to be. Beauty? Not worth the risk to notice. With each step he took deeper into the lair, his instincts grew more wary. He felt like the walls were closing in on him, stripping him of his freedom to walk away, closing off exits. Deep beneath the ocean, what options would they have if they needed to bail in a hurry? The only exit he'd seen was the one they'd left far behind. It wasn't simply the walls that were trapping them. It was also the millions of gallons of salt water stretching for miles around them.

He moved closer to Alice and put his hand on her back, keeping her close. But the moment he touched her, all thoughts of escape were subjugated by his need for her. The feel of her body beneath his hand made a dark hunger rumble through him. Desire. And even carnal lust. He had to get her alone. He had to rebuild their connection. He had to find out what was going on with the mark. How was she blocking the bond? It was getting worse and worse to be around her, harder and harder to deal with the distance. Her distress after killing that woman had nearly sent him over the edge when he'd been unable to help her deal with it the way he'd wanted.

He had to get her alone, and fast.

The fact that they were not making progress toward Cardiff was upping the stakes. Time was running out for them, and he had to find a way to get them out of there and back on track. Could Jada help? The deal needed to be closed quickly.

Yet even as he walked, pain shot through him with each step, and he could feel the internal bleeding seeping into his abdomen. He'd been able to slow down the damage from the knife in his back, but to truly mend it, he needed to go into the Calydon healing sleep for a few hours. Though many blades had cut him, that first one that had gone all the way through his kidney was the biggest issue.

Even big, badass immortal warriors needed internal organs in order to get through the day.

"We shall meet in here," Jada said as two huge French doors swung open, revealing a massive ballroom swathed in bright light.

Ian stopped the moment he saw the massive glass chandeliers hanging from the ceiling, their white bulbs shining like a New Year's Eve gala. There were no fish illuminating those suckers. It appeared to be electricity, pure and simple... but a thousand leagues under the sea? That wasn't possible. "You have electricity down here?" he asked the question anyway, probing for answers.

Jada didn't look back as she walked across the shell floor and set Chloe down on a red silk couch in the center of the room. "No," she said as she pulled a beautiful woven quilt over the girl. "This retains life," she said. "It will give her more time." She bent down and brushed her lips over Chloe's forehead. "Be strong, sweet girl. I will find a way to save you."

Distress emanated from Alice, and Ian glanced over at her. Her eyes were shining with unshed tears, and her fists were clenched as she watched the exchange.

Ian touched her arm. *You tried, sweetheart. Sometimes, that's all we can do.*

Alice jutted her jaw out even as she took a deep breath, reining in her regret and drawing upon that same strength that he was getting to know so well. *It's not enough.*

I know. Shit, he knew that. His father's death was evidence of that. How similar were they? He got her, and he knew that she might understand what drove him as well. Suddenly, his need to get her alone was more than lust or sex. He wanted to talk to her, find out what drove her, and tell her things he hadn't been able to tell his teammates.

Jada's shoulders hunched with weariness. "You like the

chandeliers?" she asked, drawing his attention back to the room. "They were a gift."

"A gift?" Ian walked under the nearest chandelier, carefully assessing the structure. There were no cords. It wasn't even attached to the ceiling. It was simply hovering there. In midair. Emanating light. Magic? Magic, definitely. Suddenly the taint and stink of the palace became clear. It wasn't simply magic. It was demon magic. And he knew only one wizard who played in that sandbox. *Cardiff was here.*

I know. Alice was staring at a small porcelain bowl on a side table. *I can feel his taint. That bowl is his, too.* Then she grinned at Ian, her face alight with such excitement that he felt his heart stutter. Since he'd known her, he'd seen only her tension, her fear, her worry, but in that moment, her optimism and courage was lighting up her face, making her look beautiful and alive. *We're close, Ian. They know him. They can help us.*

"Come sit." Jada rose from the couch and gestured to a long blue-green table made of coral. There was a bench on either side, and an armchair at each end. All of the items were intricately carved by hand, so complicated that they looked as if they'd been created by someone who'd had nothing else to do for too many years...which was probably the case. Not much to do down here if there were no visitors to swarm and attack.

Alice quickly sat on one of the benches, and Ian stood behind her, his hands on her shoulders.

The leader looked at him. "Sit."

"No." He inspected the myriad of tunnels breaking off from the main room. "I don't trust you. I prefer to be ready."

She raised her brows. "Eternity is a long time to be on your feet."

"I won't be here for eternity," he said without hesitation.

Alice touched his hand in solidarity, the small gesture jerking his attention back to her. She gave him a small smile, and his heart almost stopped. That subtle affection was incredible. Her voluntary touch was, in some ways, far more intimate than making love had been. Fresh determination swelled through him, and he squeezed her shoulders. Deep beneath the ocean in hostile territory, they were a team, and he liked it.

Being part of a team was part of who he was, and without the Order at his back, having Alice's support felt damn good.

"Very sweet," the Mageaan said, but her tone suggested she didn't agree with her words. Instead, she leaned forward, her hands clasped loosely on the table. "My name is Jada Skye. I was bound as Esmeralda's co-leader a hundred years ago, after the existing leaders were slaughtered in a battle."

"Bound?" Alice asked, a slight edge to her voice.

"Yes." Jada held out her hands, and Ian saw green and blue tendrils tattooed on the backs of them. "These are my handcuffs. Ordinary Mageaan have white and gray tattoos, but the leaders are different."

Ian frowned. He hadn't noticed any marks on the hands of the other Mageaan. Had they already faded to the point of invisibility, etched on their spirits instead of their skin? Shit. He felt itchy at the thought, and his determination to get them out of there quickly ramped up.

Alice moved her hands beneath the table, and Ian saw her look down at them. He frowned at her actions, realizing what Jada was saying: if Alice was the new leader, she, too, would have handcuffs. *Are there marks, Alice?*

She didn't answer, and his sense of danger grew stronger. It didn't matter what was on her skin. There was no chance they were going to spend their lives eating seaweed and growing gills. "Look," he said, no longer willing to play the polite hospitality game. "We need to find Warwick Cardiff. We know you've got something going with him, because his magic is all over the place here. Where is his lair?"

Jada sat up, her eyes flashing. "It is hidden in the middle of the ocean. Only those with his invitation can find it. It's a land of dark magic, illusions, and danger, except for those who are invited."

Ian's adrenaline kicked on. "Can you find it?"

She shot him a look of pure condescension. "Of course I can. We are always on his guest list. We protect his island when he isn't there."

In exchange for chandeliers, no doubt. The call of luxury was a powerful thing for some people.

"Will you take us there?" Alice asked. "I need to get into his castle."

Jada shook her head impatiently. "You are water bound. You can't go onto his land."

"Am I?" Alice set her hands on the table, and Ian could see that they were as devoid of the tattoos as they were of his brand.

Ian grinned, relieved that his mark wasn't the only one that seemed to have trouble claiming Alice. Sometimes, elusiveness was a damned good thing. "That's my woman. No one's going to claim her against her will."

Alice glanced at him, as if surprised by his statement of approval. *You hate the fact you can't claim me.*

Yeah, but it makes me feel better to know that some ancient angel fate can't land you either. He shrugged. *I'm a guy. My ego needs the boost.*

Alice rolled her eyes at him, but Ian didn't miss the hint of a smile.

Jada grabbed her hands, staring in shock. "That's impossible. There's no way Esmeralda's crown didn't transfer to you. I don't understand."

"Join the club. Alice defies nature, that's for sure." Ian grinned and eased down on the seat beside Alice, no longer able to be that far away from her. He kept his back to the table, facing outward so he could spring into action if he needed to, but he kept his shoulders turned toward Alice. He leaned in close to her and took over her space, shrugging his shoulders when she raised her eyebrows at him. *I can't give you room,*

Alice. I need more of you, not less.

Her lips tightened, but she didn't move away, allowing his body to rest snugly against hers. It didn't do much to assuage the need burning through him, but it was enough to keep him from dropping to the floor and impaling himself on his own weapon. For the moment.

"We need you to take us to Cardiff's island," he said. "Now."

Jada laughed softly. "There is no possibility of that, warrior. My job is to protect my people. I will not endanger them by making an enemy of that man." "Protect them? You sent them to their slaughter against me," Ian snapped, fresh anger surging through him at what had happened. "How is that protecting them?"

Jada's eyes glittered. "We did not expect you to defeat us. We expected no casualties." She looked at Alice. "Since you are not our leader, I no longer owe you respect. It changes everything." She rose to her feet, her eyes glittering. "You murdered our leader. You will die in the morning."

Ian didn't bother to respond. Instead, he studied her intently for weaknesses and lies that he could exploit. There was no chance he was going to let himself and Alice die in the morning, or any other time in the foreseeable future. He did, however, need to figure out how he was going to make that happen.

"Wait!" Alice leapt to her feet, the desperate edge in her voice suggesting she didn't have nearly the faith in Ian's skills as he did, which bit deep. As his mate, she should believe in him even when he didn't believe in himself. "Since I'm still an angel and not a Mageaan, the pearl will work if I offer it to you. You want it, don't you?" She braced her palms on the table and leaned forward, her stance and tone a challenge the Mageaan could not ignore. "It could save Chloe or Esmeralda, and you know it."

It occurred to Ian that it was time he found out exactly

what was so damned special about that pearl. He'd been so focused on all the other shit that he hadn't realized that the pearl might be a key tool for them. Alice had downplayed it as something useless, encouraging him to dismiss its importance, but he was beginning to realize that she hadn't been all that honest about the pearl.

Women. Can't trust them. Can't bond with them. Can't live without 'em, even for a minute.

Jada's eyes darkened. "As an angel of life, you could have saved them both. Many of my people are dead because you wouldn't help. Why would I trust you with the pearl, or honor you by giving you anything?"

Angel of life? Ian studied Alice, surprised by the news. If she was an angel of life, how was it that she had such difficulty staying alive? His mate was getting more complex by the moment, and a part of him liked it. She was a miasma of secrets and barriers that needed to be unraveled, and he was the guy to do it. Challenges kept the day interesting, and as long as she let him get up close and personal with her, it was good.

"Why should you trust me?" Alice stiffened. "Because you need that pearl too badly to do anything else but trade for it."

Jada stared at her. "You know nothing about us."

"I know enough."

For a long moment, Jada said nothing. Then she surged to her feet, anger crackling off her. "You are my guests tonight. Tomorrow you will die, or I will bargain with you. It is my decision." Then from the folds of the harness that covered her breasts, she pulled out a small thin stick.

Ian swore at the sight of one of Cardiff's wands and dove across Alice to shield her, but it was too late. A razor-thin stream of light hit them both. Turquoise light swelled around them, and when it was gone, they were no longer in the ballroom.

They were in a small, barren chamber with no windows,

no doors, and no way out.

† † †

Two hours after being transported into the cell and searching for a way out, Ian finally had to accept the fact that escape was not going to happen. Feeling caged and impotent, he paced across the floor, clasping his hands behind his head, trying to mask his frustration.

Their prison was small, maybe ten feet in diameter, with an arched ceiling that went up at least twenty feet. The walls, floor, and ceiling were smooth oyster shell, but must have been protected by magic because his mace was powerless against it. The only furnishings were a cot and tiny bathroom, as if it were designed to keep prisoners for a long time.

They were in jail, and he didn't like it. Not one bit. "There's no way out."

Alice was sitting on the floor, leaning back against the wall, her forearms draped over her knees. She had accepted their fate long before he had. "I know. We'll have to wait until morning."

The frustration of inactivity gnawed at Ian. He didn't like being incapacitated. Being trapped in the small room reminded him too much of the months he'd spent in the Order's dungeon, fighting for his sanity.

Shaking out his arms, he paced restlessly, needing to do something to further their mission. For a split second, he debated trying to reach out to Ry and have Kane teleport in, but he quickly dismissed that. Turning himself over to the Order would not get them to Cardiff. He would not give up that easily. Plus, he suspected they were too far away anyway. Since he wasn't blood-bonded with either of them, the range of their telepathic communication was limited. "We need a plan for the morning," he said. "Tell me what you know about these people."

"As I said, they are fallen angels. They were originally

133

in human form, but they lost that when they were cast aside." Alice shrugged. "They were once like me, Ian. Then they did something terrible and were banished."

"What kind of terrible?" Those hadn't been women with good hearts out there. He'd felt their need to destroy him, their thirst for his pain and suffering. If he hadn't sensed that about them, he wouldn't have been able to fight to kill. But he'd realized instantly that it was his death or theirs, and the choice had been made.

"It depends." She leaned her head back and studied him warily. "But once an angel loses her status, it isn't just her body that decays. It's her mind and her soul. They become what they chose to be when they broke the rules." She bit her lip. "Chloe was brand new. She was still so close to her humanity. I don't even think she is full angel. Maybe a half or a quarter. She doesn't belong here. She's not even dead yet, Ian. What kind of suffering is she going through right now?"

Ian reached the end of the room by the foot of the cot and turned back. "I'm the one who delivered the blow. I take responsibility." Once he'd seen Chloe's humanity after he'd struck her, he'd replayed that fight again and again in his head, haunted by the fact that he had made a mistake and struck an innocent. But no matter how many times he revisited the moment that he'd struck her, he was always absolutely certain that there had been not even a whisper of decency in the foe he'd been fighting. She had become something else in that battle, or been possessed by it. But how was that possible? He was a highly experienced warrior, taught from day one to know who was the enemy and who was the innocent. During the battle, Chloe had not been an innocent.

What had happened out there?

He knew there would be no answers tonight, and solving the mystery of the Mageaan wasn't his mission. He had to stay focused. "We're not leaving without directions to Warwick's," he said. "We have to convince Jada she needs that pearl." He looked over at her. "Why *do* they need that jewel, Alice?"

"The pearl of Lycanth can save an angel's soul," she said, sounding too tired to play games anymore. "It's like a get out of jail free card. One soul, one pearl. Only three exist. I have... had one of them."

He whistled under his breath. "No wonder they would want it." He nodded with satisfaction. "We can leverage this. There's no chance she's going to let us go without giving her the pearl."

"She might. The pearl of Lycanth will send the angel straight to hell if she doesn't have a pure heart." She looked wearily at Ian. "Is she willing to take the chance? Does she look like someone who has a pure heart? Even life as a Mageaan is better than hell."

Ian had sensed the darkness in Jada, and in all the creatures he'd fought. There hadn't been a pure heart among them, at least not during the fight. But then he thought of the one Alice hadn't let him kill, the one who had chosen not to eat them. He thought of Chloe, who had clearly been an innocent once she was out of the battle. Was there some kind of humanity left in those creatures or not? He wished he knew.

"They'll be ready for you this time," Alice said. "Your fighting ability caught them by surprise, but you've revealed yourself. If Jada chooses to kill us, she now knows what it will take."

Ian ground his jaw. "I have more than what I showed today."

"She commands the oceans, Ian. You may have more, but she has *everything*." Alice pressed her hands to her face. "We really might die tomorrow."

"I won't allow it." Despite his claim, however, he was grimly aware that without his team to support him, there were limits to what he could defeat. But if he called them to aid him, he would lose the chance to go after Cardiff, and he would die the same death as his father. The Order would come to retrieve

Alice, not to join him on a mission to find Cardiff.

If he could prove Cardiff was the one threatening the Order, they would help. Or, if they already knew it was Cardiff and had chosen to block him from the mission anyway, then he'd have to prove that he was sane enough to take on his personal enemy. Either way, calling them in now meant he'd get the boot. But he didn't like being without his team. It was what he was bred for.

"I don't know if I can come back again if I die," she said. "It was hard this time."

Ian swore at the reminder that it wasn't simply his life and his mission at stake. Could he risk Alice like that by not asking the team for help? Shit. He had to. His obligation was bigger than a single woman. But how could he risk her? Scowling, he walked away, giving her his back as he paced the room. "If I call in the Order as backup, we will be unstoppable. No chance Jada will be able to kill us." He left the words hanging in the air, offering them to her.

For a moment, Alice was silent. "They'll take me to their mansion."

"They will."

"They'll take you off Warwick."

"They will." Ian didn't turn to face her. He simply waited.

After a heavy moment of silence, she spoke. "I would rather die than give up. Don't call them."

He spun to face her, but her eyes were closed and her head was resting back against the wall. The body language of a woman too exhausted to cope. "You're sure?"

She nodded. "It has to be us, Ian. We give it our all and either die or succeed. I can't walk away, and neither can you."

Grim resolution flooded Ian, but with it was a deep admiration for the woman before him. Her bravery, her commitment to her sister...she was like a ray of white light shining into his darkness. "I'm in," he said.

She managed a faint smile. "It's settled, then."

"Yeah." Ian resumed his pacing, his mind working hard now as he tried to predict all possible scenarios for the morning, and to establish a plan for each one. He had an hour or two to plan, and then he had to go into his healing sleep and regain his strength for tomorrow.

"Can you stop pacing?" Alice sounded tired. "You're making me dizzy with all your circling."

The weariness in her voice broke through his focus. He swore when he saw how pale her face was, and how drawn her features were. "You okay?"

Her head was still propped up against the wall, her green eyes at half-mast. "I killed a woman, Ian. I killed someone. I felt her life bleed out the moment I did it."

Ian remembered the first day he'd taken a life. It was never easy, even in self-defense. "You had no choice," he said, walking over to her. He crouched down in front of her and brushed a lock of her hair back from her face. "You did good. It's my fault you had to defend yourself. I should have been able to keep you safe."

"You were keeping me safe. You were keeping hundreds of Mageaan away from me." She shook her head, and tears glistened in her eyes. "I'm an angel, Ian. An angel of life. I'm supposed to protect lives and give people a second chance, not kill them."

Ian sat down beside her and leaned back against the wall, resting his shoulder against hers as he propped his knees up and draped his forearms over his legs. "Sometimes angels have to save their own lives."

"We're supposed to let ourselves be killed."

Ian snorted with disgust. "That's total crap. Break that rule, sweetheart, and feel good doing it."

But Alice didn't acknowledge his comment. "Did you see what happened with Chloe?" She closed her eyes and pressed her palms to them. "I can't do this again," she whispered. "All I had to do was give her an angel's kiss and I couldn't do it. She's dying right now because I could do nothing." Her shoulders started to shake, and Ian swore softly, his soul aching for her anguish. "Two women died today, and both of them were my fault." She looked at him, her face full of so much self-loathing that his gut clenched. "All I'm supposed to do is bring life to others, and I do the opposite. Do you know what it's like to want to save someone and not be able to?"

"Yeah, I do." To his surprise, she leaned into him when he answered her, as if the weight of the world was too much for her to handle alone. And it probably was. He knew exactly what she was feeling. There was nothing as horrific as the feeling of impotence when watching harm befall someone and being completely unable to do anything about it. "I was ten when my father killed himself in front of me."

Alice glanced over at him, tears still glistening in her eyes. "You saw it?"

"Fuck yeah, I did. I caused it to happen."

Her brow puckered in a small frown. "How? You were only ten."

"I thought I could save him from the curse." Ian threaded his fingers through her hair, grounding himself in her presence as he relived that moment from so long ago. "He'd explained to me about the curse. My grandfather had killed himself when my dad was a kid. He'd ordered my dad to restore the family honor by breaking the curse, and he banned my dad from ever speaking to a woman, let alone having sex with them. Of course, it's not that easy to do when you're out there saving the damn world and running into women all the time. My dad wanted to give me the same command, but he knew it was impossible, so he instead taught me to identify women who might bring me down and to get out before they could get to me." The irony of the moment, that he was telling his story to a woman he'd made love to until his soul had exploded was not lost on him. "By the time I was ten, my dad was suffering. The curse was pressing him hard for a woman he'd seen from a distance once. It was killing him."

Alice raised her brows. "Was it his *sheva*?"

"Yeah. She wouldn't have been able to affect him so intensely from such a distance otherwise." Ian closed his eyes, remembering that night all too well. "He came to me in the middle of the night and told me that he couldn't fight the curse much longer because the separation between him and this woman was killing him. He gave instructions on what I was supposed to do after he killed himself."

Alice put her hand on his arm, her face softening. "I'm so sorry. That's terrible." She couldn't imagine what it would be like to have your parent tell you that they were about to kill themselves. How helpless and vulnerable would that make a child feel? And how terrified? "Did you try to stop him?"

"Of course I did. I went out and found the woman and brought her home. I figured that if he couldn't take the separation, then maybe it would be better if he had her in his life." He flexed his hands restlessly, and Alice could feel the raw strength he was exerting trying to keep the memories superficial. "The moment he saw Helen, their connection was instant." He looked over at her, his dark eyes hooded. "Like us."

Alice felt heat flood her cheeks, but there was no way to deny it. Even just sitting beside him on the floor, she was aware of the rhythm of his heart, the strength emanating from him, and the potent sexuality that seemed to heat up the very air between them. She'd chosen to sit on the floor instead of the cot, because the bed seemed too dangerous in this small room with him. "So it worked?"

"For a couple days. He even told me he was feeling better."

Alice could hear the edge in his voice, the precursor of something terrible. "So, what happened?"

Ian lifted her arm and traced his fingers down the smooth expanse of her skin. "They completed the *sheva* bond. All five stages." He raised her arm to his lips, pressing a kiss against it.

Desire and awareness pulsed through her. "So, that's good, right? For them? I mean, he had cemented the bond, which is what you want to do with me." She wanted to pull her arm away from Ian, but she couldn't make herself do it. Not with the feel of his breath drifting over her skin, the delicate way his fingers were clasped around her wrist, as if she were a fragile porcelain doll that would shatter.

"No. Not good." He pressed another kiss to her arm, never taking his gaze off her face. "Remember the *sheva* legend?"

"Oh...yes." She'd forgotten about the ill-fated destiny of the Calydon and his mate, having been slightly occupied with clear and present dangers instead. But even remembering it didn't lessen her need for him. She could barely resist the urge to melt into him. Was her response because she really was his *sheva*? Or was there something else about him that made her come to life? "Has anyone survived the bond?"

"In the last two thousand years four couples have survived, but it's unclear whether they defeated fate, or simply delayed it. The jury is still out." He leaned back against the wall, resting his head against the luminescent shell. "But the curse changes it for us, for my father. He lost Helen, the way destiny commanded, but instead of going rogue, the despair of the loss was so great that he took his own life." He was staring across the room, not looking at her. "She'd simply gone to buy bread," he said. "That was all. But that loss was enough. I was screaming at my father that she would be right back, and it didn't matter. He grabbed me by the throat and shouted at me to end the curse, to restore honor to our family's name. Then he called out his axe and chopped off his own head right in our kitchen."

Dear God. Alice was horrified. "Ian—"

"When Helen came back and saw my father, she killed herself, per the fate of the Calydon and his mate. Two people dead, same ending, but if destiny had been allowed to play out, he would have at least died with honor. But this way? Just shame." He grimaced. "The tragedy of Romeo and Juliet is not so romantic in real life. Two people dead because I thought I could save them by bringing them together."

"I'm so sorry, Ian—" Alice wanted to touch him, to hug him, to take away his pain, but she knew it wouldn't change anything. She knew that all too well.

"Even though my father had been one of the most admired Order of the Blade members, they weren't able to honor his death because it was by suicide. He lived for his mission, and he believed the only oath worthy of obeying was the one he'd made when he was sworn in as one of the elite. Nothing else mattered, and yet he lost it in the end. It was stolen from him by the curse. His body didn't disappear at death the way Calydons usually do because he had violated the sacredness of life. To this day, his body and soul lay trapped beneath the earth in my family's burial grounds, along with the other Fitzgerald males who have died."

Alice stared at him, the reality of his words sinking in. No relief for the soul? No afterlife? "Like the Mageaan," she said. "They're banned from the Afterlife as well. Trapped here."

He glanced at her. "Hell."

She nodded.

"I made a promise that day," he said softly. "I vowed to restore honor to my family's legacy as Order of the Blade members, to free their souls, and to bring back honor to my father's memory. The only way to do it is to break the curse. It was my fault he died, and I have to fix it."

She understood now what drove him. What a terrible burden for a young boy to carry. A burden for a grown man to carry as well.

He managed a grim smile. "And now my team has taken me off duty. If I go back to them, they'll boot me out of the Order. I haven't even died yet, and I've already fucked up my family's legacy." He turned his head slightly to look at her. "And you, Alice, my *sheva*. Are you my salvation or the doom that will destroy me forever?"

She swallowed at the sudden hunger in his tone. "I could ask you the same question."

He studied her for a long moment, his gaze so intense she wanted to squirm. "I know so little about you, Alice. Tell me something. Tell me your secrets."

"I can't. It's against the rules."

He uttered a low growl. "I don't care about rules." He threaded his fingers through hers, and tugged on her hand, pulling her toward him. "I want to know why you don't carry my mark." His eyes were blazing with possessiveness, and excitement rushed through her.

"Don't ask me that, Ian."

"Oh, I'm going to ask you." He slid his hand around the back of her neck, pulling her toward him. "I need to know how to break down your walls."

Her heart began to hammer as he moved closer, his mouth inches from hers. "Don't—"

"I won't stop until all the barriers between us are gone." He brushed his mouth over hers, and desire leapt through her, a white-hot flame too hot to withstand. "I want to know everything about you."

He kissed her forehead. "I want to know your dreams."

He kissed her left temple, his lips the softest caress. "I want to know your fears."

He kissed her right temple, a decadent temptation of tenderness and demand. "I want to know what makes you laugh."

"Laugh?" She closed her eyes, fighting against her body's desire to respond to him. "I don't laugh."

"Is that against the rules, too?" He kissed one eyelid, and then the other. "Or is your heart too heavy for laughter?"

She scrunched her eyes shut. "Stop it," she whispered.

"Just please stop."

His breath was hot against her ear, his voice a caress to her soul. "Why am I such a threat to you, Alice? Why do you resist me?"

"I... I can't tell you—"

Ian swore violently, and before she knew what had happened, he'd swept her up into his arms and tossed her on the bed. Her back hit the soft mattress, and then he was on top of her, his weight pinning her to the sheets. He grabbed her wrists and locked them down above her head, heat blazing in his eyes. "Stop it," he commanded. "Just stop shutting me out, for hell's sake!"

Alice knew she should have been afraid of him, but she wasn't. As trapped as she was, he wasn't hurting her. The despair was pouring out of him, nearly flooding her senses. She felt his pain, so much pain, and so much stress trying to fight it off. Her heart broke for him, for his suffering, and suddenly she didn't want to be apart from him anymore. No one had shared emotions like this with her before. It made her feel alive. It made her feel like there was a reason she came back to life every time she got killed. It made her feel like there was hope in this world of something better than her life, and something better than her future. "Kiss me, Ian," she whispered.

He groaned and closed his eyes, throwing his head back. "Hell, Alice." His voice was raw and harsh. "I'm not made of steel. If I kiss you, I'm not going to stop. I need you so badly."

"I need you, too." The words were a whisper, barely audible, but when he stiffened, she knew he'd heard her.

Slowly, he brought his head back down and opened his eyes. "Say it again," he commanded.

She almost smiled at his fierceness. *You make me feel wanted. It's so beautiful.*

Say it again.

She met his gaze, and anticipation began to pulse through her. She could feel the rigid restraint he was exercising, and she knew that if she gave him any leeway, he would take over and she'd never be able to stop the flood of passion once he unleashed it.

Her heart began to pound. Did she really want to do this? No. Yes.

"Alice," he whispered, lowering his head until his lips were grazing hers. Not kissing. Not taking. Tempting her with sinful decadence. "Tell me you need me. We are never going to get through tomorrow morning if we aren't connected. I can't do this alone."

The desperation in his voice touched her in that place deep inside that only he could awaken, and the words came of their own accord. Words that were a truth she'd never spoken to anyone. "Yes," she whispered, her heart racing and desire roaring through her. "I do need you, Ian. I need you to bring me back to life."

His low growl was his only response before he claimed her.

CHAPTER NINE

Alice's kiss was intoxicating.

Her lips felt like the softest silk of a new rose. She was a purity that Ian had never deserved, and yet, here she was, in his arms, her fingers tunneling through his hair, responding to his kiss as if she'd been waiting her entire life just for this moment.

Alice. He whispered her name into her mind as he deepened the kiss, sinking his hips against hers. Sweet Jesus, it felt unbelievable to have her body beneath his, to feel the softness of her flesh below him.

Ian. Her voice was breathless, the magnitude of her desire striking deep, igniting a fire within him so powerful he felt like it would doom him if he didn't let it come to life. Which, given the curse, was probably not far from the truth.

He ran his hands down her arms as he kissed her throat, her skin so soft and delicate. He brushed his lips across her collarbones and her chest, his mouth teasing over the low neckline of her tank top. His soul screamed for more, demanding he make her his, but he knew it wouldn't be enough to simply connect physically. He had to have more than that. He had to break through that metaphysical wall keeping them apart. "Tell me what you are, Alice." He flanked her waist with his hands, sliding his fingers beneath the hem of her tank so her stomach was bared to him.

She didn't answer his query. Instead, she groaned and arched her back, writhing beneath him. He could feel the intensity of her physical response, and he could also sense her awe and confusion. It was new for her, feeling like this, and an unfamiliar sense of ownership and propriety swelled within him. He was the first man to awaken this side of Alice, and that was how it should be.

He bent his head and swirled his tongue in her belly button, teasing her, taunting her, stoking in her the very fires she was fighting so hard to suppress. "Are you a fallen angel, Alice?" he asked again.

"No," she gasped, her fingers digging into his hair. "I'm an angel of life."

"You mentioned that earlier. But you can't save anyone. It doesn't fit." He kissed his way across her belly, holding her twisting hips still, stealing from her the freedom to move, and trying to break through the barriers keeping them apart. He assaulted her defenses on all levels: sexually, telepathically, and emotionally.

"Ian, I can't tell you—"

"You can." He trailed his tongue over her ribs, working his way up her belly. "No more walls, Alice. Tell me the secrets you can't share." He slipped the built-in bra over her breasts, and she gasped as the elastic brushed over her taut nipples.

Raw desire began to build inside him at the sight of her full breasts, at the way she was responding to him. But her body wasn't enough. He needed all of her. He needed her spirit to accept and welcome him. Having her this close, but not completely accessible, was brutal. Frustrated, he pinned her arms on the pillow and kissed her breast.

The moment his mouth closed around her nipple, Alice shuddered, her whole body twisting beneath him. "How can you be affecting me like this?"

"Because I'm hot as hell, and you know it," he said as he

lightly bit the puckered tip of her nipple, satisfaction pulsing through him as she yelped in response. "And because your soul craves me," he added, even as the mere voicing of those words made the curse pulse within him, taunting him that he was wrong. That the woman he was made for didn't need him the same way. That she would walk away. Reject him. Cut him down.

The voice seemed to swell in his mind, ruthlessly hammering away at him, stripping away at his foundation. *Isolation. Loss. Rejection.*

Swearing, Ian slammed his mouth down over hers, trying to fight off the voice of the curse with her kiss. He thrust his tongue into her mouth, and she responded instantly, matching him with each stroke, a dance of seduction and desire so intense it seared his very soul. *More, Alice. I need more.*

Alice was shocked by the sudden crush of emotions from Ian. It was as if he'd dropped all his shields and was flooding her with who he was. His despair and desperation were almost overwhelming, as was his need for her. Her heart ached for him, and she wanted to help him, to ease his pain. *What can I do, Ian?*

Stop fighting me. Just let me in.

Alice closed her eyes, tears brimming as Ian consumed her with desperate kisses. She wrapped her arms around his neck, clinging to him, trying to hold him tighter. Never had she felt so close to anyone. Never had she felt so alive. She wanted more. She wanted to see how far it could go. She wanted to reach out for this man who was calling to her so urgently.

Her mind and heart screamed for him, and she kissed him deeper, trying frantically to somehow open the connection between them, to somehow overturn the barriers keeping her isolated.

I can feel your need. Ian pulled back and tore her shirt over her head.

Alice's heart pounded as he sat up, his gaze sweeping

possessively over her body. Her breasts tingled, her nipples taut in anticipation. Without a word, he pulled his own shirt off, revealing that same chiseled body she'd seen in the water.

Her breath caught at the sheer magnificence of who he was. The breadth of his shoulders and arms, the indomitable strength of his chest, the hardness of his toned stomach. He was all male, pure, raw male, and his need for her blazed in his eyes.

Desire pooled in her lower abdomen, and anticipation roared through her as he came down toward her, his hands braced on either side of her head. He said nothing. He gave her no chance to turn him down. He just kissed her, a kiss designed for the sole purpose of stripping her defenses and claiming her to the very marrow of her bones.

Longing swelled within her, and she kissed him back just as fiercely. She braced her hands on his chest, and electricity leapt between them. He groaned and lowered himself on top of her so that her bare breasts were against his chest. So much skin. An electrifying connection. Unreal. Unbelievable. Incredible. And yet not enough.

She shifted restlessly beneath him, craving more, trying to kiss him deeply enough to ease the ache in her body.

Ian broke the kiss and trailed his way down her body. Hot, wet kisses on her breasts, tantalizing nibbles on her nipples, and daring bold swipes of his tongue on her belly... lower... and lower...

With a growl of possession, Ian grabbed the waistband of her shorts and tore them off her in a single quick move. Anticipation poured through her, and her body began to tremble as he grabbed her hips and pulled her toward him.

He locked his arms around her thighs and braced them apart. *You are going to burn for me, Alice.*

God, I hope so. She gasped as he kissed the inside of her left thigh. Then the right. Then the left again, all the while working his way closer and closer to her core. His hands were tight around her thighs, holding them apart while his thumbs circled at the edges of her labia, teasing, touching, tantalizing, so close, so very close. Desire seemed to flood her senses as he neared her most sensitive spot, and the anticipation seemed too much to take. *Kiss me, Ian!*

Demand more from me. He kissed the inside of her thigh, right next to where his thumbs were still working seductive circles. *I want you to need me so badly that you can't take it anymore.* His tongue darted out, striking her folds with a tease that made her cry out. *That's what I want. Burn for me, Alice. Let yourself crave me until I consume every thought in your mind, every breath you take.* He kissed her again, and this time he didn't stop. He tugged at her folds with his teeth, drove her to the edge of ecstasy with his tongue, and teased her to uncontrollable frenzy with his kisses.

Alice was stunned by what Ian was igniting within her. The sensations he was creating were incredible. Like waves of hot lava flowing through her body. They seemed to inflame her very soul, and she wanted more, so much more. *Ian—*

Let me in, sweetheart. It can be so much more. His fingers slipped inside her, and she gasped at the invasion that felt so right. They were supposed to be together. They were supposed to be connected.

She wanted to feel this all the way to her spirit. Damn the rules! She wanted to be free! She didn't want to play by these stupid rules anymore! *How? How do I let you in?*

Soften your shields. He kissed her again, and she writhed under him, desperate for more. *Stop protecting yourself.*

Tears burned in Alice's eyes at his words. *I have to protect myself.*

Why? He broke the kiss and moved back up to frame her face with his hands. His eyes were no longer the glittering stones of a warrior, or the tormented pits of the cursed. They were a deep rich brown of such beauty and warmth she felt her soul cry for him. *Why do you need to protect yourself?*

She laid her hands on his cheeks, feeling the roughness of his whiskers. *Because my mother was murdered, and it was supposed to be me.* The words were out before they could be stopped, and she held her breath, waiting for the repercussions, for the punishment, for the payback.

But it was only Ian, still watching her, still holding her. *Tell me what happened, love.*

And with that kindness, the story she'd held inside for so long came tumbling out in a desperate rush to cleanse her spirit before the barriers could rise again and lock her away from him. "I was six years old and I was living in an angel enclave with my mom and hundreds of other angels. That's where I was trained in all the rules and protocols of being an angel of life. The leaders were extremely strict, and they pretty much terrified all the little girls into never breaking the rules."

Ian narrowed his eyes. "I thought angels were supposed to be loving and nurturing."

She laughed softly, but it was with years of suppressed pain. "It was for our own good. Mistakes are too costly if you're an angel."

He grunted, but she could see the disapproval in his eyes. "Kids should be uplifted into their powers, not cowed into fear of them. That's how great warriors are made. With arrogance, bravery, and attitude, not fear. Fear is the enemy."

Alice shook her head. "Fear is sometimes the only thing we can hear when our heart is trying to get us to make a bad choice."

Ian leaned closer. "Sweetheart, your heart and your instincts are always right. Fear is the thing that sends you in the wrong direction. Fuck fear."

Alice stared at him, her heart starting to race at his intensity. A life without fear? Really? The thought was terrifying, but at the same time, it sounded exhilarating. And dangerous. "Do you want to hear the story or not?" She had to stop thinking such dangerous thoughts. Fear was what kept her safe and breathing air instead of seawater.

He gestured with his hand to keep going. "Yeah, continue. Sorry."

She nodded. "Catherine was there, and she was a little older than I was. We met when I was four and became best friends."

Ian's eyebrows shot up, but he didn't interrupt.

"One day Catherine and I went out to play in a nearby stream. While we were gone, the camp was attacked by demon specters, which are like the shadows of the demons that come for me when I die. We heard the screams and hid, just like my mom had always told us to do. We were in that cave for days. It was four nights before the screams stopped." It had been so cold in that cave. So damp. So terrifying. She remembered curling herself into a tiny ball behind a rock, the two of them trying to make themselves so small that no one would be able to see them from the entrance. "We waited two more days after the screaming stopped. We were so weak from hunger, we had to crawl out."

Ian began to stroke her hair, and she closed her eyes, focusing on his comforting touch.

"We could smell the blood from a mile away, but we didn't know what the scent was. Just this awful, acrid smell that burned our noses." She tried to rub the grit off her hands, remembering what it had felt like to crawl that mile back to camp. "Our hands and knees were bloody by the time we got there. When we got to the hill above the camp, we saw angels strewn everywhere, their bodies caked in blood. Around each one was a circle burned into the ground, and inside the circle was a pentagram."

"The devil's symbol? In an angel enclave?"

"It's not just the devil's symbol," she said. "It's the symbol of eternal life. If they harvest life from an angel of life, then demons can harness that magic and use it to try to break the barriers between our world and theirs. They can use it to give themselves real life." She looked at Ian. "They tortured every single angel looking for me, and not one of them told them where I was. When we got back, the only one still alive was my mother." She swallowed, remembering that frantic run across the scored earth when she saw her mother's body. "My mother was an earth angel, and they'd put her on a slab of cement to keep her off the ground. When I reached her..." Alice stopped, trying to steel herself against the agony of that moment. "She told me to get some earth and pack it in the wound above her heart. That was all she needed to live."

She couldn't say anymore. She couldn't relive it again.

"You couldn't do it?" Ian brushed his finger over her cheek, and she realized he was touching tears she hadn't noticed.

"No. All I could do was watch her die. I just sat there next to her, crying hysterically while her soul moved on. When she realized that I couldn't help her... God, the disappointment in her eyes was horrible. She turned her head away from me and died without looking at me again. Catherine couldn't save her because she's...well...she just couldn't do it either. But I am the one who is supposed to be able to do it, and I'm the one they were looking for. It was my fault she was attacked, and my fault she died."

"Shit, Alice." Ian kissed her lightly. "It's not your fault."

"It is," she said. "I'm an angel of life, and I couldn't save my own mother. What kind of angel am I?" She looked at him. "Do you know I've never been able to save anything in my life? Not even a bug. If they are dying around me, I can't help them. Not even if it's as simple as handing someone an EpiPen for an allergic reaction. I can't do anything." She pressed her hand to her forehead, trying not to let the memories overwhelm her. She didn't know how she was telling him, why this time, for the first time in her life, she could talk about these things, but it felt desperately good to be able to share it. To admit her failures to a man who she knew wouldn't judge her.

And he didn't. He simply kissed her nose and rested his forehead against hers, in an intimate, private gesture between two people who have no secrets from each other.

For a long moment, neither of them said anything. Ian gently rubbed her shoulders, his heavy weight comforting on top of her. "How does this relate to the fact you can't connect with me?"

Her arm began to itch, and she absently rubbed it. "As an angel of life, I'm bound by rules that don't apply to other angels. Our gift of being able to restore life is too powerful and too dangerous. If we get emotionally invested in someone, it can obscure our judgment and make us choose to interfere when we shouldn't. We can't save lives just because it suits us. We have to be driven by the greater good, by forces bigger than us."

He lifted his head. "The greater good?"

She smiled faintly. "I guess that sounds like your mission, doesn't it?" The itch on her arm became more intense, and she scratched it restlessly. "If you love someone, you will do anything to save them, so we can't love. We can't connect. We can't share secrets. No bonding. It's against the rules, but in addition, we literally can't do it."

Ian studied her. "But you just did it. You shared with me."

She nodded and took a deep breath. "I know. I've never been able to do that before." She managed a shy smile. "It felt good."

He grinned. "Aye, it did. Must be because my allure is so compelling that you can't hold yourself back from me anymore."

She smiled at his silliness. "Yes, that must be it. Your animal magnetism."

He shrugged. "I'm a raging inferno of manliness. Things like this happen from time to time."

"Well, it feels good. Really good. But why am I even

constrained by these stupid rules?" Her arm was burning now, and she dug her fingernails into it, trying to get relief. "I can't save anyone anyway, so what would it matter if I fell in love with the world? I couldn't save them even if I wanted to— Argh!" She shook out her arm. "I think I got a bug bite or something—"

Ian's eyes narrowed. "Your arm hurts?"

"Yes—"

He grabbed her wrist and placed his hand on her skin. A look of raw possession filled his face. "It's hot. Feel it?" He splayed her palm over her forearm, and she felt the intense heat emanating from her skin.

"What is it?" She propped herself up on her elbows, looking at it. "There's no mark—"

"Not on the surface, no." But there was an edge of excitement to Ian's voice. "But it's beneath the surface, trying to form." He raised her arm to his mouth and pressed his lips against the burning flesh. It didn't cool it. It just made it hotter and more uncomfortable. "One of the stages of the bond is trust," he said. "It has two parts—you trusting me, and me trusting you. When you told me the story of your past and your inability to save your mother, you shared your darkest secret with me. It satisfied your half of the trust stage. We've done two and a half stages so far. Halfway there."

She caught her breath. "Telling a secret satisfies the trust stage?"

"Yes. It can be that, or giving the other one the power to kill you and trusting them not to actually do it." He grinned. "We're bonding, Alice. The mark is there, beneath your skin, and it's trying to get out."

Alice rubbed the mark. "That would be a bad thing, Ian."

"Why?" He was suddenly looming over her, frustration etched on his face. "Tell me why it's so damn wrong for us to bond."

"You mean, other than the deadly *sheva* destiny?"

Because even assuming that all the angel stuff could be worked out, that was still a major problem.

"Yeah. Why else? Because I'm not buying that you're thinking about that right now."

She met his gaze. "Because angels who break the rules are stripped of their powers and thrust into exile. If I go far enough astray, I will become the Mageaan." She held up her hand, showing him the tiny gray mark on her palm that she'd noticed. "I've already started to fall."

† † †

I've already started to fall.

Alice's words reverberated in Ian's mind as he sat on the edge of the cot the next morning. Alice was still sleeping, but he had his weapons out. He was ready for Jada to come for them.

After Alice's revelation that his need to connect with her might drive her into the hell beneath the ocean, he'd shut it down for the night between them. There was no way he could take responsibility for turning her into a Mageaan. He'd just have to man-up and allow her to keep her angel secrets.

But shit, her story about her childhood still bothered him. There was no doubt Alice had learned her lessons well. The fear of making a wrong step dogged her constantly, and he didn't like that. Fear was hell. What angels taught fear? After his bout with the Mageaan and hearing the story of training she'd gotten as a kid, Ian was beginning to suspect that angels were like any other beings: some of them were good, quality people, and some of them were bad seeds whose influence was like the rot of poison infecting the world.

He thought of Ryland's obsession with angels, and wondered what he would think of the truth that not all angels were perfect.

Ian twirled his mace restlessly, wanting Jada to show up and get this thing going. Sitting on a bed beside Alice wasn't

155

good for either of them, which is why he'd dragged himself out of the bed when he'd made the inconceivable decision not to make love to her.

Once he'd removed himself from temptation, Alice had slept hard, but restlessly, calling out repeatedly for someone to save her mother, her cries desperate and agonized, until he felt his own heart ache for her pain. He'd hit the floor and gone into his healing sleep long enough to chase away the worst of the damage. Afterward, he'd spent the rest of the night alternating between comforting her in her sleep and preparing for the morning.

He also hadn't missed her comment about how she had met Catherine when they were at the encampment. She'd said they'd become good friends, which was different than how she would have described a sister. Alice had been so caught in the story that she hadn't noticed her slip, but he had. Catherine was not her sister, despite Alice's claims. It made him rethink all that had happened between them. What exactly was her deal?

The day he'd first met Alice, when she'd fallen off the cliff and Elijah had struck her down, she'd been carrying a wallet with Catherine Taylor's driver's license in it. The picture had been tattered, making it difficult to get a clear read on the visual, so he'd assumed the license he'd found belonged to the woman who'd been carrying it: Catherine Taylor.

Yet last time he'd met her, before she died, she'd told him that Catherine was her sister, and *her* name was Alice Shaw.

Last night, she'd revealed that Catherine was not her sister, but a friend who had witnessed carnage with her.

Too many tangled threads intersecting. Too many secrets she was trying to keep track of.

Ian studied the woman sleeping beside him. After the unsettled night, her face was finally relaxed in sleep, and there were no lines of stress or tension. Her auburn hair was spread over the pillow like an autumn halo around her head. Her lips were soft pink perfection, the skin on her throat delicate and tempting. In this moment, she looked every bit an angel. Was it really possible that she could end up as a Mageaan?

After a moment, Ian sheathed one of his maces into his arm, and he spread his palm over her heart, pushing aside the tank top so he could feel her skin beneath his. Her heart beat in a steady rhythm, and he closed his eyes, opening his mind to her. Asleep, her defenses were lowered, and he was able to easily slip past her barriers into her mind. It was a cascade of brilliant, vibrant colors. High-pitched, warm energy flowed through him, the spirit of a warrior with a pure soul.

He saw no poison, no taint. Just a woman filled with fear, passion, guilt, and intense determination. There was nothing to explain why she couldn't fulfill her duty as an angel of life. No sign of the walls that she claimed bound her against her will. There was nothing foreign inside her. Simply her spirit, along with the deep-seated protections that were hers alone. Deep, deep fear that was almost paralyzing in its intensity. But her spirit wasn't the unfettered simplicity of an angel. There was so much more to her: a complexity and depth that he suspected an angel wasn't supposed to have. *What are you really, Alice? What secrets are you hiding, even from yourself?*

Her luminous green eyes fastened onto his. "Are you invading my privacy?"

"Yep." He didn't remove his hand from her chest, tracking the rhythm of her heart as it began to speed up. From his nearness? He suspected it was, and he was glad to know she wasn't immune to him.

She frowned at his admission, and he expected her to get angry. But to his surprise, she smiled. "It feels nice to have you in my mind."

He grinned and leaned forward to kiss her. She kissed him back, and desire flared hot and powerful almost instantly. With a curse, he broke the kiss and stood up, pacing to the other side of the room. "I can't believe I didn't finish ravishing you last night."

"I know." She sat up, swinging her legs over the edge of the bed. Her shorts had ridden up, revealing a long expanse of leg that made his groin tighten. "I thought we were going to."

"Yeah." He watched her as she stretched, her tank top riding up to reveal the same flat belly he'd been kissing last night. Shit. He needed to get his mind off sex and fast, or they'd be caught *in flagrante delicto* when Jada showed up to announce their fate. "Catherine Taylor isn't really your sister, is she?"

Alice sucked in her breath, her face turning white. "What?"

His heart softened at the look of shock on her face. His woman was as open and real as it was possible to be. She might be lying, but she was becoming utterly transparent to him. "Tell me, Alice," he said, keeping his voice conversational. "Do you really want to rescue her, or are you going after her for another reason?" He was willing to make himself respect her angel rules if that meant helping her avoid a life as a Mageaan, but in terms of the mission they were on, he needed full disclosure.

Alice's face grew even paler. "Of course I want to rescue her. Warwick kidnapped both of us, and I was the one who got away. I couldn't save my mother or anyone else, so I can't let her die, too. I have to save one person in this world. And since I just want to free her and not actually save her life, it should work, right?"

"No. Not right." He walked over to her. She stiffened, and he saw the wariness in her eyes as she pulled her shoulders back. For a moment, neither of them spoke, and Ian reached out with his mind, gently probing hers. She immediately slammed up her mental barriers, but not before he sensed the cold chill of deception. Ah, the conveniences of the *sheva* bond. It might not work as well as it should, but it was good enough for him to find out what he needed from her. "I don't believe you," he said. "I think you want to make sure she never leaves that island alive."

She stared at him, aghast. "What are you talking about?"

It was a guess, only a guess, but he threw it out there anyway, just to test her reaction, to push her to the edge so he could force some truth out of her. He'd been a warrior long enough to know the importance of having full and accurate information when going into battle. "I think, sweetheart, that you want me to kill Catherine Taylor when we find her. Not save her. Kill her."

Ian was a little shocked by the revealing look of horror on her face, confirming that his wild stab in the dark designed to goad her into revealing more, was actually dead right.

His sweet little angel of life was actually a bloodthirsty murderer? No. That was impossible. It had to be something else, something he hadn't figured out, something he didn't know. "Why? Tell me why, Alice. Tell me what's really going on."

But before he could take it further, the room filled with a turquoise glow.

Jada had arrived.

† † †

Alice whirled around at the intrusion, her mind still whirring from Ian's question. Why had he asked that? How had he known? What would he do? What—

"Oh, shit." Ian lowered his mace. "Jada isn't even going to have the decency of a polite conversation before making her decision? It's just rude to try to drown someone without even discussing it first."

"Drown us?" Alice's feet felt cold, and she looked down. The floor of the room was being flooded with ocean water. It was already up to her ankles, and filling fast. She immediately started backing up, then caught herself. Like retreating would do any good. "I'm thinking that in about two seconds, we're going to discover we can't breathe underwater anymore."

"I agree." Ian sloshed across the room through water that was already up to his thighs. The room was filling so fast that there was foam churning across the surface of the water. "I can breathe for you. We'll do it like last time."

Alice hurried over to him, not even hesitating. "How long can you breathe under water?" The seawater was already up to her ribs, and she started to shiver. "It's really cold."

"I know." Ian wrapped his arms around her, infusing her with his warmth. "I can sustain us for a while, but no, I'm not a fish. I can't do it forever."

"So, then, maybe this isn't going to really solve our problem, is it?" Even as she protested, she wrapped her arms around his neck, tucking herself against him. As before, the raw strength of his body seemed to infuse her with power. It felt amazing, and eased some of her fear. It was getting less scary to turn herself over to him, but at the same time, the fact she was getting used to it wasn't a good sign. How far off her assigned path was he leading her? And at what point would the payment be a fast trip to become Jada's underling? Unless, of course, she finally died for good before then, which was looking increasingly likely.

"Yeah, good point. Much as I love the fact that breathing for you means I get to suck face with you indefinitely, I'm thinking we need a more long-term solution. Tread water," Ian said. "Breathe for yourself as long as you can." His eyes were darting around the room. "I need to figure out where the water is coming from. There has to be an opening somewhere, a portal that she opened to let the ocean filter in."

Alice twisted in his arms, and looked down into the water. "It has to be coming from the floor," She said. "I didn't hear it dripping down from the walls, and the walls and ceiling are dry above the water line."

"Then let's check the floor." He released her and readied himself to dive. "We can't stay here forever. We need to get out."

Alice took a deep breath, then nodded, trying to quell the panic. "Okay."

"Search for any kind of opening," Ian instructed. "It'll be a weak point, and maybe I can break through the rest of the way. Go!" He dove, disappearing under the water instantly.

After taking one last look at the ceiling, which was now far too close, Alice sucked in her breath and followed him. The aqua glow still filled the room, casting everything into a strange tint not unlike the color the moon had been when she'd tried to break into the Mageaan stronghold earlier.

She kicked down to the floor and began running her fingers over the surface. It was smooth and hard, like an oyster shell. She couldn't find even a tiny hole. She could hold her breath longer than an average human, but eventually her lungs began to burn, and she looked over at Ian. He was moving quickly along the seam between the floor and the walls, running his palms over the seam, apparently not yet affected by the lack of air.

Alice quickly swam upward, reaching the top of the water just as her lungs felt like they were going to burst. She sucked in air, watching the ceiling get closer and closer, even in the brief moments she was at the surface. It was only two feet away now. Two feet left of air, and they were hundreds of feet below the surface of the ocean. A cold chill began to gnaw at her bones, and she shivered, her lungs getting heavier and heavier as panic tried to set in.

You okay? Ian's voice was in her mind, a warm breath of reassurance. She wasn't alone.

Yeah. For a few more minutes. She knew she couldn't waste time. They had to find a way out, something they had to have missed last night when they'd been looking, something that Jada had opened. She prayed urgency would give them answers they hadn't found before. With mounting trepidation, she took another breath from the shrinking airspace and forced herself to dive again. She went for the far corner opposite Ian, and frantically began probing the floor.

She could feel the current of water, but she couldn't find where it was coming from. *Come on!* Frantic now, her lungs burning, she kept searching, but she couldn't find the opening the water was flowing through.

A loud clank echoed through the water, and she spun around to see Ian raise his mace over his head, as if he'd just punched the floor with it. *Did you find something?*

Not sure. There's a stronger current here. I'm checking. He slammed his weapon into the floor again, his muscles straining with the force of his blow. A chunk of floor exploded into the room, and Ian let out a roar of triumph. He swung back and hit it again, and another piece flew out.

Hurry! Her lungs began to hurt. Alice quickly kicked herself back toward the surface. She popped out of the water, and yelped when her forehead smashed into the ceiling. The rebound dumped her back under the water, and she accidentally sucked in water instead of air. She shoved her head back out of the water just as a violent cough caught her, and her nose bumped the ceiling as the spasms wracked her body. Less than an inch of air left.

Her throat ached. Her lungs were spasming as they tried to expel the water she'd sucked in. Frantic, she fumbled for purchase on the smooth ceiling, desperate to hold onto something as coughs wracked her body. Her chin dipped below the surface just as she coughed, and she sucked more water into her lungs. *Ian!*

Coming!

Alice coughed again, her lungs contracting as they tried to expel the water. She couldn't stop coughing, and the space for air got smaller. Frantic, she pressed her face against the ceiling, smashing her nose and chin against the hard shell as the coughs wracked her body. She couldn't stop coughing long enough to hold her breath, and she knew if she went under again, she'd be in real trouble. *Ian!*

Shit!

Shit? What did 'shit' mean? This wasn't the right time for him to run into trouble! The water was over the edges of her mouth now. "Ian!" she screamed, smashing her face against the ceiling as another cough assailed her. "Where are you?"

Trapped.

Oh, *no.*

CHAPTER TEN

The floor had come alive, and it had trapped him.

Ian slammed his mace down on the vine that had snaked around his ankle, fighting desperately against the slimy green tentacle that was winding its way up his calf. Who the hell has seaweed growing out of the floor? Seriously.

Above him, he could hear Alice coughing, and her terror was like cold ripples in the water. *Shit!* He slammed his mace down again, and the tip of a second seaweed appendage poked out of the hole he'd made in the floor. He swung at it, but it grabbed his mace and yanked it out of his hand.

He swore and called his weapon back as a third vine shot out and gripped his other leg. So, yeah, the good news was that he'd figured out how to break out of the room. The bad news was the appearance of killer kelp that could manhandle Calydon weapons.

"Ian!" Alice screamed. "Help!"

"I'm coming!" Desperate terror tore through him. Ian spun around, lunging for Alice. Her feet were kicking frantically only a few yards from him, but he couldn't reach her. He stretched as far as he could, but she was just beyond his range. "Swim down here!"

"I can't—" Another violent cough wracked her body, and he knew she'd drown before he could get to her if she went under.

Swearing, he threw his mace in her direction. It slammed into the ceiling next to her jaw. "Grab it!" he yelled.

She lunged for it, and he called his mace back with all the strength he could summon. It tore out of the ceiling and streaked back to him so quickly it left a trail of bubbles. Alice's fingers were locked around it, her eyes wide with terror as it yanked her toward him. *Alice.* Just as he reached for her, a vine shot out and yanked the weapon out of her hands, and her momentum stopped.

Swim the rest of the way, Ian ordered, stretching as far as he could to reach her. Not enough! He needed another six inches!

Then her eyes widened, and he saw her muscles contract. Another cough was coming, and she was completely underwater. *No!* If he could reach her, he could breathe for her through their kiss, but he was helpless if he couldn't reach her. *Come on!* He strained for her just as another cough wracked her body. She sucked in the ocean water, and he screamed with rage as her pain flooded him. He could feel the weight of the water filling her lungs, and he bellowed with fury and frustration at his impotence. *Alice!*

"You have two choices, warrior." Behind Alice, Jada appeared in a flash of turquoise light. She was a misty blue-green, and her face was pinched and drawn.

Ian swore, rage filling him at the sight of her standing there so smugly while Alice was drowning. "Let me save her," he shouted as he called back his mace from the vines. "She killed Esmeralda in self-defense, and you know it!" He hurled the mace toward Alice. *Grab it!*

But as the mace went past her, Alice's arms went limp, and she began to drift. Horror filled him. *Jesus, no.* He went into a panicked overdrive, fighting his seaweed shackles as he tried to reach her. He could save her if he got to her within a few seconds, if he could breathe for her before her brain died, if he could clear the water from her lungs fast enough. *Alice!*

"Go find Warwick, and retrieve from him a spell to save Chloe's life," Jada said calmly, as if Alice wasn't dying right in front of her. "You will return here within three days. If you do not save her, you will be killed. Do you agree to these terms for both you and Alice?"

"Yes, fuck, yes!" He shouted his agreement, even as the curse began to shout in his head, taunting him, screaming at him that Alice was dying. Despair surged over him, and his body bowed under the agony, as his will was shredded.

"So be it." There was a flash of turquoise light, and the vines released him. Ian lunged toward Alice, catching her in his arms. His head was spinning, the curse piercing and shrill, but the moment he held her, he willed his focus onto her, sending all his life force into Alice as he hauled her against him and kissed her, sharing his oxygen and life with his *sheva*.

She didn't respond, and he swore, kissing her more deeply, more frantically as the curse grew in power, screaming at him that he was wasting his time. That she was already dead. That his life was worth nothing. *No! Leave me the fuck alone! She's not dead!*

There was a flash of light, and then he was suddenly on his knees on the floor. The water had been drained from the room as quickly as it had come. He threw Alice onto the bed, her skin ash-white, her lips blue, her eyelids closed. "Come on, Alice! This is not the fucking time to shut me out!"

He had to tighten their connection, and there was only one way to do it, one way for him to get close enough to pull her back from the brink of death. The blood bond between a Calydon and his mate. Frantic, he grabbed his mace and raked it over the tips of his fingers, not even noticing the pain as he sliced his skin.

His mind blurring from the impact of the curse, he blindly grabbed Alice's arm, willing himself to go on despite the noise in his head. Only six hundred years of training gave him the discipline to keep going with what he had to do, even though he could barely think, was barely aware of what he was doing because the curse was screaming at him so relentlessly to kill himself.

Ian jerked the blade across her wrist, his agony doubling when she didn't even flinch at the pain. Was she dead already? "No!" He howled his protest as he pulled her into his arms, thrusting his fingers past her lips, giving her his lifeblood. "Swallow, babe, as God is my witness, swallow for me."

She didn't move, and he swore as his body began to tremble violently, as the shakes began to set in. *Come on, Alice! He stroked her hair, and showered kisses over her forehead while he whispered to her. Just swallow, sweetheart. One time. Let me save you. You're not done here. Catherine needs you to kill or save her or whatever you need to do for her—*

Her throat moved, and she swallowed.

Elation exploded through him, and Ian pressed her bleeding wrist to his lips, kissing the wound and finishing the circle that would connect them forever, by taking her lifeblood into his body. The moment he swallowed, his whole body felt like it was on fire. His mind seemed to explode with pressure, and a searing liquid burned through his veins. Words sprang up in his mind, words that carried two thousand years of power for a Calydon and his mate. He welcomed the words, opening his entire soul to them, letting them fill him as he offered them to Alice. *Mine to you. Yours to me. Bonded by blood, by spirit and by soul, we are one. No distance too far, no enemy too powerful, no sacrifice too great. I will always find you. I will always protect you. No matter what the cost. I am yours as you are mine.*

Beneath him, Alice's body arched, and then her voice, her beautiful angelic voice filled his mind as she gave him the same promise. *Mine to you. Yours to me. Bonded by blood, by spirit and by soul, we are one. No distance too far, no enemy too powerful, no sacrifice too great. I will always find you. I will always keep you safe. No matter what the cost. I am yours as you are mine.*

As the blood bond was completed, sealing another stage of the *sheva* bond, Ian was suddenly flooded with Alice's emotions. Guilt, self-hate, pain, fear. Everything an angel should never feel, but it was hers, all hers, and she was open to him. Ian immersed his spirit into that opening, wrapping his energy around her heart, infusing her with his strength. He gave her his life, his immortality, plunging it into her soul and calling her back from the edge of death.

His need for her was incredible, and beautiful, and he felt her respond, her soul reaching for his in that connection he'd been seeking so desperately for so long. *Yes.* He'd done it. He'd reached her in time.

Triumph swept through him as he cradled her in his arms and kissed her, deepening the connection between them until they were one, until her spirit and emotions were so immersed in his that there was no dividing line, no separation.

Her arms suddenly tightened around his neck, and then her lips moved. Tentatively at first, then stronger, kissing him back with a fierceness that mimicked everything he was feeling. *Ian.*

Alice. He was frantic to kiss her, to touch her, to fill her with all that he was. He needed more. He needed everything. The curse still had its claws buried in him, trying to tear him away from his sanity, even with his woman alive and well in his arms.

The same desperate energy seemed to infect Alice, as her kisses were more evocative and demanding than they'd ever been. Her skin was still cold, but he could feel the heat beginning to build beneath her skin, heat he'd given her, that had become a part of who she was.

Desperate now, he slid his hand beneath her shirt, her stomach trembling from his touch. Her skin was like the softest silk, like the very heavens themselves had spun it when they'd given her life. Rightness filled him, rightness and a need to consummate their blood bond. He was burning to look at her arm to see if she carried the mark from their bonding, but he didn't dare. He was too close to the edge, and knew that if he saw only blank skin, it would be more than he could handle.

Alice grabbed his shirt and tried to pull it up. Ian sat up, ripping his shirt over his head. As he did so, he suddenly remembered where they were. In the room they'd almost drowned in...with an audience?

He jerked his gaze off Alice and searched their surroundings, but Jada was gone. The walls and floor were still dripping with evidence from their near death, but the Mageaan had left. He didn't know where she'd gone, or when she'd be back, but he didn't care.

All he knew was that right now, he was alone with his woman, and he needed her more than he'd ever needed anything in his entire life.

He was going to take her now, and nothing was going to stop him.

† † †

Alice could feel every one of Ian's emotions. His hopelessness and emotional agony were almost overwhelming, but at the same time, there was so much strength and courage. A man who would never give up. Never allow failure. The Order was strong in his heart, the driving force for who he was. It was so powerful, so beautiful: his commitment to the Order, and the purity of his belief in who he was and what he did. She'd never felt such intensity of emotion or such a revelation of the spirit, and it was incredible.

His emotions, his very soul seemed to swell inside her, touching her heart. Tears fell for his torment. Her heart danced for his triumphs. She felt everything he did, and her own emotions reflected his. It seemed like her spirit was flying with freedom to experience all the range of feelings. Not just his, but her own. Her need for him. The way she craved his body, his touch. The intensity of her desire to hear his whispers in her mind, caressing her with his voice. She wanted his kiss. His body. His skin against hers.

God, Alice. Your soul is so open to me. You're beautiful. He pulled back long enough to pull her shirt over her head, his eyes glittering with sensual heat that reached inside her and seemed to unlock the passions that had been chained up for so long.

She braced her palms on his chest, marveling at the hardness of his muscles, at the sheer power coiled beneath his skin. "How can it be like this?"

"This, my darling, is the way it's supposed to be between us." He grasped her shorts and tugged them off her hips, trailing fiery kisses down her body. His jeans and boots hit the floor and then he sank between her legs.

Skin to skin. Bodies entwined. It was a wondrous sensation that seemed to sizzle through her body, from her nipples, to her belly, to the very core of her.

"No stopping this time," Ian said, as he kneed her legs apart, sinking his hips between her legs. "Nothing will come between us."

Alice gasped at the feel of his erection pressing against her, and she shifted restlessly, wanting more, needing more. Her body felt like it was on fire, and she could feel his desire rushing through her, filling her, chipping away at her hesitations and defenses, until there was nothing left but the heat building between them.

Ian cupped her face between his hands for a deep, intimate kiss, as his hips began to move, teasing her, brushing the tip of his member across her most sensitive parts. Tremors rippled through her, down her legs, up her spine. Her muscles began to tremble. Ian's entire presence seemed to fill her. His masculine scent of woods and pine wrapped around her. The heat from his body seemed to penetrate the last residual coldness from the ocean. His spirit was so strong and protective as it enveloped her. She felt safe, as if there were room to let go and embrace everything she was feeling. *I don't want to hold back.*

Then don't. He kissed her again, deeper, harder, claiming her. His hands roamed her hips, her breasts, her spine, stoking flames within her until her entire body was on fire, until her need for him seemed to rise from her skin like steam vapors in a hot spring, scorching the air.

God, yes. His kiss grew more frantic, as if he were getting sucked into the same vortex spinning her so ruthlessly. Hunger roared through her, the urge to feel him inside her. She writhed under him, unable to control her body's response or the sparks that were igniting within. *Ian. Make love to me. I need you.* She gripped his shoulders, digging her fingernails in as if he could keep her from shattering into a million pieces of passion and desire.

At her demand, Ian palmed her hips and dragged her toward him. Anticipation rolled through her as his powerful thighs took over her space, shoving her legs wider to make room for him. She arched her back as he nudged at her core, her soul screaming for more, for their connection, for him to unify them into a single entity that could never be torn apart.

Never leave me. Ian's voice was raw demand, but before she could answer, he thrust.

His name tore from her lips as he filled her, their bodies adjusting instantly to each other. He plunged all the way, and then held still, his hips so tight against hers it felt as if they would never be separated again.

"Alice. Look at me." His voice was raw and rough, laced with an edge that made chills run down her spine.

She opened her eyes, and was captivated by the dark possession in his eyes. "Ian," she whispered, laying her palm against his cheek.

"Say you're mine," he commanded. He withdrew slightly,

and her body jerked in reaction. "Tell me you belong to me. That it doesn't matter whether my mark is on your arm or not." There was a desperate edge to his voice, a need that tore at her heart and made her soul ache for him. "Tell me that you're my soul mate, and nothing will ever change that."

Tears filled her eyes, and the most intense yearning filled her. A craving to be irreversibly connected to this man. "I want to," she whispered. "But I'm terrified of the implications. I'm scared of what would happen to me if I offer my loyalty to anyone or anything, except for what I'm supposed to be focused on."

He thrust again, and they both gasped at the sensation of him moving within her. "What do you want, Alice? Tell me."

She closed her eyes, arching as heat cascaded through her. Each thrust and withdrawal stoked her need for him. "I want to be someone else, something other than what I am," she confessed. "I want to be the woman who can lose herself in you and not be afraid." She opened her eyes. "I don't want to be an angel," she said. "I want to just be me, whoever that is. I don't want to be afraid of who I want to be."

Ian swore softly, and she felt him brush an achingly tender kiss across her mouth. *You have a beautiful soul, Alice. I wouldn't have you any other way than how you are right now. Be who you are in your heart. It's enough for me.*

Her chest seemed to expand at his beautiful words, spoken even after he'd figured out that she was on a mission to kill the woman who was as close to a sister as anyone had ever been. Somehow, he saw beauty in her. She didn't understand it, but it was such a gift.

He drove deep again, and his voice grew more gritty and strained. *But as God is my witness, give a guy a break and just tell me that there will never be another man for you. It's just me, in whatever way you can give it. Only me. No one else. I'm your guy.*

She laughed and gripped his shoulders as he rode her

harder. That was something she could promise, with absolute certainty. *Ian, there has never been another man for me, and there never will. Who knows what form this thing between us will take, but regardless, it's only you.*

His relief filled her like a great burst of sunlight, and her own soul seemed to rejoice in response. Then he thrust one more time, and an orgasm exploded through her. He shouted her name as he drove into her, and they clung to each other, holding onto whatever it was they had between them while the orgasm gave them a glimpse of what they could be together...if she wasn't who she was.

† † †

Ian felt Alice's emotional withdrawal almost immediately. Before she could retreat physically, he braced himself on his elbows and pinned her to the bed, letting his weight press her into the mattress. "Oh, no you don't, sweetheart. Making love matters, and I'm not letting you pretend it doesn't. Not again."

Her green eyes were haunted, making his heart soften. "It matters," she admitted. "I know it does."

Relief rushed through him. They were making progress, then. The angel was not made of cold steel after all. "Good." He traced his thumb over her lower lip, then feathered a kiss over it. "Then stop shutting me out."

She pressed her palms to her eyes, as if she were fighting back tears. "Don't you understand, Ian? What you give me is an incredible gift. It's so beautiful the way I can feel your emotions, and the way you make me feel things, too. That's so rare for me. It's so much more than I ever knew it could be."

Ian almost smiled at her words. "I've got more than that to show you, sweetheart. Just give me a few minutes to recover and I'll be ready to go."

She pulled her hands down and glared at him. "How can you make a sex joke? I was talking about more than sex—"

"I know." He grinned and kissed the tip of her nose,

thoroughly enjoying her discomfiture and irritation. Her tension was good, because it showed him she wasn't as unaffected by him as she wanted to be. The connection and attraction wasn't one-sided, and that felt damn good.

"So, why are you being intentionally obtuse about it? I'm trying to talk about things that matter, and you're making it about sex." She frowned at him. "This is a big deal to me."

"And to me," he agreed, feeling inordinately pleased by the entire conversation. For the first time ever, Alice was admitting that the connection developing between them was real. "My life, yours, the future of the Order. It matters."

She blinked. "Then why are you teasing me?"

"I just made love to the most incredible woman I've ever met, and her crankiness tells me that she's not as immune to me as she pretends." He gave her a wicked grin, delighted to see the flush of awareness flood her cheeks. "I'm a guy. Amazing sex is enough to put me in a good mood, and the fact that it was with my *sheva* who is starting to fall madly in love with me... well... it's a good day."

"What?" Her eyes widened in outrage, and she smacked his chest. "I'm not falling in love with you."

"I know, I know. It's impossible for you to do, and all that stuff." He shrugged. "So is telling me your angel secrets, but we're getting around that. Makes me realize that if I'm a stubborn enough bastard, I might get what I want."

Her eyes widened. "And what exactly is that?"

You. Ian's amusement faded at the word that had burst into his mind. Her? What kind of answer was that? The answer was supposed to be that he wanted to break the curse, restore his family's honor, and reclaim his place on the Order of the Blade team. The answer was not supposed to be some mooning adulation of one particular almost-fallen angel.

Alice was simply the key to getting what he truly wanted. His interest in Alice couldn't be more than that. If he started having true feelings for her, the curse would destroy him before he got close to Cardiff. And if the curse didn't, then the *sheva* destiny would. With the way he'd reacted to losing her when they weren't even bonded, he knew damn well that if he lost her after they were bonded, he wouldn't be one of those rare exceptions who didn't go rogue and destroy everything that mattered. He'd lose his marbles and bring everything around them down into ruin. And then some.

So, then, what was he doing getting up close and intimate with her? Talking about love and getting all starry-eyed? He had to tread that fine line of keeping her close enough to keep the curse at bay, but not so close that it gave the curse too much power.

He needed some man-space. And now.

Swearing, he rolled off her and grabbed his jeans off the floor. "Jada will be back soon. We need to get dressed." He picked up her tank top and handed it to her. "Here."

Alice sat up, embarrassment flooding her at Ian's sudden coolness after she'd tried to get personal. For a split second, when she'd asked him what he really wanted, she'd *thought* she'd heard him whisper "*you*" in her mind, but his rapid withdrawal made it clear that she'd heard wrong.

Which was good. She couldn't get involved with him emotionally, and it was already pretty clear that she had minimal defenses against him. She quickly tugged her tank top on, pulling the built-in bra over her breasts that were still tender from his kisses. Her breasts were sore from being nibbled on by an immortal warrior? Really? That was so not her.

But there was no way to pretend she'd fabricated *that* lovemaking session. She could remember every delicious detail, and her skin still hummed from his kisses and his touch. Oh, yes, it was true. She, Alice Shaw, dedicated angel, had flagrantly thrown herself into a man's arms and loved every single minute of it.

Oy. She was becoming a wanton woman, and that was

just not good for an angel of life who wasn't allowed to have any connections with anyone else.

She scratched her forearm, and realized her skin was burning hot. Quickly, she looked down and saw that her flesh was bright red. There was no brand, but there was no doubt that her skin was fighting it, that his influence was growing stronger. What if the brand appeared? Would that mean she'd transferred her loyalty from her angel duties to Ian? That couldn't be a good thing. That brand had to stay away. He couldn't claim her. He just couldn't. Nervously, she pressed her palm to her arm, as if she could will it away—

Then she frowned as she noticed new markings on her skin. A tangle of blue and green vines was tattooed all the way around each wrist. Almost five inches wide, they looked like gladiator wrist cuffs. Her stomach dropped in fear as she recalled Jada's comment about what would happen if she became the leader of the Mageaan. "Ian! Look!"

He looked up sharply, and his eyes became hooded when he saw what she was pointing to. "Yeah," he said, holding up his arm. "I have them, too."

Alice realized he had the same thing around each wrist. "What is it?" If Ian had them too, it couldn't be that she'd been conscripted by the Mageaan into being their leader.

Ian looked at her grimly. "You didn't hear it?"

Her heart started to pound. "Hear what?"

"When you were drowning, I made a deal with Jada so I could save you."

She sat up straighter. "What kind of deal?"

Ian fetched his shirt from the floor and pulled it over his muscular shoulders. "She wants us to get Cardiff to use his magic to save Chloe's life. Our passport out of here expires in three days. At that point..." He held up his arms. "I'm guessing these will magically haul us back here regardless of whether or not we're finished. If Chloe's life is saved by then, we get to go free. If not..." He shrugged. "I agreed that we would die here."

Alice leapt to her feet. "What? What kind of deal is that? How are we supposed to save Chloe? Isn't she dead already?"

"Apparently not." Ian fished her shorts out from under the bed and tossed them at her, but there was no mistaking the heat in his eyes as his gaze sizzled over her body. She responded instantly with need and desire that seemed to come alive inside her with only the slightest provocation from him. "So, that's good," he said. "One less death on your shoulders."

Hope rippled through her at his words. Was it possible she could change fate and save someone, at least once? She pulled the shorts on, her spirits falling when she realized the impossibility of what Jada was asking. "Warwick can't bring people back to life." That was why he'd wanted Alice, but he'd been sorely disappointed to discover the angel of life he'd kidnapped hadn't been able to bring his beloved back to life after a couple millennia of being dead.

She'd become expendable, and he'd immediately traded her life for more black magic from the demons. She had to give Cardiff credit. He was a pretty flexible guy, and the moment he'd realized that his former love wasn't going to be waltzing across his ballroom with him again, he'd recycled Alice to a more lucrative use and decided to keep Catherine for more nefarious purposes.

"I know he can't bring people back to life. That's not something that can be done by magic." Ian shoved his feet into his boots, giving her a thoughtful look.

Alice buttoned her shorts, her thighs still feeling sensitive from his attentions. "So, what does Jada think we're going to do?" she asked, trying not to think of all they had just done. Her arms were brand-free, and that was what mattered.

"I think," he said, as he stood up, meeting her gaze, "she believes that you will find a way to do it with your angel of life powers."

Alice's heart dropped. "But I can't save anyone. You know that."

"She doesn't believe you." Ian walked over to her and caught her chin. "And you know what, sweetheart?"

Her heart began to race at his nearness, hammering frantically. "What?" she whispered, her very breath taken away by his touch.

"I don't believe you either."

CHAPTER ELEVEN

The look on Alice's face told Ian all he needed to know: she hadn't told him everything about her ability to save lives. Or her lack thereof. What the hell was she hiding from him? "I'm tired of the lies," he said. "What gives, Alice?"

She raised her chin, anger flashing in her eyes. "I didn't lie. I can't save lives—"

"No. It's not that you can't. It's that you won't." He took her hand and held it to his chest, placing it over his heart. He could feel the pulsing warmth of her hand. "I can feel the life force beating inside you. I felt it when we made love this time. You hid it before, but this time, I felt it. You're more than simply a bad angel, Alice. You're more than an angel of life. You *are* life. I know it, because the ability to squeeze life from a stone is the only way that I've fought off death a thousand times over the last six hundred years. I know life, and if I was dying, you would save me." It was a challenge, words he hadn't even thought over before he'd said them, but as he spoke, he knew they were true.

Alice could save the world if she wanted to. She had that much power.

And when she shook her head in denial, it was too much for him. Too fucking much. Why was she denying who she was? Why was she cutting off her own power? "You have

181

a gift," he snapped, tightening his grip on her hand. "And yet you sit there in fear, afraid to use it because you're so afraid of rules. Fuck rules. You're an angel. No one can strip that from you if you don't want to lose it."

"No one can strip it from me? Are you serious?" Alice gaped at him in apparent disbelief. "You didn't see the Mageaan? Are you refusing to understand just to irritate me? Because I don't know how you can deny what you've seen with your own eyes."

"You can never fully trust what you see with your own eyes," he retorted. "Any warrior knows that."

"I'm not a warrior!"

"Because you're too afraid to be one." He threw out the challenge, frustrated as hell by her continued adherence to the path of keeping him out, of refusing to acknowledge her power. The woman practically bled strength. When she'd climaxed, he'd felt a burst of white light so intense his heart still burned from being seared. Yeah, he'd felt her anguish at not being able to save Chloe, and he knew that had been real. She'd wanted to save the girl, but hadn't been able to. So what was really going on with her? Fear?

Ire flashed in her eyes. "I'm not afraid," she snapped, but he didn't believe it. Not one bit. "I'm trying to find out how to do what I was born to do. I'm trying to be the angel I'm supposed to be, and you're trying to get me to reveal secrets to you is not helping."

Adrenaline raced through him at her anger. She'd been so careful with her emotions, and to see such passion on her face ignited something in him. He grabbed her around the hips. "Come alive, Alice," he challenged as he hauled her against him. "Stop being afraid, and come *alive*." She opened her mouth to protest, but before she could speak, he slammed his mouth down over hers.

This time, it wasn't a tender, seductive kiss. It was raw, angry passion. It was dangerous lust. It was unbridled sex and untamed testosterone that needed to unleash themselves onto the world, and onto her. It was the raw, ugly emotions of humanity, exactly what Alice needed to accept about herself.

Alice gasped at his aggression, but he gave her no room. He shoved her against the wall, using his weight to pin her there as he grabbed her thighs and yanked them around his hips. He kept up his assault, his kisses too relentless for her to escape them.

He knew the moment he accomplished his goal. Suddenly, Alice seemed to suck in all the energy in the room, like she was harvesting every ounce of power out of the environment and into her. She threw her arms around his neck and kissed him back. Her kisses were fierce and desperate, screaming with the raw aggression of a woman unleashed into her own being.

With a growl of triumph, he unzipped his fly and shoved the crotch of her shorts to the side. He wasted no time and plunged himself inside her. Her body was so primed and ready for him that he was instantly sheathed so deeply he felt his entire world shift.

"God, Ian," she groaned, her fingernails raking across his back, as she trembled in his arms. "What are you doing?" "Showing you what it's like when you stop fighting who you are." He plundered her mouth with kisses as he thrust himself even deeper, buried inside her until there was nowhere else to go. Then he grabbed her thighs and jerked them upward, and he went even deeper. "Do you want more, Alice? Tell me you want more." He fisted her hair, pulling her head back as he savaged her throat with kisses.

"I can't do this—" she gasped.

"Fuck that!" He withdrew and thrust again, and Alice screamed as her body convulsed. The orgasm tore through her, but he didn't stop. He caught her screams with his lips, and grabbed her hips with his palms, holding her at his mercy while he withdrew and thrust again, prolonging the climax, giving her no relief, no mercy, driving her to the point of insanity, from which he knew that she would no longer be able to stop what was inside her.

Alice shuddered in his arms, and then the orgasm finally faded, but already he was stoking a new fire inside her, a fire that was igniting desire and lust inside him that he'd never allowed to come to life before. Never had he embraced his need for a woman like this. Never had he allowed his lust and desire to rule him. Never had he embraced his hunger for the feel of a woman's skin against his. Never had he allowed himself to be consumed by a woman the way Alice was doing to him right now. It was too dangerous, but to allow things between them to continue as they were was even more risky.

Alice needed to come to life, and it needed to happen right now. *Alice.* He demanded her response with a kiss of ruthlessness and passion as his hips moved in an undulating motion, faster and slower, hard then soft, a constant assault on her senses, giving her no room to adjust or predict his moves. *How badly do you want this? How much do you want to explode?*

Her fingers were digging into his shoulders, her breath coming in deep gasps, her body trembling violently. "It's too much, Ian. It's too much."

"No, it's not enough. Not yet." He kissed her again, and then hoisted her higher, his mouth clamping down on her nipple. He was merciless with his attentions, taking advantage of every shudder of her body that told him what she wanted and what she needed. He preyed upon her vulnerabilities. He took advantage of her need. He ruthlessly used her body to force her mind to stop fighting so hard.

Her body began to tremble more violently, and tremors raced down her legs. Her nipples were taut peaks, and heat was rising from her skin. He could feel the power straining to be released, the hugeness of the energy that was amassing inside her, and yet it was still locked down. Fear. So much fear. "Come on, Alice." He grabbed her face. "Look at me. See whose arms are wrapped around you. Who are you with? Who?"

She opened her eyes, the green depths pulsing with fire and need. "Ian," she gasped even as her thighs tightened around his hips. "It's you."

"Damn right, it's me. Your soul mate. The man destined to protect you and keep you safe." He palmed her forearms, where they were wrapped around his neck. Her skin was fiery, so hot he could smell burned flesh. The brand was searing her as it fought to break through. "You're killing yourself by fighting me," he said. "Stop it." Need and possession rushed through him, so intense he almost shouted with rage. He shoved her harder against the wall and thrust again.

This time, he couldn't stop the orgasm for either of them, and it ripped through them with merciless ferocity, unleashing its wrath into both of them like a tornado ripped from the earth itself. He shouted her name, his fingers digging into her forearm.

Heat burned through his hand, and with a furious roar, he lifted her arm and pressed his lips against the burned flesh, taking the heat and the pain away and drawing it into his own body. The moment he did it, an electric shock exploded through them both. Alice yelped, and he gripped her, fighting to hold onto her as the violent current tore through him.

Smoke burned through the air, and he stumbled, using all the strength he could summon in his thighs to keep them upright. Alice clung to him, her face buried in his shoulder as her body convulsed, almost in perfect sync to the contractions of his own muscles. It was out of control, so far out of his control that all he could do was hold onto her and hope he could protect them both until it finally ended.

Minutes...seconds...hours later, it ended. Everything faded into stillness and silence, until all that was left was the sound of them both panting. Steam rose from their sweat-slicked bodies, and the room was filled with the scent of lovemaking and burned flesh.

Alice's face was still buried in the crook of his neck, her

arms and legs wrapped around him so tightly he felt like she'd never let go. His arms were locked so hard around her, they were beginning to cramp, but he didn't move.

He couldn't move.

He wouldn't move.

"Ian?" She sounded breathless and exhausted, so drained that regret flickered through him.

"Yeah?" Summoning immense effort, he lifted his head from hers.

"What just happened?" Pain edged her voice, and fear. More damn fear.

"I'm not sure." He managed a deep breath. "You okay?"

"No." She tightened her grip on him and pressed her face more tightly against his shoulder. She wasn't rejecting him physically. She was connecting them even more closely.

Yeah, baby. That was what he wanted. He laughed softly, and set his hand on the back of her head, supporting her. "Did I hurt you? Did I go too deep?"

There was a moment's hesitation. "No, that was okay."

"Okay? Only okay? Hell, woman, you call that okay?"

There was a ripple of laughter from her. "No, Ian, I can't call that only okay. If I die in the next minute, I am sure I'll remember that one."

He grinned. "That's better." He could still smell flesh burning, and he trailed his hands tantalizingly along her back. "You aren't on fire by any chance, are you?"

Silence.

He pulled back, nudging his shoulder to get her to look up. "Alice?"

She finally pulled her face out of his neck. Her hair was curled against her neck in damp tendrils, and her cheeks were flushed. Her eyes were full of fear, and the corners of her mouth were tight with pain. Possessiveness roared through him, along with a tenderness he wasn't used to experiencing. He suddenly saw her not as an all-powerful angel who needed to be brought into her powers, but a vulnerable woman who he'd dragged into a battle she hadn't wanted to participate in. Sudden regret coursed through him, and he grimaced. "Listen, I'm sorry—"

"It's my arm. Both of them," she interrupted. "They hurt. I mean, they really, really hurt."

He went still at her words, and he saw the trepidation in her eyes.

Without another word, he clasped her elbow and tugged lightly to pull it free from his neck. For a moment, she didn't let go of her death grip on his neck. Her arms were locked tightly around him, keeping them out of sight behind him.

"Alice," he said softly. "We have to know." He rubbed his thumb over the inside of her elbow, pressing lightly.

After a moment, she relaxed her arm, her gaze riveted nervously to his. He slowly drew her arm forward, sliding his arm down her triceps and over her skin. Her entire arm was on fire, so hot he could feel the pads of his fingers burn as he touched her. As he got closer to her forearm, the heat became even more intense.

He didn't look at her skin, didn't take his gaze off Alice's as he brought her arm within view. She didn't look down either. They just stared at each other. There was the sound of crackling and sizzling as he laid his palm over her skin, and he felt the sharp sting of hot iron burning his hand. The scent of burning flesh stung his nose, and Alice sucked in her breath. "What just happened?"

Without a word, he pulled his hand off and inspected his palm. His skin was black and charred, ashes of burned flesh flaking from his hand. Hot, black lines crisscrossed his palm, a pattern that he knew all too well.

Alice touched his hand. "That's the head of your mace," she whispered. "How did it get burned on your skin like that?" She met his gaze, her brow furrowed "I thought I was supposed to get the marks?"

"I think you did." This time, when he clasped her wrist and moved her arm, he did look down. Alice bent her head next to his, her hair soft against his cheek.

On her arm was the partial outline of his mace, just like a *sheva* should have, reflecting the three and a half stages they had completed. But it wasn't the thin silver lines of a *sheva* mark that would have had him leaping up in victory and shouting his pride to the entire world. No, it wasn't that at all.

Instead of being a smooth, delicate consummation of their bond, the lines were dark, angry burn marks that had charred the skin so badly that they were puckered and raised. The flesh was black and damaged, and smoke rose off her skin. Sparks flickered and sizzled, as if the mark was still on fire. The fact that it had burned its image into his palm suggested that it still was.

It was his brand, yeah, but it didn't look how it was supposed to.

It didn't look like a *sheva* mark.

To him, it looked like the dark, angry brand of a demon. Holy shit. What had he done?

† † †

Alice didn't have to ask to know that something had gone egregiously wrong. The shock on Ian's face sent a cold chill right to her core. "Ian? What happened?"

"They're supposed to be silver marks that blend with your skin. Like tattoos painted by angels." He gestured to the charred flesh and the burns etched into his own palm. "Not this. I've never seen it like this."

The bile of fear rose in the back of her throat. "What is it?"

"What does it look like to you?"

There was only one thing she could think of, only one time that she'd smelled that exact scent of burning flesh before. "Demons," she said. "It looks like demons."

Ian closed his eyes for a brief moment, and she felt his adrenaline surge. "Yeah, that's what I thought, too."

"Demons?" She couldn't keep the squeak of fear out of her voice as she quickly looked around the room. "But how?"

"I think—" Before he could finish his answer, the room filled with a brilliant turquoise glow. Ian swore and immediately unsheathed himself from her body. "Jada's coming."

Alice shivered as Ian broke the physical connection between them, and her legs trembled as Ian lowered her to the floor, helping her fix her shorts before he yanked his jeans back over his hips. They were barely dressed when Jada appeared in the room.

She was an ashen-gray mist now. The blue seemed to have faded into the pallid pallor of a gravestone. "You're ready to go?"

Ian moved in front of Alice, tucking her arm out of sight behind his back. Why was he concealing it from Jada? How bad was it? What had he been about to say? And *demons?*

Trepidation rushed through Alice, and she folded her arms under her breasts, tears burning in her eyes when her tender, charred skin brushed against her shirt. Gone was the high of that place Ian had taken her to when they'd made love, replaced by a rising terror she couldn't contain. Why had she finally gotten his marks? And why did they hurt so much? And *demons?*

"Yeah, we're ready." Ian held out his arms to show his cuffs. "These are your assurances we will return?"

Jada nodded. "Exactly seventy-two hours from now, you will be recalled to this room. Chloe will be here waiting for you. You will have ten minutes to save her. If you don't, you will die." She smiled at them, a smile of grim reality. "You would have died last time. You know I can do it."

Alice thought of the young half-angel, and her heart started to ache. "Can I see her?"

"No," Jada snapped. "You've betrayed your kind enough."

"How do you know she'll still be alive when we get back?" Ian asked.

Jada met his gaze. "I know. That is all the information you need."

Alice closed her eyes, filled with regret for the young woman who didn't belong. An angel who was so barely an angel that she shouldn't have been subject to the same fate as the Mageaan. "I'll give the pearl to her," she said softly. "I'll offer it to her—"

"It won't work on her," Jada snapped.

Alice opened her eyes to study Jada. She'd felt Chloe's energy. There was goodness there. "She's not tainted—"

"I won't take the risk," Jada said. "When you return, you will give the pearl to me. I will use it. Both conditions must be met, or you die."

Ian stepped up. "That isn't what I agreed to—"

"The pearl wasn't yours to offer," Jada snapped, her attention riveted on Alice. "Alice needs to add her agreement. Agree to the deal, or you both die now."

"I—" Alice hesitated, all too aware of the throbbing pain in her arms, of the demon taint pulsing through her. Now she could afford even less to release the pearl and strip herself of the protection it offered. Was it really worth it just to get to Catherine? Or would she be better off letting herself die one more time and coming back to life again far from this underwater hell?

Except she didn't know if she could come back again.

She was so close to using up her lives. If she died before she found Catherine... No, she couldn't take that chance. And there was no way to reach Catherine without the Mageaan's help. It was too late to start over. Dammit. "I agree," she said, even as fear bit at her, and regret filled her. "I agree to give you the pearl willingly." The moment she said the words, a cold chill pricked her, and the tattoos on her wrists flared brighter before fading.

The added terms had been woven into the brands by magic. Now that all three parties had assented, the terms were locked down. It would bind Jada, forcing her to free them both if they fulfilled their requirements, but it would also bind Alice and Ian. She would have to give Jada the pearl. There was no out.

Ian swore under his breath, and his arm went around her shoulder, pulling her close. This time, she didn't resist him. She burrowed under his shoulder, drawing on his strength, hoping that somehow, someway, together they could accomplish that which had started off a daunting task and now had become impossible.

Sometimes, impossible odds were the best ones you could get. At least they were better than none at all.

Jada nodded. "It is done, then." She slipped her fingers into a crevice on her harness, pulled out the pearl. Alice gasped as Jada handed it to her. "I can tell you're on the edge, and you need to stay surface-bound long enough to track Cardiff. Keep it, and then you will willingly offer it to me when you return."

Alice fisted the pearl as if she'd been given the most precious gift ever, and Ian felt her shudder in relief at having it back in her possession.

Jada pulled a thin wand out of the harness covering her breasts. "My guides will take you. It will take you one day to arrive at your destination. One day to return. Which gives you one day to find the wizard and secure his assistance." She pointed the wand at them. "May the oceans favor you. May the wind carry you swiftly. May the sunlight dawn in your favor."

There was a flash of light, and then one of the walls dissolved, revealing the murky green of the deep ocean. Like before, the sea did not enter the room, held at bay by some invisible force that Alice now suspected was Cardiff's magic.

As they watched, four dolphins swam up next to the edge of the water barrier. They were wearing black seaweed harnesses similar to that which crisscrossed Jada's breasts, and they were attached to an old wooden dinghy that looked like it had been dredged out of a shipwreck on the bottom of the sea.

Despite her trepidation, Alice couldn't contain her gasp of delight. "We're getting a ride from dolphins?"

Jada nodded, the faintest of smiles nudging at the corner of her mouth. "Our dolphin friends are the one beauty of our fate. Be kind to them, and they will return the favor."

Alice looked over at Ian, and he shrugged. "Dolphins it is, then." He set his hand on Alice's back as they headed across the room. Just as they passed Jada, he paused. "I'm sorry that fate has handed you this life," he said. "If you hate it, don't accept it."

Jada's face darkened. "You know nothing of which you speak, warrior."

"Are you so sure about that?" Ian turned away, but not before Alice saw the look of pain flash across his face. It was gone instantly, but it had been enough. She knew that he was referencing the curse that had doomed his family, and the fact that he was refusing to acknowledge its victory.

Only the will to live had kept his heart beating all these years, reflecting an inner strength that was more than all the great warriors of his lineage had possessed. How could a man like that ever understand the repercussions that faced angels? How could he ever understand her?

As Alice stepped out of the room into the cold chill of the undulating water, she wondered exactly what Ian hadn't had a chance to tell her about the marks, and whether he could explain the fact his mark was that of a demon.

Perhaps he would give her answers during the day of travel that it would take them to reach the wizard. The calm before the storm.

She climbed into the rickety boat, gripping the algae-slickened rails as Ian settled beside her. He locked one arm around her waist, then grabbed the seat with his other hand. Jada moved closer to watch their exit, and for a split second,

Alice thought she saw a flicker of gold in Jada's turquoise hair. The gold of the angel she'd once been?

Then she nodded at the dolphins, and they exploded forward with a squeal of delight, taking off so quickly that Alice would have fallen over the back of the boat had Ian not grabbed her.

Hold your breath, Ian said. *She didn't give us back our ability to breathe under water.*

Alice nodded, peering upward as the dolphins headed toward the surface, toward fresh air, toward freedom, toward Catherine. What would happen if Alice found her? And what would happen if she didn't?

Ian wrapped his palm around her burning arm, and she knew that Catherine was no longer her only problem.

CHAPTER TWELVE

He'd never been a sunlight guy, and he'd never been the one to notice the wind on his face or the freshness of the air.

But when their algae-covered boat popped out of the ocean and landed with a splash on the surface of the water, Ian felt like he'd just been granted a slice of heaven.

As the chirping dolphins gallivanted merrily across the sea, dragging the little dinghy behind them, Ian raised his face to the sun. It was warm, healing, and seemed to seep right into his cells.

"Oh, wow." Beside him, Alice flopped back on the wooden seat, throwing her arms over her head and arching her back, exposing herself to the sky. "Returning to the surface after being underwater feels as amazing as coming back to life after being dead." She took a deep breath, her breasts straining against the blue fabric, her flat belly peeking out from under the hem of the shirt as she stretched. "Can you feel the heat of the sun? Unbelievable. It never gets old, does it?"

Ian tore his gaze off her limber body and did a careful inventory of their surroundings. As far as he could see, there was only ocean. Nothing else. Not an island. Not a beach. Not a single piece of land. The only living creatures other than their escorts were a few seagulls circling above. Their rough calls to each other were the only sounds beside the splash of the water against the hull of the boat and the happy squealing of the dolphins.

He sensed no threats. Not at the moment, at least. He let out his breath and looked back down at Alice, who had closed her eyes, as if she were drinking the sun into her very pores. "You look like you're relaxing on a tropical beach."

She grinned and flipped her damp hair back from her face. "I feel like I am." She held up the pearl. "I have a respite for now, and it feels good." She pressed it to her lips, and then carefully zipped it back into the front pocket of her shorts.

Ian looked around again, uncomfortable with how relaxed she looked. "Now isn't the time to relax. We're on our way to deal with a black magic wizard who was one of the most deadly Order members in existence a thousand years ago. The shit's about to come down."

"I know what he is. He killed me, remember?" She stretched her arms above her head. "The thing is, Ian, life is too short. Not only is it brief, but it's full of so many hard things that there's never a time to breathe or recover. So, when you get a moment like this, you have to drink it into your soul to sustain yourself when all that's around you is darkness." She sighed. "I was so stressed down there that I forgot about slowing down and appreciating each moment that I have. This moment is a blessing, and I need to notice it."

Ian looked down at her again, astounded by the expression of serenity on her face. He didn't understand how she could turn it off like that. He knew how tormented she'd been beneath the ocean. Worried about Catherine. Almost dying. Guilty over not being able to help Chloe. Upset about the brands. And it was all gone. Completely vanished. "Where did it go?"

"Where did what go?"

"Your stress."

She laughed softly. "Oh, don't worry. It's still there. I'm just taking a minute to regroup, so I don't crash and burn before I need to."

"By basking in the sun?" Yeah, it felt good, but there was too much to do, too much at stake. He shifted restlessly, needing to do something.

Alice turned her head to look at him. Her dark eyelashes were shading her eyes, looking decadent and innocent at the same time. "Is there anything we can do right now about all this we're trying to accomplish?"

He thought for a few minutes before answering. "No, not really. We're kind of stuck in the boat for the moment."

"Right. So, this is our breather. A gift from the heavens to recharge." She patted the bench beside her. "Join me. Look at the clouds."

"Look at the clouds?" he repeated, unable to keep his disapproval sheathed. "I need to be alert. We could come to Cardiff's at any moment."

"Jada said twenty-four hours." Alice closed her eyes again. "And aren't your senses so overly developed that you could kill a flea with exact precision without even looking where you're throwing your mace? And couldn't you hear a butterfly approach from five miles away?"

He grunted. "Yeah."

"So, you're fine." She patted the bench again. "No one is going to sneak up on us in this ocean with you around. Take a load off, warrior. Recover. This might be your only chance."

Ian hesitated, but she looked so damned appealing the way she was stretched out on the bench. One knee was bent, showing too much of her thigh, and her wet hair was a disheveled mass of auburn highlights under the bright sun. If he closed his eyes, he could almost imagine the scent of sunscreen and piña coladas, and the feel of a beach, of soft sand beneath his bare feet. "Damn, woman, you're making me soft."

She laughed softly. "Nothing could make you soft." She held out her hand and crooked her fingers at him. "Join me, Sir

Knight, and see what you've been missing all your life."

He stared at that small hand, inviting him into her world, and suddenly, he couldn't resist it anymore. He called out his mace so he had it ready, and then stretched out beside her on the narrow bench. They were so close that his shoulder was on top of hers, and he had to loop his left leg over hers to keep from sliding off the edge. Casual intimacy, not about sex, and he had to admit, he liked it.

Alice pointed at the sky. "See that cloud? The one in the shape of a poodle?"

"Poodle? Seriously?" Ian followed her glance, and was surprised to see that he could figure out which cloud she was talking about. "Yeah, I see it." He could discern the arrogant head, the fluffy tail, and even a little cloud shaped like a bow.

"Whenever I see a poodle in the clouds, I think it's my mom," she said. "She had a toy poodle growing up and always said that when we got settled somewhere we'd get one. I like to think that she's in heaven now, and when she shows me her poodle, it's her way of saying she loves me."

He remembered the story of how her mother had died without forgiving Alice, and his heart broke a little for her story. "You think she's forgiven you for not saving her?" Her hand was next to his, and on a whim, he slipped his fingers into hers and tangled them together.

She smiled slightly, and her fingers tightened in his. "No, I don't think she has forgiven me," she said quietly. "But I think that's her way of saying she hasn't given up on me. That there is still an opportunity for redemption."

Ian frowned as he rubbed his thumb over the gray circle in her palm. "Why are you so hard on yourself? It wasn't your choice not to save her."

"I know. But I still feel there had to have been something I could have done." Alice sighed. "I'm an angel of life. Even you said that you thought I was too scared to act the way I should."

Ian grimaced at the reminder of the violent lovemaking

that had brought his mark to life on her skin. "Yeah, sorry about that. I was a little rough."

"No." She sat up, looking down at him as her hair tumbled over her cheeks, framing her face like a halo of auburn rainbows. "It was beautiful." She touched his cheek, her fingertips so soft. "I've spent my whole life straddling the line between being a stoic, impassive angel, and trying to find meaning in life. I spent hours observing strangers, trying to experience the moments when they fell in love, or felt pain, joy, triumph, and all the other human emotions, and now I've been able to live it myself. As much as it may cost me, and as dangerous as it is for me, that lovemaking was such a gift that you gave to me." She smiled. "Thank you."

He clasped her hand and pressed his lips to it. The smile on her face was so beautiful, so real, that it made him want to show her the world.

"Tell me, mighty warrior," Alice said, her voice teasing as she rolled on top of him and propped her elbows on his chest, resting her chin in her palms. "What kind of childhood spawns a great warrior like you?"

Childhood? They were on their way to take on the man who had cursed generations of his family and killed Alice, yet she wanted to talk about his childhood? But even as he snorted at the idea, it appealed to him, this chance to retreat into simple humanity and connection, like normal people might do.

Alice was right, he wanted this moment. Ian set his hands on her hips, relishing the sensation of her body on top of his. She was so relaxed that her weight was sinking into him, and he loved the sensation of her trusting him enough to let go. "I was an only child. I never knew my mom, but I was really close with my dad."

Alice raised her auburn brows. "That's so ironic. I never knew my dad. My mom was my world. You and I are like twins."

He laughed softly. "Not twins. Maybe comrade souls."

He began to work his fingers through the tangles in her hair. "My dad was the eleventh Order member in my family. He was a brilliant warrior. All the Fitzgeralds were. At the time, he and both of his brothers were Order. They were young for the Order, only in their late thirties, whereas most of the team were many centuries old."

Alice smiled, her face contented, as if she were enthralled by the story of Ian's past. "How old were you when you joined the Order?"

He liked her attention. It felt good to just talk. Who knew that there could be such pleasure from this kind of simple interaction? "Nineteen."

"Nineteen? That's amazing!"

Her eyes widened so much that he chuckled. "Now you're making fun of me."

"No." But she smiled too. "Tell me about your dad."

"Great guy." Ian hadn't thought much about life as a kid for a long time. "He taught me to hunt and fish. We spent a lot of time on survival skills and honing my Calydon instincts. Of course, I didn't come into my powers until I was eighteen, but he trained me so thoroughly that I was already tapping into my abilities by then." He grinned, thinking of those times. "Once, I decided he was too serious and conservative, so I booby-trapped the house when he was out hunting. When I got back inside after setting it to wait for him, he was already in there. He jumped out at me and scared the living shit out of me. I screamed bloody terror and ran my ass outside as fast as I could. Of course, in my crazed flight for safety, I triggered the traps I'd set and caught myself in them. He gave me grief about that for years. That incident taught me not to take anything for granted or to assume I'm smarter than the enemy." Alice smiled. "He sounds like a good father."

"He was." Ian thought back to all those nights in the dark woods that his father had spent teaching him, giving him the tools to survive. "He always thought the curse would take him, so he tried to make me self-sufficient from an early age, so I would know what I needed to do once he was gone." He pulled his hand from her hair and showed her the black onyx ring on his index finger. "This was the ring that the Order gave him when he took his oath. They gave up the ring tradition shortly afterwards, so he was the last one to receive one. He always told me that wearing the ring reminded him of his commitment to the Order. It gave him strength to resist the curse so he could fulfill his oath and honor his family's legacy."

Alice ran her fingers over it, and Ian stiffened, shocked by how right it felt to have Alice touching it so reverently. He'd never talked about that ring with anyone, never told anyone what it meant to him. Why bother? Everyone's response was always disgust, because the Fitzgerald men had betrayed their oaths and honor by taking their own lives.

But not Alice. The look on her face was admiration and empathy, and it made something in his chest tighten. "You get it, don't you?" he asked softly.

"Get what?"

"Get why my dad is worth admiring."

She looked up at him and smiled. "Of course I do. He was a good father, and he taught his son about honor and survival. The curse wasn't his fault." She wrinkled her nose. "Warwick is very powerful. His spells are unstoppable."

Ian was suddenly filled with awe for this tiny woman draped across him. With those few words, she'd given him a gift, the freedom to admire his father and try to uphold his honor. "Thank you." He kissed her once, gently, a kiss of tenderness, not the mad rampage of earlier. Yeah, he still wanted her naked and writhing beneath him, but right then, in that moment, it was a different kind of perfection.

"Why did Cardiff curse your family?" She folded her arms over his chest and rested her chin on them, using them as a pillow. "How'd you get so lucky?"

Ian resumed the untangling of her hair, one cluster at a

time. "You know how I told you the *sheva* bond doesn't have a happy ending?"

She wrinkled her nose. "Yes, and I appreciate the reminder now that I have half your mace incinerated on my arm."

He laughed softly and kissed the top of her head, appreciating her ability to laugh about it. Here, in the sunshine, in the middle of the ocean, being towed by dolphins, all the battles they would soon be facing seemed distant and removed. Alice was right. The respite was good. "Well, traditionally, the Order of the Blade's job is to kill bonded males when they go rogue, to keep them from killing innocents. But when it's an Order member who has bonded, the Order kills the mate instead. It's a brutal choice, but the Order is all that can stop a rogue Calydon. Without us, too many innocents will die. Our *shevas* must be sacrificed to save the greater good."

Alice paused. "You did mention something like that before. That's why your teammate killed me the first time?"

"Yeah. Sorry about that."

She burst out laughing and shifted her head so she could see him. "An apology feels a little inadequate for the fact I was murdered, but I'll let it go." She raised her eyebrows. "How does this relate to Warwick?"

"Pretty simple. He found his *sheva,* and immediately quit the Order so he could be with her. My ancestor, Augustus Fitzgerald, was his closest friend, so Warwick told him what he was doing."

Alice's expression softened in understanding. "So, let me guess. Augustus killed Warwick's woman?"

"Yeah. Warwick was enraged. He was especially angry that his best friend could be so blasé about murdering the woman he loved. Augustus apparently told him to man-up and take it like the warrior he was supposed to be. Warwick was so enraged and felt so betrayed that he cursed my ancestor and all his progeny to suffer the same fate: to meet the woman of his soul, and to lose her. But he didn't just want them to get a freebie by going rogue and losing their minds. He wanted them to suffer, so he cursed them to experience the loss so brutally that they killed themselves." Ian ground his jaw. "And one by one, that's exactly what has happened. I'm the only one left."

Alice studied him, her green eyes wise with comprehension. "And now I'm the woman both standing in the way of the curse and hurling you right into its claws at breakneck speed, all at the same time."

He shrugged. "Something like that."

Alice sighed. "So, let's clarify this. In addition to the fact I'm going to drive you to suicide, you are quite possibly going to be responsible for me losing my angel status and becoming a Mageaan until I finally die for good and wind up in demon hands for eternity."

He grimaced. "Yeah. We're like a match made in heaven, aren't we?"

"Not so much." She rolled off him, landing beside him on the narrow bench. Side by side, they lay in the rocking boat, under the vibrant azure sky, absorbing the warmth of the sun into their bodies. "Well," she said finally, "our relationship may be doomed, cursed, and ill-fated, but at least the sex is great." He burst out laughing at her comment. "Isn't the guy supposed to say that? And the woman is supposed to say that at least she got to experience true love before heading off to an eternity of hell?"

"Love." She said the word as if she'd never heard it before. "What would I do with love?"

"I don't know. Enjoy it?"

She sighed. "It's too dangerous to enjoy. It's kind of like sucking on a poisonous thorn and trying to enjoy the flavor. Not that easy."

Regret filled Ian at the truth he heard in her voice. His angel of life truly didn't believe in love. She couldn't save lives, she didn't trust love, and she couldn't even keep herself alive. Anger began to build inside him, outrage for the life that had been thrust upon this woman who had endured so much, yet could still lie in an ancient boat in the middle of the ocean and think her unforgiving dead mother had sent her poodle clouds to tell her she was loved. Shit. She deserved more.

Suddenly angry, he sat up. "Why do you keep dying?"

She didn't flinch at the intrusion of reality into their idyllic moment. "I told you. Cardiff killed me, and I'm hard to kill, so I keep rebounding." She shook out her hair, which was still dripping onto the bottom of the boat. Now that Ian had cleared most of the tangles, it fell in smooth waves that glistened in the sun as they began to dry. Her thick hair curled into soft tendrils that begged for him to run his hands through it.

He did, marveling at the softness of her tresses as he combed his fingers through them. He'd never paused long enough in his quest to do his Order duty and to find Cardiff to do something indulgent like bask in the softness of a woman's hair or enjoy the sun on his flesh, but this moment... it was perfection. He liked the fact that he could touch her without asking, and in return, he got a warm smile and encouragement. He didn't know what was building between him and Alice, but it felt good.

He didn't want it to end. To change. To be destroyed. "Why do you continue to die? He killed you only one time."

"This is true." Alice didn't open her eyes. Instead, she linked her hands behind her head and seemed to just ease into the sway of the boat, her relaxed body moving rhythmically with the waves. "I'm actually quite difficult to murder, believe it or not. But he hit me with black magic, demon magic, actually, which works on angels." She sighed and rubbed her arm, which was still smoking slightly. "So, he did kill me, and I went straight into the arms of demon central. But I'm an angel of life, so I keep coming back to life. It won't go on forever, though." She pulled down the neckline of her tank top, and he saw six faded slashes across her chest, claw marks he hadn't noticed when they'd been making love. Why hadn't he seen them? Because he'd been too overwrought with lust, or because he had seen only her true self, which didn't include demon scars?

He ran his finger over the marks. They were cool and seemed to be healed. "I didn't notice those before. What are they?"

"When I die, the demons torture me. Usually when I come back to life, the marks are gone." She released the shirt so it eased back over the scars. "This time, I didn't heal entirely. I think I'm out of recovery options. Next time, dead may be dead."

Ian mulled that over as he watched the dolphins bound through the water. "It doesn't bother you?"

"It is what it is, Ian. I can't change it, so why get worked up about it?" But even as she spoke, her mouth tightened ever so slightly, revealing that she wasn't quite as at peace as she was trying to be. Her fingernails were digging into the wood, and her breath had become a little more rapid and shallow.

Frowning, he stretched out beside her again and propped himself up on his elbow. He needed to be closer to her. "You okay?"

For a long moment, she didn't answer, but she finally shook her head. "I'm scared," she whispered. "I'm scared of so much. I try to ignore it, and to enjoy the sun, but dammit, Ian. I'm really scared."

"Aw, come here, sweetheart." Ian scooped her up in his arms, setting her on his lap. Alice didn't resist. Instead, she just leaned against his chest, her head resting on his shoulder as she let her feet dangle.

"You were right," she said, moving her head slightly so that her damp hair tickled his neck. "When we were making love and you said I was afraid, you were right. I'm terrified of dying for good. I'm afraid of being tortured again. I'm scared of being a Mageaan. And most of all, I'm afraid of failing someone I love again."

Ian's chest ached for her pain, and he rested his chin on her head as she snuggled closer against him. "Fear is okay, Alice. You'd be stupid not to feel fear. But the fact that you get up and continue your battle anyway is what makes you a warrior."

"I don't want to be a warrior. I want to be the girl who wakes up in a little cabin in the woods, takes a walk with her dog in the morning sunshine, and feels safe all the time to be whoever she wants to be."

Ian tried to picture that, but couldn't. The Alice he knew was a fighter who never slowed down... except for now. Except for this moment. He had to admit that as much as he admired her toughness, he appreciated that she'd forced him into this quieter moment. He hadn't stopped trying to survive for hundreds of years, and it felt incredible to simply be at peace. "Fight for what you want, Alice. You can do it." He kissed the top of her head again, wishing he could grant her the peace that she craved so badly.

"Can I?" She held up her hand, and he saw it was trembling. "Why is your brand a demon mark, Ian?" She raised her head to look at him. "Is that what you are? Are you the demon who has come to claim me?"

Ian frowned. "I'm not a demon—"

"Calydons were formed from demon magic," she said. "You know that. It may have been two thousand years ago, but that's what gives you guys your power." Her voice was shaky, not the strong courageous one she'd put on for so long. "I can't consort with demons, let alone bond with one. I'm kind of thinking that would be a deal breaker to my angel status."

"All Calydons have the same ancestry, and their *sheva's* marks are the thin silver lines. Yours is the only one that's different. So it's not coming from my demon ancestry." He paused, debating whether to tell her his suspicions. Then he realized he owed it to her. The woman was fighting for her life, for her soul, and for him. She might wish for a life of shelter and safety, but she deserved the truth, even if it was ugly. "I think it might be you, not me."

She stared at him. "Me? You think I'm the demon?"

"Yeah, maybe. You've got a lot going on with them right now."

"Oh, God." Alice pressed her hand to her forehead. "I really hope you're wrong. If this—" She held up her arm, showing the angry black brands. "If this is from me, I'm in such trouble."

"No, you'll get through it. I'll help you. We can handle it. The brand may be tainted by demons, but it's still mine and it still connects us." Ian traced his fingers over his mark that was on her arm. It might be black and charred, but it was still his symbol, and he liked that it was there. It eased some of the tension and loosened the grip of the curse. But if he lost her, he knew it would be much worse now that they were bonded.

Instinctively, he tightened his grip on her and looked out across the water again, checking to make sure they were safe. "What is with the demons? Why do demons come after you when you die?"

Alice slid off his lap and moved to a seat across from him. She leaned forward, her forearms resting on her thighs. "Angels and demons are two sides of the same being," she explained. "We're connected. For angels, purity trumps and it gives us the freedom to live in this world. For demons, there is no purity or goodness, which bans them from our world." She fingered her arm. "They're always trying to gain access to the physical world."

Ian nodded, well aware of that razor-thin line that Calydons lived by. When Calydons went rogue, they lost their sanity. They weren't demons, but they were damned close. And Ryland...well...Ry was as close as any living creature had ever been to demon. "So, how does that affect you?"

Alice bit her lip. "If the demons can harvest my spirit, they're hoping they can use me as a way to get into the physical realm." She met his gaze. "Cardiff uses demon magic, but in order to do so, the demons have to offer it. He gave me to them as a trade, and he killed me in a way specifically designed to send me to them." She waved her hands. "Demon magic. Rah, rah. Good time for all."

Ian stared at her, outrage for her plight mounting inside him. "So, when you die for good, you'll go to hell? There's no other option for you?"

Alice closed her palm. "My soul is not clean, Ian. As long as it's not completely clean, the demons have access, because we're so closely connected. I would have to become truly pure to avoid it now that I have demon magic in my body." She opened her palm, and he saw a one inch gray circle on her skin. It was bigger than it had been. From their making love? Shit, he hoped not. "I'm losing my angel status, Ian. They're gaining hold."

He took her hand and tried to rub the circle off. It didn't move. "How do you become pure? How do you stop it?" Even as he asked the question, he knew it was stupid. The woman was a fucking angel, a thousand times more admirable than he was. Why should she have to do *anything* to become pure enough to keep her status? She was already good.

She took her hand back, closing her fist. "I don't know. Standards are high for angels of life because we are so powerful." She rolled her eyes. "Or we're supposed to be powerful, but we all know how great I am."

"So, who makes the rules? Is there some all-powerful council that evaluates you and makes the decision?" Because if there was, he was going to find those bastards and make sure they understood what Alice deserved.

But she shook her head. "There is no one looking over my shoulder. It's just a part of the fabric of my being. It's like your Calydon destiny. It's just the way it is. A metaphysical force that is part of who I am. I don't understand exactly how it works. None of the angels do. We just try to follow the rules as we were taught."

"That makes no sense." He didn't want it to make sense. He didn't like the idea of fate controlling her the way it controlled the *sheva* bond. It was damn hard to break ties like that.

Shit, this was complicated.

Ian pressed her hand between his palms. "Why do you want to kill Catherine Taylor?" He was burning with the need to understand Alice. She was so complex, a woman of so many facets that he still didn't grasp all that she was, or all that she was struggling with. He felt like he needed to get a handle on it to figure out how to help her. "That can't be good for your soul, can it?"

Alice looked away, focusing on something on the horizon. "It's a long story," she said evasively.

"My calendar's pretty open for the next few hours. I've got time." Ian saw from the look on Alice's face that she wasn't going to tell him, so he leaned forward. "In less than a day, we're going to be in Cardiff's territory. I need to know what I'm walking into, Alice, or I can't ensure our safety."

She bit her lips and finally sighed. Not meeting his gaze, she said, "I promised her I would kill her."

Ian blinked. That wasn't the answer he'd expected. What was up with all these angels running around with demons and dealing with death? This wasn't the world of angels he'd have predicted. "Why?"

She finally looked at him. "I owe her."

"If you kill another angel, doesn't that put you over the top with regard to the purity you're trying to attain?"

Alice nodded, and she sat up straighter. "There's a good chance of that. Killing another angel is pretty high up on the list of things I'm not supposed to do."

"But you'll do it anyway?"

She grimaced. "I don't know if I can. She's extremely difficult to kill." She met his gaze. "I might need you to help me." He saw the relief in her eyes, and realized that she'd been dreading asking for his help this whole time, worried that he'd say no.

Ian ran his hand through his hair. "Why does she need to die?"

Alice shook her head. "I can't tell you. It's her secret to share."

Ian narrowed his eyes. "What kind of angel is she?"

Alice hugged herself, again looking past Ian at the horizon. "When my mother died, I freaked out," she said, avoiding his question. "I couldn't cope. Back then, I hadn't developed any protection from emotions, so I was eviscerated by her death and the fact I couldn't save her." Alice fought against the swell of emotion that was so dangerous to her. "I tried to kill myself, and Catherine stopped me. She could hear the demon shadows coming back, so she grabbed me and dragged me out of there. She saved my life that day. I owe her." She looked at Ian. "It's that simple."

"Asking your friend to murder you is never simple," he said. "Originally, you said you were going to rescue her."

Alice met his gaze. "I am."

"Killing her rescues her?"

"Yes."

Well, shit. What kind of situation was Catherine in? "Does she come back to life like you?"

"No. She dies only once."

Hell. Ian shoved his hands through his hair, trying to wrap his mind around what Alice was telling him. He couldn't commit to helping her. As an Order of the Blade member, he was sworn to protect innocents, and slaying an angel in cold blood didn't fit within those limits, no matter what the reason. Just as Alice had been unable to break the rules that bound her by giving Chloe an angel's kiss, he was unable to slay an innocent in cold blood. "All I can kill are rogue Calydons who are endangering innocents, and I can kill in self-defense. That's it, Alice, and I wouldn't violate that oath even if I could." He met her gaze. "Just as angels of life wield power of extraordinary means that could be abused with devastating consequences, so do the Order of the Blade members. There have to be lines we never cross."

She looked sharply at him, betrayal burning in those green eyes. "So, you won't help me? Really?"

He didn't want to disappoint her, but he knew there were limits to what he would do, and this was one of them. "I won't kill Catherine Taylor," he said. "I can't."

The anguish in her eyes was devastating, and Ian swore as he instinctively reached for her.

But Alice held up her hand to block him, and he stopped. She turned away, facing the front of the boat and cutting him off. Ian swore, his body starting to ache at the distance she was putting between them. But he knew it didn't matter what she did or how far she pushed him. He would not betray the oath he'd made to his family, to his father, and to the Order. It defined him, and it was what had made it possible to get through the last six hundred years.

There were no choices to be made.

So, what the hell happened now? What would happen when they got to Cardiff's? Were they still on the same team, or had he just acquired another enemy? He swore and thudded his fist into his hand. What next?

CHAPTER THIRTEEN

Alice didn't move from the bow of the boat as she watched the sun begin to set across the horizon. They'd been in the dinghy for almost twelve hours now. By morning, they would be almost there. To Warwick's island. To Catherine. With no way to save her. Or kill her, rather.

Amazingly, Jada had been interested enough in their survival to pack food for them, so at least they weren't hungry. Alice had napped, so she wasn't as tired either. But it wasn't enough to decrease the stress building inside her, despite her best efforts to get into the tropical vacation mindset.

Frustration beat through her, and she glanced back at Ian. He was sitting astride the rear seat, his mace held loosely in his hand. The man was on edge, not at all relaxed, as if he expected a sea monster to leap up out of the water and try to eat him. It made her feel safe, but at the same time, seeing him sitting there looking so lethal was a tease, showing her what he could do if he chose. He could help her kill Catherine if he wanted to, but his commitment to some ideal about the Order was making him blind to what mattered. Shouldn't the bond make him want to help her? Shouldn't the fact that half his damn mace was burned into her arm shift his loyalties to her over the Order and a family that was long dead?

But no. It hadn't. He wanted to make love to her. He

would die if she rejected him. But trust her enough to help her without full information? Not a chance. Bastard.

I can hear you, sweetheart. I'm not a bastard.

Alice felt her cheeks heat up and she spun away from him, staring back across the water. After hearing him talk about his father, she knew he wasn't a bastard. Ian may have grown up in the shadow of the curse, but he'd had a father who'd loved him, and that was an incredible gift. If he didn't appreciate and honor that gift, *then* he would be a bastard. She was envious of the way he'd spoken about his father. She'd never had that bond with her mother. As a little girl, she'd tried to impress her, but her mother had been more concerned with angel duties than showering love on a little girl.

Yes, she was an angel of life, but she was a sucky one, and that meant that she could yearn for connection and emotion. She could see it in others. She could scent it as it drifted across her path. She could feel the loss of it, agonize over the absence of it, and envy those who had it. Envy. For an angel? God, what kind of angel was she? How much further would Ian pull her off track if she let him get to her?

Biting back frustration, she took a deep breath, trying to pull her emotions back under control. She focused on the scenery, trying to absorb the beauty of it into her soul. The sun was low in the sky, casting the most magnificent shades of orange, pink, and purple across the water, as if it were lighting up the path the dolphins were supposed to follow. She focused on the sunset, trying to raise her mental shields against him, trying to eliminate his ability to unsettle her.

It's going to be more difficult to block me out since we're blood-bonded. We're locked into each other now.

Alice said nothing, hating how her body and her mind craved him. His deep voice sent waves of comfort and warmth through her, and it made her ache for him. Why could he make her feel like that? If she fell in love with him, she'd become irretrievably broken as an angel. If she fell in love with him, she would try to make the same choice that she'd made before with her mother, saving him out of love, which is why she'd lost the ability to save anyone. She knew it had been taken away from her because she'd proven incapable, and it wouldn't return until she proved herself worthy. As far as she could figure, the only reason she hadn't been fully stripped of her angel status was because she'd been a child when she'd made the decision. And ever since, she'd been gradually falling.

"Shit, Alice. Why didn't you tell me all that?"

Alice spun around, furious that he'd been in her mind. "What is wrong with you? Don't you have any respect for my privacy?"

Ian's eyes glittered. "You were broadcasting. I'd have to be dead not to hear your thoughts."

"I wasn't broadcasting! I was thinking! Privately!"

"You'll have to try harder than that to keep me out." Ian rested the mace across his thigh. "Listen, Alice, I'm sorry I can't help you kill Catherine. Isn't there another way to 'save' her?"

She closed her eyes. "I wish there was."

"You're willing to sacrifice your soul for her?"

"Yes." She didn't hesitate. "Of course."

There was a long silence, then she felt a wash of warmth from Ian. "I respect that," he said. "You're an amazing woman, Alice. Courageous. Committed. I admire you."

Alice scrunched her eyes shut, fighting off the swell of warmth at his kind words. "I'm not," she said. "I'm just not. Don't tell me lies."

"Okay," he agreed. "I just have one question."

She looked over at him. "What is it?"

"Do angels of life protect everyone, or are they assigned to certain people?"

"They get assignments."

He mulled that over for a moment. "Have you ever gotten an assignment?"

"No." She turned away. "No, I haven't."

"Are you sure?"

She looked back at him. "Of course I am."

"Because..." He turned his mace to reflect the sunset. "Ry seems to think that you're part of the angel trinity protecting the Order. If you are our angel of life, then maybe you're the reason that we're so hard to kill. Maybe you've been doing your job all along. Did you ever think of that?"

She stared at him in disbelief. "That's impossible. I would know. I would have sensed you all."

"Are you so sure?" He set the mace down. "Here's the thing, Alice. All Calydons are immortal and damned difficult to kill. But for some reason, the Order of the Blade members are tougher than any of the rest of them. We survive battles that no one should survive. We recover from wounds that no Calydon should heal. Hell, Quinn Masters actually died a few months ago and then revived. It's inexplicable what he did." He leaned forward, his gaze intense. "I thought it was because we're badasses, but now I'm wondering if we're actually protected." He pointed the end of the mace in her direction. "By you."

She gaped at him. "What on earth makes you think that it's me?"

He grinned. "Because we're a bunch of fucked-up bastards, and it would take a pretty fucked-up angel to handle us. You fit the bill."

She stared at him. "You're calling me fucked-up? Are you serious?"

"I mean it as a compliment," he said.

Tears filled her eyes and she turned away, throwing up her mental shields as hard as she could. She felt Ian's grunt of pain, and she knew she'd shut him out. Fucked-up was not what she needed to be. How could he call her that? But though she denied it, she knew it was true, and she understood that he'd intended it as a compliment. But he was a warrior, not an angel, and the standards were different. She couldn't afford to be fucked-up, as he'd so eloquently put it. And there was only one way she could possibly save herself, and that was to make sure Catherine died. Yes, killing Catherine might doom her forever, or it might be the key that would save them both. It was dangerous, but it was a risk she had to take. She had no other options, and regardless of what happened to her, she had a debt to pay off.

If Ian wouldn't help her, there was only one man she knew of who was powerful enough to kill Catherine: Flynn Shapiro, her former best friend and the man who was currently on a mission to murder her.

Flynn would kill her at first chance. But if she could get him to use that energy against Catherine at the same time so that he killed them both... She nodded. It could work. Risky, but her only chance.

She was going to have to let him find her. Back at the beach, Ian's teammate Vaughn had told her that Flynn had infected her with his blood, and he could find her that way. How far would it work?

She gritted her teeth and looked back at Ian. His mace was sitting on his lap, ready to defend or attack at a moment's notice. For a moment, she hesitated as fear rippled through her, then she thought of Ian's words while they were making love, that she was afraid to be who she was, to tap into her power.

Dammit. She wasn't afraid. Well, she was, but she wouldn't let everything around her be destroyed just because she was terrified. Ian was right. She had to be stronger. She had to be braver. She had to stop running away from all of it.

Taking a deep breath, Alice narrowed her eyes and focused on the mace. For a moment, nothing happened. Then suddenly it shot off Ian's lap and into her palm. As Ian looked at her in surprise, she fisted the handle and raked the blade across her palm. Blood spewed out, and she flung her arm into the air, spraying the droplets into the mist before he could stop her. The wind caught some of them, and others fell into the ocean.

The trail had been set.

She could only hope that Flynn found her at the right time. Not too early. Not too late. Or else all was lost.

Ian grabbed her wrist, his eyes blazing. "What did you just do?"

She met his gaze. "I asked for the help you wouldn't give me."

† † †

Flynn Shapiro.

She'd called Flynn Shapiro.

She'd called in the man who'd murdered her two months ago.

Two hours later, Ian was still reeling from Alice's confession. The dark clouds of the curse had begun to close in as he was haunted by the memories of Flynn's poisoned disc slicing across her belly. He couldn't escape the images of Alice writhing in his arms as the toxin killed her, and how he'd been unable to help her.

Restlessly, he shifted in the boat, his brow beginning to sweat as he recalled that horrific moment when Alice's soul had left her body, stripped away by the demons. How he'd stood there with her in his arms, utterly helpless to save her after Flynn had killed her.

Fuck. Ian pressed his forehead into his palm, trying to block the memories, but they were too strong and too vivid. He could feel all the anguish of that moment when he'd called out his weapons to use them on himself. How he'd been a fraction of a millisecond from killing himself. It was the closest the curse had ever come to taking him. And now, the mere realization that Flynn was on Alice's trail again was almost enough to send him back there.

Alice looked back at him, and her brow was furrowed. "Are you okay?"

"Fine." Swearing, he clenched his fists. There was only one solution. He had to keep her alive. *He had to keep her alive.* But shit, he had to find Cardiff first. How could he focus on both? What if Alice wanted to go off after Catherine, and he needed to track down Cardiff? How could he let her walk away unprotected? *Shit!*

"I did what I had to do," she said.

"No. You didn't." He glared at her. "There are other options besides inviting an assassin after you. You have no control over how that will play out. What were you thinking?"

Defiance flared in her eyes. "I told you! I owe Catherine, and you wouldn't help—"

"There are other solutions," he snapped. "There always are."

"There's no other option. Catherine has to die!"

"Why?" He grabbed her arm. "Tell me why!"

"Because—" Alice hesitated. "I can't betray her. It's her secret. But trust me, she needs to die."

Ian closed his eyes at her request. Trust her? Trust her that some angel he'd never met should be killed in cold blood? "How do I trust that request?" he asked. "It goes against everything that defines who I am."

"Killing her goes against everything that defines who I am as well," Alice said. "That's why you should trust me. If I am willing to do it, there must be a reason."

Ian met her gaze and reached out with his mind, brushing against hers. She stiffened and raised her shields against him. "You want me to trust you when you won't let me in?"

"You have loyalty to the Order. I'm loyal to Catherine. How is that different?"

He ran his hand through his hair. "My loyalty didn't compel me to invite an assassin to find me. That's the difference."

She pressed her lips together, and he suddenly saw the pinched skin around her mouth, and the tightness around her eyes. He realized she was terrified of Flynn coming after her. Shit. What had she done? "Alice, I will do what I can to help you. But you need to trust me. If you see Flynn, tell me. I can't help you if I don't know what's going on."

For a long moment, Alice said nothing, then she gave a slight nod. "I feel like I'm so out of my depth," she admitted.

He grinned, relieved that she was connecting with him again. "Yeah, well, you got me, so don't sweat it. I'm a good weapon to have—"

The boat suddenly stopped.

They both turned around as the dolphins shed their harnesses and dove out of sight. There was a slap of their tails on the surface, and then they were gone, leaving the dinghy drifting in the vast sea.

Alice frowned and looked around. "We must be at Warwick's."

They were surrounded by ocean on all sides. Blue sky. Green ocean. Nothing else. "Do you see it?"

"No." Alice leaned over the edge of the boat and touched the water. "But Jada said it was hidden to all except those who know."

"So, we must know, then, right?" Ian closed his eyes and opened his preternatural senses. He breathed in the fullness of the air. He tasted salt in the wind...and soil. He smelled grass and flowers. He could hear the sounds of tiny claws skittering along dead leaves and the sound of leaves rippling in the wind. "We're here," he said. He opened his senses further, using the powers and skills his father had taught him so many years ago in the woods, to see with his mind and not with his eyes. He sensed the life force around them. Plants, animals, and the pulsing call of the earth itself. Tangled in the midst was the cold, dank energy of black magic, coating his pores like a heavy syrup of death and danger.

The brands in his arms began to burn, and he instinctively reached out for Alice, drawing her closer against him while he called out his mace with a crack and a flash of black light.

"Where is it?" Alice asked.

"Can't you feel it?" Keeping his eyes closed, he turned in a slow circle, using his preternatural senses like a radar, sending it out into the air. So much space and air over the water to the north and the west. He turned again to the east. More open space. He turned again, facing due south, and sent out a wave of energy.

It vanished, absorbed by whatever was in front of them.

He opened his eyes, but saw only ocean.

Alice was leaning forward, her gaze riveted in the same spot his was. She was holding out her palm, the one with the gray mark. "I can feel him," she said. "I can sense his magic."

Ian leaned over the edge of the boat and peered into the water. Just ocean. No sand. "Where is it?" It was here somewhere. He knew it was. But where?

Alice went down on her knees and stuck her hand in the water. It came away wet. She frowned. "I could swear it was right here."

"Me, too."

He crouched beside her and shoved his mace into the water. It sliced through easily, and he could see the blade beneath the surface of the water. "Just ocean."

For a moment, the two of them sat there, staring at the island that wasn't there. "Cardiff believes in angels," Alice finally said.

"So?"

"So, angels can't be proven. We don't look special or wear halos or float down from heaven." She chewed her lip. "You have to take us on faith."

Ian looked back across the expanse of water. "Faith." Faith wasn't a word he'd believed in. He believed in making things happen, in fighting relentlessly to discover the right solution. Faith was for people who didn't take action. He looked over at her. "Do you have faith?"

"Not really," she said, and there was no mistaking the regret in her voice. "And I should." Slowly, she rose to her feet. "Faith is the most powerful tool any of us can have," she said. "As powerful as angels are, there's nothing we can do for those who don't believe in us and allow us to help."

He raised his brows. "So, maybe that's why you can't save anyone. Because the people you want to save don't believe in you."

She looked over at him. "My mother was an angel. Of course she believed in me."

"So maybe you're the one without faith. You don't believe in yourself."

Her mouth tightened, and she inclined her head. "Entirely possible." She turned back toward the water again. "Cardiff has faith," she whispered. "Faith is what it's all about." She took a deep breath, and before Ian could stop her, she stepped up onto the edge of the boat.

"Hey." Ian eased toward her, his heart starting to race. "What are you doing?"

"I'm taking a leap of faith." And then she jumped.

Ian lunged for her, but his hands closed around empty air. He stopped in surprise, realizing that she had literally disappeared. Not into the water. She'd just vanished. Into Cardiff's hidden kingdom?

It didn't matter where she was. Alice was unprotected, and he was going after her. Without a second thought or a moment of hesitation, Ian threw himself off the edge of the boat and into the air, his mace ready.

† † †

Alice startled, jumping to the side when Ian burst out of the mist and landed beside her, his boots thumping on the damp earth. When she saw it was him, she relaxed...slightly. He was better than an insane, murderous wizard, but he'd made it pretty clear he wasn't the shiny-cheeked answer to her dreams.

Ian let out his breath in a low whistle. "Holy shit," he said as he looked around.

"I know. It's incredible." They were deep in a jungle, with massive trees towering so high they blocked out the sun. The vegetation was thick and green, with vines and moss dangling from branches. Bushes with leaves two feet wide surrounded them, and the squeaks and chirps of animals were a tremendous cacophony of noise. But the most incredible things were the flowers that towered above them. Pink, blue, yellow... every color imaginable, in every shape possible. They twisted around tree trunks, dangled from branches, squeezed out between leaves, and popped up from the dirt. The fragrance was astonishing, the deeply rich scents of flowers so vibrant that she wanted to close her eyes and simply breathe.

It was a sanctuary, an oasis in the middle of a vast ocean. A place of beauty and nature, so unlike what she would have expected from a wizard steeped in black magic and death. "It's beautiful." She started to walk toward a bush of violet flowers, but Ian grabbed her arm and yanked her back.

"Stop."

The urgency in his voice made her freeze. "What is it?"

"Give me a sec." He looked around, and she felt his energy rippling through the air. After a moment, he looked at the ground she'd been walking toward. He hurled his mace at the earth, and the moment the blade made contact with the ground, there was an explosion. The earth vanished, replaced by a bottomless pit seething with black and purple smoke.

"Oh, wow." Alice started to retreat, but Ian forced her to stop again as he recalled his mace from the pit.

He jammed his mace into the earth behind them, and the same thing happened. It simply crumbled beneath his weapon, revealing another gaping hole bubbling with noxious mist. Ian swore under his breath, and recalled his mace as it plummeted down the bottomless hole. "The beauty is a trap," he said. "A distraction."

A trap. The most beautiful things she'd ever seen were simply a facade for death and destruction. The realization was almost devastating, as if she'd finally opened her heart enough to trust the good, the beauty, and it was all a lie. Was how she felt about Ian a lie as well?

"Stay here." Ian hurled his mace all around them. Hole after hole after hole opened up, until the only solid earth was the four-foot piece of ground they were standing on. Everything beautiful was gone. Had it ever been there, or was it all simply an illusion?

"Don't throw it at our feet," she said as he looked around, ostensibly for another spot to test. Not that there was anything left. He'd opened up the entire area around them, so they were perched on what felt like the head of a pin, standing precariously in the middle of bottomless chasms of torment and death.

Not her first choice of places to be, she had to admit.

"It wouldn't make a difference if I hit the earth we're standing on. We're on solid ground. The dolphins knew where to deliver us." He looked around. "The question is, how do we get out of here?"

He slung his arm around her shoulder and hauled her against him, as if to ensure that she didn't accidentally step off the ledge and free-fall to a gnarly conclusion. There was nowhere else to go given their tiny sanctuary, but she had to admit that being tucked up against his strong body felt like the right place to be. She could feel his calmness, and it soothed her nerves, giving her the ability not to panic. Ian gave her security and stability, and it felt amazing. But were her feelings no more real than the beauty that had welcomed them? Was Ian just one mace strike from disintegrating into a poisonous death for her?

Probably, he said. *You gotta watch out for the guys who carry weapons. We're an unpredictable bunch.*

Alice stiffened at the brush of warmth in her mind that

seemed to cascade through her, igniting her body the same way he always did. *Do you really have so little sense of privacy?*

I've spent half a millennium running around the earth with a bunch of sweaty guys who wind up naked, almost dead, and bleeding several times a week. Privacy isn't going to keep us alive, babe. I don't believe in it. Well, I do!

He tightened his grip on her and looked down at her. His eyes were blazing with adrenaline and heat. *Well, I don't.* And before she could stop him, he bent his head and kissed her. Not a simple kiss designed to ease her terror at their predicament, like a nice guy would offer her.

It was a statement of ownership from a soldier in the middle of a battle, a man whose testosterone was raging, who was in the mindset to dominate, outsmart, and survive. And of course, it plunged straight into her soul, awakening everything that made her a woman. She didn't care that they were balanced precariously on the tip of the earth. She forgot that there were noxious fumes and a bottomless pit surrounding them. She lost sight of the betrayal of the beautiful flowers being so deadly. All that mattered to her was the feel of his mouth on hers, the heat from his body consuming her, the untamed power in his arms as they crushed her against him. She melted into the kiss, accepting all that he thrust at her, loving every bruising kiss he gave her.

As she kissed him back, the tension and fear that had been dogging her melted away, replaced by the sensation of being cradled in a basin of warmth, safety, and unstoppable desire. The world became about the two of them, and the magic they could create with their kisses. She wanted more. She wanted all of him. She wanted him to make love to her like he'd done before, only this time, she wanted it to be about them, not about him trying to make his brand appear on her arm or break through her barriers.

She wanted Ian to make love to her, Alice Shaw, simply

because she was the woman who touched his heart.

Hell, Alice. Ian wrenched his mouth off hers, breaking the kiss. *We can't do this right now.*

She almost cried out in protest as he deprived her of the kiss, and she had to struggle to resist the need to beg for more. Ian was right. Of course he was right. This wasn't the time or place for anything like this. What was wrong with her? Had she completely lost her mind?

No, you haven't. Ian caught her under the chin and raised her face so she met his gaze. *I heard your thoughts when we were kissing, and I want you to know that there is nothing I would like more than to make long, slow, leisurely love to you for no other reason than that you are the woman who brings light into my life.*

Alice's throat tightened. "Stop it," she said. "Don't say things that you don't mean—"

"Oh, I mean it." He cut her off with a kiss, a long, tender kiss that made tears sting her eyes. *When we get out of here, that is exactly what I am going to do to you.* He pulled back so she could see the promise in his eyes. "Because I want it even more than you do. Got it?"

Alice nodded, her throat too tight to answer. No one had ever said anything like that to her, making her feel like she was special simply because of who she was.

He grinned. "Hell, woman, you're a lot of things that make me crazy, but special? You're in a category that no one else can touch." He squeezed her once, then turned away to scan their surroundings, keeping her anchored against him. "I have to admit, the thought of making love to you is a damned good incentive for getting us out of here alive. I'd hate to die and miss it."

She almost laughed at his comment. "That is such a guy statement, not wanting to die because you might miss out on some great sex."

He rubbed his hand seductively over her lower back,

even as he continued to evaluate their surroundings. "It was great sex, wasn't it?"

She felt her cheeks heat up. "Yes," she admitted.

"And just think, I got better than that to show you." He winked at her. "Now you don't want to die either, do you?"

"I don't want to die for other reasons."

"Yeah, but the sex is a good one."

She poked his side. "You're such a dork."

"But a hot one." His eyes narrowed as he zeroed in on the trees nearest them, and she saw the moment he stopped being a playful lover and stepped fully into his role as a warrior.

With a happy sigh that was so incongruous to the situation they were in, Alice wrapped her arms around Ian's waist and peered past him at their surroundings. So weird that she felt safe and content right now, given everything that was going on, but she did. At least, she felt secure enough to be able to think rationally and not be overwhelmed. The power of a good kiss and a hard male body could not be underestimated. She pointed out at the trees. "The trees must be on solid ground, right?" There had to be something around them that wouldn't disintegrate from Ian's mace.

"Maybe." Ian hurled his mace at a tree, and it instantly exploded into a raging inferno so hot that she felt like her skin was on fire. Ian swore and pulled her behind him, his body blocking the heat. As they watched, the other trees caught fire in a weirdly surreal domino effect, until they were in the middle of a towering firestorm of orange and purple flames. "So, the answer to your question about the trees being on solid ground seems sort of irrelevant now," he observed. "Given that they all just blew up."

"Yes, I would agree." Alice tensed as the flames leapt across the gap to the patch of earth they stood on, landing on her bare foot. She jumped at the pain, and Ian stomped out sparks as they flickered at their feet. Fire raged all around them, and toxic fumes poured out of the earth below them.

There was nowhere to go, and the smoke from both sources was getting thicker and thicker. Alice coughed as her lungs started to burn, and Ian pulled her shirt up so it covered her mouth and nose.

"What now?" she asked, shouting over the roar of the flames.

He swore. "Do you trust me?"

She stared at him. What kind of question was that to be asking right now? All she wanted was for him to maybe pound his chest and let out a Tarzan yell before he grabbed her around the waist and carried her to safety. "I thought we already established that I don't!"

"Do you want to change your mind?"

"I—" Alice coughed as the toxic smog coated her lungs. Above her, thick smoke raged, blocking out the canopy of trees and flowers that had seemed so welcoming. Below her, chasms of death. Was there really a choice? Was there anyone to trust other than the man who would kill himself if anything happened to her? She let out her breath. "Yeah, okay. I can be willing to negotiate."

He grinned, a grim smile that made her heart leap just a little bit. He didn't look as worried as she felt. Did he really have a plan for this? "Time for a ride." He held out his arms. "Climb on."

Alice gritted her teeth as she leapt up on him. His strong arms pulled her legs around his hips, and she locked her arms around his neck. "Make sure you don't let go," he said. She tightened her grip and tucked her head against the curve of his neck. "What are you going to do?"

"Jump."

"Jump?" She couldn't keep the squeak of fear out of her voice. "Jump *where*?"

"Through the flames. I can smell soil on the other side." He backed up two steps to the edge of their mound of turf, enfolding her in his iron grip. "I can make it."

The flames were a good thirty yards away, and she had no idea how thick they were. How long could he stay airborne? And would the earth disintegrate when they landed? "Um, Ian? I don't think this is a good idea—"

"Let's go!" His body flexed beneath hers, and she felt power coil through him.

And then he leapt, straight into the fire.

The flames were hot, scorching Ian's skin, tearing at his flesh. He kept Alice cradled to him as they crashed through burning branches that whipped at his face. Swearing, he turned his body in the air so that his shoulders took the brunt of the impact, blocking the flaming whips from Alice's flesh.

He began to lose altitude, falling back down toward the ground, but they weren't through the flames yet. He needed more air time! He lunged for one of the burning branches. His palm was instantly fried as he grabbed it. He swung off it, flinging them further though the flames. "Come on!" he bellowed as he grabbed another one, and another, his skin melting from the heat as he swung them forward through the branches.

His muscles were screaming with pain as more branches lashed at him, tearing at his flesh, and still he went on. He couldn't let Alice fall. He couldn't let her down. He had to make it. Again and again, he grabbed for branches, hurling himself to the next one while Alice clung to him.

His hand slipped off a branch and he lunged for another one, but his fingers slid off that one as well. He knew that his hands were too burned to work. That he'd destroyed them. "No!" he yelled as he grabbed one more branch and flung them forward with every last bit of his strength.

They careened through the air, and suddenly the flames were gone. Fresh cool air gifted their lungs, and he cradled Alice as they plunged to the earth. He took the impact when they landed, using his body to protect her as they rolled across the bumpy earth.

Finally, they came to a stop, and Ian released her with a groan of pain. He struggled to his feet, shouting in pain as he called out his mace and the handle slammed into his palm. But he didn't relax, spinning around to assess their situation, needing to assure himself that they were safe before he went down.

They were in a pasture, filled with grass that seemed to undulate on its own and flowers that sparkled with mist that they shouldn't have. But he sensed no threats. No dangers. It was safe, for a moment at least.

He dropped to his knees, releasing the mace, fighting for consciousness as the pain raged through him. Never had he felt such agony. It was tearing at him, not just his hands, but through every cell of his body.

"Ian!" Alice knelt before him, her cool hands like a gift of salvation on his skin. "Are you okay?" Ian lifted his head and was shocked to see Alice was untouched. Her skin was unmarred, and even her clothes were pristine. He blinked, certain he'd seen wrong, but when he looked again, she was the same. Her green eyes were focused on his, full of fear and worry. "You're okay?" he rasped out.

"Yes, I'm fine." Her face grew darker with worry. "But you're not."

"No." His stomach began to contort with pain and he went down on the ground, fighting to stay conscious. "What's going on?"

Alice rolled him onto his back, her hands moving over his skin. "Oh, God, Ian. This is bad."

"You know what it is? Black magic?" But it didn't feel like black magic. It felt like he was dying from the inside out.

"No," she said. "It's Catherine. That was her trap. That's why it didn't hurt me. Her power doesn't work against me. We cancel each other out."

"Catherine?" He struggled to open his eyes, but his vision was streaked with patches of red and black. "What the hell is she? An angel of death?"

"Yes," Alice said. "And she just targeted you."

Chapter Fourteen

Panic hit Alice as she watched the black taint spread across Ian's skin. It was moving fast, faster than he could heal. Of course it was. It was death.

Alice leapt to her feet, spinning around as she shouted at the idyllic setting. "Catherine," she screamed. "Stop it!" Her voice echoed and bounced across the fields, but there was no reply. Of course there was no reply. That was why she had to kill the woman who was so close to her that she might as well have been her sister.

"Dammit!" Alice fell to her knees beside Ian, her stomach churning when she saw the necrosis moving over his skin. Dear God, he was rotting alive. "Ian!"

His eyes were closed, and his lungs were rasping with each labored breath. "Now's the time," he rasped out. "Now or never, babe."

"Now or never, what?" She was horrified by the sight of his hands. They'd been incinerated by the tainted flames, and now were crumbling, rotting flesh, contaminating his arms. "Oh, God," she whispered.

"Angel of life," he managed.

"What?" She jerked her eyes toward him. "I can't save you!"

"If you're assigned to the Order, you're wrong," he said.

"You can save me."

"Save you?" God, if there was a way, *if there was a way.* Frantic, she pressed her hands to his chest, reaching through their bond to connect with him. He was wide open to her, and she immediately found herself deeply merged with him. She could feel his guilt and grief, but she was astonished by the sheer, raw determination pulsing through him. She knew now why he was the only one of his family still alive: he was too damned stubborn to die. Until now. No one could stop the angel of death.

As immortal as he was, he was no match for Catherine. No one was.

No one except an angel of life. His voice was raw and painful in her mind. *Come on, Alice.*

I'm trying! She could feel the blackness spreading through him, but she had no idea how to stop it. *What do I do?*

You're the angel. You— He stuttered with pain, and his body convulsed. *—decide.*

Me? Sweat broke out on her forehead, and tears burned in her eyes. *I don't know what to do!*

What do other angels do?

Alice frantically thought back to the angel compound she'd grown up in, trying to remember what the other angels had done when they'd tried to call upon their supernatural powers, something she'd never come close to figuring out how to do. Every time she'd been thwarted in trying to save someone's life, she'd been attempting an easy, obvious solution, like giving her mother dirt or Chloe a kiss. The answer had been obvious; she just hadn't been able to do it. But now? He was being poisoned by the angel of death. There was no easy antidote to that!

Alice, Ian gasped. *Now, sweetheart.*

Don't pressure me! Tears burning her eyes, Alice tried to quiet her mind and her spirit. She reached inside herself, trying to find the inner glow that Catherine always talked about, the place of quiet that was the source of her powers. But she couldn't find anything. There was just fear, anger, and guilt. A miasma of churning emotions that made it impossible for her to focus.

Ian's body jerked, and she grabbed his shoulders. *Mom,* she beseeched, reaching out to the heavens, *if you're out there somewhere, show me what to do! Show me how to save him!*

She held her breath, waiting, but of course, there was no response, no great illumination of knowledge filling her mind. *No!* She screamed, suddenly so angry that her mother had died. That she'd blamed Alice. That she'd left her alone. *I hate that you left me! I hate you!* The violent emotion tore through her, the fury and anger at being abandoned and rejected by her mother. Years of dark feelings erupted, and tears poured from her, so much pain, so much agony, and so much sadness. It rolled over her, like the darkest of hells, filling her with more than she'd ever felt before. It was too much, too overwhelming, and she cried from the force of it all.

Ian's hand moved, and his fingers entwined with hers. *I knew you had it in you,* he said. *I knew you were more than a reserved shell.* His warmth filled her, seeping through all the agony trying to consume her, and she lunged for it, holding onto it so desperately.

I don't know what to do, Ian. I don't know how to help you.

Ian's energy and his spirit began to fade, and she knew she was losing. *If you were part of the Order's trinity, you'd know what to do to save me. I thought you were my angel...*

There was a sudden hum in the air, and Alice spun around. The air was becoming translucent about ten feet away. Oh, God. Flynn? He was too early. Alice immediately called out Ian's mace, and she leapt in front of him, clenching her hands around the handle, putting herself between him and whatever threat was coming. *Ian! Don't die! Please hang on!*

The air seemed to shimmer and darken, and then three warriors appeared. Ryland and Vaughn, the men who had been at the beach with Ian, plus Kane Santiago, who had appeared at the last moment to transport them out of there.

Were they here to take Ian back? To kidnap her? "Stop," she shouted, holding out the mace. "Don't come near here!"

Ryland's eyes went black with rage, and there was so much taint rolling off him she could actually see a muddy black and brown aura forming around him. His gaze went past her to Ian, who was writhing on the ground, and he let out a roar of outrage. "What did you do to him?" He called out his machete, and hurled it at her as he sprinted toward them.

Kane shouted at him to stop, but Ry didn't hesitate. Alice yelped, and swung the mace. To her shock, it seemed to take on its own power, and it crashed into Ryland's machete inches from her face. The shock of the impact threw her back, and she fell to the ground next to Ian. Ry reached her just as she landed, and he called out his other machete, his face twisted with rage. "You killed him!"

"Stop it!" Kane suddenly materialized next to Ry, grabbed him and teleported him away, reforming at the other side of the field.

Ryland let out a roar of rage. A black light flashed, and suddenly Kane was down on the ground and Ry was racing toward her again, thick black and purple steam rolling off him. Dear God. He was insane!

Alice leapt to her feet, and grabbed Ian's mace, moving between Ry and Ian. "Stop it!" she shouted. "Ian's dying, and he needs your help! I didn't kill him! I'm an angel of life! I don't kill people!" But even as she shouted the words, she remembered how Esmeralda had fallen to Ian's weapon while she'd wielded it. She did kill people. For a split second, she hesitated, and then fury raced through her.

She was tired of being an angel of life who got it all wrong, the one who couldn't help those she cared about!

"Ryland, stop!" she screamed. "Don't be a fool! I need your help!"

But Ryland was enraged, his sanity torn to shreds at the sight of Ian dying. There was no way to stop him. "Dear God," she whispered in horror, watching as he bore down on her. "He's gone mad." She raised the mace, preparing to fight him, afraid he would accidentally kill Ian in his rage. "Get away from him," she shouted, but even as she said the words, Ry put on a burst of speed—

Vaughn stepped in front of her, into Ryland's path. He held out his hands, spread his palms, and raised his hands to the sky. His skin began to glow green, and the earth began to tremble and bubble below his feet. Lightning cracked across the sky, and dark purple clouds surged above their heads, cutting out the sunshine. The muscles across his back twitched and spasmed, and his skin began to undulate as if the very gods themselves were coming to life within him. "Stop!" he commanded, and his voice seemed to thunder through the pasture. He held his hands so that his palms faced Ryland, but the warrior didn't slow down.

Alice caught her breath as Ry neared Vaughn, neither warrior backing down. Ry raised his machete. "Get out of my way—"

Vaughn shoved his palms in Ryland's direction, as if pushing an invisible barrier at him. The Calydon was flung backwards with a violent explosion, his body twisting and contorting as he sailed through the air.

He slammed into a pile of rocks and didn't move.

Vaughn went down on his knees, his whole body shuddering from the force of what he'd done. To Alice's shock, he actually faded from sight, and then reappeared again, as if he were losing his solid form. Stunned, she gripped the mace tighter, not sure who was friend and who was foe now. Behind her, she could hear Ian's labored breathing, and panic began to hammer at her. "Someone help Ian," she shouted. "He's dying!"

Vaughn turned toward her. His eyes had the faintest glow of green around the edges, and his muscles were straining against his skin. The tendons in his neck were bulging, as if he was fighting to stay in control. She braced herself, waiting for him to turn it on her as well. But he didn't. Before her eyes, he seemed to suck all that power back into his body. The earth stopped moving, the sky cleared, and his eyes returned to a dark brown. The only sign that he'd just blown Ryland across the clearing was the fact that a faint green glow emanated from his palms. "You called," he said.

Alice blinked. "What?"

"You called Flynn. I heard it." He looked past her, searching the woods, where the flames were beginning to fade. "He'll be here soon. He wouldn't have missed your call either." Vaughn's eyes were hooded and dark as he looked at her, troubled, even. "Why would you call him? He wants to kill you."

Alice raised her chin. "I know he does. That's why I called him."

"You want him to kill you?" At her nod, Vaughn narrowed his eyes. "You're a woman of courage."

She was so surprised by the statement, that she wasn't sure how to respond. "I'm not—"

"You are." Vaughn strode forward, and laid his hand on her cheek. His hand was cold, ice cold, as if he'd drained himself of all life during his attack on Ryland. For a moment, she thought he was going to say something, then he turned and walked away, his body moving with lithe, predatory grace as he blended in with his surroundings, disappearing in plain sight. What in heaven's name was he?

Before she could ask, sharp pain began to resonate through her arm. She looked down and saw an angry dark line cutting through the brand on her arm, filling in the outline even further. She tensed as she watched it form. Another stage of the bond? What had she done?

"You satisfied your half of the death stage when you risked your life to save his by jumping in Ryland's path," Kane said, startling her when he spoke from right behind her shoulder. His voice was heavy with respect. "You're a crazy woman, aren't you? No one in their right mind would stand in front of Ry when he has snapped." He sounded impressed, and it almost made her smile. "Ian's lucky he's got you. The bond is almost complete. How many stages do you have left?"

"His half of both the trust stage and the death stage. That's it." Two half stages away. So close to the Calydon destiny that would destroy them. As lovely as it was to have Kane's warmth and approval directed at her after a lifetime of being on the outside, Alice knew it wouldn't matter, not if Ian died. She jerked her arm down, fighting off the mixture of emotions arising from seeing Ian's mark on her arm: satisfaction, fear, uncertainty. "Can you help him? He's dying."

Kane strode over to him and crouched down. "Save him."

"I tried." She hurried over and knelt beside him, taking Ian's hand between hers. "I can't."

There was a grunt, and she looked up as Ryland rolled to his knees. He was bracing his hands on the ground, his head bowed. She tensed, but he raised his head, and she saw that the poisonous aura around him had faded. It was still there ever so slightly, but it no longer controlled him. "Ian," he rasped out as he stumbled to his feet.

This time, no one stopped him as he sprinted across the clearing, falling to his knees beside Ian, whose skin was now mottled with black and purple that was creeping up his neck, dotting his cheeks. It had almost consumed him. Once it covered him, it would be the end.

"Son of a bitch," Ryland said. He looked at Alice, his eyes simmering with rage. "Save him," he demanded.

"I can't—"

"You can!" He lunged for her, grabbing her by the throat

before Kane could stop him. His fingers were tight, but not hurting, not yet. "You're an angel of life. You're the angel of life that protects the Order. It's your job!"

"I tried," she shouted, screaming at him. "Nothing works!"

"Son of a bitch," Kane said. "He's not Order right now. That's why. Quinn and Gideon suspended him when he took off with you."

Alice's stomach dropped. "You actually expelled him? How could you do that?" The one thing that mattered to Ian was the Order and honoring his oath, and yet he'd lost that? Ian convulsed, and she felt a stab of pain from him. Quickly, she put her hand on his forehead, trying to comfort him. *I believe in you, Ian.*

He didn't respond.

Ryland's eyes glittered. "Ian betrayed the Order. There was no choice."

"There's always a choice," she snapped.

"Is there? Then choose to save him," Ryland said.

"I can't!"

Disgust flared in Ryland's eyes, disappointment so bitter that she felt it in her own heart. When she'd first met Ryland, he'd gone down on one knee to honor her. Now? He looked like she wasn't worth the effort of saying her name.

"Shit!" Ryland released her with such force she fell back. "We need to reinstate him. Right now."

Kane shook his head. "We don't have time for an entire ceremony. There's no way to do it that fast. He's dying right now."

"Fuck!" Ryland slammed his fist down so hard a crack split the earth. "We can't lose him." His face contorted with anguish, and he bowed his head, his body trembling with the effort of holding back the dark forces within him. Alice didn't know what he was, but she knew she'd seen that kind of taint before. Slowly, he raised his head, his eyes glittering as he looked at Alice. "It's up to you, angel. How do we make this right?" He called out his machete and held it to her throat. "And you *will* find a way."

Alice stared at the machete, her heart hammering. She knew she couldn't save him. She'd already tried. "Why can't you save him? Can't you offer him your healing capacity, like he did with me?"

Ry and Kane exchanged grim looks, then they nodded. Alice's throat tightened as both warriors bent over Ian, their hands on his chest. The air between them began to hum, and she heard their voices reaching out to their fallen Order member.

Ian. Kane's voice was first. *Come back to us.* As he spoke, Alice felt a rush of healing warmth fill Ian. It poured into the atmosphere, a burning hot strength that seemed to ignite the air. It was like what Ian had done for her, but without the sexual undertones.

Fitz. Ryland's words were rough and dark, laced with a lethal force that made her skin crawl. *Dante would kick your ass if you gave it up right now. Get your shit together.* Then his energy joined Kane's and filled Ian's body.

Alice's throat tightened at the sight of the two massive warriors fighting so hard to save the life of their fallen comrade. It was obvious that it didn't matter that Ian had been kicked out of the Order. Their commitment to him was absolute, and she felt the urgency of their need to save him.

"Alice," Kane said. "Connect with him."

She shook her head, feeling so useless and isolated. "I can't help him—"

"Maybe not as an angel, but you can as his mate." Kane's voice was rough and low, laced with the energy he was pouring into Ian. "Trust me when I tell you that the power you carry for him is off the charts. You can make a difference, just you alone, not as an angel."

Alice hesitated, all too aware of her limitations. "You

241

don't understand. I truly can't save anyone's life—"

"He doesn't need you to save it," Ryland snapped, glowering at her. "Just be there for him, tell the bastard you love him, and give him a reason to fight to come back."

Heat fused through her. "I don't love him—"

"Fuck that you don't." Ryland's eyes had turned a turbulent shade of purple. "You're an angel. Don't you love everyone? Isn't that what angels do? You're his damned mate. Be an angel to him!" As he spoke, he grabbed Alice's hand and slammed it down on Ian's chest. "Love him!" he commanded. "Now!"

The minute her hand touched Ian, Alice was inundated with the pain ricocheting through him. Her heart tightened, and she huddled over him, suddenly overwhelmed with the need to bring him peace, to take away the pain. *Ian. It's me. You can do this.*

"Offer him your golden healing light," Ry demanded. "You have that, don't you?"

Alice shot him a surprised look. "How do you know about our golden light?" Golden lights were something angels could give only once every thousand years, to a soul deemed worthy of receiving it, a soul that was so important that humanity would suffer if it died. Only souls of the greatest power and in the deepest agony could handle it. Every angel had it to offer, but it was a great risk because it would overwhelm all but the strongest souls. It wasn't a life-saving light. It was a light of peace and comfort. A light to heal the soul. It was a gift from one pure heart to another, a finding of serenity through the blackest of nights. Had an angel once given it to Ryland? Is that how he knew about it? No. It was impossible. No one who carried the amount of darkness that Ryland did could have been able to receive it. So, how did he know about it?

"Give it to him!" Ryland grabbed her shoulders and shook her, his eyes blazing ruthlessly. "Give him your golden light!"

Kane was staring at her. "Ian's my friend," he said. "You better not hold back anything you can offer him."

"It won't save his life," she explained. "That's not what it's for. It's for the healing of the soul and the offering of peace. It can be offered only to someone of great importance to angels, someone deemed worthy—"

Alice?

Alice looked down as Ian's voice wafted through her mind. His body was arched in pain, and his mouth was twisted in discomfort. Tears filled her eyes at his torment. How could she let him suffer like that? She couldn't save his life, but Ryland was right. This man, her soul mate, the man who had touched her heart, he deserved all that she could give him.

Suddenly, she didn't care that Ian wouldn't fit the requirements of a soul worthy of receiving the golden light. Screw that! He had opened her to feelings and emotions she'd craved her whole life, and now he was dying because he'd tried to save them. What could be more deserving than that? Yes, maybe he couldn't make the earth spin, but dammit, he made her world spin, and that was enough.

Screw angel rules. She was giving her light to him, and that was the way it was.

Leaning over him so her hair dangled on his chest, Alice pressed her palms to his chest. She'd never called upon her golden light, but she instinctively knew exactly how to do it. She closed her eyes and took a deep breath, reaching inside her for the golden light that burned so brightly in every angel. The one that could never be shared, except for that one moment, that one rare moment when it was right.

She inhaled again, opening her heart to the beauty of the golden light. It began as a small glow, and she gently called to it, asking it for help. *Please offer peace to Ian,* she asked. *He is in pain.*

She was vaguely aware of Kane and Ryland bent over Ian beside her as they infused Ian with their healing energy, offering to him what they carried within themselves. It was strangely comforting to be wedged between their broad shoulders, to be sandwiched between their bulky frames as they all worked together as a team. She could feel their energy infusing her through her connection with Ian, and it was incredible how pure and strong their life forces were. They were completely committed to Ian, giving him everything they had, their low voices talking to him as they helped his body fight off the poison.

The golden light began to swell inside her, and Alice held out her hands and cupped them. As she watched, her arms began to emanate a faint golden energy that slid over the brands to her hands. A golden ball formed in her hands, a whirring sphere of energy so bright that Kane shaded his eyes.

But not Ryland. He was staring at it, riveted by the orb, even as he continued to pour his healing strength into Ian. He raised one hand and brushed his index finger through the glowing light that was reflected like the flames of candles in his eyes. "I can't feel it," he said.

"That's because it's not for you." Alice moved her hands over Ian's heart as the golden light sparkled and drizzled between her fingers. A large droplet splashed on Ian's chest, melting right through his shirt. He sucked in his breath and shuddered. *Ian.* She reached out, connecting to his mind. *This is my gift to you. The peace you've never had.* Then she tipped her hands, and the orb spilled out and landed on his chest. For a moment, it glowed brightly, as if it were the sun itself, and then it melted into him, spilling out across his body. His skin turned gold, radiating the most beautiful orange and amber colors.

"It's incredible," Ryland whispered as his energy suddenly surged, blasting Ian with unbelievable amounts of healing power.

Ian gasped and his body convulsed.

"Bring it back, Ry!" Kane ordered. "It's too much!"

Alice's heart jumped as the two warriors tried to balance the energy they were feeding Ian. She tried to shut them out as she focused on Ian. Putting the golden light in him was only part of it. The other part of the healing and peace had to come from her.

She closed her eyes and concentrated on the warmth of his skin beneath her palms. She focused on the steady thump of his heart, slowing hers until it matched his. She allowed the golden light to spread through her, lifting her own heart. The most astonishing sense of serenity seemed to take over her, releasing the tension that she'd held for so long. Her shoulders relaxed, her arms felt limp, and her heart seemed to take a giant breath and simply let go. It was the purest of emotions, the gift of complete peace in her soul, and she gave it to Ian.

CHAPTER FIFTEEN

Serenity.

Peace.

Tranquility.

Beauty.

Words foreign to Ian filled his mind and took over his consciousness. He felt the most incredible sensation of peace cascade through him, like millions of sparkling snowflakes on a moonlit night. Six hundred years of tension and hardship floated away, leaving him with a quietness in his soul that was incredible.

Ian. Accept this gift I offer you.

Alice's voice was so soft and beautiful in his mind, like the sound of angels singing just for him. Her presence seemed to fill him, an incredible gift of peace and love. Golden light blossomed in his mind and before his eyes, but it didn't blind him. It simply wiped away six centuries of grit and hell, until all that was left was the sensation of rightness, that all was well. *Alice.* He wanted to reach for her, but he couldn't seem to move his hands. He became vaguely aware of a searing pain in his body, of Ryland and Kane chanting in his mind, but he couldn't bring himself to worry about it. He just wanted to see Alice, to feel her touch, to breathe her into his being. She was all he needed. *Where are you?*

Right here, Ian. Her fingers slid between his, squeezing gently. *Will you accept my gift?*

Yes. He couldn't believe how right it felt to have her hand in his, and to feel the delicate warmth of her touch. He couldn't remember the last time anyone had touched him like that, as if he were a treasure that needed to be soothed. He liked it. Really liked it. He tried to squeeze her hand, but he couldn't make his fingers respond. *Why can't I move?*

You had a bit of a run-in with an angel of death. You need to heal yourself. Can you feel Kane and Ryland? They're helping you.

Her voice was like magical bells in his mind, and he sighed deeply, basking in the sensation of her presence. *They're saving me? They're trying. But you need to help.* The golden light seemed to glow brighter, and Ian took a deep breath, cleansing his lungs. Tension seemed to dissolve from him, and the despair that had weighed him down for so long seemed to vanish. He had no fear of Alice or their connection or the ill-fated *sheva* destiny. It simply felt good and right.

Come on, man. Ry intruded upon his moment of tranquility. *You gotta help us. If you don't save your ass, then I'm going to take your angel and keep her. She's fucking incredible.*

Possessiveness thrummed through Ian, and urgency began to simmer inside him. A need to claim his woman, to make her his. He began to struggle to regain consciousness, to move his body. *Alice. Where are you?*

Here. Her fingers tightened in his. *Always here.*

Ian focused on her hand in his, on the tightness of her grip. She was there with him. She wasn't leaving. All was well. *All was well.* The words seemed to free him, and he felt power begin to build inside him, strength that had been deteriorating as he'd fought the curse. Without the fear or despair holding him back, there was no longer a drain on his resources. He focused on the healing energy coming from Kane and Ryland and fed it through his body. He found the black pockets of poison in his soul, and he summoned his own healing strength and joined with his teammates to purge it. One by one they attacked the poison spots, and Ian never let go of Alice's hand. The golden light continued to burn brightly, filling him with her spirit, and the most incredible sense of calmness and hope.

He didn't need to die today. He didn't need to die ever. *Alice?* This time, he managed to tighten his fingers slightly, and he wanted to shout at the victory of locking her hand more securely in his, of claiming her.

I'm still here, Ian.

I'm not giving up. It can work out. We can make it all work out okay.

A wave of her emotions crashed over him. A yearning so powerful it seemed to come alive and plunge into his chest. *Don't say that, Ian. I can't deal with that—*

It's true! Fierce determination flooded him, and he fought the poison even harder. He needed to open his eyes. He wanted to see her face. He had to make her understand that there was hope, that there was always a chance. With a roar, he and his teammates blasted through the last of the taint, the part that had locked around his heart. It shattered like a crystal ball, its fragments dispersing harmlessly through him as the unified Calydon healing energy swallowed the last bits up.

Air rushed back into Ian's lungs, and he gasped, sucking in oxygen as he bolted upright. The first thing he saw was Alice leaning over him, her auburn hair framing her face like a silk curtain. "Alice!"

Joy flashed across her face, and he heard Kane and Ryland whoop with triumph. But his team didn't matter. Nothing mattered except Alice. He framed her face with his hands and pulled her to him so he could kiss her. Her lips were soft and warm, and sudden hunger exploded through him. He needed her, this woman who had given him the first peace he'd ever experienced in his life. *Alice.* He infused her name with all that he felt, with his gratitude, his awe, and his need for her.

A soft noise of desire echoed from her throat, and she kissed him back, a kiss of desperation, joy, need, and promises of so much more. Ian slid his hands around the back of her neck and—

Kane cleared his throat, jerking Ian back to the present. He swore and broke the kiss, grinning at his teammates as he slung his arm around Alice's shoulders so she tumbled against him. "Can't a guy get some privacy around here?"

"Shit, man." Ryland's hand slammed down on Ian's shoulder. "Good to have you back."

Kane let out a low whistle and sat back on his heels. His face was drawn from the effort of healing Ian, making Ian realize exactly how hard they'd all had to push to bring him back.

"Thanks, man." Ian slugged a handshake with Kane, who nodded once, then he glanced at Ryland. "Thanks, Ry—"

His words died in his throat when he saw the darkness in Ryland's eyes. It was getting worse, a man so close to the edge that it looked like he'd snap at any moment. "You okay?"

Ryland wiped his forearm over his forehead, leaving a streak of dirt through the beads of sweat. "Yeah, fine." His gaze flickered to Alice, and there was no mistaking the hint of awe in his expression. "Shit, man," Ry said. "You're one lucky bastard."

Ian grinned and pressed his lips to the top of Alice's head. "Yeah, I know."

She smiled up at him, and his heart almost stopped at how beautiful she was.

"You need to smile more," he said, tracing his fingers over her upturned lips. "You're radiant."

Her smile widened. "I'm just feeling the high of that golden light. It affects me, too."

"You're not basking in the joy that I lived to see another day?"

A mischievous light glinted in her eyes. "Of course not.

You're trouble." She held up her arm. "You're reeling me in, and last I heard, Calydons who fully bond with their mates meet a terrible demise. I want romance, not ugly endings."

A smug possessiveness thrummed through Ian at the sight of his almost-complete brand. "I'll romance you," he said. "I'll bet there's a lot of info on the internet about how to romance a woman."

"Flowers," Kane said. "Chocolate. Foot massages." He grinned, looking like a freaking Cheshire cat who'd just swallowed a whole can of caviar. "And get her knocked up. Women go soft for babies."

Alice's cheeks flamed red, and a strange emotion settled in Ian's chest. Something that made his lungs feel sort of thick and heavy.

"Babies?" Ryland snorted, moving away from them. "Jesus, Kane. We're in a war zone and you're talking about babies?" Tension radiated through his body again, and he shifted restlessly. "Why in God's name would you bring a kid into this world when it's crumbling down around us?" The venom in his voice was virulent and sharp. His eyes were a turbulent purple and black, and there seemed to be a faint black cloud around him. He shook his head. "No kids. No fucking kids." Then he turned and walked off, his body rigid.

Ian pulled Alice closer to him as he watched Ry. "He's going to go any day," he said. "Now that Dante's dead, there's no one to keep him in balance." Dante had been the Order's leader since before any of the current team had joined them. He'd brought them all together, and created a unit that had been struggling to hold together since his death.

"Thano had a connection with Ry," Kane said. "If Thano's really dead, Ry won't hold out. His only mission since Thano disappeared has been to get him back."

Ian thought of the irreverent warrior who never missed a chance to remind them that they were all old geezers in comparison to his thirty-five years of life. Thano was the one who was always there with a quip to diffuse the tension when things got too heated. Resolution flowed through him. "I want him back, too."

"Me, too." Kane's eyes glittered. "If he's alive, we'll find him." He glanced at Ryland, then leaned toward Alice. "Can you give Ry some of that golden light? He could use that peace."

Alice shook her head. "An angel can offer it once a millennium. I can't."

Ian looked sharply at Alice. "Once every thousand years? That's it?"

She nodded. *I wasn't supposed to give it to you. But I did.*

Son of a bitch. She'd chosen him to receive it? Suddenly, he felt overwhelmed by the moment. He took her hand and pressed his lips to her palm, not even sure what he wanted to say or how to say it. As he kissed her, he suddenly noticed that the pocket of her shorts was glowing blood-red. He paused. *Alice? What's that?*

She looked down, and her face paled. *It's activated.*
What is?

The pearl. It glows only when it is called into duty to protect an angel from becoming a Mageaan. I must have crossed that line when I gave you my golden light.

Ian scowled. *Take it back. I don't want you to risk yourself like that.*

But instead of the fear he expected to see on Alice's face, she gave him a serene smile and touched his jaw. It was a tender, incredible smile that touched his very soul. *It's okay, Ian. I knew that might happen. It was worth it.*

Shit. Ian knew then and there that he had to find a way to save her. End of story.

"Ryland needs some of that golden light." Kane sighed and ran his hand through his hair, oblivious to the revelation Alice had just shared with Ian. "I'll ask my wife if she can give him some."

"Wife?" Ian looked sharply at Kane. "You married her?"

The soul mate bond was so powerful that Calydons rarely bothered to get married. They were sucked into the bond, and then went rogue. No time for flowers and wedding processions.

Kane grinned. "Hell, yeah." He held up his hand, and Ian saw a black and silver band on his ring finger. Engraved on it were two spiked flails, his weapon, with their chains interwoven by a halo. "Wedding band and everything."

"Shit." Ian looked over at Alice, and sudden regret filled him that he'd never have that chance. He would die. She would die. One or both of them would die.

Alice seemed to feel the heat of his stare, and she glanced at him. In her eyes was such stark longing that his chest tightened, but at the same time, her jaw was tight with grim resolution and the acknowledgment of reality.

"Nice work, by the way." Kane held out his hand. "Welcome to the team, Alice."

Her expression softened with warm surprise as she shook his hand. "Thank you."

Kane nodded. "My *sheva* is Sarah Burns. She's our angel of hope. She's been looking forward to meeting you. She hasn't met a lot of angels."

Alice cleared her throat. "Well, I look forward to meeting her." But her voice was flat, and Ian knew it was because she was thinking that she wouldn't live long enough to make that trip. Despite the residual glow of the golden light, the reality was that she had still been killed by the wizard, and eventually death would catch up with her.

The idea settled darkly around Ian as he slid his hand around Alice's arm and gently helped her stand, emotions warring at him. She'd given him a gift of such incredible power, a gift she'd never be able to give to anyone else, not even Catherine. She'd saved it for *him,* breaking rules so he could have it. He couldn't let her suffer for all eternity on his behalf. He had to find a way to stop the slide.

Kane grinned. "Sarah's pregnant. Did you know that?

Three months along and going strong. I didn't even know angels could get pregnant!"

Ian stared at Kane. "You're going to be a dad?" He hadn't heard that news. Shit, what planet had he been hiding on? "You're shitting me." He'd been teammates with Kane for centuries. He'd been in battles with him. They'd dragged each other from death, and they'd shed more blood than anyone ever should. And for him to be a *dad?* Ian couldn't imagine Kane hoisting some infant on his hip and making googly noises after getting home from taking out a bunch of rogues.

"No joke." Kane stood up, and there was no hiding the gleam of satisfaction on his face. "How about that, huh? We don't know if it's going to be a boy or a girl. It might be a demon. It might be an angel." He grinned. "Who the hell knows? But it's gonna be great."

To his surprise, a flicker of envy ran through Ian. And sadness. Kane's enthusiasm reminded Ian of his own father and what a great dad he'd been. Ian had never contemplated fatherhood, unwilling to risk his own children's future until he was able to break the curse. But as he felt the satisfaction rolling off Kane... Hell. Ian looked over at Alice, unable to keep his thoughts away from her when thinking of starting a family. She might not have had a mother who appreciated her, but he'd felt the depth of her soul, the warmth that was buried so deeply.

She'd be a great mom. He knew she would be.

Then Alice shivered, and his thoughts of some fairytale family vanished in the face of the reality they were dealing with. Alice was standing slightly away from them, her arms wrapped around her belly, her face pinched and worried as she distanced herself from the picture Kane was painting for her, a world he knew she didn't believe was accessible to her.

Protectiveness surged through him, a need to change her future, to make her feel safe, to make her face glow the way Kane's was.

She looked over at him, realized he was watching her, and smiled...a smile so beautiful it made his heart stop. *I'm so glad you're okay, Ian. It was worth it.*

I'm never worth that kind of sacrifice, sweetheart. But even as he said the words, he reached for her, drawing her into his arms for an embrace. As he buried his face in her hair and felt her body melt into his, he couldn't stop looking at Kane's goofy-ass grin. A child? A family? With Alice? Really?

"Son of a bitch." Ryland's explosive epithet had them all spinning around. He was standing at the end of the woods, staring into the trees that had been burning so fiercely before.

"What is it?" Ian's mace burned in his arm, and Kane called out his flail. "That pit you guys jumped over." Ryland turned to face him, his eyes blazing. "It's the same exact thing that took Thano." His eyes flashed. "Thano's here. He's fucking here. I know it."

Adrenaline rushed through Ian, and he strode over to stand beside Ryland. The pits that had nearly taken him and Alice were still there, bottomless holes of purple, green, and black smoke. "Thano got sucked into one of *those*?"

"Yeah. Almost got me too." Ry went down on one knee, peering over the edge. "Thano!" he bellowed. "Can you hear me?"

There was no response.

A long silence filled the night as all three warriors reached out with their minds, trying to connect with Thano telepathically. If he was near, they'd be able to reach him. If he was far away, only a warrior he was blood-bonded with could reach him, and none of them fit that bill.

Ian didn't pick up anything from Thano, and from the frustrated expressions on his team's faces, Ian knew they'd come up short, too. Ian grimaced, studying the seething cauldron below them. "You think he could have survived that?"

Alice walked up beside him, setting her hand on his arm. Ian instinctively pulled her against him, needing the physical connection with her. "It's not Catherine's trap," she said. "It's not death. So, he might have a chance."

"Catherine?" Ry looked up sharply, not bothering to rise from his knee. "Your sister? Her trap is death? What does that mean?"

Alice hesitated, and Ian knew she was retreating to her old self of holding back and playing by the rules.

"Alice." He took her hand. "What the hell does it matter if you contradict precedent now? There's no going back. You broke the rules by giving me that golden light. You've gone too far. It's time to do whatever the hell you want to do. Being safe gets you nowhere. You know that."

"But—" Alice started to protest, and then she stopped as Ian's words registered. She slipped her hand into her pocket and felt for the pearl that was protecting her, the pearl she would have to give up when they returned to Jada. What did it matter if she broke the rules now? She'd killed a woman. She'd given Ian the golden gift. Ian was right. There was no salvation for her.

A strange sense of liberation began to flow over her. After a lifetime of trying to play by rules that she hated, rules that stole from her everything she wanted to be, she'd crossed that line. She'd used the golden light on Ian, a light that was supposed to be preserved and offered only to someone who represented a greater purpose than themselves. Ian was simply himself, and she'd done it anyway. She'd never be able to go back, no matter how she tried to atone for what she'd done. She could only go forward, and make the most of what she had. To be free. *Free.*

Fierce determination flooded her, and she clenched her fist around the pearl as the reality of what she'd done settled on her. Yes, she would still die. Yes, she might be trapped as a Mageaan without the pearl to protect her, but right now, in this moment, she was free. Truly *free.* She smiled, a small smile that grew.

Ian grinned back, though there was no mistaking the worried shadows in his eyes. "Freedom," he said.

"Freedom," she agreed. She strode forward to the edge of the pit and crouched beside Ryland. "Catherine Taylor isn't my sister," she said. "She's my best friend, but not my actual sister."

Ry's pitch-black eyes were fastened on hers, as if he were riveted by her words. "What is she?"

"An angel of death."

Ryland's jaw flexed, and he closed his eyes, as if the news was more than he could handle. "An angel of death," he whispered. "Just like the oracle said."

"Oracle?" Ian crouched beside them. "What oracle?"

Ry's eyes opened, and recognition flared through Alice once again. Ryland was more than a Calydon. He was more than Order of the Blade. Something that rang a bell...

He stood up, breaking eye contact and moving out of range before she could place it. "Thano is here," he said. "And an angel of death." He called out his machete. "We need to find them both."

Kane was staring down into the chasm. "It really is exactly like the one that took Thano. I thought it had been made by demon magic."

"It is demon magic," Ian said. "Demon magic controlled by Warwick Cardiff, a black magic wizard. He's here. And if you saw the same pit before, then he must have created that one, too."

Kane looked up, his eyes glittering with fury. "Warwick Cardiff? Who is he?"

Ian felt a flash of triumph. Kane and Ryland were giving him their full attention now. For the first time in six hundred years, they were on board with his mission. "He's a wizard who harvests demon magic. He's the one who cursed my ancestor for killing his *sheva*. If he was the one trying to kill Kane's *sheva*, then he's the one targeting the Order. Not just me. The entire Order."

Kane ran his hand through his hair. "Why would he target the Order? Whoever is trying to kill our angels is after the Order." He gave a grim smile. "I get why he'd be pissed about his *sheva* getting killed. I'd probably go after you guys too if you killed Sarah. But why the entire Order?"

"I know why." Alice spoke up, and all the men turned to look at her. She was looking at Ian, and only Ian. "You all make choices in accordance with your Order oath. If it didn't drive you, you would be free to make the right choice—"

"The Order choice is the right choice," Ian interrupted. "I honor my duty—"

"Exactly!" She looked around at them. "Warwick believes that the oath the Order members take obscures their ability to do the right thing." She looked at Ian. "Didn't you say that Warwick's best friend was your ancestor? But that Augustus put his Order duty over their friendship?"

Ian nodded. "He did what was right—"

"He did what the Order oath convinced him was right." She looked around at the three stoic faces. "Don't you understand? Warwick is trying to free all of you and future Order members by destroying the Order, by giving heroes the freedom to think for themselves instead of playing by the rules."

Ryland's scowl deepened. "He wants to destroy the Order to free us? Fuck that." His fist tightened on the machete. "The Order is sacred. Dante's mission will be upheld by those carrying his torch."

"Sacred? Like murdering *shevas* to protect their males?" she challenged. "Would you really kill me if Ian and I finished bonding and he went rogue? Protect the greater good by killing me?"

Ian growled and moved in front of her as Ryland scowled. "If you are part of our angel trinity," he said, "then no. Ian would be the one to die. Protecting the Order assets to protect Dante's legacy is all that matters. Ian is one member. You protect us all. You are more important."

She blinked. "You would kill your teammate in cold blood?"

A muscle twitched in Ry's cheek. "I do what I have to, angel. It's what I live for." His eyes darkened. "Don't look for what I'm not," he said. "I don't give a shit about anything but making sure Dante's legacy is protected."

Kane studied him. "And angels," he said. "You care about angels."

Something flashed across Ry's face. "Our guardian angels, yeah. Because they're part of the fabric of the Order."

"No. Not just them," Kane challenged. "Any angel. Why?"

Ry's face darkened. "I honor Dante. Nothing else matters. If Warwick is trying to bring down his legacy, then I'll stop him."

Alice groaned in frustration. Didn't they understand what she was talking about? "What about the fact you're following the rules to kick Ian out of the Order, when you both know he's one of the best warriors you've ever had, and one of the most loyal?"

Guilt flashed through Kane's eyes. "We do what we need to do. He made his choice."

"Seriously?" She looked at Ian. "And what about how you're unwilling to help me kill Catherine because your first job is to find Warwick and end the curse because you owe your ancestors this great honor? All you think about is honor, and not the situation."

Ian's face darkened. "Are you trying to say that I should walk away from my oath to the Order and my family honor?"

Alice hesitated, knowing that those two things were what defined Ian. They were what had been driving him his whole life. The resistance on his face made her heart sink. She would never be most important to Ian. Just as her mother had always been more interested in angel activities than her own daughter, Ian would never put her first. Suddenly, the love that had blossomed so brightly in her heart when she'd offered him her golden light seemed to flicker and die.

None of the men standing before her would put their women first. Their first love was the Order. Blind, mindless adherence to traditions formed two thousand years ago. Fury boiled through her, anger that she'd finally broken through her boundaries, and yet these men were too stubborn to do the same. God, she almost understood why Warwick wanted to break them up. She understood, because she had been bound so deeply by rules for so long, and her mother had died for it. If she'd become brave earlier, her mother might still be living. With the pearl in her possession, who knows what she could have done? Instead, she spent her life hiding. Now, she had only days left to live. Well, dammit. She was going to make the most of those last days.

"Wait a second." Ryland held up his hand. "Did you just say you're here to kill Catherine? You're here to kill the angel who might be the third part of our trinity?"

Alice hesitated at the threat in his voice. "I'm here to do what I promised her I'd do." But as she thought of Catherine, she felt a vast warmth spread through her, a beautiful sensation so pure and amazing she wanted to cry. She'd always said she loved Catherine, but suddenly, for the first time in her life, she felt it in her heart. It was so powerful that it almost overwhelmed her. She knew it was so vivid because she was no longer fighting what she was, or allowing the strictures of her kind to rule her. Catherine was the source of support and friendship and family that had kept her heart beating her whole life, and suddenly, for the first time, she could feel, truly feel, how much Catherine meant to her.

She didn't want to kill her. She didn't want to lose her. Dear God, she didn't want to.

"What did you promise her you'd do? Kill her?" Ryland

pressed.

Alice took a deep breath, recalling that moment when she'd made that promise to Catherine, and she knew that no matter how badly it tore her up to do it, she had to make it happen. She owed it to Catherine to do what Catherine couldn't do herself. But as she studied the dark denial in Ryland's eyes, she knew that he would never allow it. "Catherine asked me to rescue her," she said evasively. "So, that's why I'm here."

"By killing her?" he asked.

She didn't need to answer him to know that she'd just acquired an enemy. Instead, she lifted her chin and faced his challenge. "What if killing her was the best thing for the Order?"

He said nothing, and she saw the conflict warring in his eyes. As loyal as Ian was to the Order, Ryland was even more intense, almost rabid with his commitment to their deceased leader. But so was his connection to angels, despite his denial. Which would win?

"I think," said Ian, breaking up the moment. "We need to find Warwick. He has answers all of us need. Let's start there."

For a long moment, Ryland didn't move, then he gave a curt nod. "Agreed."

Kane inclined his head. "Agreed."

Ian looked at her. "Alice?"

There was no need for her to find Warwick. His spell had already been cast on her. There was nothing that could help her now. She was there for Catherine, and only Catherine. But as she looked around at the determined trio, she knew that there was only one answer to give at the moment. "To Warwick," she said. If they got to Warwick, he would lead her to Catherine, and Catherine was what mattered. *Dear sweet Catherine, why do I have to find my love for you right before I have to kill you?* There was no answer from Catherine, and no answer from anywhere else. Would she rather have never felt this, or felt it and lost it? She knew the answer. Even a minute of being alive was worth all the pain that came with it. "Let's go."

She met Ian's gaze, and she couldn't help the feeling of loss that echoed through her. The brand burned on her arm, mocking her. She was his soul mate, but she would never trump his code of honor. She'd given her soul for him, yet his would never be offered in return.

But as she turned away, he caught her arm, pulling her back. *Alice.*

She resisted the personal intimacy. "What?"

I will find a way to do it all. The fierce determination in his voice caught her attention, and she looked up. *To do right by you. You will not end up in the ocean or in demon hands. I swear it.*

His stare was intense, his jaw flexed with conviction. There was no doubt he meant it, and her heart fluttered at his promise. He'd uttered the words from the depths of his soul, imbuing them with the beauty of true emotions. God, to have him look at her like that, as if his world would be right only if she was okay... it was incredible. A gift. Even if, in the end, he wasn't able to do it.

She knew why she'd given him the golden light. His intense loyalty and commitment to family honor was so admirable and so beautiful that she couldn't help but treasure it. Ian had shown her how to break her bonds and follow her own heart. He'd given her freedom, and for that, she would never regret her choice, even if he would never love her the way she wanted to be loved. "Better to have lived and lost," she said softly, "than to never have lived at all."

His eyes narrowed. "Isn't it 'loved' not 'lived?'"

Her throat ached for what she felt for him, with the need to tell this solitary warrior that she loved him, but she couldn't do it. She wouldn't do it. Not when he couldn't give it back to her. So she shrugged. "I'd never truly lived until I saved you. You gave me the gift of life. That's what matters."

But as she turned away, she knew it wasn't all that mattered. Love mattered. Love was why she'd saved him. And love was why she had to kill Catherine. Love might be beautiful, but it had a razor edge of pain that hurt more than anything she'd ever felt before.

Ryland was perched on the edge of the pit. "I'm going in. If Thano's down there, I'm going to find him."

Alice stiffened. "You're going to jump in there?"

"Why not? I got an angel of life here to keep me alive, right?"

Alice's jaw dropped at his assumption. "We have no reason to believe I'm one of the Order's trinity. Don't do something so—"

Ryland jumped, instantly swallowed up by the hell below.

"Ry!" Kane swore and dematerialized. He was back in a split second, his body streaked with black and purple slashes. His hair was on fire, and his skin was sloughing off. "I can't find him. It's a nightmare down there. We can't go in there." His face was grim. "I don't know how Ry or Thano could have survived that. It almost killed me and I was only in there for a split second." Kane looked at Alice. "Do you feel Ryland? Has he called to you for help, as his angel of life?"

Alice blinked, and shook her head. "No, I haven't felt anything." Should she? She had no idea what it was supposed to feel like to save anyone.

"Well, shit." Ian ran a hand through his hair. "We need to get to Cardiff fast then, and have him shut it down."

"Yeah." Kane looked around, searching their surroundings. "Which way?"

Alice followed his glance. They were at the edge of the forest. In one direction was the meadow that they'd landed in. In another was the pit. To the left and right stretched more woods. There was no sign of civilization or any kind of inhabitants. "What if his house isn't on the surface? What if the pit is the front door?"

The three of them stared grimly at the seething chasm. Jump, or not?

Chapter Sixteen

Ian stared into the grisly depths of the sinkhole that had taken Ryland, and shook his head. "No," he said. "We can't take the risk by going in after him. If we all die, there's no one to finish the job." He met Kane's grim gaze. "If Thano's alive, Ryland will find him. The rest is up to us."

Kane grimaced, but he nodded. "I'll take us quickly. We'll scour the island. Come on."

Ian grabbed Alice's hand, dragging her away from the edge, even as discomfort with his choice raged through him. How could he walk away if Ryland needed him? But his mission was bigger than that. He had to see it through. Even if the team felt he wasn't up to Order standards, he would never withdraw his oath. Stopping Cardiff from destroying the Order was part of his oath. Breaking the curse was his other duty. Nothing else. He had to stay focused on the big picture.

Alice stared at them. "What? You're going to leave him in there?"

Ian spun around. "We have to," he said, even as the words ripped him apart. "We have no choice. It's our duty."

"Screw your duty! What is wrong with you guys?"

"Nothing's wrong with me," he snapped, drawing her close. "Do you have any idea how fucking hard it is to walk away from him? But if he's dead, then we'll die too. If he's alive, then he'll take care of himself until he finds Thano."

"But what if he's alive and in trouble?" she challenged.

Ian couldn't hide the wave of regret, but he ground his jaw. This was why the Order was for only the elite. Because sometimes it was hard as fucking hell to make the right choice. "We won't let him down," he said. "All he has to do is stay alive until we find Cardiff and get him to shut it down."

Alice tried to pull out of his grasp. "No, we have to help!"

Kane touched her arm. "I tried, Alice. There's no way to find him in there. If there was a way, I would do it." Rage flared in his eyes. "He stood by me when I needed him, and I'm going to fight for him. Come on."

Ian felt Alice's turmoil, but after a moment, she looked over at the pit and nodded. "Okay." But even as Ian took her hand and put his hand on Kane's shoulder, completing the circuit, he felt her unease.

Something was wrong. *Alice? What is it?*

She looked at him with troubled eyes. *I don't know. I just feel like he needs our help.*

We're going to give it to him. Don't worry. Ian glanced over at the pit as they began to dematerialize. *Remember, the Order is more immortal than any other warriors.*

She met his gaze. *Yes, but if it's because I'm your angel of life, then we have a problem. Since I broke the rules and the pearl started glowing, I'm not sure whether I still have those powers or not. You all might be unprotected. You might not be so immortal anymore.*

Ian gripped her hand more tightly. *Or, now that you're not constrained by your limitations, you might be even more powerful than you were before.*

Her face was tense. *How do we know which it is?*

I don't know, but I expect we'll find out. Before they could finish the conversation, they dematerialized, and the hunt was on.

†††

"We found it," Alice whispered in stunned disbelief when Kane helped them materialize for the eleventh time, having taken them from spot to spot around the island in search of Warwick's domain.

This time, they'd hit the jackpot. Towering above them was a castle made of black stone. Six towers, with black flags billowing from the ramparts. Stone gargoyles perched beside every window, the glittering rubies in their eyes so realistic it made chills run down her arms, as if they were living creatures trapped heartlessly in a casing of rock.

The sky above was a conglomeration of purple and black clouds, churning and rumbling. The castle was perched on the far edge of the island, the back half of it built on rock pilings that suspended it over the ocean. The ocean was whirling and raging beneath the shadowed structure, whitecaps crashing against the walled side.

It stretched nearly a hundred yards along the coast, with stone railings lining the upper decks. Alice almost expected to see the ghost of an ancient sea captain's wife leaning on the rail, staring out over the horizon, still waiting for her true love to return, her tattered dress lashing against her legs in the harsh wind.

It was a haunting sight, and she could hear the howl of the wind as it whipped through the ramparts, down empty corridors, through windows that had no glass. It was a place of loneliness and isolation. No beauty. No salvation. Just the cold, harsh existence of a life battered by storms and surf so brutal that not a single weed clung to the stone, not a single blade of grass braved the sandy ground around the building.

Kane and Ian went low, crouching behind a massive boulder that was covered in patches of green lichen. She knelt beside them, but the emptiness of the existence before her tore through her like a great vacuum. There was no life in that mausoleum. Just death. Suffering. Emptiness. She knew what that felt like. It was what she'd carried with her for so many years, until Ian had finally freed her.

"I need to see where I'm taking us," Kane said softly. "Otherwise we could end up in the middle of a wall." During their search of the island, each time Kane had teleported them, it had been to a place close enough that that he could see where he was going to materialize. Ian searched the building. "Take us to the ramparts on the north side. It's well covered. We'll go from there—"

"No." Alice couldn't take her gaze off the center widow's walk where she'd felt that presence of the ghostly widow. She pointed to the spot. "There. That's where he'll be. That's where he spends his time."

Ian looked over at her. "How do you know?"

"Because if the person I loved was murdered in my arms, that's where I'd wait for his spirit to return to me. The ocean brings life. He built this castle for her." She could feel it in every fiber of her body. She was absolutely certain.

Alice, other people aren't like you. They don't come back to life when they die.

She didn't look at him. *The spirit never dies, Ian. Not unless Catherine—* She stopped, suddenly realizing what she'd been about to reveal.

Ian stared at her. "Catherine kills the spirit?"

Alice didn't answer, and this time it wasn't because she was bound by angel rules. This time, it was because answering his question would unlock secrets that were too dangerous for the world. This time, the secret was her choice, and it felt good.

Ian probed at her mind. *Alice. Talk to me about Catherine. Help me understand.*

You have to choose whether to trust me, Ian, even without knowing all the facts.

He swore softly. *Alice—*

"I see him." Low, dark venom undercut Kane's words. "That's him. The man who tried to make me kill Sarah."

Alice looked toward the castle, and her breath caught in

awe. Galloping toward them across the surface of the ocean was a massive black stallion, his rider wearing a black cape that billowed out behind him, flapping in the wind. The horse's hooves were silent, despite the water splashing up all around him. Together, they were a shadow in the wind, streaking across the ocean as if the seas themselves had granted the duo passage. Warwick's head was bent low as he urged his horse on, hiding his face from sight, but she recognized the animal and the breadth of the rider's shoulders. "That's him," she whispered. "That's the man who killed me with the death spell that's haunting me."

"Deathbringer. The winged demon horse." Ian went still beside her, his fingers digging into her arm. "I've never seen him before," he said. "All I've ever found were his hoofprints."

As they watched, Deathbringer leapt from the surface of the water, his sleek body stretching out as he vaulted toward the top of the ramparts, a good hundred feet in the air. His tail was gorgeous and shiny, his mane almost two feet of silken strands. But the true beauty came from the supreme grace of his rider, who seemed to move like the angels themselves as his horse sailed to the rooftops.

Deathbringer landed with total silence on the widow's walk that Alice had pointed out. The horse spun to face the ocean, raising his majestic head toward the water. The pair went utterly still, facing out across the expanse of frothing waves, immobile in the swirling wind.

"They're waiting," she said. "They're waiting for his woman to return to him." How many hours had he spent standing there, waiting? Suddenly, her heart ached for that kind of love, for that kind of loss, for the strength of a commitment that could span so many centuries. She looked over at Ian, and her heart fell. His attention was riveted to Cardiff, his eyes cold with the lethal focus of a warrior.

What happened to the man who had been so consumed by her that he couldn't be apart from her without falling into despair? Was it the fact that the bond locked her to him? Had that given him the security he needed to forget about her?

She looked down at the brand on her arm. All that was left were two small lines. His half of the death stage, and he'd never satisfied his half of the trust stage either. Despite all that they'd been through together, despite the fact that she'd shared with him her deepest secrets and offered everything to him, he hadn't trusted her enough to satisfy the bonding stage.

Ian needed her alive. He needed her in his life. But it was simply self-preservation. He didn't trust love, because it had failed everyone in his family. Love meant death by the greatest dishonor. It wasn't simply that Ian was focused on his missions. He believed that love was the greatest demon there was. Which left no place for her.

"On three," Kane said quietly.

"You stay here," Ian told her. "I don't want anything to happen to you."

Words that formerly would have made her heart sing now felt empty and dull. He didn't want to protect her from harm because he cared. He wanted to keep her safe so he didn't kill himself.

He looked over at her and frowned. *What's wrong? You feel sad.*

She lifted her chin. *Nothing.*

Ian narrowed his eyes. *I don't believe you. When this is over, we're going to have a talk.*

Yay. A talk. What a way to melt a girl's heart.

"One," Kane said.

Ian put his hand on Kane's shoulder. *Alice, I promise you that after we take care of Cardiff, I'll find Catherine for you. If she's in there, I'll find her.* Alice knew he was telling the truth. The whole truth. He would find her, but he wouldn't kill her.

"Two," Kane said, moving into battle stance.

Ian stood beside him, flexing his hands. Both men were ready to call out their weapons the moment Kane teleported them. They were waiting until the last second, so that the crack and flash of black light wouldn't alert the wizard before they attacked. *Alice. Tell me you'll stay here and wait for me. I won't be able to focus if I'm worried about you.*

He was worried about her? The words were cruel, because she wanted them to mean so much more than they did. *Fine,* she lied, not even trying to hide the fact she wasn't telling the truth. She wanted him to be tuned into her enough that he sensed her lie. *I'll stay here.*

Good. His approval filled her, and she knew he was barely focused on her. *I'll be back.* He grabbed her suddenly and hauled her over to him, kissing her so fiercely that she felt her head spin. Desire and passion rushed through her, stripping away her defenses. Her heart cried for him, for what he wouldn't give her, and for a split second, she clung to him, not wanting to let go.

"Three!" Kane shouted.

Ian released her instantly, grabbing onto Kane as the night split with the resounding crack of four Calydon weapons being called out. Black light exploded through the air, and she saw Deathbringer rear up as he whirled around to face them.

Kane and Ian shimmered and then faded—

At the last second, she lunged forward and brushed her fingers across the back of Ian's shirt, a touch so light he could never feel it. A touch that was enough to make Kane's magic include her and spin her away with them to the ramparts where the battle awaited.

The moment they landed, Alice saw Cardiff spin toward them. Not wanting to be seen by Warwick or noticed by Ian, she immediately scurried through the nearest doorway, darting down the steps just as he turned and faced Ian and Kane.

She couldn't see Warwick from where she was, but she had a clear view of Ian's profile. His face morphed into shock at the sight of the man who had destroyed his entire family. Six hundred years of his emotional burdens rolled through her. She hesitated, torn between going back there and supporting him, and trying to find Catherine.

But why go back to Ian? He'd keep her from Catherine, and he was so obsessed with the wizard that he hadn't even noticed her slipping past him. A warrior who would hear a butterfly sneeze from a thousand miles away hadn't noticed her holding onto his shirt and then running past him into the stairway.

She had her answer. Ian wasn't for her.

It was time to leave him behind and go find Catherine. So she did.

† † †

Ian materialized on the widow's walk just as Deathbringer whirled toward him. For a split second, he was frozen in awe at the sight of the man who had haunted his family for generations. A dark hood enveloped the wizard's face, casting it into shadows. But Ian could see the sunken hollows of his cheeks, the thin black line of his lips, and a nose misshapen from too many battles.

He was not a man who had survived immortality well. Was that because of the loss of his soul mate? Ian's mind flashed to Alice, and he suddenly understood what had driven Cardiff for so many centuries. If he lost Alice, he knew it would destroy him. At the thought of Alice dying, grief surged over Ian, so violent and so powerful that he went down on his knees, gasping as stark desolation raced over him. He was suddenly overwhelmed with fear for Alice's well-being, and he turned his head, searching the woods for the sight of her standing safely by the rocks he'd left her near.

She wasn't there.

True fear attacked him. *Alice? Where are you?*

There was no answer for a split second, and terror tore through him. *Alice!*

I'm here, Ian. It's okay. Don't worry about me. She sent soft waves of reassurance, instinctively understanding his fear for her safety.

But it wasn't enough. He needed to see her. The sense of doom was too strong. *Where are you?*

Again, a hesitation, then an answer that made his heart freeze. *I'm looking for Catherine. I'm in the tower.*

What? She was in Warwick's castle? Ian spun around and saw a stone doorway behind him. He inhaled and caught the faint scent of flowers that he associated with Alice. *Alice! That's too dangerous!* He sprinted for the door, driven by the instinct to go after her, to protect her, to—

"Another Fitzgerald. Still alive. Amazing."

Ian spun around as the voice of the curse boomed through his mind, only this time, he wasn't imagining it. It was the real voice of the warrior in front of him. It was his voice that had haunted Ian all those years. "It's been you in my head?"

Deathbringer pranced restlessly, and Cardiff steadied his mount. "I thought you were all dead by now." His eyes gleamed with delight as he surveyed Ian's body. "You look thin, warrior. You've been suffering, haven't you?" He leaned forward. "How does it feel? Too much to handle?"

Ian's muscles tensed with the need to strike out and cut down the man who'd been responsible for his father's death, but he forced himself to remain still. Killing Warwick would not end the curse. The wizard had to undo the spell before he died.

"You bastard." Kane's voice was low, seething with disgust as he stood beside Ian, his weapons clenched in his fists. "You tried to make me kill my *sheva.*"

"Tried?" Cardiff raised his brows. "It's not over yet, warrior. None of it's over." He raised his wand, his fingers grasping it loosely. "The circle must be broken. The new Order must be born, and the old Order expunged."

Adrenaline thudded through Ian as he lined up beside Kane, rapidly assessing their chances. *Ry. We got the bad guy. Get up to the ramparts.* Ian had no idea if Ryland was in any shape to hear him, but he had a bad feeling they were going to need backup. Warwick Cardiff had been a legendary warrior, and now he also had demon magic.

Beside him, Kane was absolutely still. The calm, focused energy of a warrior in battle was rolling off him. "Turn yourself in," Kane commanded. "The Order is not yours to destroy. It is a legion of honor."

Fury hissed in Warwick's eyes. "Shut up." A streak of purple light shot out of his palm. Kane blocked it with his weapon, but another one hit a split second later, nailing Kane in the chest. The warrior crumpled to the ground instantly, a spiral of black smoke rising out of his chest.

"Kane!" Ian hurled his mace, but Deathbringer danced to the left, dodging the blow with ease.

Warwick laughed and unleashed another flash of light at Ian. Ian swore and blocked it with his mace. The beam bounced off his blade and slammed into the wall. Stones exploded from the castle, cascading all over the rooftop. The nearby gargoyles seemed to flinch, as if they were alive and had felt the impact.

"Hey," Warwick snarled. "That's my home you're destroying. I'm saving it for my woman."

The wizard's insanity was evident, and Ian swore as he blocked another blast from Warwick. He called back his errant mace and threw it again. And again, the horse spun his master out of the path of the weapon while Warwick blasted him. Ian ducked, and a stray spark hit his shoulder. The agony was incredible, and he stumbled as pain cascaded through him.

Deathbringer danced around him as Ian fought to remain standing. Warwick's bitter laughter echoed through the night. "Don't worry. I won't let you die yet. You need to lose your woman first." Then Warwick shot another slash of light at Ian, knocking him to the ground.

Ian swore, his fingers digging into the roof as he fought against the pain, but his body was frozen, his muscles rigid. He could do nothing but shout in protest as Warwick spun his mount away and the stallion clattered down the stairs, in pursuit of Alice.

"Shit!" Ian tried to get up, but his body was immobilized in some sort of lockdown spell. "Kane! Wake up!"

There was a low groan from across the roof, but Ian couldn't turn his head to see if it was Kane. *Kane?* Since they weren't blood-bonded, they couldn't talk mind-to-mind across long distances, but short distances were no problem. *You with me?*

I'm here. Can't move, though. You?

No. My muscles are frozen. Sweat began to bead on Ian's brow as the clatter of Deathbringer's hooves grew fainter. The wizard was closing in on Alice. He had to get to her. Had to get up. *Can you teleport?*

Not sure. There was a pause, then an affirmative. *Yes.*

Relief rushed through Ian. *Go back to Dante's mansion. Get help.* He didn't hesitate to ask for backup from the team now. Cardiff was after his woman, and he would call upon any assistance he could. *I'll stay here and deal with the wizard.*

What the hell are you going to do? Lie there and yell at him? Come back with me. Maybe Lily can figure out how to break the spell.

Lily Davenport was their research expert, and the *sheva* of one of their teammates, Gideon Roarke. She'd once been their nemesis, but after falling in love with Gideon, the world-famous researcher had become their greatest asset by providing information that none of the rest of them had. *I'm not leaving Alice. Just go! I'll be back as soon as I can.* There was a ripple of energy in the air, and then Ian sensed that he was alone on the roof.

Below him, he could hear the fading echoes of the horse's hooves as the duo thundered after Alice. Ian fought the invisible restraints that rendered him motionless, but he couldn't break them. Frantic now, he reached out to her, brushing against her mind. *Alice. Watch out. He's coming after you.*

There was a ripple of fear from Alice. *He's already here.*

Chapter Seventeen

Alice raced around a bend in the hallway, her bare feet sliding on the cobblestones as the thundering sound of Deathbringer's hooves echoed through the corridor. She knew Catherine would be in the lowest portion of the building, the closest to the center of the earth that she could be. There had to be a basement, a dungeon in this castle—

A streak of green light crashed into the stones beside her head, and they exploded out of the wall.

Alice! Ian's frantic voice filled her mind. *Get out of there!*

Trying! Ahead of her, Alice saw a narrow hole in the ancient stone walls. A dumbwaiter slot? She raced over to it as Deathbringer and Warwick rounded the corner. The rider was carrying a wand, a wand that looked just like the one that had killed her. "No!" She reached the opening and dove through it, not even taking the time to look where it led.

When she started to plummet into the darkness, she knew she was in trouble. *Ian! I'm falling!*

She felt Ian's burst of tension, and then his calm, warrior focus filled her. *Let me into your body. Open yourself to me.*

What? Her head cracked against a wall, and she yelped, pressing her hand against the injury.

Just do it! Suddenly he was filling her with his entire being, like a great summer storm. She felt the strength of his body seem to take over hers, and her body felt like she had just acquired a new surge of life. *Call my weapon*, he commanded. *Now!* Alice immediately pictured the mace in her mind and called it to her. There was a loud crack and a flash of black light, and then it was in her hand, startling her. There was no way she would ever get used to that. *What now?* But the question hadn't even formed in her mind when Ian showed her that moment when she'd been falling into the crevasse in the ocean, and he'd used the mace to stop the fall. She immediately slammed the end of the mace into the wall, but it bounced off, sparks flying. *I can't get it to stick!*

Do it again! This time, she felt the sheer force of his will flooding her, and it felt like his hands were on hers as she slammed it into the stone again. This time, the blade caught, and she yelped as it jerked her to a stop. Somehow, she didn't lose her grip on it, and she knew it wasn't her own strength that had held her there. It was Ian's. Her chest heaving, she dangled from the handle, her fingers trembling from the effort. *How did you do that?*

I'm just a great boyfriend. Remember that next time you run off on me.

Heat washed over her. *Isn't 'boyfriend' kind of a weak term for a guy whose brands are all over my arms?*

You seem commitment-averse. I was trying not to scare you. His voice was calm, but she felt his tension. *You okay?*

For the moment. Alice peered below, trying to determine how far above the ground she was. She could see a faint light about thirty feet below her. The ground, or an illusion? She glanced up and saw only darkness, indicating that she'd fallen a long distance before Ian had helped her break the fall. Cardiff wasn't peering down at her, and she sighed with relief, realizing that she'd lost him for the moment. It was his castle, though, and she had no doubt he would find her again soon.

Come back to the roof where I can protect you, Ian ordered.

For a split second, yearning burned through Alice. The idea of rushing back up to the roof and falling into Ian's arms sounded like the best idea she'd ever had. But then she thought of Catherine, and she knew she had a promise to keep. *I can't. I need to find Catherine.*

Alice! No! Cardiff is after you! We'll find Catherine together after we deal with him.

Tears burned in Alice's eyes at the idea of leaving him. *You don't understand, Ian. I've failed at everything important my whole life. I have to get this one right.*

You didn't fail. You saved my life.

Alice's throat tightened. Yes, she'd helped him find peace so he could save his own life, but in return, he'd renewed his focus on his duty and his family's honor. *Catherine loves me, Ian. How can I walk away from that?* She waited, giving him a chance to speak up, to give her a reason to trust that he would help her kill Catherine in the end, despite his oath and his promise never to do such a thing.

You'll do her no good if you get caught by the wizard. Get back here, Alice! Now!

She closed her eyes, regret filling her. She'd given him an opening to tell her that he loved her, and instead, he'd given her a command. *I'm sorry, Ian.* Then she let go of the mace and let herself fall.

† † †

Alice! Ian bellowed her name, but she cut him off like a blast of cold death. His body went rigid as the loss tore at him and fear for her well-being sliced through him. He fought it off, struggling to fend off the debilitating grief, but he couldn't get the image of Cardiff out of his mind. Cardiff closing down on her. Grabbing her. Hurting her. Killing her, all to punish Ian. "No!" His voice was a tormented scream, and he tried to channel all the anguish, thrusting it into his body to try to regain the use of his muscles.

But it didn't work. He just lay there, like a useless piece of driftwood, cast upon the shore by a storm that had no use for him. Nothing to be done. He couldn't help her. Couldn't save her. His failure beat at him, stripping away what little sense of self he had left. Gasping for air, he forced his mind off Alice, picturing the graveyard where Augustus and his father were buried. He imagined the headstones in his mind, reading the words inscribed on the marble of his father's memorial.

Here lies Rudolph Fitzgerald, a great father, a mighty warrior, and a legendary member of the Order of the Blade. Honor shall be restored to his name.

Honor. *Honor.* Ian pictured the word that he'd carved into his own palm that night. *Honor.* He had to restore honor to his family's name. He had to regain the Fitzgerald place within the Order. Dying over Alice would not accomplish that. He had to be stronger than what she made him, because fear of losing her made him weak. He had to be prepared to fight Cardiff when he came back. He had to be the warrior that no one else in his family had been able to be.

Ian took a deep breath and focused on the starry sky. He breathed in the vast expanse of the night. He studied the full moon, drawing strength from its magic. Its brilliant light filled the night, radiating the same bizarre shade of turquoise that it had the night that Alice had dived into the ocean. Around the moon circled undulating crimson clouds, as if they were stalking the lunar sphere.

Ian focused on the clouds, watching each one carefully until his mind was clear of all thoughts except the clouds. Alice was but a distant buzz around the periphery of his subconscious, almost out of the way. Drawing upon all the years of training with his father, Ian slowly, carefully, intentionally, eradicated Alice from his thoughts, sealing himself off from her. As he did so, he felt the curse recede, replaced by a humming power that he hadn't felt in months, not since the first time Alice had died in his arms.

At the same time, there was a distant ache of loneliness, sadness, and regret, as if he were losing the very thing that made his heart beat... Then it was gone, replaced by the steady, focused mindset of a soldier prepared for battle.

Alice was gone from his heart.

All that was left was a Fitzgerald warrior.

† † †

Alice bit her lip to keep from crying out in pain as she hit the stone floor after releasing the mace. Tears burned in her eyes as her knee throbbed, but she didn't pause to assess it. She just looked around, quickly checking out her surroundings. The cold dampness in the air and the musty smell told her that she was below the earth.

She crawled out of the crevice and into a long hallway. Doors went off on all sides, heavy steel barriers with bars on the windows. The dungeon. But there were too many! How would she search them all? "Catherine?" She whispered the name, afraid to shout.

No response.

Alice hurried up to the first door, biting her lip against the stabbing pain in her knee. She hoped it was just a momentary twist, because she didn't have time to worry about it. Cardiff would be on her at any moment. She peered through the bars and saw an empty cell.

Quickly, she hurried to the next one. Empty.

The next one was unoccupied as well.

"Catherine!" she whispered more urgently, getting worried about how long it was taking. This was Cardiff's castle. He would know exactly where that hole had dumped her, and he'd be here shortly... Realization dawned on her. If Cardiff already knew where she was, why was she being quiet? He was most likely well on his way to her, delayed only by the fact he'd had to take the long way around because he hadn't yet figured out how to shrink himself and the horse to fit through the dumbwaiter passage. This was the time for speed, not stealth! Galvanized by urgency, she didn't hold back anymore. "Catherine!" she shouted, starting to run down the long hallway. "Where are you?"

Again, no response.

But above her head, she heard the faint, distant thudding of a horse galloping.

Frantic, she ran harder, not even feeling the pain in her knee anymore. "Catherine!" she screamed. "It's Alice! Where are you?" She reached a split in the hallway, two passageways extending outward in the dark with rooms off them. Which way?

She peered down each corridor, and realized that the one heading east, toward the ocean, was significantly darker. Almost no light penetrated. "Catherine," she breathed, a chill rippling down her spine. Was Catherine absorbing light rays? Not that. Not yet.

Frantic, she sprinted down the gloomy hallway, right into the darkness that seemed to swallow her up as soon as she stepped into it. It was thick and cold against her skin, the way death would feel. She didn't bother to call Catherine's name anymore. If she was preying on light, there was no point.

Alice focused on the darkest spot in the hallway, on what looked like a bottomless black hole in the atmosphere. That was it. That was where Catherine was. She hurried down the passageway, fighting against the pain in her right knee. She reached the door and grabbed the bars, standing on her tiptoes to peer through.

At first, she could see nothing.

After a moment, her eyes adjusted, and she could discern a faint white blur in the corner. It was as if all the light that was left in the room had concentrated on that one place, like a faint spotlight was shining down from above. As she looked more closely, she could see a woman sitting on the floor, her arms wrapped around her legs, her face pressed to her knees.

Ragged blond hair tumbled down around her, the tattered ends dragging on the floor. She was wearing a white robe that had slid up to reveal arms so skinny that Alice's breath caught. "Oh, Catherine," she whispered. Dear God, what had happened during the months that Warwick had stolen her? Suddenly, her resolution vanished. How could she kill this woman? Catherine was all she had left, a friend who was as close as a sister. How could she strip Catherine of life?

There had to be a way. Ian had to be right. There had to be some solution that neither of them knew about. "Catherine!"

The woman in the corner didn't move. She didn't lift her head, even though Alice knew that Catherine had to know she was there.

Alice quickly tried the door handle, but it was locked. She rattled it, and the noise was loud in the hallway. Frantically, she stood up on her toes and peered through the bars again. "Catherine," she said, keeping her voice as calm as she could. "It's Alice. I've come to get you out of here."

Catherine shuddered at Alice's words, and she slowly raised her head. Her formerly blue eyes were a lifeless gray, and there were dark shadows beneath them. Her face was drawn, and her lips were a bluish purple. Alice's throat tightened, and she gripped the bars. "Oh, my dear Catherine," she whispered, her heart breaking for her friend's anguish.

"Ally?" Catherine's voice was raw, as if she hadn't spoken for days. "Is that really you?"

"Yes, it's me." Alice tugged on the bars. "We're leaving."

"No." She shook her head, her face becoming even paler. "You made a promise, Alice. It's time. You have to do it."

Tears trickled down Alice's cheeks. "No. There has to be another way. I have the Order of the Blade with me." She thought of Ian on the roof. *Ian? I need some assistance, here.* "They'll help—"

"They can't help! No one can help!" Catherine tried to stand, but her legs were too weak, and she fell, her knees

283

cracking on the hard floor.

Alice instinctively reached through the bars, trying to help her. Ian had not responded to her call, and she couldn't feel his presence. *Ian. Are you there?* "I helped someone save his own life tonight, Cat. Someone who I'm not supposed to protect, an Order of the Blade member. I helped him live by giving him my golden light."

Catherine stared at her in disbelief. "But that's impossible. You can't do anything even close to saving a life. And how could you give the golden light to an Order of the Blade member? He would never qualify."

"I know, but I did it. Don't you see what that means? It means that maybe our fate isn't determined. Maybe we can save you—"

"It's not worth the risk." Catherine grabbed the wall and dragged herself to her feet. "I love you, Ally. I knew you'd come for me." She staggered, her fingers digging into the cold stone as she fought her way to the door.

Alice extended her arms through the bars and caught Catherine as the other woman reached her. Through the bars, they hugged. Alice was shocked by how cold Catherine was, but at the same time, she felt a wave of warmth and love from the other angel. Love she'd never felt before. She realized instantly that it was because she was no longer blocking it. Ian had freed her, and now she could even feel love from other people. "Cat." She wrapped her arms around her, holding her tight through the bars. "I'm so sorry I took so long to get here."

"I missed you." Catherine hugged her back, her cheeks mashed against the bars as she tried to get close to Alice. "I know you tried. I knew you'd come." She managed a smile, a haunting smile that made Alice want to cry. "It's not too late. You can still kill me."

But Alice shook her head. "I can't," she whispered. "I love you, Cat. I won't give up."

Catherine's eyes filled with fear. "But you have to kill

me. It's already started. I wake up in the morning and I—" She stopped, and Alice knew what she had been going to say. "It's already starting. You have to stop me."

Alice closed her eyes. How could she kill the one person she loved? But even as she thought it, she knew Catherine wasn't the only person she held in her heart. She loved Ian, which was why she'd helped save him. How could she save one and kill the other?

Cat's fingers dug into Alice's arms. "Ally? You did figure out a way to kill me, didn't you? You didn't come without a way, did you?"

Alice grimaced. "I—" Suddenly, she heard the thud of hooves in the distance, and her heart stuttered. "He's coming."

Cat gripped her arms. "No, no, no, he can't get me. Do you know what he's trying to make me do to the Order?"

Alice stared at her. "The Order? Then you're...you're one of their guardians?" She was so shocked she didn't know what to say. If Cat was one of the trinity, did that mean Alice was, too? She hadn't really believed it. Hadn't thought it was possible. And if she was, what did that mean?

Catherine nodded. "He tested me on one of the Order members that he brought here." She grimaced. "It was so awful, Ally. The poor man—"

Footsteps pounded on the dirt floor, and Alice gripped Catherine's arms. "He's here." Frantically, she looked around, desperate for something to use to defend herself. But before she could even think about it, Ian's mace appeared in her hand with a flash of black light and a crack.

Catherine gaped at her. "What is *that*?"

"It's an Order of the Blade weapon." She held it up, moving away from the door, her heart racing. What in God's name she was planning to do with it, she didn't know, but—

"It's an Order of the Blade weapon?" Catherine's voice raised several octaves. "I might be able to make it deadly enough to destroy me. Bring it over here. We'll try that. It might work."

Alice hesitated as the footsteps grew nearer. *Ian? Is that you?* There were no hoofbeats. Just the footsteps of a person. Was it Ian? But there was still no answer, and she couldn't feel his presence at all. Fear began to build inside her. Ian had never cut her off before. Was he hurt? Was he dead? "I don't want you to die, Cat."

"It doesn't matter! I have to!"

"If you're a guardian angel for the Order of the Blade, what will happen to them if you die? What if they lose one of their trinity?" Even as she asked the words, she realized that it applied to her as well, if she were the third part of the trinity. What if she died for good? What would happen to them? If, of course, she was part of their trinity. But what if she was? What if, all this time, she'd been saving lives?

Catherine looked grave. "It will be worse for them if I live." She thrust her hand through the bars. "Give me the weapon, Ally. Let me try it."

"I—" Alice looked back and forth between Cat and the hallway that was echoing with the sound of encroaching footsteps. *Ian. Please tell me it's you who is almost here.* No reply. Was he dead?

"Alice!" Catherine screamed at her. "Don't you dare let me live! You made a promise to me!"

"Is he dead?" She couldn't focus on anything else but the gaping void in her mind where Ian was supposed to be. "Is Ian Fitzgerald dead? Can you tell?"

Cat's jaw dropped. "Are you kidding? We don't have time for that. Give me the weapon." But as Alice looked at Cat's fierce gaze, she suddenly saw in her dear friend the same emptiness and loneliness that she'd lived with her whole life. An agony of guilt, and a terror so deep it made her bones ache. She'd lived with that her entire existence, the fear of what would happen to her if she screwed up, and in the end, she'd finally broken through those walls, and it hadn't been so bad.

It had been, in fact, beautiful. She could feel the love for

Ian and her worry that something had happened to him. She could feel the love that she and Cat had for each other. It was beautiful, a gift so pure that it made everything worthwhile. She looked down at her shorts and saw the white light from the glowing pearl through the fabric. The pearl was the only thing keeping her an angel, and soon it would be gone. Did she feel any regret? No. She'd rather be alive for two hours than die without understanding what love was. And as she looked into Catherine's eyes, she saw the same emptiness that she'd lived with.

She couldn't let Cat die never having lived.

"No." She stepped back from Catherine. "I won't kill you. We're going to find a way—"

A huge dark shadow morphed out of the darkness and grabbed Alice from behind. A hand clamped over her mouth, and she was hauled back against a hard, well-muscled body.

But it wasn't Ian's body.

"Alice," a husky voice said in her ear, and she went ice cold.

It was Flynn. The man she'd lured here to kill her.

† † †

Alice's heart began to pound furiously as Flynn crushed her against him with his massive arms. He was solid muscle, more than he had been before that terrible night when everything had changed for them, for him. The night that she'd betrayed him, at least in his eyes. "Flynn," she said, trying to keep her voice calm, trying to reach the man who had once been her dearest friend. "I'm so glad you're here. We have to get Cat out of the cell—"

"No." His arms tightened around her, and she saw a faint green glow beneath his fingernails. "This is about you. And me." He spun her around, and she gasped when she saw his face.

Eyes that were once a beautiful rich brown were glowing

green. A mouth that used to quirk in laughter at her jokes was a grim, brutal line. His cheeks were shadowed, his eyes heavy with torment. She saw the burdens that haunted him, including those she hadn't been able to spare him from. Suddenly, she didn't see him as the man who had been about to kill her. He was someone who'd been tormented and abused for so long that he was trapped in his own hell.

She hadn't been able to see it before. She hadn't been able to see his pain. But now, she felt like her heart was going to break for him. Suddenly, her fear of him was gone. Simply gone. "Flynn," she whispered, laying her hands on his cheeks. "I'm so sorry I wasn't there for you that night. I'm so sorry for it all."

He stared at her, and for a brief second, she thought she saw a flash of brown in his green eyes, an attempt at sanity trying to break through. "Alice?" His voice was rough and harsh, as if he were speaking for the first time in too long.

"Flynn. Please, don't cross that line again. You don't have to do it. You know you don't."

He stared at her, and she felt the internal battle within him. How had she not felt his torment before? How had she not sensed his agony? How much time had they spent together, and she'd never seen the anguish beneath the surface? All he'd been was a partner in her loneliness, someone who understood hell.

But now, in his eyes, she saw more. Love. Yearning. Longing. For her. Guilt filled her, and shock. He loved her? Dear God, no wonder he'd felt it was such a betrayal when she hadn't been able to save that person for him on that awful, terrible night.

"Alice," he gasped. He suddenly thrust her back against the wall and stumbled away from her, clutching his hands to his head. "No," he roared, as if he were fighting a demon from within. "No!"

"Flynn Shapiro. Your time is done." A deep voice boomed through the hallway, and a massive shadowed figure walked toward them. It was Vaughn, but he seemed to be even larger than before, moving with a silent, ominous stride too dangerous for any living creature.

Flynn spun toward him, and a low growl echoed from deep in his chest. "No," he spat. "You walked away. You don't get to come back."

"I can do whatever I want," Vaughn said, closing the gap. His eyes were glowing green, and there was a dark turbulence flowing off him. "Come with me, Flynn. Don't make me kill you." Vaughn's hand twitched, and Alice felt the sudden surge of power roll off him. There was something about Vaughn that was so much more than Flynn, so much more than anything she'd ever seen before.

"Dear God," whispered Catherine. "What is he?"

Lethal power. Power ready to kill. *No.* Not again. No more death. "Flynn," she urged. "Don't let him take you. Run. *Run.*" She didn't believe for an instant that Flynn would be able to defeat Vaughn. His only choice was to flee.

Flynn looked over at her, and she saw the torment in his eyes. The violence, the years and years of taint from what he'd been forced to do, but she also saw the humanity that she'd connected with before. He deserved a chance. "Run," she said. "Just run."

He closed his eyes for a split second, as Vaughn drew even closer. Then he opened his eyes, looked right at her and said, "I will always love you, Alice. Good-bye." Then he whirled around, charged the stone wall of the hallway, and burst right through it. He let out a howl of agony as he sailed through the air down toward the ocean.

Vaughn streaked by her, a flash of darkness too fast to register, and then he followed Flynn through the hole in the castle wall. She heard two quick splashes in the ocean, and then silence. *Please, Flynn, get away from him.*

"That was it, wasn't it?" Catherine was staring at her through the bars. "Flynn was how you were going to kill me, wasn't he? And you didn't let him."

Alice gritted her teeth and strode toward the door. "Yes, you're right. I'm not going to give up on you, Cat. There has to be a way—"

Out of the darkness, a massive figure burst forth and suddenly Deathbringer was there, bearing down on her in a dead gallop. Alice swung her mace, but Warwick scooped her easily off the ground, throwing her over the back of his horse as they sped down the hallway.

She gasped as he pinned her with one hand, pushing so hard that she couldn't breathe. She felt her ribs crack, and she grabbed his leg, fighting to hold on, to stay conscious, to stay alive.

She raised her head and looked back to see Catherine reaching for her through the bars. Regret filled her heart. She couldn't leave her sister behind. Cat didn't believe, and would never be able to save herself. "Cat! Don't give up!" Then Deathbringer turned a corner, and Catherine vanished from sight.

Chapter Eighteen

Forcing himself to stay calm, Ian closed his eyes. He focused all his energy into his body, sending healing into all his cells. He could feel his muscles trembling as they tried to fight off the spell that had immobilized them. He concentrated even more intently, drawing upon a lifetime of trying to fight off the spell that had haunted him for so long. Magic sucked, but there had to be a way to defeat a spell as simple as this one.

His little finger twitched, and triumph shot through him. *Come on!* He drilled down harder, willing all his focus into his right hand.

His thumb moved.

Then his index finger.

Then—

Ian! Alice's desperate plea burst through his shields, and he faltered, his mouth going dry at the desperation in her voice. The shields he'd erected against her so carefully shattered, and her anguish filled him.

He couldn't stop his response to her, and he didn't want to. *Alice! What's wrong?*

Cardiff has me— A wave of her pain washed through him, and a dark sense of fury rose through Ian at the thought of that bastard with his hands on Alice.

With a roar of rage, Ian broke through the spell in one

swift, violent move. He leapt to his feet and immediately opened his mind to Alice, latching onto her through their blood bond. He knew instantly that she was three floors down and moving quickly up the stairwell.

Cardiff was bringing Alice to him.

Ian bolted over toward the doorway that Cardiff had sprinted down previously, and he lined up beside the open door. He called out his maces and gripped them, ready to take him out.

The clatter of hoofbeats was getting closer, and Ian readied himself. *Stay low, Alice—* Before he could finish his warning, Deathbringer burst through the doorway. Ian instinctively swung, aiming for Cardiff's chest. But as he moved, he realized that Cardiff had Alice in his arms and was using her as a shield to hide behind. He'd put her right in Ian's line of attack.

Alice's face went white with horror at the sight of Ian's mace heading toward her chest, and Ian swore as he fought to alter his trajectory. *Alice!* He threw every bit of strength into his blow, dragging his mace to the side just as the trio blew by him. His mace slammed into the stone wall with a brutal clatter, missing Alice's face by a fraction of an inch.

"Jesus." The terror of what he'd almost done tore through him, and Ian staggered as the image of Alice's bloodied body filled his mind. For a second, he was frozen, overwhelmed by what had nearly happened. He couldn't move as Cardiff reined in his mount, spinning the massive beast toward him, Alice still locked in his arms.

All Ian could do was stare at Alice. Her face was streaked with dirt and taut with fear, but there was a fire blazing in her eyes. A courage he hadn't seen before. And as he stared at her, he felt his heart stutter. The woman who he'd blocked from his heart only moments ago filled him, and suddenly his world became only about her. No one but Alice.

"You're free." Cardiff whipped out his wand, but this

time, Ian didn't hesitate. He dodged the beam of light from the wand, circling the horse as he tried to get closer to Alice to pry her out of the bastard's arms. But the horse was too quick, and there was no way to free her. It was a standoff, because Ian wouldn't strike for fear of hitting Alice, and he couldn't afford to have Cardiff die until the curse was lifted.

Then there was a shimmer of low pressure in the air, and Ian grinned as Kane appeared at his side, accompanied by six members of the Order of the Blade. Gideon Roarke, their interim leader. Quinn Masters. Elijah Ross. Zach Roderick. Gabe Watson. Plus their deceased leader's young son, Drew Cartland. Ian swore when he saw him. The youth was a dangerous wildcard, too untrained and unpredictable to be brought into battle.

But there was no time to argue. Upon arrival the Order went directly into formation, spreading out in a circle around the wizard. All of them were armed, their gazes focused and intense. A team meant for war.

Rightness surged through Ian as he felt the familiar power of the team around him. This was what he lived for. This was what he was meant for. His team.

Gideon was the one who spoke. "You want to destroy the Order," he said to Cardiff.

Cardiff glowered at him. "I want justice."

Ian knew that the conversation was simply for distraction while the team moved into position and established a plan. If this battle were to be simply hand-to-hand combat, it'd be an easy win for the Order. But as he and Kane had learned, the rules changed when a wizard was involved. They had to be smarter than he was, not simply better fighters.

But even though Ian tried to focus on his team and listen to the commands going back and forth in silent telepathy, all he could think about was the woman in the wizard's arms.

Alice was gripping his forearm, as if she were trying to keep it off her throat. Her mouth was twisted in pain, and she was staring at Ian.

Hang in there, Alice. We'll get you out.

She nodded once. *I don't want to die.*

The moment Ian heard her confession, he felt something inside him stop. Ever since he'd first met her, she'd shown no fear of death or of the future that was coming her way. And now she'd changed her mind? She was afraid? Shit. That was unacceptable. Fierce protectiveness surged though him, and he knew that there was no choice. He had to save her. Not just now, in this moment. He had to save her from her fate.

Warwick glared at them, then he looked past them and muttered something. Words to a spell? "Shut him up!" Ian shouted. "Don't let him do that!"

Elijah was closest, and he unleashed his weapon at the wizard. His throwing star cut through the air as something moved to Ian's right. He glanced over, and then spun around when he saw that one of the stone gargoyles was watching him. "Incoming," he shouted, wielding his mace just as the creature came to life, tearing out of the wall with fearsome strength.

All around him gargoyles erupted off the walls. Ian heard the shouts of his team as they fought creatures made of stone that their weapons could not dent. The air filled with the grunts of men as they took hits from the monsters. Ian joined the chorus, shouting as he slammed his mace into the chest of the nearest combatant.

His blade bounced off, and the gargoyle lunged for him, slamming a cement fist at Ian's head. He ducked, and the stone glanced off his temple, still hitting him hard enough to send him spinning. As he fought to regain his balance, he glanced around at his team. They were all heavily engaged and losing badly. Even Drew, with his assortment of weapons, was no match for the two gargoyles bearing down on him. Their weapons were useless against the stone creatures.

Shit. They were not prepared to take on magic.

Ian!

He spun around at Alice's call and saw Deathbringer charge down the stairs with Alice and Cardiff. Ian sprinted past his current opponent, who stood back and let him go, making it clear that, by pursuing the wizard, Ian was doing exactly what Cardiff wanted him to do.

It was a trap, but he wasn't about to let Alice or Cardiff go. It was time to end this. *Now.* He was going after them, right into the trap the wizard had set.

Ian bolted around the corner, and a streak of green light hit him flat in the chest. It flung him back against the wall of the room. As he hit the stone, there was a loud clanking sound, and steel cuffs slammed around his wrists and ankles, trapping him against the wall like he was a sacrificial virgin.

Magic was a pain in the ass. Seriously.

He jerked at his restraints, but they were locked down with relentless force.

He was trapped. Again. And he didn't like it any more than he had when the killer kelp had decided to become his anklet.

Deathbringer stopped, and Cardiff swung him around to face Ian. Alice was pinned against his chest, her face pale, and the wizard's hand covering her mouth.

Ian focused on her terrified face. *I'm with you, Alice. We'll get through this.*

She nodded once, but he could taste the bitterness of her fear. Shit, as hard as it had been to deal with the constant threats to her life when she wasn't concerned about dying, seeing her afraid of death made it a thousand times worse. He could feel the cold draft of fear in every cell of her body, and it made terror settle deep in his bones. What had changed for her? Why was she suddenly afraid to die?

"Why are you here, soldier?" Cardiff demanded. "Why did you track me down at my home?"

Ian met his gaze, knowing that he couldn't defeat the wizard through battle. He had to find another way. "Free my family from the curse. Take the death spell off Alice." Hey, it was worth a try, right? One never knew when an insane, murderous wizard would suddenly become reasonable.

But today wasn't the day for miracles, because Cardiff simply barked with derisive laughter and pointed his wand at Alice's temple. "Why would I do that? When Alice dies for good, the Order loses their immortality. Think how easy they will be to kill."

Alice's eyes widened, and Ian swore. "What does killing the Order do for you?" he challenged. "Does it bring back your *sheva?*"

"It saves all the other ones, you stupid fuck!" Cardiff shouted. "It's not about revenge! It's about fixing the Order and giving it the vision that it was supposed to have!"

Well, gee, that was helpful. Ian was sure Dante would be thrilled to know that his Order was so bad that the only way for life to flourish on earth was to expunge the whole damn crew from existence. Stupid crazy bastard, but hey, if he was into *sheva* preservation, Ian had an answer to that one. "Alice is my *sheva*. If you kill her, you'll perpetuate that which you hate."

Cardiff waved his wand with a dismissive snort. "You are all tainted. We need to start over with a clean slate." He looked past Ian. "With the next generation."

The next generation? Ian followed the wizard's gaze and realized Cardiff was watching Drew. The youth was fighting on the landing at the top of the stairs. Two gargoyles were engaging him, but Drew wasn't getting hit as hard as the other Order members. Ian realized that the gargoyles were not attacking Drew with deadly intent. They were simply keeping him busy enough that he couldn't help the rest of the Order. "Dante's son? He'll never join you. He believes in his father's legacy."

"He carries far more than his father's legacy," Cardiff said. "He's already changing sides. You will see. He's the future. Even if I die, the seed is planted."

There was a shout from above, and Ian saw Elijah fall, then roll to the right, barely dodging a blow that would have crushed his skull. "Can't you see it?" the wizard laughed. "You all are already losing your immortality, because your angel of life is so close to death."

Close to death? Ian jerked his gaze back to Alice, and his heart seemed to stutter. *Alice. You okay?* She grimaced. *I'm having trouble breathing. It feels like I'm drowning. Like he's filling my lungs with fluid of some sort.*

Tension started to ripple through him. Fear. Despair. He could feel her struggle, and it plunged right into him. Shit. He had to stop overreacting and stay focused. He couldn't help her if he lost his shit right now.

But never had he felt anything as devastating as the idea of losing Alice now that they were so tightly bonded. It was horrifying. No wonder Warwick had gone insane. Ian would do anything to save Alice... An idea burst into his mind. "Stop," he gasped. "Alice can bring her back to life."

Cardiff froze, his black eyes sharp. "What are you talking about?"

"Alice. She's an angel of life—"

"For the Order. She can't help anyone else. I already tried."

"She's broken the rules now." Ian looked at Alice. "I got expelled from the Order, so she couldn't help me, but she did. She brought me back. She's no longer constrained by angel limitations."

Alice gaped at him. *I didn't bring you back. I gave you peace and serenity with the golden light. You healed yourself. I did nothing.*

Warwick stared at him, and suddenly Ian felt the wizard's emotions blasting through the room: crashing waves of longing, so intense, so powerful, and so crazily desperate. He jerked Alice around so he could look at her. "Is he telling the truth? Can you bring Audrey back to life?"

Tell him yes, Alice, Ian urged.

I'm an angel, Ian! By nature, we tend to be pretty horrific liars.

Then don't lie. Tell him the truth. You know you can use your powers on anyone. You've broken through your restraints. You can do it if you want to. He sent his confidence into her, trying to help her see what he saw in her. He'd been awed by the immense strength of her powers when she'd given him the golden light. There was no doubt in his mind that she could save the entire world if she wanted to. *You know you can.*

Alice shook her head, and he felt her denial. *You're wrong, Ian. I can't.*

Furious, he fought his shackles. *Of course you can! Stop living the role that you've locked yourself into! Tell him you can save his* sheva *and believe you're speaking the truth!*

Cardiff shook her with such fierceness that anger tore through Ian. He struggled against his bonds, desperate to get free and help her. *Tell him! It's the only way!*

Alice swallowed, and Ian felt her summon her courage as she answered the wizard. "As long as her soul didn't die, she's still alive. Just in a different place." Her words rang true, and Ian knew that she'd chosen her words carefully to enable her to speak the truth. She hadn't said she could save the woman, because she believed she couldn't. *Ian! I can't bring the dead back to life.*

Her words were a fierce denial, but he could feel the faintest undercurrent of hope that he could be right, that she was more than she'd let herself be. *You can.* Ian shot Cardiff a hooded gaze. "Take the death spell off Alice and the curse off me, and then we'll help you."

"I won't do it unless you free Ian," Alice said quickly. "I don't care if I die. I know what death is, and it doesn't matter if

I stay alive unless Ian does too."

Ian's gaze shot to Alice, shocked by her statement. Despite her aversion to dying, she was claiming his future as a condition to her assistance? Something tightened in his chest, something he didn't understand, but it made him want to tear across the room and sweep Alice up into his arms.

"You lie. You're afraid of death. Everyone is—" Cardiff stopped when Alice held up her arm, showing him Ian's brands on her skin.

"We're almost fully bonded," she said. "Of course his life matters to me. How can I live without him?"

The strangest feeling of awe began to roll through Ian. Alice was really fighting for him. It was unreal. Incredible. Something so powerful and inspiring rolled through him, making him want to shout to the heavens that she was his woman.

Cardiff looked sharply at her arm. "The brand has demon taint. What the hell's that?"

Darkness jarred Ian at the reminder of how disfigured the marks were. The ugly black scars marred what should be symbols of the ultimate beauty and purity, marks that symbolized the incredible bond between a male and a female. It was wrong that they were tainted. Just wrong.

As Ian scowled at her arm, he sensed the faintest hint of demon shadows beginning to form around the edges of the room...and that's when he knew. The demon taint in her brand wasn't because of him and the fact he carried a trace of demon in his genes. It was because she was so close to death, so close to being owned by the demons, that they were staking their claim on her, trying to trump Ian's.

Son of a bitch. They were claiming her.

No way. He couldn't allow that to happen. No fucking way.

Tension ran through him as he twisted his arms, trying to get free of the bonds. He needed to liberate himself so he could protect her against the encroaching death, but again, he made no progress. The things were locked down, secured by magic. Shit! The fact that the shadows were there told him that she was about to die again, and they were ready to take her. Had Cardiff made a deal with them? A bargain? How was he going to kill her for good? She always came back.

The door opened and a young woman was carried in by two Calydons that Ian had never seen before. They were strapping and strong, men who were clearly warriors. The new Order already being created? The woman was being dragged between them, and her head was lolling to the side as if she'd been drugged.

"Catherine!" Alice screamed, fighting to get free of Warwick.

This was Catherine? Ian narrowed his eyes as he inspected her more closely. The Calydons dropped the woman at Deathbringer's feet, and she slumped to the ground. There was a dark cloud surrounding her, almost as if it were bleeding out of her pores. Her skin was spotted with black, and even her blond hair was tinged with a putrid brown.

"This is your death," Warwick said, bringing his mount closer. "Alice Shaw, bring my *sheva* Audrey Beckett back to life, or die at the hands of the angel of death."

Alice felt her heart stop as she looked down at Catherine, and suddenly she understood why Catherine had been so desperate to die. She was dangerous now, a scourge that would contaminate all who came near her. Guilt filled Alice for the fact she'd let her need to feel love trump what she'd promised Catherine she would do. "Oh, Cat, I'm so sorry."

"Now!" Cardiff threw Alice to the ground.

She landed next to the woman that Alice knew in her heart was her sister, even if they weren't connected by blood. "Cat!" She touched her hands, and immediately jerked it back when her skin burned.

Alice. Ian's voice broke into her mind. *Get away from*

there. She's too dangerous. The demons are coming for you.

Alice looked back, and her heart began to race when she saw the familiar dark shadows easing out of the walls. She looked at Warwick. "You promised them that they'd get me today, didn't you? That you would kill my soul so I couldn't come back this time?" Terror began to beat at her, and fear. If Catherine killed her, it would be over. Her soul would be dead forever, locked down in an eternity of hell. After a lifetime of not really caring if she died, she didn't want to anymore. She wanted to be with the man she loved. She wanted to take care of her sister. And—

A warrior came tumbling down the stairs, his body limp and bleeding. He landed beside Alice, his shoulder resting against her leg. He was immobile, his head almost entirely crushed by stone. Alice immediately sensed that his spirit was leaving his body.

"Shit! Gideon!" Ian shouted.

The moment Gideon's skin brushed Alice's, the most tremendous sense of power filled her. Before she could even think about what she was doing, Alice laid her hand on his chest. Her hand glowed white, offering him the same blessing that had always come to her when she'd been suffering in the afterlife with the demons. It spilled through him until his entire body glowed white. There was a burst of brilliant light, like an explosion, then complete blackness and silence for a split second, and then the room returned to normal.

Gideon was still lying on the floor, but she could feel his healing energies racing through him, working to repair the head wound. He was no longer on the edge of death. His body was working the miraculous healing that the Calydons were so famous for.

Stunned, she stared at him as the aftermath of her powers continued to rush through her like a torrent. "Oh my God," she whispered, shocked by what had just happened. Had she really just saved Gideon?

"Yes, you did." Ian's pride flowed over her. "You did it. You gave life back to Gideon. You're one of our angels. You're our guardian angel."

Alice couldn't believe it. All this time, she'd had a mission, and she'd been doing right by it. It was exhilarating and amazing! She wasn't a pathetic angel with no talents. She'd been feeding the Order their life force this whole time. "How did I not know?"

But even as she asked the question, she realized she had known, but had not been ready to understand it. How many times had her hands glowed with that white light? Sometimes faintly. Sometimes bright. She'd never thought of it as significant, just another sign that she couldn't control her powers. In reality, it must have been the Order drawing on her. Her hands hadn't started to glow until after her mother had died...

And that's when Alice knew. Her mother must have been the Order's guardian angel before she'd died, and she'd passed it on to Alice. She'd never told Alice what her assignment was, or how to do it, or how to connect with her charges. An angel of life was supposed to be trained by her mother, but her mother had never done that for her. Would she have helped Alice if she hadn't died? Or... would she simply have abandoned her for good?

With a sudden burst of clarity, Alice began to wonder if maybe her mother hadn't been the flawless angel she'd always believed. She remembered the bitter tilt to her mother's lips, the weariness that always seemed to be pouring off her. She'd thought it was because her mom was burdened with a daughter she didn't want. What if that wasn't it at all? What if her mother hated being an angel, and she'd wanted a different life for her daughter, so she'd withheld her assignment and given Alice the pearl of Lycanth, so that Alice could be free to live however she wanted?

Maybe her deathbed disappointment hadn't been Alice's

failure to save her, but her disappointment that her daughter could not break free of the rules... Dear God. As she had the thought, Alice knew it was true. She was certain of it. Her mother had not only loved her, but she'd loved her enough to want her to be free of the hellish life of an angel. She'd had a lifetime of freedom with that pearl, and she'd never understood that freedom was the true gift her mother had tried to give her.

Not until now. Not until it was too late.

But even as she realized it, a part of her felt violated. She could have been connected to the Order her whole life, and instead, she'd been alone and isolated, trying to find her way.

Ian watched the expressions warring on Alice's face: the awe, the excitement, and the wash of loneliness. He swore as he picked up on her thoughts about her mother, so many questions she would never be able to answer. *You have always known who you were,* he said. *You've been keeping us alive for a long time.*

She looked at him, and he saw anguish in her eyes. *What about Dante? I didn't keep him alive. Would I have been able to if I'd been there?*

Her question shocked him. She was right. How had she not been able to save Dante? What had been different about his death? They'd seen the replay of his death, and it had been a single strike by a Calydon weapon that had brought him down, something that should never have been able to hurt him. *I don't know, sweetheart.* But he was going to find out.

"See?" Cardiff's hand closed on Alice's hair, yanking her back toward him, making Ian strain at his bonds again. "She is part of the Order's trinity. Without her, the Order will not be able to continue. Since she has no daughter, there will be no replacement for her when she is gone. You'll die. The Order will die—"

"And Audrey will never come back," Ian interrupted, desperate to distract the wizard.

Ian's exhilaration at discovering Alice's true calling

vanished, chased away by the fact that her saving Gideon had just given the wizard all the reason he needed to make sure she stayed dead because he now knew for certain that Alice was their guardian angel.

Alice's death wouldn't just destroy Ian. It would take down the entire Order. Ian had to stop him, had to find a way to reach him. "Do you really want to be alone for the rest of your life?" Ian challenged the wizard.

As he posed the question, he felt himself answer it as he looked at Alice, still kneeling beside Gideon and Catherine, both of whom were unconscious.

No, he didn't want to be alone the rest of his life. He wanted Alice to be a part of it.

For a long moment, Warwick hesitated, and Ian could feel him warring with his choice. Bring back the woman he loved, or change the future? Ian knew what he would do: he would choose Alice. "You'll be with Audrey again," Ian urged. "You'll kiss her. You'll see the beauty of her smile." Still straining against the cuffs that wouldn't budge, he looked down at Alice, his heart awakening for the first time in his life. No longer did he see a woman who would strip him of his ability to stay alive, a female who was too dangerous to connect with. He simply saw the reason he wanted to live. "You'll hear her voice again," he said, thinking of all the things about Alice that mattered, that were so beautiful. "You'll hear her say your name. You'll see that smile on her face when she looks at you. You'll hold her again, and never have to let her go. You'll be the one to cheer for her when she finally finds her path, and you'll be the one she'll reach for when she needs help."

Alice dragged her gaze off Warwick and looked at Ian, confusion in those beautiful green eyes. *Are you talking to me or Warwick?*

Both of you. Something strained inside Ian, something that was fighting to get out. *I've stayed alive for six hundred years because I've avoided women. When I met you, I did my best to block you and prevent you from getting inside me.*

She rolled her eyes. *I know that, thanks.*

The truth would destroy his reputation and dishonor his family, but Ian didn't care. He needed her to know the truth before it all ended and he lost the chance to tell her. *I resisted you, and all other women, because I was afraid, Alice.* The ultimate sin by a warrior: to shirk his duty because he was too fearful to do what he needed to do. *I was afraid that I wasn't strong enough to handle a woman. To handle you.* The words burned through his mind, the admission that a warrior as great as he was had burned in fear, true, deep fear for so long. *I was afraid of what I felt for you.*

Really? Hope burned in her eyes, emotions so bright and so beautiful that his chest seemed to expand. As she spoke, she looked down at her arm, and he saw the black line traveling over her skin, filling in his brand. The trust stage. By trusting her with his secret, he'd brought them one step closer to sealing their bond forever. All that was left was his half of the death stage. *That was your deepest secret?* She looked at him. *That's what it is? That you were afraid?*

Yeah. Like a yellow-bellied sapsucker sobbing for his mama at the sight of his own shadow. It's not a thing for a man to be proud of, but I need you to know who I am, who I was.

She laughed slightly, her gaze meeting his. *And now?*

And now I know that you're the one thing that's worth living for. Fuck fear. I'll face down anything for a chance to be your guy. You've changed my world, Alice. That's the thing you really need to know.

Tears filled her eyes, and she leapt up. Ignoring Warwick's shout, she raced across the stone floor and flung her arms around Ian. He buried his face in her hair, drinking in the feel of her body against his, the pure scent of her skin, the strength of her arms as she held onto him. His arms were still trapped in the restraints, and his soul screamed with the need to hold her, to draw her against him and make her his, but hell, having her hugging him was pretty fucking good.

Warwick's low chuckle broke through the moment. "No, no, no. How can I bring Audrey back to a world that is still wrong? No. I can't." He leaned forward. "If one angel of life can bring Audrey back, then so could another. When the time is right, I'll bring her home. Right now, I want to make things right. Alice will die. You will kill yourself and end the Fitzgerald line, and the Order will be destroyed by gargoyles. Life will begin anew."

Alice spun around to face Cardiff, her fists clenched by her sides. "Don't be a fool," she shouted. "Love is more important than destruction! How could you choose death over love?"

"I'm not choosing anything over love," Cardiff snapped. "How dare you judge my commitment to Audrey?" His wand flashed, and a green laser hit Alice in the chest.

She gasped and stumbled, and fury roared through Ian. He bellowed his protest as he fought his bonds, straining so fiercely against the metal that blood poured down his wrists. "You don't get to take her," he bellowed. *Gideon! You awake yet?* His teammate didn't respond. Shit!

Ian yanked at his arm again, and this time he felt a small movement of the steel. It was coming free from the wall! Come on! He jerked again, and felt a tiny bit more movement.

Cardiff laughed, his mount prancing restlessly. "How much does it hurt to see your woman suffering, and to be helpless to protect her?" He shot another blast at Alice, and she went down on her knees, gasping.

"Shit!" Ian fought even harder, and his left wrist moved a tiny bit. Crumbles of stone trickled to the earth. "Alice! Get up! Get away from him!"

"I'm trying." She dragged herself to her knees, and he saw tears burning in her eyes. Tears of pain and fear.

Cardiff laughed, twirling his wand like a baton. "See? Isn't it hell to see your woman suffer? Don't you feel like a failure?"

"Fuck!" At the top of the stairs was Drew, still fighting, but not hard. Ian started to call him, and then hesitated. Was he calling the enemy if he called the kid? But as quickly as he thought it, he dismissed it. Drew was Dante's son. Blood ran thicker than anything else. *Drew. Get your ass down here.*

The youth turned immediately and started fighting his way down the stairs. *Coming!*

See? A good kid.

Gideon didn't move from his comatose pose on the floor, but his voice touched Ian's mind. *I'm good now. What's the plan?*

We have to get him to take the curse off Alice. She can't die.

Keeping our angel of life alive would be a good plan. Gideon's concurrence was strong and steady. *How are we going to get Cardiff to retract it?*

Shit. He had no fucking idea! There had to be something he could do! Ian frantically inspected the room, searching for a solution. He noticed the demonic shadows building in the corners. Why had the demons always been there when she died? How were they so connected to her? There had to be an answer in the demons...

Cardiff waved his hands at the specters, pointing them toward Alice. "That's the one you'll get," he said. "Not the other."

The other? Ian realized that some of the shadows had been circling Catherine, as if they'd sensed her death too. But that made no sense, not if they were there for Alice... Son of a bitch. They weren't there for Alice, were they? They were there for an angel's soul, and it didn't matter which one. Alice was the one they kept getting, because once she died, they'd gotten their claws into her and had a link to her. They were the ones dragging her back toward death, but it didn't have to be her, did it? Any angel would suffice, and once they got their angel, it would be done.

Son of a bitch. Could it be that easy? Could that be right?

He looked up at Cardiff, needing to confirm his suspicions. "You bastard," he said. "It doesn't have to be Alice, does it? You made a deal with the demons that you'll kill an angel and give them her soul. But it doesn't have to be her, does it?"

Cardiff's face was impassive. "Death is death. It's all the same."

No, it wasn't. It wasn't the same at all. One was a debt that could be satisfied only with Alice's soul. The other was a contract that wouldn't end until it was honored, one that would be satisfied with *any* angel's soul. Son of a bitch. That was it. Cardiff's answer had given Ian the solution he needed.

Another flash of light from the wand hit Alice, and this time she screamed. The demons began to circle more closely, creeping down the walls. Despair tore through Ian as he watched his woman fading, as he saw her life ending. He twisted his right arm, but the bolt didn't move any further. He couldn't get it! He needed more strength, and he knew what it would take to get it.

There was one emotion that would make him strong enough to break the bonds, and that was how he felt about Alice.

He focused on Gideon and Drew, who was working his way down the stairs. *When I give the word, attack him. Drew, you've got twenty-one weapons to call. He can't defend against them all. You hit from the front. Gideon, you come from behind and deliver the final blow while he's distracted.*

Both warriors assented to his plan. *What about you?* Gideon asked.

Ian focused on Alice as she crumpled to the floor, right beside Catherine. The dark shadows were only a few feet away from her. *I'm going to save Alice.*

Warwick laughed, a booming, psychotic chortle as he

pointed his wand at the two women. He muttered something, a trickle of green sparkles dusted out of the tip of the wand, and then the women's hands began to move toward each other: the tainted, blackened palm of death, and the beautiful, pristine hand of the woman Ian loved. As their hands moved, Catherine's head came up, her eyes haunted and deadly, focused on Alice like a predator.

Ian knew Alice had no defenses against her sister. The moment she touched Catherine, she would die. Despair coursed through Ian, and he heard that same voice haunting him that had been after him his whole life. *You have failed her. She is lost. You have no honor. Die by your own hand, warrior. Die.*

And this time, for the first time in his life, Ian didn't fight the voice of doom.

He embraced it.

He let the despair consume him, like the dark cloud of grief. His soul screamed in agony. The weight of loss overwhelmed him, berating him until he screamed in pain so great that he felt like his soul was being torn apart. He gave himself over to the howl of gaping, raw loneliness and he let the immensity of his failure consume him.

Die, warrior, die! The voice shouted at Ian, and he accepted its command.

It was time for him to die.

"Now!" he shouted to Gideon, then with the strength of one gone mad with grief, he ripped the manacle out of the wall, called forth his mace with a flash of black light, and plunged it straight into his heart.

CHAPTER NINETEEN

Alice screamed as Ian plunged the head of his mace into his chest. The moment the weapon made contact, fire raged through her. His entire being seemed to fill her, bursting through her like a hurricane knocking her off her feet. Strength surged through her, and she lunged to her feet, her weakened body suddenly reverberating with intense power. "Ian!" She lunged for him, her entire soul aching for him as he sagged in his bonds.

As she reached him, a young warrior leapt off the stairs with a battle cry as he unleashed a relentless arsenal of weapons at Cardiff, throwing them so fast that they were a blur as they flashed past her head.

Cardiff whirled Deathbringer around, shooting streaks of magic at the weapons, knocking them down as fast as they came, but then more came, until the room was a volley of green lights and weapons.

Not that it mattered any more who won, not with Ian's life bleeding out of his chest. Her throat raw, tears blurring her vision, Alice reached Ian. When she touched him, the most intense feeling of rightness filled her. Ian seemed to expand through her spirit, her soul, and her world. "Ian!" She caught him as he sagged in his bonds, his freed arm hanging limply by his side. "You killed yourself!" Guilt ripped at her. He'd finally succumbed to his worst nightmare because she'd been almost dead. "This is wrong! Please don't give up! We can—"

"It's perfection." He raised his head, his eyes glazed. "By killing myself, I saved you. There is no greater honor than that. I offer my life for you freely."

Tears streamed down her face, her heart breaking into more pieces than she could ever have imagined. "But—"

"Cardiff made a deal with the demons for angel magic. It won't end until he meets his end of the deal." His voice was laced with pain. "So I offered myself."

"You did it on purpose?" She stared at him, not understanding. "But you're not an angel."

"No, but my *sheva* is. My soul will count, because you're a part of me." He tried to grab her arm, but he was too weak. "I gave my life for yours. The final stage is done. We're connected forever."

She looked down. Her heart stilled and then seemed to blossom when she saw that the brand was complete. Every line of his weapon was carved on her skin. He was a part of her, and she was a part of him. Merged together. Forever. "Oh, Ian," she breathed in awe. "It's done—" As she watched, the angry black began to fade. The lines became thinner, and the color fainter. "Oh, no! It's disappearing!"

"No." His eyes were bloodshot now, barely open as he fought to watch her arm. "It's turning into what it should have been all along."

"What do you mean?" But then she saw what he meant. As she watched, the lines turned into beautiful, elegant silver marks. No longer was their connection blackened by demons. It was simply them, simply the beauty of what should be between them.

The demons had released their claim on her. Now their bond was pure and magical, everything it was supposed to be. Intense rightness filled her. "I'm yours," she whispered. "Forever."

"Forever," he agreed, brushing his fingers over her cheek in a gesture so tender that it made her soul ache with longing. "You're a part of me. Which means I fulfill the contract—" He gasped suddenly, and Alice saw black shadows winding around his ankle. The demons that had come to take her were taking him instead. "No! Stop!" She shouted and batted at them, but they just kept coming. "Ian!"

His fingers drifted off her cheek. "I love you, sweetheart. You'll always be my angel." Then his eyes closed, and his body relaxed. The dark shadows swirled over his body, and she felt them taking his soul. "No, no, no!" She screamed, frantically trying to remember how she'd saved Gideon. She called the white light, but it didn't come. Nothing came. Because he wasn't Order anymore. She couldn't save him. "No!"

He'd relinquished his legacy for her. He'd given up his chance to restore honor to his family name. He'd taken the road considered least honorable. Everything that mattered to him, he'd given it all up for her.

And she'd lost him. Dear God, he was gone.

††††

A weapon whizzed by Alice's head, and she numbly looked up as the young warrior continued to pummel Warwick. A dagger nicked the wizard's shoulder, and another grazed past his horse's chest. There were too many for him to fend off. He glanced down at Ian, and then threw his arms in the air in victory. "It is done!" he crowed in delight.

Victory because he'd caused an amazing man to kill himself? "You bastard!" She lurched to her feet, anger blazing through her. She'd never felt so much fury, never allowed such intense emotions to flow though her. "You don't get it! You didn't dishonor him! Ian just made the most powerful choice a warrior can make! You didn't ruin him. He died with glory and honor because he took back what you stole from him, his ability to love!" She was screaming at him now, tears streaming down her face.

Warwick glanced at her. "What are you raving about, woman?" In the split second he took his attention off the battle to focus on Alice, a spear plunged into his shoulder.

He shouted, whirling back to face his young attacker, but Alice grabbed his horse's bridle, yanking the massive animal back toward her with surprising ease, as if the horse himself was on her side and not the wizard's. "You failed! Don't you get it? You failed to destroy him! He defeated you!"

The wizard yanked the horse's reins free of her grasp, and she saw pink foam frothing at the animal's mouth. Blood? He was hurting his horse too? "You bastard!" She called out Ian's mace, and it appeared in her hand. "How dare you!"

Cardiff laughed. "You think you can kill me with that?" He held his arms out to his sides in a defenseless position. "Just try! If you kill me, it will destroy you even more! Try!"

Alice raised the mace to strike, her arms shaking with fury as he waited for her to strike him down in cold blood. She hesitated, the weapon heavy in her hands. How could she do that? How could she take a life? How could she become like him?

She could make herself do it. She knew she could break the rules. She was already damned. But at the same time, did she really want to become the person with even more blood on her hands? Tears filled her eyes, and she lowered the mace. "I am an angel, not a monster," she said, claiming her birthright with pride for the first time in her life. "I will not be that person. You will find your death by hands other than mine."

"Like mine!" With a shout of triumph, Gideon sprang up from the floor behind Warwick, and slammed his axe into the side of the wizard's neck. It went clean through, severing the life from him instantly.

Cardiff tumbled off his mount, but before he hit the ground, his body shimmered once and then vanished from sight, his cloak dropping to his horse's saddle. It stayed there for a minute, then the animal stepped sideways and the cloak slid silently off the leather and landed in a soft heap on the ground beside his massive hoof.

Beside him, Catherine moaned, and she slumped on the wood as the stains on her body faded.

Alice cried with relief as Catherine looked up, her eyes blue again. "Alice?" she croaked.

"Cat!" Alice dropped to her knees beside Catherine and hugged her. The wizard's death had broken the spell he'd cast that had been dragging Cat toward that horrific fate. "You're okay."

Cat hugged her fiercely, her body trembling. "For now, Ally. Just for now." She pulled back and met her gaze. "It won't end."

Alice brushed the hair out of her sister's eyes. "I know. We'll figure something out. But we have time now."

"Not much, Ally. Not much." The women hugged again, both of them treasuring this moment, all too aware that Catherine's battle was far from over.

The sounds of fighting on the roof stopped, and there were shouts of triumph from the warriors still up there. In their tower room, Drew let out a whoop of victory, but Gideon just looked at Alice, his face grim. "Ian?"

Grief surged through Alice. Grief, and the most powerful love she'd ever experienced. "He killed himself for me."

Gideon looked past her, and hope sparked in his face. "His body hasn't vanished yet. He still has a chance."

Alice's heart jumped, and she whirled around to look at Ian. "What?"

"Calydon bodies vanish at death. The older they are, the quicker they disappear. Ian's should be gone by now." He sprinted across the room and knelt beside Ian as boots began to thud down the stairs. With a few slashes of his axe, he broke the manacles that had been trapping Ian and caught him as he slid to the ground.

315

Alice squeezed in beside him, and put her hand on Ian's chest. His body was empty. His spirit was gone. "He's not there."

"No!" Gideon swore, grabbing Ian's shoulders. "Quinn Masters died for two minutes, and then came back to life. Ian! Come on! Don't give up!"

God, if there was a way...but she knew there wasn't. He was gone. Tears blurred, and she realized she was clutching Ian's hand, as if she could bring him back to life with her touch.

Gideon grabbed her arm. "Save him, like you saved me. Give him that white light shit that you did."

"I can't. He's not Order of the Blade! You guys kicked him out and now I can't help him!"

Gideon blanched, and the other Order of the Blade members charged down the stairs. Kane let out a shout and teleported himself right beside Ian. "Shit, we have to heal him!"

But unlike last time, when his team could help him, this was different. "He's dead," she whispered. "There's nothing left to save."

Kane turned his head. "Then you're the only thing that can help him."

"He's not Order—"

"Who the fuck cares? Just do it." Kane's eyes glittered. "I'm married to an angel, and I know damn well that you can break the rules if you want to badly enough."

"I do want to! I love him!"

"Then save him!" Kane commanded. "Now!"

Alice looked down at Ian, knowing that it wasn't anything like how it had been with Gideon when she'd saved him out of instinct and duty. It wasn't Chloe, who was just a person to her. This was *Ian,* the man who had saved her so many times, pushed her past her limits, and made her laugh when she had no reason to. He'd awakened her emotions, and he'd given her the ability to feel and connect in a way she never had before. The man who'd given up what mattered most to him, just so he could give her love.

She didn't want to save him because it was her duty.

She wanted to save him because she loved him—

Oh, God. Did she really love him? That was the ultimate betrayal of her duty as an angel of life. The ultimate failure. Had she really crossed that line?

But as she gazed down at Ian, the pain in her heart was so deep, so intense, and so agonizingly terrible, that she knew the answer was yes. And she didn't want it any other way.

Kane's flail pressed against her neck. "Save him," he said, his eyes darkening with a fury that made her skin crawl. "I won't lose two of my teammates. Get him back for us. *Now!*" His eyes were blazing with such torment and hell that her skin went cold.

Something was seriously dangerous inside him. Slowly, Alice reached out and touched his face. His skin was cold and hard, almost brittle. "You need help," she said.

Surprise flickered in Kane's dark eyes, and for a split second, she saw the desperate humanity within them. A vulnerability he kept hidden deep inside, from others but also from himself. "I know," he said softly, in a voice so low she felt his words more than heard them. "Sarah keeps me in control. I need to get back to her. But right now, Ian needs help."

"Save him like you saved me," Gideon said. "I can feel the white light pouring out of you. It's still in there. Use it on Ian. Now."

"The white light is for the Order—" But as she protested, she realized there had been times when she'd used white light on someone other than the Order: herself.

Every time she died, just at that moment when the demons had taken her beyond what she could endure, a white light had come for her. It had always started as a glow, but it eventually took the shape of a woman before plunging into her and taking her back to the physical world. She'd always thought it was something external coming to rescue her, but now, for the first time, she realized that she'd been wrong.

That light was inside her. It was her own powers, coming to save her when she was at her most desperate, when she was so desolate that she called it even without meaning to. She wasn't Order, but she used the white light on herself. Could she call it for Ian, for the man who was such a part of her that his brands were on her arms?

Sudden, fierce resolution flowed through her. Determination. No fear. For the first time in her life, she felt no fear or insecurity, just the same intense focus that she'd seen in Ian every time he'd prepared for battle. "Come on, Ian." She slid her hands under his head and bent her head to his. *Just as you offered me your healing and your strength to save my life all those times, I offer you mine.*

Then she pressed her lips to his cold ones and offered him everything she had, just as he had offered it to her so many times. She opened her heart to him. She let him feel her love for him. She showed him her terror at what would become of her for saving him, and at the same time, let warm reassurance flow through her that it was the right choice. That she would do it a thousand times.

His lips didn't respond, and his soul was gone...no...no... wait! She could feel him! Distant. Not in his body, but hovering close, connected by mere threads, still trying to hang on and resist the demons. There was still a chance!

Ian. Come back to me. Alice continued to kiss him, trying desperately to erase a lifetime of protective shields around her emotions. She let herself feel the agony of a future without Ian. She allowed herself to experience the anguish of what his death would feel like. She let the trauma of it all fill her, until the grief and desperation were so strong that they tore at her heart. She welcomed all the pain and let it fill her.

She opened herself to Ian's suffering, and nearly staggered at the feeling of how fiercely he was fighting to live. She brought that will to live into her, and she absorbed it as her own until her lungs began to labor under the effort of taking one more breath, as if she were the one who was dying.

She let his death fill her, merging them until she felt her soul join him in death. Further and further she fell into the crevasse, winding her soul around his, until his last breath tried to steal hers, until death was their only future. *No! I'm not ready to die!* Just as she had all those times while in demon hands, Alice lunged for the one thing that would save her: the white light.

She screamed to the heavens, calling for her life, for help, and for salvation. She turned her existence and Ian's over to a power far greater than she. And as she did so, she reached the end of her capacity and her lifeline. Immediately, that familiar white light formed in her mind, coming to save both her and the man so connected to her that they were one.

As she and Ian fought together for breath, the white glow began to spin, faster and faster. It took the shape of an orb, stretching longer and longer, and then suddenly morphed into the form of a woman. And for the first time in her life, Alice saw that it was herself. She screamed for help, and the white light transformed into a glowing sphere and plunged right through both of their hearts.

She gasped and her body bowed in unison with Ian's, and their screams joined in agonizing relief as their spirits returned to their bodies.

Alice. Ian's arms went around her, catching her as she collapsed onto him. His pride filled her, a sense of pride so beautiful that she wanted to cry. *I knew you had it in you.*

"Way to go!" Kane thumped her shoulder, and she was vaguely aware of the rest of the team's cheers of triumph.

All she could focus on was Ian. *I lo—* But before she could get the words out, her thigh began to burn. Alice yelped and grabbed for the front of her shorts. Smoke was rising from them, and a charred black hole was in her front pocket. She cupped her hand beneath the hole as the pearl rolled free and landed in her palm.

It was no longer the inactive swirl of reds and oranges. Now, it was glowing with a blazing white light, so bright that she had to shield her eyes. Ian sat up, bracing himself on his elbows, his eyes clear and focused as if he hadn't been a whisper from death. "What's that?"

She held it up. "The pearl of Lycanth. It's activated now."

Ian looked at her, and his eyes were grim with comprehension. "Saving me damned you, didn't it? The pearl is on overdrive trying to protect you."

She nodded and closed her fist around it. "Without it, I'd already be in the ocean."

"And when you have to give it back when we return—" He didn't finish the sentence. They both knew what would happen.

Alice shrugged. "You don't need to go back. I'll go—"

"Fuck that. We're going back, and we're going to face the deal we made. If you're going to wind up living a mermaid's life, I'll buy some scuba gear and rule the underworld with you."

"But what about the Order? You can't be in the Order if you're stuck under water."

Ian took her hands and met her gaze with unflinching intensity. "The bastards don't appreciate me. Why would I trade what I have with you to run around with a bunch of guys who sweat too much?"

Tears burned in Alice's eyes and she saw the depth of sadness in Ian's face at the idea of walking away from the Order. "No," she said, "Don't do that for me—"

He put his index finger across her lips, silencing her. "I love you, Alice. There's no other life for me besides the one I share with you. I'm sure there are sharks and shit down there that I can protect the girls against. Because those women need protection, don't they?"

Alice nodded. "They do—"

"So, I'm the man to do it." He winked at her, and behind the sadness at leaving his friends, she saw an inner peace, a man who had found his calling. "You really mean that, don't you?"

"Of course." He kissed her hard. "I gave my life for you, sweetheart. Giving up oxygen and poker with the guys is a no-brainer."

Alice laughed, suddenly feeling giddy. And to think this was the man she'd thought could never put her first. She felt light and glorious, a woman finally alive. "I love you, Ian."

"I love you, too." He kissed her for a long moment, then raised her arm to press his lips to her marks. He stopped suddenly and grinned at her brands. "Now, that's what it's supposed to look like."

She followed his gaze and smiled at the thin, silver lines. She pressed her hand to them, and found they were cool to the touch. "It's over."

"Yeah, it is." He grinned. "The demons no longer have any claim on you. They got me, and that satisfied the bargain."

"But you came back, like I did." She looked at him. "So, they'll come back again, won't they? The deal isn't done."

"I think it is. Unlike you, I was actually dead for a minute. The deal was complete. They got their angel soul; they just couldn't hang onto it." He framed her face with his hands. "Don't you get it sweetheart? They won't be stalking you anymore. No more dying. We've got a whole life ahead of us."

Hope began to hammer in her heart, hope for all the things she'd craved for so long, but had no chance of having. "What about the bond? Don't you need to go rogue since we bonded?"

He paused for a moment, then shrugged. "I feel fine. My guess is that I died too quickly to go rogue, but since I died, that fate is taken care of as well."

"Or it could still come after you," Gideon said, clamping his hand down on Ian's shoulder. "Welcome to the unstable world of being fully-bonded and always looking over your shoulder to see if fate's going to grab you by the ass."

Ian grinned, and slung his arm around Alice. "I've been stalked by magical shit my whole life. Keeps life interesting." He kissed the top of her head, his eyes growing serious. "Hey, Alice?"

She smiled at him. "Yes?"

"Since the new trend appears to be that we marry our soul mates, I'd hate to be out of the club. Will you marry me? And..." He cleared his throat. "I'd be a good dad," he said, not quite able to keep the thickness out of his voice.

She grinned, the most incredible emotions filling her up. "I will," she whispered. "I really will. And you will be an amazing father, one that will make yours proud." A flicker of sadness drifted through her heart. "But I don't know how to be a good mom."

"I'll help you." He laid his hand over her heart. "All you need is in here. I believe in you, and I'll help you find your way."

Alice put her hand over his, and she knew he was right. She might be a guardian angel, but she'd just found the guardian angel who was meant for her.

As they stood there, Alice became aware of a loud chirping from the ocean. Frowning, she walked over and peered out a window. Beneath them, cresting the whitecaps were two dolphins towing an ancient dinghy. Alice caught her breath as Ian's hands clasped her shoulders. "It's time."

"It is."

Anguish filling her, Alice turned toward Catherine and hugged her. "Let the Order protect you. They'll help," she whispered.

Catherine hugged her back. "I love you, Ally."

Alice pulled back, searching Catherine's eyes for a promise. "Stay with them, Cat. Seriously."Catherine pulled back, wrapping her too-thin arms around her torso. "It's bigger than you know, Ally. I can't stay."

"But—"

Cat held up her hand. "Trust me, Alice. Let me do what I need to do. Don't come after me."

Alice's chest hurt with sadness, but she'd already broken one promise to her sister. She couldn't betray her again. "I'll always be here for you."

"I know." Cat hugged her again, then turned and ducked wearily down the stairs, slipping unnoticed past the men who were talking solemnly with Ian, not happy with his disclosure that he was off to become a merman. Guilt swept through her at the heaviness of the atmosphere, all jubilation from their defeat of the wizard gone.

The tightness of the bond between the men was evident, and Alice knew that they would have welcomed Ian back into the Order if he weren't leaving it to be with her. How could she let him give that up?

She knew then that she couldn't. He was compelled to come back with her, but if she could save Chloe, they would be allowed to leave. She would be trapped as a Mageaan without the pearl, but Ian would be free.

She would not let Ian stay with her. She would save Chloe not just to save the girl, but also to liberate Ian, and then, she would let him go.

It would be easy. As a Mageaan, she would control the sea. If she commanded it to reject him, it would. He would have no choice.

The dolphins squeaked again, and Ian met Alice's gaze, his warm smile not hiding the weight in his heart as his team stood in a silent semi-circle around him. "Ready to start our new life, sweetheart?"

Sadness filled Alice's heart as she put her hand in his, because she knew that this was the last time they would be together. She managed a smile, but not words.

It was just too hard.

†††

Ryland leaned against the wall of the tunnel, his lungs heaving with each ragged inhale. His skin was hanging in shreds. His clothes had burned into embers. Around him on the floor lay the putrid remains of the poisonous substance that had tried to claim him once he'd entered the pit. What he'd had to do to break free of it...it had been a thousand times worse than what had happened when he'd been at the other pit with Kane.

He looked down at his hand and saw glittery scales shifting beneath the skin. Shit. He leaned his head back against the wall, summoning the same intense control that had kept him going for so long. But he couldn't find it. All he could think about was Thano going through that same hell. And the angel of death, somewhere in this morbid castle. And Dante's demise. Shit, he missed Dante.

His upper lip curled, and his teeth began to lengthen.

"Shit!" He slammed his head back against the wall and pressed his hands to his eyes, his body straining with the effort of holding it in. *Dante. Why the fuck did you have to die? What kind of plan is that?*

Ryland.

Ryland's eyes snapped open at the sound of his mentor's voice. He spun around desperately, almost frantically, searching the dark tunnels. "Dante!" he shouted. "Dante! Where are you? Are you down here?" He staggered down the hall, bumping off walls as he tried to regain his equilibrium. "Dante!"

Stop.

Ryland froze, going instantly immobile at the command. *This war has become your battle.*

"Yeah, okay." He clenched his hands as his fingernails began to lengthen, the sharp barbs digging into his fisted palms. "Tell me what to do."

You don't need that from me anymore. You know your path.

"My path is your path. I'm here to serve you."

This is bigger than I am, Ryland. You need to move beyond me.

Denial roared through him. "No!" he shouted. "I will not abandon you!" Scales shifted on his arms, and Ryland's face contorted. "Shit!" He went down on his knees, fighting as his muscles began to contort. "I can't do this without you, Dante. I can't." He gasped the last words. "Help me. Please, help me."

He felt Dante's disappointment, and then a wave of calmness washed over him as Dante provided that same protection he'd given him so many times before. Ryland sucked in his breath as the scales receded and his muscles relaxed. He hung his head, shuddering as his body reclaimed itself. "Thank you."

No more help from me, Ryland. You are on your own now. Deviate from the path you think you're supposed to be on. There's no other way.

"No other way to do what?"

What needs to be done.

Ryland felt his mentor's spirit vanish. Loss and grief roared through him. "Dante!" He lunged forward, his hands clutching at empty air as if he could somehow reach the man who'd given him a second chance at life, who'd snatched him from the bowels of hell and taught him how to be a warrior.

But Dante was gone, and the emptiness of his existence filled Ryland again, the same pulsating doom that haunted him day after day. With a groan, Ryland hauled himself to his feet. His palms were bleeding, three cuts on each hand. A reminder of how close he was to that edge.

But Dante had given him a reprieve, and he would not waste it.

He wiped his hands over the wall of the passageway, leaving his blood behind as he continued down the dark hallway, allowing his instincts to continue to guide his path.

Thano. He tried again, for the thousandth time. *I know you're alive. You don't get to shirk your duties anymore. Man up, kid, and get with the program.*

There was a faint ripple of Calydon energy in Ryland's mind, and he went utterly still. *Thano. Your manicurist misses you. You gotta come home.* He focused all his energy into his mind, thrusting out feelers in all directions. *Come on, Thano. Answer me. I'll do the rest.*

And then he heard it. The sound that he'd been searching for so hard. *You're too old for this shit, Ry. Go back to bed and let the young guys handle it.*

Thano! It's about damned time you spoke up! Elation rushed through Ryland, and he immediately locked onto the warrior's mental energy. He broke into a run, not caring about his half-burned foot or the bits of silvery scales drifting in the air behind him. He sprinted down the hall, took a right, two lefts and then stopped in the middle of a long hallway. Thano's energy was all around him. It was weak and splotchy, mingled with something else, but definitely Thano. *Where are you?*

Right where I've been, waiting for one of you guys to show up.

Ryland looked down at the ground beneath his feet. Solid rock. Fuck that. Rock wasn't enough to stop him.

He called out his machete as he rubbed his foot over the floor, searching for the weakest spot. Thano's energy suddenly came through stronger, and Ryland marked it. He took a step back, focused on the location he'd identified, and then slammed his machete into the rock. Stones exploded everywhere. Three more hits, and then the hole was big enough for him to fit through.

Ryland immediately dropped through the hole, not even bothering to check and see what he was descending into. It was pitch black as he landed, so dark that not even his enhanced vision could penetrate the darkness. "Thano?"

A faint violet glow appeared in the corner, and Ry

whirled toward it, his machete ready...until he saw what it was.

Sitting in the corner, his forearms draped over his knees, was Thano. His palm was faceup toward the ceiling, and a small violet flame was burning brightly on his hand. His face was shadowed by the light, showing hollowed-out cheeks. He was covered in dirt, and his shoulders were bone-thin, as if he'd been deprived of food for a thousand years, not for just the short time that he'd been missing.

But he was alive. Conscious. "Thano." Ryland lowered his machete, his throat actually tightening at the sight of his teammate.

Thano looked up, and in those haunted eyes was the same glittering attitude there had always been. "Where have you been?"

"Looking for you." Ryland walked across the room, and after a moment, he sat down beside Thano, draping his arms over his knees like Thano was. He leaned his head back against the wall, suddenly too exhausted to move. "You forgot to leave your new address, which made it a little tough to find you."

"Sorry about that." Thano held out his hand. "I've never been able to start fires before. Not sure what that means."

"You'll have to ask Zach. He knows fire." Zach Roderick was one of the Order members. He had a special relationship with fire that none of them really understood. Ryland passed his hand through the flames. "It's ice cold."

"Yeah. Zach's isn't." Thano turned his head to look at him. This time, now that he was closer, Ryland could see shadows in Thano's eyes that hadn't been there before. "Ry?"

"Yeah."

"I want to go home."

Ryland nodded. "Let's do it, buddy." He stood up, but Thano didn't. No words passed between the warriors, but Ryland understood. He sheathed his machete, then crouched down, slid his arms beneath the warrior and picked him up.

As he carried Thano back toward the hole in the ceiling,

Ryland thought of Dante's words. The battle was his now. His to win or lose.

There was no choice. Nothing else mattered but Dante's legacy.

Whatever the battle was, he was going to win it.

Chapter Twenty

Alice perched on the bow seat of the dinghy, watching the sun rising over the horizon as the dolphins carried them back toward Jada and Chloe. The dawn was a beautiful but quiet array of yellows and oranges, the start of a new day, of her new life as a...yeah...water dweller.

Sigh.

She took a deep breath, inhaling the fresh air. "This is the last time I'll breathe air like this," she said. "It's the last time I'll belong to the land instead of the ocean." It was a bummer, but at the same time, she felt weirdly liberated. She may have condemned herself, but she'd done it willingly and knowingly, and she was proud of what she'd accomplished.

If she were going to be doomed to life beneath the sea, at least she'd done something sort of amazing to actually deserve it. There was a certain amount of pride in that.

Ian was sitting on the rear seat, his hands clasped loosely as he leaned on his quads. "There has to be another way," he said. "A way to stop the ocean from claiming you."

The urgency of his voice made it clear that he hadn't fully accepted life as fish bait. He didn't really want to join her there, and why would he? She wasn't high on it either, to be honest. As amazing as she was, she wouldn't blame him for not being entirely committed to a lifetime of soggy sex, with electric eels as house pets.

She thought of those horrific wails emanating from the Mageaan and all the suffering they endured. Yeah, and *that*. Quietly, she fisted her hands, reminding herself that she could survive anything. Except it wasn't simply about suffering and torture. The bigger issue was leaving Ian. God, she didn't want to do that. She really didn't.

"Alice," Ian pressed. "Let's talk about this. I'm not giving up."

"You have to relinquish that dream, Ian." With a sigh, she turned away from the sunrise and faced him, wanting to drink in every last bit of time with him that she could. "The thing is," she explained, "becoming a Mageaan is kind of like the *sheva* destiny. It just happens when an angel goes bad. My legs will disappear and become a tail. My lungs will change so that I become a water-breather." She shrugged. "It's not something you can will away by deciding to break the rules."

Ian ran a hand through his hair. "There has to be a way. There are five couples now who have defeated the *sheva* destiny, right?"

Alice raised her brows. "Gideon said that we may have just delayed it. No one knows if it's going to keep coming for us."

"Well, at least we got it to stall. That's a step forward. So, how can we do that here?" He started going through assorted options, none of which would stop the unstoppable.

As Ian expounded upon ways to change a predetermined future, Alice couldn't help but smile at his unwavering commitment to finding another solution. It was that same unflinching resolve and determination, along with his refusal to walk away from what mattered to him, that had made her fall in love with him. Somehow, she'd made it to the top of his list, and that was worth all the tears and suffering in the world.

She might have to dropkick him out of the ocean for his own good, but he would forever be in her heart. "Ian?"

"Yeah?"

She held out her arms, asking him to come to her. "Make love to me," she said. "Not to save us from some terrible fate, or to get your marks to appear on my arm. Just make love to me because you want to." She somehow managed to summon a flirty smile. "Once we get to Jada's, we don't know how long it will be before we'll have a chance to be alone again." But she knew when it would be. It would be never. This was their farewell.

Ian's face darkened, making chills of anticipation run down her spine. Without another word, he stood up, his weight balanced perfectly in the small boat. He crossed the vessel in two strides, then knelt before her, sliding his torso between her thighs and putting his hands on her hips.

Her heart began to pound as he tightened his hold on her. Without saying a word, he dragged her across the seat toward him until she was pressed up against his hard stomach. "You," he said, as he ran his hand through her hair so it was trapped in his fingers, "are the woman I was meant to be with."

Then he bent his head and kissed her.

It wasn't a kiss of ownership or possession. It was a kiss of absolute reverence, of tenderness, and Alice's heart filled with aching beauty for what they shared. *You make me feel like I'm cherished beyond words.*

You are cherished, my love. Ian kissed her again, a kiss so beautiful, so magical that Alice's heart seemed to take flight and sail to the heavens. He slid his hands beneath her shirt, his touch warm and seductive as he traced circles on her lower back and around each vertebra.

God, Ian. It feels so good to have you touch me. How could she give this up? How could she walk away from this? This man was all that mattered to her. But even as she thought it, she knew that was why she had to give him up: because she loved him, she could not take him away from what was important to him.

331

But for the next twenty-four hours, she had him. Under the sun, under the stars, under the moon. She would have to make the next day last for a lifetime. No, not simply a lifetime. An eternity, because that's how long she might live now that there was no price on her head. Funny how eternity didn't sound so wonderful now that she was going to have to face it without Ian.

Ian scooped her up and laid her in the bottom of the boat, stretching out beside her on the hard planks. Greedily wanting access to all of him, Alice tugged his shirt over his head. He did the same to her, then his jeans and her shorts were tossed aside, until it was just them, with nothing between them.

Reverently, Alice ran her hands over his chest, his marvelous strong chest. "I never had time to bask in you before," she said. "You were too busy pounding me into oblivion."

Ian grinned, a wicked gleam in his eyes as he rolled on top of her, his weight pinning her to the bottom of the boat in the most delicious and erotic manner. "I plan to pound you into oblivion some more," he said. "But feel free to bask while I'm doing it."

Alice laughed, loving his sense of humor. It felt so good to be here with him, not in a rush, with nothing to focus on but each other. A flash of sadness touched her, knowing that it wouldn't last— "Hey," Ian tucked her hair behind her ear, his brown eyes so tender and gentle. "Why the sad face?"

She smiled, tracing her finger over his whiskers. "I'm worried about Catherine," she said. It was true, but not the whole truth. "And I feel bad about you leaving the Order for me—"

"No." He cut her off with a kiss, a kiss that was more intense now, more powerful, designed to strip away her thoughts. *I'm a big boy, Alice. I know how to make my own choices.* His kisses grew more demanding and more devilishly manipulative. She felt her resistance sliding and crumbling under his sensual assault. Desire began pulsating low in her belly. Hunger for him crawled through her. Untamed passion rose to a crescendo.

She wrapped her arms around his neck, gasping as his hands roamed her breasts, her hips, her belly, and her thighs. *God, yes, Ian. This feels so incredible.*

Sweetheart, you ain't seen nothing yet. Then he wedged his knee between her thighs and thrust deep, connecting them in one swift move.

Alice gasped, her body convulsing at the feel of him inside her. It felt so amazing, so perfect, and she knew she would hold this moment, this man, in her heart forever. Then he began to move, sliding in and out in the most addictive and compelling rhythm, stoking fires inside her that seemed to ignite her very soul. He caught her mouth in a ravenous kiss, as if he were equally lost in the sparks flying between them.

As amazing as it had been between them before, now it was so much more. It was as if the heavens had brought them together, as if their souls had never been complete until they'd found each other. The orgasm began to build inside her, sending streaks of searing desire humming through her.

Ian began to move faster, driving harder and deeper, ruthlessly binding them together. Scorching fire suddenly exploded between them, catapulting her over that beautiful, magical edge into a whirlwind of ecstasy. *Ian.* She clutched his shoulders as his body went rigid. He shouted her name as he was thrust over the precipice, freefalling into her arms and her soul.

You will always be mine, Alice. Ian's voice was raspy and intense, fighting for words through the searing blaze of the orgasm that raged between them, merging their spirits and souls into a single unit of forever and ever. *And I will always be yours. I love you.*

Tears filled her eyes. *I love you too, Ian.*

As they crested in a surge of unmatched, untamed, and unstoppable passion, Ian sealed their declarations with a kiss of intense commitment and love, and she knew she was lost to him. And for this last time, she decided to simply allow herself to be spirited away by the moment. Life would intrude again too soon. But for the next day, she was going to stop obsessing about what was coming for her. Instead, she would simply let herself live.

And love.

And be loved.

And to be ruthlessly manhandled by the man who made her heart sing.

† † †

Ian straddled the rear seat of the boat, his mace out and ready as the dolphins eased to a stop beside the base of the large coral reef they'd escaped such a short time ago. Prepared for Jada to try something deadly, he had one hand locked on Alice's wrist. He could feel her pulse fluttering nervously.

It was time.

Ian looked over at her, frowning at the tight press to her lips. After an entire day of lovemaking that had been the best day of his life, no exaggeration, Alice had begun to withdraw. She'd barely spoken since the dolphins had taken them below water. He didn't like the emotional distance she'd erected, but he felt none of the grief or despair from the curse. When he'd died, the curse had apparently been satisfied, and he'd been freed.

Now that the curse was obsolete, Ian knew that his feeling of isolation about her distance was simply his own need for her, not something fabricated by a spell. It was all real, and that was good. So, yeah, it was great to know he wasn't going to stab himself in the heart every time his woman decided to get moody, but he damn well wasn't going to let her shut him out.

That wasn't what they had between them. *Alice.*

She glanced over at him, and he saw trepidation in her eyes. *What?*

Are you worried about not being able to save Chloe?

Her face paled, as if she hadn't even considered that possibility until now. *I'm not sure how to save her.*

You'll find a way. Do not, for even one minute, consider the option of not succeeding. Be ruthless in your confidence. Accept nothing less than success.

Alice managed a smile. *I know, I know. Failure is not an option.*

He sensed her commitment to doing what she had to do, and nodded with satisfaction. How far his angel had come. While she was figuring out how to save Chloe, it was his job to try to find a way to break that damned Mageaan fate. Just as he told her not to give up, he had to do the same.

There had to be a way out...but at the same time, he knew enough about the powers of fate and destiny to realize that, in this case, there really might not be a loophole that would allow Alice to remain an angel.

Failure was possible.

There was a loud grinding, and then a portion of the coral reef vanished, revealing the same room where he and Alice had been trapped. On the cot where they'd made love was Chloe, under a turquoise blanket.

Alice stood up, her gaze fixed resolutely on the girl. As she stepped off the boat into the room, Ian knew that she was going to succeed in saving Chloe, and grant them the chance to live. She had that aura about her, the attitude of a warrior who would not be defeated. *Damn, I'm proud of you, Alice.*

She glanced back at him, and this time the smile was real. *Thanks.*

Never forget it. As Ian prepared to follow her, he couldn't help but glance up toward the surface of the ocean, toward the life he was leaving behind. Would he ever set foot on solid ground again? Or would he be completely severed from his old life? Would he grow a tail, too? Damn, he hoped not. There was something sort of girly about iridescent tails.

He saluted the surface of the water, and the team that had meant so much to him for so long. *See ya later, guys.* He sent the message out to his team, having no idea if they would hear him.

There was no reply, and a strange sense of isolation settled over Ian. It was fucking weird not to be with his team, and not to have a future with them. Even after they'd kicked him out of the Order, he'd still felt his bond with them, and he'd had no doubt that they would stand by him, exactly as they had.

This was different, though. This was forever, and it made him feel adrift and aimless. What the hell would he do with his life if he wasn't fulfilling Order duties? Then, as he stepped into the room and saw Alice kneeling beside Chloe, her auburn hair streaming down her back, a sense of absolute rightness settled over him, and he knew that it was the correct choice.

Alice meant everything to him, and if she had to stay there, then so would he. Even if he grew a damned tail, it would still be a better life than a thousand years on the front lines of the Order without her. She was what mattered. If she had to stay, then he would remain there with her.

End of story.

† † †

Alice focused on the young woman before her. Chloe's face was dangerously pale, her eyes were closed, and her lips were ashen. Her heart was barely beating, but she seemed to be in a suspended coma of some sort, as if Jada had put her in that state to keep her from dying before Alice could come back.

The kiss of an angel of life was all she needed. So simple, and yet, so difficult.

For a long moment, Alice studied the girl, knowing that

if she simply tried to kiss her, it wouldn't work. So, what now? How could she do it?

"Alice? You got any ideas?" Ian crouched beside her, looking at the girl.

"I need to kiss her."

"Well, try. See if anything has changed."

Alice glanced at him, then shrugged and bent down toward Chloe. When her mouth was a fraction of an inch from Chloe's cheek, her muscles froze, locking her down. Frowning, she shook her head and retreated. If she pushed it again, the repercussions would be worse. "No, not working."

"Well? Can you save her?"

They both turned around at the sound of Jada's voice. The Mageaan was standing behind them, her body a misty blue, fading in and out of view. Since the water was being held at bay by an invisible barrier over the entrance, she had legs, but they were iridescent and tinted turquoise, as if the legs were simply an illusion.

Ian immediately stood up. "Cardiff is dead."

Jada paled. "Dead? Are you sure?"

"Yes. You are free from him."

"Free?" The Mageaan hissed. "He was our protector, you fool! The oceans are not a safe place! We are so close to demons, and it is a constant battle to fend them off and to protect the earth from them. His magic was what kept us safe." She strode across the room, fear and tension rolling off her in thick waves. "What am I supposed to do now?"

As Ian watched her, an idea began to form. "If your people need protection, I can arrange for that."

Jada looked back at him. "At what cost, warrior?"

"One pearl." Ian ignored Alice's gasp of surprise, and walked toward Jada. "Alice is of great importance to the Order of the Blade. If you allow her to keep the pearl so she can return to the surface with me, the Order will be forever indebted to you. We will extend our circle of protection to you, and you can call on us at any time."

Jada stared at him, and then looked at Alice, who was still on her knees beside Chloe. For a long moment, Jada closed her eyes and Ian could see her struggle. He knew the thoughts she was having: liberate herself and sacrifice the people she was supposed to be protecting, or accept her role as leader of the Mageaan and commit to saving them.

He'd seen how much she cared about Chloe, and he knew which she would choose. She was a leader first. After a long moment, she opened her eyes. "If Alice can save Chloe, she may keep the pearl for as long as the Order protects us."

Triumph surged through Ian, and he grinned. Hot damn! "It's a deal. We'll be here for you."

"No." Alice stood up and walked over to Jada. "I can't save Chloe while I'm still in this form. I can't buck the system." She reached into her pocket and pulled out the pearl. It was glowing bright white. "Jada, I hereby give this pearl to you of my own free will." Then, to Ian and Jada's shock, Alice dropped the pearl into Jada's hand.

"Wait—" Ian lunged for Alice, but she was immediately swept up in a swirl of turquoise and red mist. Ian plunged into the cloud, blinded by the fog as he tried to find her. After a terrifying moment, he finally found her. Just as his hand went around her wrist, the mist faded, revealing her again.

She was a pale blue ethereal creature, and where her legs had once been was a tail. Ian went cold. "Dear Lord, Alice—"

"I had to do it to save Chloe. Once I'm a Mageaan, the angel rules don't apply. But because of what Chloe is, my kiss will still work to save her." Her green eyes beseeched him to understand, and then she returned to Chloe's side, leaping across the floor on the end of her tail.

On her fucking *tail*. What? Did only the leaders get legs when on solid ground? Shit. Jesus. He was stunned, unable to take his gaze off her scales as she settled beside Chloe.

This time, as she bent over the young woman, nothing

stopped her as she pressed her lips to Chloe's forehead. The moment that her angel kiss was delivered, Chloe's body shimmered once, turning a brilliant gold.

She sat up, her mouth open wide in shock. "You did it," she gasped. "Thank you!" She threw her arms around Alice, hugging her. Then, before their eyes, she turned into a luminescent swirl of pinks, purples, and golds, and then disappeared.

Jada let out a cry of relief and fell to her knees, tears of joy cascading down her cheeks. "You did it," she whispered. "You freed her. Dear God, you set her free."

Ian stared in shock. "What the hell just happened?"

Alice turned back to him, and her eyes were radiant. "I freed her," she said. "She went home."

"Freed her? Went home to where?" He still couldn't believe what had just happened. Alice had given up their freedom to save one woman?

"She wasn't meant to be down here," Alice said, her smile radiant. "Did you see that Ian? I saved her. She's so important to the world, and I made it right. On my own. I did it."

The pride shining in her eyes was so riveting that Ian felt his heart expand. He knew now, that this was what Alice had needed to do. Just as his mission as an Order member was to save innocents from rogue Calydons, hers was to use her angel powers to help others. After a lifetime of failing to help those she cared about and being afraid of breaking the rules, she'd finally become the woman she wanted to be.

Jesus. She was the bravest, most honorable person he'd ever known.

Overwhelmed with admiration, he went down on his knee before her and took her hand, pride bursting within him. "You are so incredible, Alice. You honor me with your love."

Her smile faded as she looked at him. She placed her hand on his head, and he saw tears of sadness fill her eyes. "I trapped us here."

He shrugged. "That's fine. I don't care. I'll adjust."

"I care, though. I can't let you give up your birthright to live here with me. The world needs you, and I won't be so selfish as to take you from your mission, or to steal you from those who need you." She smiled. "That's not what an angel would do, is it?"

Ian stiffened. "What are you talking about?"

"Be well, Ian. Every time you save the world, think of me." Then she waved her hand. "I love you."

The invisible barrier across the doorway suddenly burst. Water flooded into the room, and swept Ian off his feet. "Hey!" He called out his mace and jammed it into the floor as an anchor. "What are you doing?" "Freeing you!" Tears were burning her eyes.

"Fuck that! I don't want to be freed! I killed myself for you, Alice! The other shit doesn't matter!" The current grew stronger, and Ian's grip began to slide off the mace. "Alice! Call it off!"

Alice shook her head. "Don't you understand, Ian? I can't take you away from it! It's wrong!"

"Alice! Shit! Of course I'll miss it, but if I have to make a choice, I choose you every damn day of my fucking life! Every fucking day! I love you, you crazy woman. When are you going to figure that out?" He lost his grip on the mace, and he howled as he was tumbled out the door, away from the only thing that mattered to him.

Away from Alice

Away from the woman he loved.

Sudden anger roared through him, and his vision went red. Burning, insane rage ignited within him, and he unleashed a roar of fury. His mind blanked out until all that he saw was white-hot insanity. Alice was gone. She'd left him. He'd lost her.

And then the man he used to be was gone, swept up in a firestorm of destruction.

He went rogue.

CHAPTER TWENTY-ONE

Alice gasped when Ian's eyes glowed red. "Oh, no! He's gone rogue—" Before she could finish stating the obvious, he hurled his mace. It crashed into the reef, shattering a chunk of it.

"No!" Jada screamed in protest. "We'll die if he destroys our home! Stop him!"

"Ian!" Alice shouted at him, but it was no use. The man he had once been was gone, replaced by a raging lunatic intent on destroying the reef. "Stop it!"

He hurled his second mace, and it took out another chunk. Alice realized grimly that they hadn't escaped destiny after all; it had come screaming after them just as it had for all the other Calydons before them. Fate decreed that Ian was destined to lose her, and he'd done exactly that when she'd banished him from her world. The result? He'd gone rogue.

And now what? She frantically tried to remember the rest of the story. After losing her, he was destined to destroy everything that mattered to either of them...which is why he was tearing apart the reef. It was her home now, the only place of respite she would have in this lonely existence.

After he finished ripping apart her world, she was supposed to kill him to stop him, and then kill herself. Seriously? After all they had been through? No way! That was patently unjust. She couldn't let that happen. Destiny wasn't going to take them.

Alice swished her hand through the water, cutting off the ocean's expulsion of Ian. It stopped shoving him away and allowed him to move as he wished, allowing him to return her. "Come back to me, Ian! I'm here now!"

Too little, too late. No longer having to fight the waves, Ian launched himself at the coral, preparing to finish it off, even over Jada's screams.

"No!" Alice called his maces to her, stripping him of his weapons. Ian roared with rage, and she could see there was no humanity in his eyes. No man. Just monster. Beast. Demon. Just as all the other Calydons over the last two thousand years had been fated to become after meeting their *sheva*.

Jada swam up beside him and attacked with a flash of a dagger. He flung her aside, barely even noticing her. Alice tensed, realizing that Jada might call the rest of the Mageaan. In the state he was in, they would have no chance. A thousand women would be slaughtered. Dammit! She had to stop him!

She threw one of the maces, willing it to obey her. As always, it seemed to take on a life of its own, and it slammed unerringly into his shoulder. Alice gasped with horror as Ian howled with pain, regret filling her at hurting him. "Stop it!" she screamed. "Come back to me!"

But as he charged the reef with his fists balled, she saw only deadly intent in his eyes. There was no man left to hear her.

"Ian!" Kane suddenly materialized beside her, and he swore when he saw Ian. "No way, man, not you." He sounded pissed as he called out his double-spiked flail. "Pull it together, Fitz! Now!"

At the sound of Kane's voice, Ian whirled around. His weapons jerked out of Alice's grasp and slammed into his palms. Instantly, he launched into a full attack, striking right for Kane's heart. Kane blocked the blow and leapt aside, still shouting at Ian to come back to him.

But even as Alice called to him and Kane fought him, she could see Ian was sliding further and further away into his insanity. The Order was what mattered to him, so that was what he had to destroy. His Order, her home—

Then he turned suddenly and faced her, blood-thirsty rage seething in his eyes. "You die," he said in a raspy, haunted voice. "You have to die."

"Me?" Alice scrambled backward as he came at her, apparently forgetting about his need to destroy Kane or the reef. He simply wanted to annihilate her. "But why? That's not part of the legend, is it?"

"Apparently, you're what matters most to him," Kane shouted as he tackled Ian, knocking him off course. "He has to destroy you first!"

Alice's jaw dropped open as she watched Ian hurl Kane aside and come after her again. There was no doubt that he was coming for her. Was it really because she was the most important thing in the world to him?

There was no other explanation. She was what he cared about most.

Not the way she'd dreamed of discovering a man's commitment to her, but still, there was something amazingly romantic and undeniable about a love so powerful it could turn a man insane.

And as she looked into his seething red eyes, she realized that their relationship was the most important thing to her as well. Their love was what mattered most to both of them.

Despite all the responsibility both of them had for the greater good, somehow, someway, their love had triumphed over it all. How ridiculous that she had tried to ban him from the oceans for his own good. Being together was what was best for both of them, regardless of the cost. She finally understood that nothing else mattered as much as what they shared.

Tears burned in her eyes, and she held up her arms,

welcoming him as he charged her. "Oh, Ian," she said. "I love you, too." And then, for the first time ever, she truly dropped every single barrier around her heart. She'd thought she'd done it before. She'd thought she knew what love was. But suddenly, she was filled with the most amazing sense of peace, and she knew she had finally found her place.

It wasn't as a guardian angel.

It wasn't as a protector of the Order.

It wasn't as Ian's *sheva*.

It was simply in the arms of the man she loved, who loved her back.

This moment, this man, this love... it was what life was about.

Ian raised his mace to slam it into her heart, and she pressed her palms together, summoning all that was good and loving within her soul. The mixture of golden and white light flared brightly, like a bomb had ignited. It flashed through the ocean, blanking out everything around them. But it wasn't simply angel light. It was her love, that which she had been forbidden to feel or embrace. She unleashed it into the monster trying to take over the man she loved, cracking through the insanity attempting to steal him from her.

The white light hit Ian, and he screamed in agony. Alice utilized their bond to touch his mind, offering him all the love she had. *I love you, Ian. Come back to me.*

His mind was filled with thousands of images, of all the rogues he'd killed, his father dying, the gravestones of his ancestors, and then, finally, an image stayed with him. One image. Alice. Holding out her hands to him, offering him her heart.

Ian felt the strangest sensation roll through him, like a golden sun gifting him with its warmth on a cold day. Hundreds of years of suffering and torment seemed to vanish. The rage disappeared. All that remained was one image, one thing, and one vision. "Alice?"

She smiled, and he realized she was real. Not his imagination. He blinked, and suddenly the red haze affecting his sight vanished. "You're real?"

"I'm real." She flung herself at him, and he caught her, wrapping his arms around her and holding her tightly against him.

He buried his face in her hair, absorbing every facet of her being into his soul. *How did you do that? How did you bring me back from rogue?*

She pulled back, smiling at him with so much love in her eyes he was almost overwhelmed. "I combined my love with a little angel power. But you had to accept it in order for it to work." Her smile broadened. "And you did. I guess you do love me."

"Of course I do." He kissed her hard, savoring every touch of those lips, the taste of her tongue. *Sweetheart, that was far more than a little angel power. You are way more of a badass than I ever was.*

Alice chuckled, making him smile. After all they'd been through, to hear her laughter was one of the most beautiful gifts he'd ever received.

"I guess I'd have to be in order to protect a bunch of testosterone junkies who go rogue over their sweethearts," she teased.

Ian knew then that Alice had finally accepted who she was, on every level: a guardian angel, a lover, a partner, and a woman. "I love you, sweetheart."

"I know." Her smile faltered. "I guess I have to let you stay here with me, then, huh?"

"Wait." Jada swam over, the pearl still clenched in her hands. She placed it in Alice's hand. "I hereby offer you the pearl of Lycanth willingly." She closed Alice's fingers around it. "Take it, Alice. It's yours."

Alice stared at her. "But—"

Jada shook her head. "It's been hell down here, Alice.

I lost hope and even my humanity a long time ago, and have been basically waiting for someone to kill me. I was envious when you killed Esmeralda. I wanted to be freed from this hell." She sighed. "When Chloe arrived here, and then was dying, it was the final blow. How could she have wound up here? How could the earth lose her? It made no sense. I had nothing left. No hope, no faith, nothing."

Alice touched her arm. "I'm sorry—"

"Don't be." Jada smiled, the first smile Ian had seen from her. He was surprised by how pretty she was. "You've given me hope again, a mission, and that is beautiful."

Alice frowned. "What do you mean?"

"During my time on earth, before I became a Mageaan, I saw many, many Calydons go rogue from the *sheva* bond. I thought it was unbreakable. Everyone did." Her eyes were bright with hope. "What I saw happen just now was a miracle. You used your angel power in ways that should have been impossible. Not only did you channel it into forbidden directions, but it worked, both to save Chloe and to break the *sheva* destiny." Determination flared in her eyes. "If you can break through your restraints, so can I, and so can the angels trapped here with me. I have to stay, Alice, until I can free every one of these women. They need me." She smiled. "And I need to help them."

Alice closed her hand around the pearl in disbelief, but she knew exactly what Jada meant. Saving Gideon and Chloe had been incredible, and she wanted to do more of it. She was so happy to hear that Jada was fighting back, that these women would resist this terrible fate they had been sentenced to.

Jada nodded at her. "Take the pearl. Go to the surface. Come back when you need something."

Ian touched Jada's arm. "And you call us whenever you need anything. Got it?"

She smiled. "Don't worry, you'll be hearing from me." She stepped back and waved them off. "Safe travels, my friends." She bowed her head in a statement of respect and honor. "Safe travels," she repeated.

And then, she turned and swam away, not into the palace, but into the ocean... no doubt in search of the fallen angels she was going to save.

Alice looked down at her hand, at the pearl that her mother had given her so long ago to free Alice from the burden of the angel rules. "I did it, Mom," she whispered. "I found my own path."

Ian hugged her close and kissed her gently. "She would be proud."

Alice looked up at him and knew he was right. "She's not disappointed in me anymore," she agreed, words that were so beautiful she wanted to cry.

Ian put his hand around her fist that held the pearl. "Accept the pearl, sweetheart, and let's go home."

She smiled and nodded, glancing behind him at Kane, who was waiting patiently to teleport them back home. "Why did you come here?" she asked him.

The warrior grinned. "Because I've got something to show you guys."

She raised her brows. "What is it?"

But Kane shook his head. "Not here. We need to go on a field trip."

Alice frowned. "But how did you know we would be able to leave?"

Kane shrugged. "Because you're one hell of a guardian angel, and I knew you wouldn't be able to stay away from all of us Order guys. We're simply too charming."

Alice laughed, and Ian slung his arm around her shoulder. "Accept the gift, Alice, and let the boy give us a ride."

She opened her hand and looked down at the pearl that was silent and inactive, with dull streaks of red and orange. "I accept the pearl," she whispered.

It immediately glowed bright white, and she felt a

humming vibrate through her. There was a burst of pink mist around her, but this time, neither she nor Ian panicked. She just held onto him while they waited for it to fade.

And when it did, she was back to herself again.

Except, she wasn't back to herself. She was a thousand times the woman she'd ever been, and it was all because the man she loved had found a way to open her heart.

† † †

Ian was shocked when he materialized on a patch of dirt, and he realized they were standing on his grave.

Kane had brought the three of them to the Fitzgerald burial ground.

Ian stared down at the headstone he'd bought for himself so long ago, the one that had been ready and waiting for him to succumb to the curse. His name was etched in the dark gray marble, with only the date of his death left blank. Around him, in all directions, extended the graves of the Fitzgerald men who had died, many of them heroically. There were no bodies in those graves, because they had vanished at death. All that remained were the markers.

But in a small circle at the end of the plot lay the graves of those who had died by their own hand, who had sentenced their souls to purgatory and lost their honor.

He walked several feet to his father's grave and went down on one knee. He bowed his head. "I broke the curse, Dad. It's over. I know it's too late for you, but the Fitzgerald name will be restored."

Ian put his hand on the earth, and to his surprise, the dirt seemed to shift beneath his touch, as if his father had heard him, and his soul had sighed with relief.

Alice put her hand on his shoulder, and he entwined his fingers with hers. Suddenly, being in the cemetery didn't feel as difficult and wrenching as it used to. Alice gave him comfort. She gave him peace.

He looked up at her, and his heart tightened when she smiled down at him. It felt damn good to have her by his side.

"You guys should be in a Hallmark commercial. You're that cute."

Ian turned sharply at the sound of Thano's voice. To his shock, Thano was just behind him...riding the wizard's horse. "Thano!" He strode over to his teammate, Thano bent down, and they exchanged a hard hug. For a moment, there were no words, and then Ian finally stepped back. "Shit, man, it's good to see you. Where did you come from? How'd you get back?"

"Ryland tracked me down. The bastard interrupted my pedicure." Thano grinned, and Ian noticed how thin he looked. His eyes were sparkling with humor, but there were shadows in them that hadn't been there before. "It's good to be back. Got myself a horse. You like?" He stroked his mount's neck.

Ian rubbed the horse's nose, surprised at how soft it was. To him, Deathbringer had always been a harbinger of evil, not an animal to be patted. "You're rehabbing Deathbringer?"

"Rehabbing him? No chance. He kicks ass exactly how he is." Thano scratched the beast between the ears, like he'd adopted a damn cocker spaniel, not a war horse. "This warrior is my new partner, and his name is Apollo, because you cynical old guys need a little more Greek power on this team. Figured having a god on our side might help." Something surprisingly dark flashed through Thano's eyes, as if he were now the one with a load of hell haunting him, instead of the rest of them.

Then Thano grinned, shaking the shadows off as if they'd never been there, but Ian didn't believe it. What had happened to Thano while he'd been in Cardiff's lair?

"If Apollo decides he likes you," Thano continued, "he may allow you to bask in his greatness. Or, he might be offended and kick you in the head. You just never know."

"Sounds like your perfect match, then." Ian grinned as Apollo reached around and began to nibble on Thano's jeans. "Never knew the Order would turn into a mounted force, but

I'll bet he'll be an asset." A warrior horse that could run on water, fly, and move in complete stealth? Yeah, that would work.

Ian had to admit, the horse looked good. His coat was a glossy black, and his stiff leather bridle was gone, replaced by a soft gray suede that draped gently over his nose. There was no bit in his mouth, no way to really control him, and yet he stood proudly beneath Thano.

There were black straps around Thano's thighs that almost looked like they were holding Thano in place. Ian noticed that Thano's feet were hanging limply, not gripping the horse's sides. "Shit, man, you okay?"

"Dude, this day is not about me," Thano said. "Get with the program, old man."

Ian frowned. "What are you talking about?"

"The party, of course." Thano jerked his chin, and Ian looked past him, shocked to discover that the entire Order was present. All of his team, plus their women.

The Order members were kneeling in a semi-circle, each of them holding their weapon in their right hand, while the women stood off to the left in a small group. Gideon Roarke, Quinn Masters, Elijah Ross, Zach Roderick, Gabe Watson, Ryland, and even young Drew...though Vaughn was nowhere in sight. The man was the dedicated guardian of the youth he loved like a son, yet he was absent. Still searching for Flynn, like Alice had indicated? After spending time with him over the last two months searching for Alice, Ian still felt like the man was an enigma, but he'd gotten used to having him around. He'd become almost an honorary Order member, and Ian hoped he was okay.

Thano rode Apollo to the spot beside Gideon, and then the massive beast went down on one knee with Thano still astride, the horse and rider assuming the position as a single entity.

At the top of the circle was an empty spot. Carved in

the ground was an outline of a mace, exactly like Ian's weapon.

He recognized the formation immediately, and his throat tightened. "Son of a bitch," he said. "You've got to be kidding."

"What is it?" Alice moved up beside him.

"It's an induction ceremony for the Order of the Blade." Suddenly, it became hard to talk. He ran his hand through his hair. *That's my weapon carved in the dirt in the vacant spot. It's for me. They're taking me back.*

Alice smiled and tucked her hand in his. *Of course they are. You're one of them, Ian.*

He swallowed again. *Walk me there.*

"Of course." She took his hand and together they walked around the outside of the circle. As part of the tradition, no one said a word. They all just watched him, so many sets of eyes following him on his ascension to the summit of the circle.

When Ian reached the spot, he stopped beside the drawing of his mace in the ground, and then realized there were more markings in the dirt. Surrounding the etching of his mace were seven other weapons. The one closest to his was an axe. His father's axe. Stunned, Ian jerked his gaze to his team.

No one said a word, but Kane nodded once. A single nod to tell Ian that not only were they inducting him into the Order, but they were bringing back all his ancestors who had been banned.

"Jesus." Sweat beaded on Ian's brow, and he was too emotional to speak.

"When you killed yourself to save Alice," Gideon said, "you showed us that death by your own hand can be the most heroic, courageous, and admirable choice there is. Just as the rules regarding the automatic death for Order *shevas* is changing, so must that rule. Evolution is the key to survival, my friend, and you have moved us forward."

Jesus. If death by one's own hand was officially deemed

an honorable death, then his ancestors' deaths would no longer be tainted. Once they were inducted back into the Order, the souls of his father and the others would finally be freed to go to the Afterlife.

Ian tipped his head back, staring at the sky, trying to regain his composure. His father's soul would be restored. Shit. He'd never thought it could happen, but it had. Centuries of guilt over his father's fate finally released him, liberating him from the choices he'd made so long ago. *I love you, Dad.*

He fought against the tightness in his throat, staring into the bright blue sky. It was vibrant and filled with puffy white clouds, just like the day he and Alice had been in the boat. One cloud floated across his view. He grinned and pointed at it. "Alice, it's a poodle."

She looked up and then laughed. "My mom must approve of you," she said. She raised her hand in a salute to the sky. "Love you, too, Mom."

Ian laughed softly as he tightened his grip on her hand. He was looking at poodles in the sky when he was on the cusp of restoring his family's honor? Yeah, he was. He grinned at Alice, who was smiling back at him, love and pride shining in her eyes. Yeah, he was, and that was exactly how it should be. *I'm glad you're here to share this moment with me.*

Me, too. So glad. She squeezed his hand, and he knew that he had finally found his place.

"Let's get a move on," Thano said. "Ry's got a date to find a missing angel of death, and he won't stay here long."

Ian looked over at Ryland. He was wearing a black sweatshirt, with the hood pulled low over his forehead. But even that didn't hide the seething darkness in the warrior. Ry was almost out of time, and everyone there knew it. *Good luck, Ry.*

The warrior didn't move, but Ian felt him touch his mind. *Take care of her, Fitz. She's a good one.*

I know. Ian looked over at Alice, who had slipped away

from him to stand by the other *shevas.* As she approached them, a woman Ian didn't recognize reached out and embraced her warmly. Kane's *sheva,* Sarah? The angel of hope? He smiled when Sarah tucked her arm through Alice's, welcoming her into the incredible group of women who had aligned themselves with the Order. First Grace, then Lily, then Ana, then Sarah... and now Alice. His woman. He grinned. It was right.

"Hey!" Thano waved his weapon. "You want back in or what?" Ian returned his attention to the team surrounding him, and felt the most immense sense of peace. "Yeah, I do." Then he went down on one knee, and the ceremony began.

Sneak Peek: Darkness Unleashed

The Order of the Blade
Available Now

Ryland spun around, engaging all his preternatural senses as he searched the graveyard for Catherine. He knew she had to be close. He'd touched her backpack just before she'd vanished right in front of him.

"Catherine!" he shouted again. He'd been so close. Where the hell was she? All he could sense were the deaths of all the people in the graveyard. Women, children, old men, young men, good people, scum who had taken their demented values to the grave with them. The spirits were thick and heavy in the graveyard, souls that had not moved on to their place of rest.

They circled him, trying to penetrate his barriers, seeking asylum in the creature that would be their doom. "No," he said to them. "I'm not your savior." Not by a long shot. He was about as far from their savior as it was possible to be.

Dismissing them, Ryland focused more directly on Catherine, opening his senses to the night, but as much as he tried to concentrate, he couldn't keep the vision of her out of his head. He'd finally seen her up close. She'd been mere inches away, the angel who had filled his thoughts for so long. Her hair was gold. Gold. It must have been tucked up under a hat when he'd seen her before, but now? It was unlike anything he'd ever seen before. He'd been riveted by the sight of it streaming behind her as she ran, the golden highlights glistening in the dark as if she'd been lit from within.

Her gait had been smooth and agile, but he'd sensed the sheer effort she'd had to expend during the run. Another few feet, and he would have caught up to her easily, but she'd sensed him while he'd still been a quarter mile away, giving her a head start that had gotten her to the graveyard first.

Shit. He had to focus and find her. Summoning his rigid control to focus on his task, Ryland crouched down and placed his hand on the dirt path where he'd last seen her. The ground was humming with the energy of death, but again, he couldn't untangle her trail from all the others. He realized that she'd mingled her own scent of death with those of all the other spirits, making it impossible for him to track her. He grinned as he rested his forearm on his quad and surveyed the small cemetery. "I'm impressed," he said aloud. "You're good."

There was no response, but he had the distinct sensation that she was watching him.

Slowly, he rose to his feet. "My name is Ryland Samuels," he said. "I'm a member of the Order of the Blade, the group of warriors that you protect. I'm here to offer you my protection and bring you into our safekeeping."

Again, there was no answer, but suddenly threaded through the tendrils of death was the cold filament of fear. Not just a superficial apprehension, but the kind of deep, penetrating fear that would bring a person to their knees and render them powerless. Fear of him? Or of the fact he said he wanted to take her with him? Swearing, Ryland turned in a slow circle, searching for where she might be. "There's no need to be afraid of me. I would never hurt an angel."

The fear thickened, like the thorns of a dying rose pricking his skin.

Ryland moved slowly toward the far corner, and smiled when he felt the terror grow stronger. She might be able to hide death, but there was no cover for the terror that was hers alone. He was clearly getting closer to her. "Look into my eyes," he said softly. "I don't hurt angels."

There was a whisper of a sound behind him, and he felt the cold drift of fingers across his back. She was touching him.

He froze, not daring to turn around, even though his heartbeat had suddenly accelerated a thousand-fold. Her touch was so faint, almost as if it were her spirit that was examining him, not her own flesh. Was she merely invisible right now, or had she abandoned her physical existence completely and traveled to some spiritual plane? He had no idea what she was capable of. All he knew was that he felt like he never wanted to move away from this spot, not as long as she was touching him. He wanted to stay right where he was and never break the connection.

He closed his eyes, breathing in the sensation of her touch as her fingers traced down his arm, over his jacket. What was she looking for? Was she reading his aura? Searching for the truth of his claim that he would not hurt her? She would get nowhere trying to get a read on him. He never allowed anyone to see who he truly was, not even an angel of death.

But even as he thought it, he made no move to resist, his pulse quickening in anticipation as her touch trailed toward his bare hand. Would she brush her fingers over his skin? Would he feel the touch of an angel for the first time in a thousand years? He felt his soul begin to strain, reaching for this gift only she could give him.

He tracked every inch of movement as her hand moved lower toward his bare skin. Past his elbow. To the cuff of his sleeve. Then he felt it. Her fingers on the back of his hand. His flesh seemed to ignite under her touch. A wave of angelic serenity and beauty cascaded through his soul, like a breath of great relief easing a thousand years of tension from his lungs.

At the same time, there was a dangerous undercurrent beneath the beauty, a darkness that he recognized as death. A thousand souls seemed to dance through his mind, spirits lodged in the depths of her existence. Her emotions flooded him. Fear. Regret. Determination. Love. A sense of being trapped.

Trapped? He understood that one well. Far too well.

Instinctively, he flipped his hand over, wrapping his fingers around hers, not to trap her, but to offer her his protection from a hell that still drove every choice he made.

He heard her suck in her breath, and she went still, not pulling away from him. Her hand was cold. Her fingers were small and delicate, like fragile blossoms that would snap under a stiff breeze. A hand that needed support and help.

Ryland snapped his eyes open but there was no one standing in front of him. He looked down and could see only his own hand, folded around air. He couldn't see her, but she was there, her hand in his, not pulling away. "Show yourself to me," he said. "I won't hurt you."

Her hand jerked back, and a sense of loss assailed him as he lost his grip on her. "No!" He reached for her, but his hands just drifted through air. "Catherine," he urged, as he strained to get a sense of her. "I—"

Sneak Peek: Darkness Awakened

The Order of the Blade

Available Now

Quinn Masters raced soundlessly through the thick woods, his injuries long forgotten, urgency coursing through him as he neared his house. He covered the last thirty yards, leapt over a fallen tree, then reached the edge of the clearing by his cabin.

There she was.

He stopped dead, fading back into the trees as he stared at the woman he'd scented when he was still two hours away, a lure that had eviscerated all weakness from his body and fueled him into a dead sprint back to his house.

His lungs heaving with the effort of pushing his severely damaged body so hard, Quinn stood rigidly as he studied the woman whose scent had called to him through the dark night. She'd yanked him out of his thoughts about Elijah and galvanized him with energy he hadn't been able to summon on his own.

And now he'd found her.

She'd wedged herself up against the back corner of his porch, barely protected from the cold rain and wet wind. Her knees were pulled up against her chest, her delicate arms wrapped tightly around them as if she could hold onto her body heat by sheer force of will. Her shoulders were hunched, her forehead pressed against her knees while damp tangles of dark brown hair tumbled over her arms.

Her chest moved once. Twice. A trembling, aching breath into lungs that were too cold and too exhausted to work as well as they should.

He took a step toward her, and then another, three more before he realized what he was doing. He froze, suddenly aware of his urgent need to get to her. To help her. To fill her with heat and breathe safety into her trembling body. To whisk her off his porch and into his cabin.

Into his bed.

Quinn stiffened at the thought. Into his bed? Since when? He didn't engage when it came to women. The risk was too high, for him, and for all Calydons. Any woman he met could be his mate, his fate, his doom. His sheva.

He was never tempted.

Until now.

Until this cold, vulnerable stranger had appeared inexplicably on his doorstep. He should be pulling out his sword, not thinking that the fastest way to get her warm would be to run his hands over her bare skin and infuse her whole body with the heat from his.

But his sword remained quiet. His instincts warned him of nothing.

What the hell was going on? She had to be a threat. Nothing else made sense. Women didn't stumble onto his home, and he didn't get a hard-on from simply catching a whiff of one from miles away.

His trembling quads braced against the cold air, he inhaled her scent again, searching for answers to a thousand questions. She smelled delicate, with a hint of something sweet, and a flavoring of the bitterness of true desperation. He could practically taste her anguish, a cold, acrid weight in the air, and he knew she was in trouble.

His hands flexed with the need to close the distance between them, to crouch by her side, to give her his protection. But he didn't move. He didn't dare. He had to figure out why he was so compelled by her, why he was responding like this, especially at a time when he couldn't afford any kind of a distraction.

She moaned softly and curled into an even tighter ball. His muscles tightened, his entire soul burning with the need to help her. Quinn narrowed his eyes and pried his gaze off her to search the woods.

With the life of his blood brother in his hands, with an Order posse soon to be after him, with his own body still recovering from Elijah's assault, it made no sense that Quinn had even noticed the scent of this woman, let alone be consumed by her.

His intense need for her felt too similar to the compulsion that had sent him to the river three nights ago. Another trap? He'd suspected it from the moment he'd first reacted to her scent, but he'd been unable to resist the temptation, and he'd hauled ass to get back to his house. Yeah, true, he'd also needed to get back to his cabin to retrieve his supplies to go after Elijah. The fact she'd imbued him with new strength had been a bonus he wasn't going to deny.

But now he had to be sure. A trap or not? Quinn laughed softly. Shit. He hoped it was. If it wasn't, there was only one other reason he could think of to explain his reaction to her, and that would be if she was his mate. His sheva. His ticket to certain destruction.

No chance.

He wouldn't allow it.

He had no time for dealing with that destiny right now. It was time to get in, get out, and go after Elijah. His amusement faded as he took a final survey of the woods. There was no lurking threat he could detect. Maybe he'd made it back before he'd been expected, or maybe an ambush had been aborted.

Either way, he had to get into his house, get his stuff, and move on. His gaze returned to the woman, and he noticed a drop of water sliding down the side of her neck, trickling over her skin like the most seductive of caresses. He swore, realizing she wasn't going to leave. She'd freeze to death before she'd abandon her perch.

He cursed and knew he had to go to her. He couldn't let her die on his front step. Not this woman. Not her.

He would make it fast, he would make it efficient, he would stay on target for his mission, but he would get her safe.

Keeping alert for any indication that this was a setup, Quinn stepped out of the woods and into the clearing. He'd made no sound, not even a whisper of his clothing, and yet she sensed him.

She sat up, her gaze finding him instantly in the dim light, despite his stealthy approach. They made eye contact, and the world seemed to stop for a split second. The moment he saw those silvery eyes, something thumped in his chest. Something visceral and male howled inside him, raging to be set free.

As he strode up, she unfolded herself from her cramped position and pulled herself to her feet, her gaze never leaving his. Her face was wary, her body tense, but she lifted her chin ever so slightly and set her hands on her hips, telling him that she wasn't leaving.

Her courage and determination, held together by that tiny, shivering frame, made satisfaction thud through him. There was a warrior in that slim, exhausted body.

She said nothing as he approached, and neither of them spoke as he came to a stop in front of her.

Up close, he was riveted. Her dark eyelashes were clumped from the rain. Her skin was pale, too pale. Her face was carrying the burden of a thousand weights. But beneath that pain, those nightmares, that hell, lay delicate femininity that called to him. The luminescent glow of her skin, the sensual curve of her mouth, the sheen of rain on her cheekbones, the simple silver hoops in her ears. It awoke in him something so male, so carnal, so primal he wanted to throw her up against the wall and consume her until their bodies were melted together in single, scorching fire.

She searched his face with the same intensity raging

through him, and he felt like she was tearing through his shields, cataloguing everything about him, all the way down to his soul.

He studied her carefully, and she let him, not flinching when his gaze traveled down her body. His blood pulsed as he noted the curve of her breasts under her rain-slicked jacket, the sensuous curve of her hips, and even the mud on her jeans and boots. He almost groaned at his need to palm her hips, drag her over to him, and mark her with his kiss. Loose strands of thick dark hair had escaped from her ponytail, curling around her neck and shoulders like it was clinging to her for safety.

Protectiveness surged from deep inside him and he clenched his fists against his urge to sweep her into his arms and carry her inside, away from whatever hardship had brought her to his doorstep.

Double hell. He'd hoped his reaction would lessen when he got close to her, but it had intensified. He'd never felt like this before. Never had this response to a woman.

What the hell was going on? Sheva. The word was like a demon, whispering through his mind. He shut it out. He would never allow himself to bond with his mate. If that was what was going on, she was out of there immediately, before they were both destroyed forever.

Intent on sending her away, he looked again at her face, and then realized he was done. Her beautiful silver eyes were aching with a soul-deep pain that shattered what little defenses he had against her. He simply couldn't abandon her.

It didn't matter what she wanted. It didn't matter why she was there. She was coming inside. He would make sure it didn't interfere with his mission. He would make dead sure it turned out right. No matter what.

Without a word, he grabbed her backpack off the floor, surprised at how heavy it was. Either she had tossed her free weights in it, or she had packed her life into it.

He had a bad feeling it wasn't a set of dumb bells.

Quinn walked past her and unlocked his front door. He shoved it open, then stood back. Letting her decide. Hoping she would walk away and spare them both.

She took a deep breath, glanced at his face one more time, then walked into the cabin.

Hell.

He paused to take one more survey of his woods, found nothing amiss, and then he followed her into his home and shut the door behind them.

Sneak Peek: Ice

Alaska Heat

Available Now

Kaylie's hands were shaking as she rifled through her bag, searching for her yoga pants. She needed the low-slung black ones with a light pink stripe down the side. The cuffs were frayed from too many wearings to the grocery store late at night for comfort food, and they were her go-to clothes when she couldn't cope. Like now.

She couldn't find them.

"Come on!" Kaylie grabbed her other suitcase and dug through it, but they weren't there. "Stupid pants! I can't—" A sob caught at her throat and she pressed her palms to her eyes, trying to stifle the swell of grief. "Sara—"

Her voice was a raw moan of pain, and she sank to the thick shag carpet. She bent over as waves of pain, of loneliness, of utter grief shackled her. For her parents, her brother, her family and now Sara—

Dear God, she was all alone.

"Dammit, Kaylie! Get up!" she chided herself. She wrenched herself to her feet. "I can do this." She grabbed a pair of jeans and a silk blouse off the top of her bag and turned toward the bathroom. One step at a time. A shower would make her feel better.

She walked into the tiny bathroom, barely noticing the heavy wood door as she stepped inside and flicked the light switch. Two bare light bulbs flared over her head, showing a rustic bathroom with an ancient footed tub and a raw wood vanity with a battered porcelain sink. A tiny round window was on her right. It was small enough to keep out the worst of the cold, but big enough to let in some light and breeze in the summer.

She was in Alaska, for sure. God, what was she doing here?

Kaylie tossed the clean clothes on the sink and unzipped her jacket, dropping it on the floor. She tugged all her layers off, including the light blue sweater that had felt so safe this morning when she'd put it on. She stared grimly at her black lace bra, so utterly feminine, exactly the kind of bra that her mother had always considered frivolous and completely impractical. Which it was. Which was why that was the only style Kaylie ever wore.

She should never have come to Alaska. She didn't belong here. She couldn't handle this. Kaylie gripped the edge of the sink. Her hands dug into the wood as she fought against the urge to curl into a ball and cry.

After a minute, Kaylie lifted her head and looked at herself in the mirror. Her eyes were wide and scared, with dark circles beneath. Her hair was tangled and flattened from her wool hat. There was dirt caked on her cheeks.

Kaylie rubbed her hand over her chin, and the streaks of mud didn't come off.

She tried again, then realized she had smudges all over her neck. She turned on the water, and wet her hands...and saw her hands were covered as well.

Stunned, Kaylie stared as the water ran over her hands, turning pink as it swirled in the basin.

Not dirt.

Sara's blood.

"Oh, God." Kaylie grabbed a bar of soap and began to scrub her hands. But the blood was dried, stuck to her skin. "Get off!" She rubbed frantically, but the blackened crust wouldn't come off. Her lungs constricted and she couldn't breathe. "I can't—"

The door slammed open, and Cort stood behind her,

wearing a T-shirt and jeans.

The tears burst free at the sight of Cort, and Kaylie held up her hands to him. "I can't get it off—"

"I got it." Cort took her hands and held them under the water, his grip warm and strong. "Take a deep breath, Kaylie. It's okay."

"It's not. It won't be." She leaned her head against his shoulder, closing her eyes as he washed her hands roughly and efficiently. His muscles flexed beneath her cheek, his skin hot through his shirt. Warm. Alive. "Sara's dead," she whispered. "My parents. My brother. They're all gone. The blood—" Sobs broke free again, and she couldn't stop the trembling.

"I know. I know, babe." He pulled her hands out from under the water and grabbed a washcloth. He turned her toward him and began to wash her face and neck.

His eyes were troubled, his mouth grim. But his hands were gentle where he touched her, gently holding her face still while he scrubbed. His gaze flicked toward hers, and he held contact for a moment, making her want to fall into those brown depths and forget everything. To simply disappear into the energy that was him. "You have to let them go," he said. "There's nothing you can do to bring them back—"

"No." A deep ache pounded at Kaylie's chest and her legs felt like they were too weak to support her. "I can't. Did you see Sara? And Jackson? His throat—" She bent over, clutching her stomach. "I—"

Cort's arms were suddenly around her, warm and strong, pulling her against his solid body. Kaylie fell into him, the sobs coming hard, the memories—

"I know." Cort's whisper was soft, his hand in her hair, crushing her against him. "It sucks. Goddamn, it sucks."

Kaylie heard his grief in the raw tone of his voice and realized his body was shaking as well. She looked up and saw a rim of red around his eyes, shadows in the hollows of his whiskered cheeks. "You know," she whispered, knowing with absolute certainty that he did. He understood the grief consuming her.

"Yeah." He cupped her face, staring down at her, his grip so tight it was almost as desperate as she felt. She could feel his heart beating against her nearly bare breasts, the rise of his chest as he breathed, the heat of his body warming the deathly chill from hers.

For the first time in forever, she suddenly didn't feel quite as alone.

In her suffering, she had company. Someone who knew. Who understood. Who shared her pain. It had been so long since the dark cavern surrounding her heart had lessened, since she hadn't felt consumed by the loneliness, but with Cort holding her...there was a flicker of light in the darkness trying to take her. "Cort—"

He cleared his throat. "I gotta go check the chili." He dropped his hands from her face and stood up to go, pulling away from her.

Without his touch, the air felt cold and the anguish returned full force. Kaylie caught his arm. "Don't go—" She stopped, not sure what to say, what to ask for. All she knew was that she didn't want him to leave, and she didn't want him to stop holding her.

Cort turned back to her, and a muscle ticked in his cheek.

For a moment, they simply stared at each other. She raised her arms. "Hold me," she whispered. "Please."

He hesitated for a second, and then his hand snaked out and he shackled her wrist. He yanked once, and she tumbled into him. Their bodies smacked hard as he caught her around the waist, his hands hot on her bare back.

She threw her arms around his neck and sagged into him. He wrapped his arms around her, holding her tightly against him. With only her bra and his T-shirt between them, the heat of his body was like a furnace, numbing her pain.

His name slipped out in a whisper, and she pressed her cheek against his chest. She focused on his masculine scent. She took solace in the feel of another human's touch, in the safety of being held in arms powerful enough to ward off the grief trying to overtake her.

His hand tunneled in her hair, and he buried his face in the curve of her neck, his body shaking against hers.

"Cort—" She started to lift her head to look at him, to see if he was crying, but he tightened his grip on her head, forcing her face back to his chest, refusing to allow her to look at him.

Keeping her out.

Isolating her.

She realized he wasn't a partner in her grief. She was alone, still alone, always alone.

All the anguish came cascading back. Raw loneliness surged again, and she shoved away from him as sobs tore at her throat. She couldn't deal with being held by him when the sense of intimacy was nothing but an illusion. "Leave me alone."

Kaylie whirled away from him, keeping her head ducked. She didn't want to look at him. She needed space to find her equilibrium again and rebuild her foundation.

"Damn it, Kaylie." Cort grabbed her arm and spun her back toward him.

She held up her hands to block him, her vision blurred by the tears streaming down her face. "Don't—"

His arms snapped around her and he hauled her against him even as she fought his grip. "No! Leave me alone—"

His mouth descended on hers.

Not a gentle kiss.

A kiss of desperation and grief and need. Of the need to control something. Of raw human passion for life, for death, for the touch of another human being.

And it broke her.

Sneak Peek: Prince Charming Can Wait

Ever After

Available Now

Clouds were thick in the sky, blocking the moon. The lake and the woods were dark, swallowing up light and life, like a soothing blanket of nothingness coating the night. Emma needed to get away from the world she didn't belong to, the one that held no place for her. Tears were thick in her throat, her eyes stinging as she ran. The stones were wet from the rain earlier in the day, and the cool dampness sent chills through her.

She reached the dock and leapt out onto the damp wood. Her foot slipped, and she yelped as she lost her balance—

Strong hands shot out and grabbed her around the waist, catching her before she fell into the water. Shrieking in surprise, she jerked free, twisting out of range. The evasive move sent her off balance again, her feet went out from under her, and she was falling—

And again, someone grabbed her. "Hey," a low voice said. "I'm not going to hurt you."

Emma froze at the sound of the voice she knew so well, the one that had haunted her for so many sleepless nights. The voice she thought she'd never hear again, because he'd been gone for so long. "Harlan?"

"Yeah."

Emma spun around in his grasp, and her breath caught as she saw his shadowed face. His eyes were dark and hooded in the filtered light, his cheek bones more prominent than they had been the last time she'd seen him. Heavy stubble framed his face, and his hair was long and ragged around the base of

371

his neck. He was leaner than she remembered, but his muscles were more defined, straining at his tee shirt. He looked grungy and real, a man who lived by the earth every day of his life. He exuded pure strength and raw appeal that ignited something deep within her. She instinctively leaned toward him, into the strength that emanated from him. His hands felt hot and dangerous where they clasped her hips, but she had no urge to push him away.

Damn him. After not seeing him for nearly a year, he still affected her beyond reason.

"You're back," she managed.

"Yeah."

Again, the one word answer. He had never said much more than that to her, but she'd seen him watching her intently on countless occasions, his piercing blue eyes roiling with so much unspoken emotion and turbulence. She managed a small smile, trying to hide the intensity of her reaction to seeing him. "Astrid didn't mention you would be here."

"She doesn't know." Again, he fell silent, but he raised one hand and lifted a lock of her hair, thumbing it gently. "Like silk," he said softly. "Just as I always thought it would feel."

Her heart began to pound now. There was no way to stop it, not when she was so close to him, not when she could feel his hands on her, a touch she'd craved since the first time she'd seen him. It had been two years ago, the day she'd walked back into her life in Birch Crossing. He had been leaning against the deli counter in Wright's, his arms folded over his chest, his piercing blue eyes watching her so intently.

And now he was here, in these woods, holding onto her.

His grip was strong, but his touch was gentle in her hair as he filtered the strands through his fingers. "You've thought about my hair before?" she asked. Ridiculous question, but it tumbled out anyway. And she wanted to know. Had he really thought about her before? Was she not alone in the way her mind had wandered to him so many nights when she hadn't been able to sleep?

His gaze met hers, and for a second, heat seemed to explode between them. Then he dropped his hands and stepped back. The loss of his touch was like ice cold water drenching her, and she had to hug herself to keep from reaching out for him.

"Tell Astrid I was here," he said. "I'm leaving again—"

"What?" She couldn't hold back the protest. "Already? Why?"

"I have a job."

That job. That mysterious job. He had never told Astrid, or anyone else in town, where he went when he disappeared. Sometimes, he was in town for months, playing at his real estate business, taking off for only a few days at a time. Other times, he was absent for longer. This last time, he'd been gone for almost a year, which was the longest that anyone could remember him being away. And he was leaving again already? "Astrid misses you," Emma said quickly, instinctively trying to give him a reason not to disappear again. "You can't leave without at least saying hi."

Harlan's gaze flickered to the house, and his mouth tightened. He made no move to join the celebration, and suddenly she realized that he felt the same way she did about invading that happy little world. He didn't belong to it any more than she did. Empathy tightened her chest, and she looked more carefully at the independent man who no one in town had ever been able to get close to. "You can stop by and see her tomorrow," she said softly.

He didn't move, and he didn't take his eyes off the house. "She's happy? Jason's good to her?"

Emma nodded. "He treasures her. They're so in love." She couldn't quite keep the ache out of her voice, and she saw Harlan look sharply at her.

"What's wrong?" he asked. "Why did you say it like that?"

"No, no, they're great. Really." She swallowed and pulled back her shoulders, refusing to let herself yearn for that which she did not want or need in her life. "She would kill me if she found out I let you leave town without seeing her. How long until you have to go?"

He shifted. "Forty-eight hours." The confession was reluctant.

"So, then, come back here tomorrow and see her," she said, relief rushing through her at the idea that he wasn't leaving town immediately. For at least two nights, she could sleep knowing that he was breathing the same air as she was.

"No, not here." He ran his hand through his hair, and she saw a dark bruise on the underside of his triceps. "You guys still go to Wright's in the morning for coffee?"

Emma's heart fluttered at his question. For a man who had held himself aloof, he seemed endearingly aware of what his sister did every day...and he knew that she was always there as well. "Yes. We'll be there at eight thirty."

He nodded. "Yeah, okay, I'll try to make it then." He glanced at her again, and just like before, heat seemed to rush through her—

Then he turned away, stealing that warmth from her before she'd had time to finish savoring it. "No." She grabbed his arm, her fingers sliding over his hard muscles. Shocked by the feel of his body beneath her palm, she jerked back, but not soon enough.

He froze under her touch, sucking in his breath. Slowly, he turned his head to look back at her. "No?"

"Don't try to make it tomorrow morning," she said quickly, trying to pretend her panic had been on Astrid's behalf, not her own. "You have to make it. Astrid needs to see you. She wants you to meet Rosie. She's happy, Harlan, but she needs her brother, too. Jason is her family, but so are you, and you know how she needs to be connected."

Harlan closed his eyes for a long moment, and she saw

emotions warring within him. For a man so stoic and aloof, he was fermenting with emotions in a way that she'd never seen before. She looked again at the bruise on his arm. "Are you okay, Harlan? What happened while you were gone?" There was no way to keep the concern out of her voice, no way to hide that her heart ached at the thought of him being hurt.

His eyes opened again. He said nothing, but he suddenly wrapped his hand around the back of her neck.

She stiffened, her heart pounding as he drew her close to him. "What are you doing?"

"I need this." Then he captured her mouth with his.

She had no time to be afraid, no time to fear. His kiss was too desperate for her to be afraid. It wasn't a kiss to seduce or dominate. It was a burning, aching need for connection, for humanity, for something to chase away the darkness hunting him...everything she needed in a kiss as well.

Her hands went instinctively to his chest, bracing, protecting, but at the same time, connecting. She kissed him back, needing the same touch that he did, desperate for that feeling of being wanted. She didn't know this man, and yet, on some level, she'd known him for so long. She'd seen his torment, she'd felt his isolation, and she'd witnessed his unfailing need to protect Astrid, even if he had never inserted himself fully into her life.

Somehow, Harlan's kiss wasn't a threat the way other men's were. He was leaving town, so he was no more than a shadow that would ease into her life and then disappear. He wouldn't try to take her, to trick her, to consume her. He wouldn't make promises and then betray them. All he wanted was the same thing she did, a break from the isolation that locked him down, a fragile whisper of human connection to fill the gaping hole in his heart.

"Emma!" Astrid's voice rang out in the night, shattering the moment. "Are you out here?"

Harlan broke the kiss, but he didn't move away, keeping

his lips against hers. One of his hands was tangled lightly in her hair, the other was locked around her waist. Somehow, he'd pulled them close, until her breasts were against his chest, their bodies melted together. It felt so right, but at the same time, a familiar anxiety began to build inside Emma at the intimacy.

"Do not fear me, sweet Emma," Harlan whispered against her lips. "I would only treasure what you give."

His voice was so soft and tender that her throat tightened. How she'd yearned for so many years, for a lifetime, for someone to speak to her like that...until she'd finally become smart enough to relinquish that dream. And now, here it was, in the form of a man who would disappear from her life in forty-eight hours, maybe never to return. Which was why it was okay, because she didn't have to worry that he would want more than she could give, or that she would give him more than she could afford. Maybe she didn't belong in the room of couples and families, but for this brief moment, she belonged out in the night, with a man who lived the same existence that she did.

"Emma?" Astrid's footsteps sounded on the deck, and Harlan released her.

"Don't tell her I was here," he said. "I'll come by Wright's in the morning. Now is not the time." Then, without a sound, he faded into the darkness, vanishing so quickly she almost wondered whether she'd imagined him.

Stephanie Rowe Bio

Four-time RITA® Award nominee and Golden Heart® Award winner Stephanie Rowe is a nationally bestselling author with more than twenty published books with major New York publishers such as Grand Central, HarperCollins, Harlequin, Dorchester and Sourcebooks.

She has received coveted starred reviews from Booklist and high praise from Publisher's Weekly, calling out her "... snappy patter, goofy good humor and enormous imagination... [a] genre-twister that will make readers...rabid for more." Stephanie's work has been nominated as YALSA Quick Pick for Reluctant Readers.

Stephanie writes romance (paranormal, contemporary and romantic suspense), teen fiction, middle grade fiction and motivational nonfiction.

A former attorney, Stephanie lives in Boston where she plays tennis, works out and is happily writing her next book. Want to learn more? Visit Stephanie online at one of the following hot spots:

www.stephanierowe.com

http://twitter.com/stephanierowe2

https://www.facebook.com/StephanieRoweAuthor

Select List of Other Books by Stephanie Rowe

(For a complete book list, please visit www.stephanierowe.com)

Paranormal Romance

The Order of the Blade Series
Darkness Awakened
Darkness Seduced
Darkness Surrendered
Forever in Darkness (Novella)
Darkness Reborn
Darkness Arisen
Darkness Unleashed
Inferno of Darkness
Darkness Possessed (Coming Soon!)

The Soulfire Series
Kiss at Your Own Risk
Touch if You Dare
Hold Me if You Can

The Immortally Sexy Series
Date Me Baby, One More Time
Must Love Dragons
He Loves Me, He Loves Me Hot
Sex & the Immortal Bad Boy

Romantic Suspense

The Alaska Heat Series
Ice
Chill
Ghost (Coming Soon!)

Contemporary Romance

Ever After Series
No Knight Needed
Fairytale Not Required
Prince Charming Can Wait
The Knight Who Brought Chocolate (Coming Soon!)

STAND ALONE NOVELS
Jingle This!

NONFICTION
The Feel Good Life

FOR TEENS

A GIRLFRIEND'S GUIDE TO BOYS SERIES
Putting Boys on the Ledge
Studying Boys
Who Needs Boys?
Smart Boys & Fast Girls

STAND ALONE NOVELS
The Fake Boyfriend Experiment

FOR PRE-TEENS

THE FORGOTTEN SERIES
Penelope Moonswoggle, The Girl Who Could Not Ride a Dragon
Penelope Moonswoggle & the Accidental Doppelganger
Release Date TBD